I0743782

Also By the Author

The Menmenet Series
The Jackal of Inpu
The Lion of Bastet
The Bull of Mentju

The Founding Fathers Mysteries
Murder at Mount Vernon

Death of a Golden State
The Blockchain Killing

HYPERKILL

Robert J. Muller

A Pirates of Khonoë Novel

Poesys Associates

San Francisco

To Raphael Lemkin

Time comes into it.

Say it.   Say it.

The universe is made of stories,

not of atoms.

> *Muriel Rukeyser, "The Speed of Darkness"*
> *From Out of Silence: Selected Poems,*
> *edited by Kate Daniels*

your face

carries the reaches of air

I know I am space

my words are air.

> *Muriel Rukeyser, "The Speed of Darkness"*
> *From Out of Silence: Selected Poems,*
> *edited by Kate Daniels*

She's been looking like a queen in a sailor's dream

And she don't always say what she really means

> *Gordon Lightfoot, Sundown*

Young man, in mathematics you don't understand things. You just get used to them.

> *John von Neumann*

CHAPTER ONE
The Ravager

PAVAN KHADOROV FOUND HIMSELF SERIOUSLY reassessing his chosen career.

Avoiding certain death when it seemed inevitable because of following orders was just common sense. After all, he had joined the Galactic Syndicate Security Service for thrills, adventure, and service to the Syndicate, not to realize a death wish. In fourteen years, he had seen dozens of situations come and go with little thought other than to get the job done. And to survive it, if possible. And he always had gotten the job done. No matter what the cost. Nevertheless, lately he'd noticed a growing disposition to resist taking actions that in a civilian might raise scruples, or at least a touch of conscience.

His latest foray into undercover work had exacerbated this tendency. Pavan and his new best friend, Tigyanor Balsteon, were part of the team of pirates assigned to take care of the prisoners. The *Ripper* had tracked down a sizable cargo ship with Chuati registry as it was leaving orbit around Trastiv-4. The *Ripper* had locked onto the other ship with a hypertractor field, immobilizing them.

Pavan was the newest pirate, which meant he got all the shit jobs on the ship. He'd befriended Tig as a start to his infiltration mission. But he had made little progress beyond that before the boarding call.

Tig grabbed Pavan and tossed away the cleanoid Pavan was using to clean the toilets. The little technoid screamed a thin scream of disapproval as it hit the floor, but the sound disappeared behind them as Tig dragged Pavan along the corridor toward the shuttle bays.

"Come on, Pavan," urged Tig. "Step it up. This is your shot at getting ahead. You don't get ahead by cleaning the heads, my man."

"OK, OK," said Pavan, pulling himself free from the hulking, bearded pirate. "Do I need anything?"

"Blasters issued from the gun locker in the shuttle bay."

They turned into the bay, joined the thirty other pirates jostling for weaponry, and packed themselves into one of the boarding shuttles. Pavan watched the approach to the big freighter with a critical eye. The connoid pilot knew what it was doing. Commercial connoids rarely learned boarding procedures, so Pavan reasoned this was a stolen military or police model or a hacked commercial one. He saw the other two shuttles making sweet approaches to different boarding ports, an unexpected level of tech for pirates. His briefing had suggested they were a ragtag bunch of outlaws, not a highly effective military force. The blaster rifle in his hands was the latest model, too.

He spotted an ion cannon above their target port. Why no defensive fire?

The answer came when he and Tig got guard detail. A skeleton crew of five, not enough for anything more than screaming insults at the boarding party. Which they didn't do either. Pavan suspected a prior arrangement with the crew by The Captain of the *Ripper* without the owners' knowledge. The crew would hand over the ship, guarded until they got their payoff. Then the pirates would cast them adrift in lifeboats for rescue by the Trastiv authorities.

The squad leader, a small pirate with a fixed sneer and wild red hair, said, "You two," pointing at Tig and Pavan. "Strip 'em and dump 'em."

Pavan looked at Tig for elucidation of these orders. Tig grinned and said, "Come on, Pavan."

He walked over to the first crew member. "Take off your clothes. Now." He lifted the blaster rifle, and the man nodded quickly and stripped. Pavan got the idea. He handled the next crew member, a small woman who gave him a dirty look as she stripped down. When all five were naked, Tig jerked his head at Pavan, and they herded the crew members down the corridor. They came to a trash portal door.

"This looks like a good place to put 'em. Open it, Pavan."

Tig pushed one of the crew in the back with his rifle. "In."

"Is this necessary?" asked the freighter's captain, puzzlement prominent in her expression. "Why not—"

"Just get in."

Pavan joined Tig and herded the crew into the trash room. They closed the door.

"Flush it, Pavan."

"But—"

Tig grinned. "Why waste all those credits on trash? Cheaper to space 'em. Flush it."

Pavan had three choices. If he refused, Tig would do it then shoot him. If he rescued the crew after killing Tig, the other pirates would kill him and then the crew with some excruciatingly painful method. Or he could flush them. Not really a hard decision.

But it was harder than usual. After fourteen years of this, he had tired of making death or death decisions for people who didn't want to die. And that's what gave him second thoughts. But now was not the time. He'd work through these unfamiliar emotions in his spare moments between toilets.

He pushed the flush button and watched through a viewport as the five bodies floated toward the *Ripper*. They bounced up against the boundary of the hyper-tractor reverse torus near the pirate ship until they stabilized. A skeleton crew.

"Let's check the plunder, my man," said Tig, slapping Pavan on the back. "You'll get a bigger share now."

Tig sat Pavan down on his bunk a few days after the freighter boarding.

"What's wrong, Pavan? You're dragging around like you got food poisoning, and we're eatin' nothing but luxury food we got from the freighter."

Pavan slumped back against the bulkhead. He needed to get past the depression that had settled over him like an ulcerating wound that wouldn't heal. But he couldn't admit the cause to Tig. Pirates didn't get depressed over dead men's tales. The alternative was a blown cover. He wasn't about to do that. At least, not yet.

He shook his head and said, "Homesick, I guess. I'll get over it, Tig. Action would help. We're just sitting here doing nothing, and all I get to do besides cleaning toilets is think about home."

"Home is that nice?"

Pavan grinned at his friend. "It's at least got dirt, flowers, and blue sky. And not so many toilets."

The burly pirate laughed and slapped Pavan on the shoulder. "I'll see what I can do to spice up your life. A better set of quarters would help. Hold on a minute."

Tig left the quarters, leaving Pavan to his own devices. His main device was his servipad, an ordinary technoid pad with some extraordinary and clandestine features. He was alone for a few minutes. Now was a good time for his report. He took out the servipad.

"Did you record the names of the murder victims from their NIUs?"

The Neuronal Identification Unit was the small bit of tech that everyone in the Syndicate had in their brain stem that provided identifying information when authorized.

The servipad was offended. "Of course, sir, the priority in mission operations is to record any death. And any agent actions that cause expiry of individuals, including authorized killings and collateral—"

Pavan grimaced. The servipad loved needling him. "Fine. Create a report for the Ducis and send it through the encrypted sub-channel as soon as you can."

"I would recommend against unnecessary use of comms, sir, as these technically sophisticated pirates may detect unauthorized—"

"Whenever you can without being detected."

The servipad stood on its dignity. "Certainly, sir. As you wish. But don't blame me for unexpected events." The servipad blanked with a short warning about an approaching life form.

Tig returned, a big smile on his face. "Pavan, pack up. You're moving to new quarters with me! Way better than here. And no more toilets. Go on, pack up."

"Packing up" was a matter of shoving various personal items and clothes into his duffel bag, which took about thirty seconds. Maybe he would finally interact with pirates closer to the command decisions of The Captain. That mysterious individual was off limits to everyone. Pavan had discovered that part of the pirate code on these ships was complete anonymity for the commander of the ship. The Captain gave orders through messages and never revealed himself to the crew. Tig had explained it as a way to control a bunch of unreliable thugs. You didn't know which thug around you had the power to have you spaced, so you behaved yourself.

Tig drew a flask out of a deep pocket in his newish jacket. Pavan had seen the jacket on one of the freighter's crew members that he'd stripped. It was a very nice jacket.

"Here, Pavan, have a drink. Lavonian whiskey from the freighter. Time to celebrate. Things are lookin' up for us!"

Pavan drank. It *was* Lavonian whiskey, the kind aged in aromatic wood for 100 years. He'd tasted it before, last month, in the Syndic's house on Gaelea, celebrating his marriage to the Syndic's niece Margona. Lovely stuff. He took another sip and smiled, remembering his wife and their wedding night. Then he blacked out.

Pavan awoke disoriented and sick to his stomach, face down on a bunk. He groaned and sat up to find a grinning Tig on the other bunk.

"What did you do to me, you bastard?" groaned Pavan.

"The oldest pirate trick in the book, my lad," responded his friend. "Shanghaied you."

Pavan looked around. Different quarters, higher class than his old ones.

"Where are we?"

"The *Ravager*."

"The…what?"

"That freighter we raided? A new captain paid The Captain of the *Ripper* to hijack the ship and recommission it. The *Ravager*." He grinned. "That's why we hove to there. They added armor and more ion cannons to the old lady, making her into a true corsair ship." He slapped the bulkhead next to him with familiarity.

"You fucking *bastard!* I've got to get back to the *Ripper!*" He half rose off the bunk, then thought better of it as his stomach heaved.

"Settle down, my lad. You're well and truly fucked, so man up."

"I've got debts to pay, Tig. Big ones. On the *Ripper*. To The Captain. I can't walk away, they'll kill me." Untrue, but Pavan couldn't come up with anything better on the spur of the moment. His *Ripper* mission was critical. The ship was a menace to navigation throughout the Syndicate, and he had to stop it. And now he was on a ship heading who knows where.

"All taken care of, I'm sure. Part of the recruiting fee."

"Fee?"

"The Captain of the *Ravager* needed a crew, and he paid for it. All those new pirates, they were the crew for this ship. The Captain is out to make his fortune, and we're along for the ride."

"I'll bet some of those credits found their way into your servipad, you ratfucking son of a bitch."

"You'll get used to the idea, my man. Now, settle down, have a little nap, and I'll show you the food ponds."

"What about the food ponds?"

"That's your new job, Pavan. Picking space lice out of the food ponds. It's a necessary job and a demanding one."

"What the hell are space lice?"

"Plenty of time for all that. Relax. Consider how you'll show your loyalty to The Captain."

"The Captain. I've got to talk to him. This can't stand, Tig."

"Nobody talks to The Captain. Told you."

"Yeah, but—"

"Easy way to learn what space tastes like, my man. Keep pushing and see what happens. Friendly advice, no?"

"But the *Ripper*—"

"Long gone, Pavan. Went into hyperspace after the crew transfer. You've been out for hours. The *Ravager* is halfway to our next raid. We'll drop out of hyperspace in a few hours."

A galactic adventure with no chance of recovering his mission. Maybe becoming a pirate would work for him after all. But what about Margona? Instead he pretended he was still on his mission, just with a different set of pirates. He could do that until he commed the Ducis for new instructions.

"All right, all right. What's this raid, and how much plunder will there be?"

Tig smiled. "More like it, my man. Knew you'd get it. Welcome to the *Ravager*."

The *Ravager*'s raid turned out to be a ruthenium mining station in the Ertes system. Pavan had heard of Ertes before. It was a red star with one gas giant planet, Ertes-1, and a huge asteroid field. Many asteroids now had small mining stations that mined rare elements. The lack of any inhabited planets meant a miner could find an empty asteroid, register it with the Syndicate, and start mining. Eventually, they would form a government and join the Syndicate. But for now, it was independent miners doing their best to make a killing on the rare metals they mined.

Since there was no government, there were no police. Some miners had gotten together and hired a security company to provide protection, but most of the mining stations were perfect targets for a pirate raid. If raids affected trade materially, the Syndicate might send a patrol ship, but that was unlikely given the number of mines. One less mine wouldn't even be a blip to the Syndicate, but it would provide a pirate ship with a nice boost to the ship's takings.

Pavan gathered all this information as the pirates on food pond duty talked. Picking space lice was a boring occupation. The lice themselves were tiny, disgusting, translucent creatures. They appeared from nowhere despite the best efforts of the ship's crew, which weren't up to the hygiene standards of a normal starship. Space lice withstood radiation and poison and so had to be manually extracted and ejected from the ship. No protein in them, either. Disgusting.

Tig told Pavan that the targeted mining station had a large quantity of ruthenium in storage because of a broken supply chain. The pirates had a buyer ready and waiting for the entire hoard.

Tig headed up the landing party of ten pirates, and he made sure Pavan was part of it. "You need the experience, Pavan."

Pavan, happy to get away from the space lice, was game. Or so he thought.

The miners had fortified the station with an automated arms system that was no match for blaster rifles. After taking out the blaster ports, the pirates stormed the building and took the couple running the place prisoner. By threatening the wife, they got the husband to open the ruthenium store and started loading the crates of metal onto the transport shuttle. It took three trips to empty the store. Then the shuttle returned to pick up the pirates.

Tig and another pirate commed The Captain and got their orders. They executed the two miners with two rifle blasts.

Tig said, "Pavan, clear the rest of the station. Blast anybody you find. Captain's orders." Tig grinned. "I gave him your name, Pavan. The Captain knows who you are, now. Don't fuck this up."

Pavan walked through the station, opening doors and checking compartments, until he came to a small room toward the back. He opened the door and found two children, a boy and a girl, sitting on a bed and holding each other. They looked at Pavan with terror in their eyes.

Pavan couldn't bring himself to shoot the two kids. That would be too much. Their parents were already dead. Nothing he could do about that. But he didn't have to kill their kids, too.

He whispered to the children, "OK, kids, here's what you do. You go into that laundry closet down the hall, quietly, without a sound. Hide under the clothes. When we're gone, you'll need to call for help on the comm system. Can you do that?"

The girl, older than the boy and showing signs of adolescence, nodded. She helped the boy up, and they crept down the hall with Pavan to the compartment. Pavan shut the door on them, then walked back to the control room.

"All clear. Nobody else in the place," he told Tig.

The pirates boarded the transport shuttle. Tig took out his servipad and said, "Activate the timer, you."

"Aye, sir," responded the servipad. "Five minutes to ignition."

Tig ordered the connoid to take the shuttle back to the Ravager. Pavan looked at the small mining building as the shuttle rose and turned away from the asteroid. Suddenly, a bright light lit up the surface.

"You blew up the station," said Pavan, watching fragments flying off into space.

"Captain's orders. No evidence left. Just in case," said Tig. "No point in being sloppy, Pavan."

The shuttle docked in the Ravager's shuttle bay, and Pavan joined the pirates, moving the new ruthenium cargo into one of the cargo bays. He had to keep busy, for now.

The pirates gathered at the door of the docked shuttle, blaster rifles ready. It was a week after the raid on the mining station. The *Ravager* had come across a nice little space yacht en route to a pleasure world, easy pickings.

The docking door swooshed open, and the pirates swarmed in, eager to see the plunder on tap.

Pavan was clear on the orders this time: no killing, find the valuables, pile everything up in the docking port and shift it back to the *Ravager* for sorting. The no-killing part pleased him. According to Tig, The Captain of the *Ravager* only killed when stealing a ship or raiding a planet. A simple ship raid was just thievery, not a killing opportunity.

"Yo, Pretty Boy. Get the hell over here and crate up this thing, then get it to the docking port," called the tall pirate in charge. He towered, covered in tattoos, with a hawklike nose and sharp teeth. He had just grunted when Tig introduced Pavan to him. Pavan looked around, but no other pirate even came close to fitting the description "Pretty Boy." He got to work on the large, silvery statue, an abstraction that was a truly poor depiction of a bird or a bizarre species of octopus. Valuable? Sure thing.

Pavan expanded a folding antigravity crate and wiggled the statue into it, then knelt down behind it to fasten the closures. The sounds of drills and saws emanated from the various rooms along the passageway, pirates freeing the yacht of its luxury items. Somebody had discharged a blaster, the ionized air smell competing with a sweet and subtle perfumery from the luxury yacht's ventilation system.

Pretty Boy. He'd gotten worse in the mess from other pirates. They seemed to have a hazing ritual or something for new crew mates, especially the ones on the food ponds crew. His dark good looks compared to the rest of the pirates seemed to aggravate them into active antipathy, even the women.

Pavan heard the pirate in charge talking and peeked over the edge of the crate. A woman he hadn't seen before was listening and nodding. The blaster rifle and spacer's boots she wore identified her as a pirate, though her costume was much less colorful than the clothing the other pirates wore. A simple jumpsuit, form-fitting but dark blue and unadorned. This woman was somebody he'd like to know; he had a sixth sense about things like that, based on her style, the shape of her lips, and the way her eyes moved. Later. He kept his head down and listened.

"The Captain says we're heading to Ravos as soon as we get this loot on board," said the woman.

"What the hell for? I was counting on Khonoë and shore leave."

"We'll get shore leave on Ravos. They've got a fine bar in the capital city there."

"OK, but why waste our time? That rock is 4,000 hypersecs from here."

"The Captain says there's a weapon there we need to check out. Could be useful. Give us an edge." The woman smiled. "Anyway, you going to complain?"

"Hell, no. At least not on the first tour. Captains get impatient about being contradicted on their first tour."

"Yeah," agreed the woman. "Where's the owner of this barge?"

"Locked himself in his cabin. You want him?"

"I checked his Syndicate background. He's the younger son of a super-wealthy Lavonian merchant family. We're going to take him and ransom him or sell him to the Bularian slavers if his family doesn't want him."

"OK, I'll bring him along. Lavonian? We can take the ransom in Lavonian whiskey!"

"Hurry it up. The Captain wants to move on before any locals respond to the raid here."

The two pirates separated. Pavan slid down out of sight. Ravos? Never heard of it. But a secret weapon? Add that to the list of things to report to the Ducis. Along with the Lavonian, of course. And his killings.

"Did you get all that?" Pavan whispered to his servipad.

"Of course, sir. My surveillance facility is more than capable—" The screen blanked.

"Like what you overheard, Pretty Boy?" The voice behind him was a growl. Pavan slowly stood up and turned around. The voice came from a leering pirate, one of the boarding party. "What's it worth to you to keep it quiet, Pretty Boy? 10,000 credits? Your share of the loot?"

"What if—" Pavan began. His blaster was too far away to grab.

"No ifs, Pretty Boy. The Captain don't like rats on the ship, and you're a rat, I can tell. Give me that pad."

The pirate moved toward Pavan, hand extended. Pavan reached past the extended hand and grabbed the pirate's vest, pulling him forward. He used the pirate's weight to move him along in the weak ship's gravity and threw him over the crate to crash against the passageway bulkhead.

There were too many pirates nearby to play nice and de-escalate the situation. Pavan leapt over to the fallen pirate, who scrambled up and pulled a knife from a sheath on his belt. The two men circled, the double-edged knife slashing the space between them. Pavan, keeping his eyes on the knife, waited for his opportunity. The pirate made a vicious thrust toward Pavan's chest. Pavan jumped forward, grabbed the pirate's arm with both hands, and thrust downward, then pulled with one hand, dislocating the man's elbow. The knife fell from the pirate's suddenly useless hand.

The pirate yelled an unintelligible obscenity and swung his other fist against Pavan's neck. Pavan, who had kept an eye on the knife, fell backward, twisting to fall next to it. He grabbed the knife and twisted toward the pirate, who was jumping to the attack. As the man dove onto the knife, his eyes opened wide and his mouth opened, but the knife in his chest stopped his heart before any sound emerged. The pirate collapsed over Pavan, pinning him down.

Pavan pushed the dead man off. Three other pirates ran into the passageway, responding to the noises of the fight. Two of them grabbed Pavan and pulled him to his feet. He left the knife where it was. More killing; not a regrettable one this time.

Tig and another pirate entered the passageway from another direction. "Pavan!" shouted Tig. "What the hell's going on?"

"This guy pulled a knife on me, no reason," panted Pavan. "The son of a bitch attacked me. I don't even know who he is."

"Maybe he just didn't like your face, Pretty Boy," grinned the pirate holding one of Pavan's arms. "Wanted to give you another scar to match that one on your cheek."

Pavan gave the man a dark glance. Tig came up and put a hand on the pirate's arm. "He's OK, honest. He wouldn't just knife a guy, he's...." Tig's mouth twisted. "He's too green. Probably doesn't even know which end of the knife to use. Got lucky. A coin toss."

"Fuck you, Tig," said Pavan, struggling a bit to give some credence to his reaction. But he gave his friend a nod of thanks.

The pirates let go of Pavan's arms. "You'll have to explain it all to The Captain," said one pirate. "Be lucky if he don't space you. But nobody liked this twit." He nudged the dead pirate with a foot. Behind him, the pirate in charge entered the passageway, pushing a scared young man dressed in an elegant leisure robe ahead of him.

"What the hell is all this? Why aren't you all getting the goods to the shuttle?" demanded the big pirate.

The pirates stepped out of the way to show him the dead body. "Knife fight. Looks like Pretty Boy got the best of it against Tiny here."

"That man is dead," stated the young man, turning an interesting shade of green.

The pirate in charge pushed the young man forward. "Get down to the docking port or you'll be dead with him," he said. He stared at Pavan. "If Tiny wasn't such a complete fuckup of a pirate, I'd kill you, Pretty Boy. Well, stuff happens. You broke it, you own it. Get the body back to the *Ravager,* along with your cargo. Now. And you, Tig—you're responsible for making sure Pretty Boy gets back to the *Ravager* all safe and sound, nice like. And you, Kolnor, you go find one of this kid's hostesses and 'recruit' her. We're a pirate short now. Got it?"

He pushed the boy, who stumbled, then kept pushing him down the passageway. He said, over his shoulder, "And the rest of you get back to work! Captain wants to leave, now! Before the local gendarmerie comes calling. Move it!" He disappeared. The other pirates dispersed, leaving Pavan to his charnel work. He packed the body into another antigravity crate and stacked it on top of the one containing the silver statue. He couldn't decide which was the least valuable.

Pavan pushed the antigravity crates down the passageway to the docking port, joining the line of pirates pushing similar crates. He didn't look back.

CHAPTER TWO
Shore Leave

PAVAN AND TIG TRUDGED OUT of the space elevator tunnel into the shabby arrivals lounge on Ravos. Pavan's eyes probed for anything threatening. Boxes and crap everywhere. Stevedores, technoids, and who knew what else lounging around. The smell reminded Pavan of a spacer's boot that had seen far too many landfalls on the wrong feet. Pavan checked that he had securely stowed his servipad and microblaster in an inner pocket.

"A bunch of us are gonna meet up in a bar in the city, Pavan," said Tig. "You gotta come. The place is a riot. They love visiting pirates, and they got everything you need. Music, girls, any drink or drug you want."

"I was thinking of a walk in a nice park somewhere," joked Pavan.

Tig took him seriously and gripped his arms and shook him. "Your problem is you need to have some fun, my man. That's what shore leave is for. Besides, things here ain't exactly a walk in the park. The planet's interdicted, so every-thing's in chaos. They'll rob and kill you within two minutes out there."

"If the planet's interdicted, how did we get down here?"

"Trade secret, my man. The Captain's connections. Makes the place exclusive to us, great for shore leave. 'Course, Khonoë is best."

"What's Khonoë?" He'd overheard the pirates talking about it on the *Ravager*.

"Pirate planet, outside Syndicate jurisdiction. Wide open for anything you want."

Shore leave. Bars with all-you-can-anything. Pirate planets. Pavan found little in the lounge to suggest his life was improving. Might as well enjoy himself before he died. Shore leave. Sure thing.

Tig pulled Pavan out to the transit platform, and they climbed into the first cab they found. It was decrepit, but it cheerily promised them it would get them wherever they wanted to go.

"So, where to, guys?" asked the cab. "There ain't that many tourists here these days. What kinda fun you lookin' for?"

Tig laughed. "The Golden Pig."

"OK, bud." The cab was silent for a minute, processing. "Ya sure you can handle it? That place…"

"Do we look like the kinda guys can't handle a little fun?"

"Just checking, bud. Say, that area of town is kinda heavy. Cost you another ten credits, hazard fee, case I get some damage needs fixing."

"Just get us there and step on it, and you'll get twenty." Tig clearly felt flush from his share of the mining station doings.

"You got it." The old cab tore off with a sharp whine of its antique ion converters.

The cab was old, dilapidated, and tired. It said so, several times. As this wasn't much of a conversation starter, Tig and Pavan ignored it. Tig closed his eyes. Pavan's servipad wasn't as insensible. Pavan had taken it out to get some background on the planet.

"I cannot myself order this mechanical coffin-dodger to mute itself, sir," said the servipad. "I would humbly ask that you perform that function."

"No, I enjoy listening to it." He didn't. But he didn't want to give any ground to the servipad.

The cab said, "What kinda flat-boy porker you carrying around, son? Ain't got no respect, that's what I say."

"I don't—"

"Sir, I must insist that you mute this ancient rust-bucket before my auditory facilities overload. Please. Sir."

"Well, since you ask—"

"I ain't shuttin' up for no little punk-pad ain't been around long enough to learn manners, bud. I take you where you wanna go, you and your paddy, but I ain't takin' any orders from nobody."

"That's fine, I don't—"

"Sir, really—"

"Will you be quiet! And stop interrupting."

"Yes, sir."

"That's telling it," commented the cab.

Tig, eyes still closed, shook his head slowly at this interaction but said nothing.

Pavan's mind wasn't on this conversation. He finally had open comms to Gaelea and had to report to the Ducis in private. Carousing in a bar full of pirates would not help with this.

The cab screeched to a halt. A man had jumped in front of it and raised his arms.

Pavan leaned forward to check things out through the pseudowindow. "What —"

"Hold on a minute, bud. Got to deal with this guy."

"What does he want?"

"Probably a robber. No worries, gents, I'm armored. He'll figure it out and go away in two ticks." The man raised a stick and pounded on the cab's roof. The noise barely penetrated.

"He'll be dead in one tick," said Tig, pulling a blaster pistol from a capacious pocket in his nice jacket.

"Whoa, whoa, whoa," said the old cab. "No guns! People are starving out there, ya know? Besides, if you go out there, his twenty friends will jump you and your friend here, tear you apart, then trash my seats. Don't do it."

Pavan said, "Tig, we're on shore leave, not on a raid. Nobody needs to die here."

Grumbling, Tig put the gun back in his pocket. "What are you gonna do about it, you? We don't want any uniforms," he told the cab.

"Hum." And that was all it said.

"Hum what?"

"Really loud. You can't hear it 'cause of the armor soundproofing."

Pavan could detect a high-pitched whistle leaking through the old cab's creaky doors. The attacker dropped the stick and backed away, covering his ears. He finally slunk out of range of the pseudowindows and disappeared.

The cab jerked forward, fast, whipping Tig and Pavan back in their seats. "Almost there," said the cab.

Pavan watched the chaos go by. He asked his servipad to summarize the planet. The pad gave him a five-minute overview of the transformation of a perfectly nice, prosperous trading world into a frenzied, starving mess, all courtesy of the Syndicate interdiction. He'd seen worse worlds, worlds held in thrall to religious fanaticism, worlds destroying themselves to make their leaders rich. This one's problem was courtesy of Pavan's employers. The chaos in Pavan's life, courtesy of his employer, mirrored the chaos he saw in these streets.

Ideas formed in Pavan's mind, ideas that could get him freed from life among the pirates. Freed from the brutality of the GSSS. But he had to talk to the Ducis. Privately.

The cab pulled up in front of a large, square building painted in garish colors with a blinking vid sign advertising all the things a pirate might want. The vid showed a grotesquely obese pig, shining gold, behaving badly with all those things.

"OK, fellas, here you are. Credits?"

Tig waved his servipad, and the cab took its fare. It said, "Commed my call signal into your pad, fella. Just call when you need a ride. And a piece of advice: watch yourself and your friend. He looks a little green, ya know?"

"Yeah," said Tig, grinning. "Green he is. Come on, Pavan."

Pavan needed time. He thought fast and held up his servipad. "This servipad is getting to me. Do you know a good place where I can get this thing an attitude patch?"

"Sir—" started the servipad in an alarmed voice.

"Flat-boy needs a wipe, way I hear it," said the old cab. "But yeah, I got a special deal with a guy can fix anything. Cost you six credits for the round trip."

Pavan turned to Tig. "I'll be back in an hour. I'll meet you in the bar."

"Don't be long, my man. All the drinks will be drunk, along with the rest of us," said the pirate, grinning. He exited the cab and slammed the door.

"Ouch!" said the old cab. "Hey bud, your pal ain't got much in the way of manners, does he?" The cab whined its ions and set off.

"Sir, I really must protest this unwarranted attack on my functionality," stated the servipad. "And I must point out that regulation 3824.6 of the Guidelines is quite clear that damaging government property—"

"Quiet, you. This is not the place. And I won't damage you."

"Sir—"

Pavan addressed the old cab. "Can you drive around the streets for an hour? I don't want to damage my pad. I just need some time alone. My friend—well, he's a bit much, sometimes."

"I get that, son. Sure, I can show you the sights. I'll cruise along the river, and you can check out the fires on the other side. Real pretty, the way the light glows."

"Thank you." Pavan wasn't really listening to the cab. He was using his fingers to instruct his servipad to set up a privacy shield. The servipad, reassured about its survival as a viable artificial intelligence, did as he asked. The shield created an image of Pavan gazing out the pseudowindows and conversing with the cab.

"Privacy established, sir." Silence descended.

"Comm the Ducis on an encrypted sub-channel, priority one."

The servipad complied, and after a short wait, the Ducis's dark, austere face appeared in front of Pavan. The set of his mouth was grim, and the image seemed to glare directly into Pavan's eyes.

"Well, Pavan? Where the devil are you? Why haven't you reported?"

Pavan touched an icon to upload his report. "It's all in my report, milord. I've had to abort my mission on the *Ripper* because they shanghaied me onto a new pirate ship, the *Ravager*. Now I'm on Ravos."

"Ravos." The Ducis's eyes flicked as he checked his vizquery. "That's 4,000 parsecs from where you're supposed to be! And it's interdicted. How did you get through the shield?"

"I'm not sure, milord. These pirates have connections."

"This does not please me, Pavan. The depredations of these pirates on Syndicate shipping need to stop." The eyes flicked some more. "Your report shows little progress, and your incidental damage tally seems excessive."

"I agree, milord, but I see no way to resume that mission. What about fixing Ravos?"

The grizzled beard jutted forward. "Fixing?"

"Interdiction has just about destroyed the planet. Surely there's something we can do about it. And I'm here and ready to do what it takes."

The Ducis cocked his head. "Your report mentions the pirates who abducted you are after a weapon on Ravos."

"I don't believe there is anything here worth their while. They'll leave soon, and I can stay and work on things here."

"Unfortunately, your assessment is quite wrong, Pavan. The interdiction is a result of our discovery of a serious threat to the Syndicate on Ravos."

"What can you tell me about it, milord?"

"Not a lot. Something on the planet can disrupt hyperspace within a hypersec. Interdiction prevents damage to shipping and trade in the vicinity. The Syndicate Security Council has decided we need not go to the expense of rooting it out and destroying whatever it is. Ravos is not very important to trade. But now that you're *there*, we can investigate and take action."

"Is there *any* information I can use to locate this weapon, milord?"

"No, we know very little more than that it exists." The Ducis smiled a grim smile. "They call it the Secret of Ravos in the reports, just to be mysterious."

"Can I get the PIS to help in locating the Secret?"

"I'm afraid not. In fact, the PIS will undoubtedly do everything in its power to stop you."

"Can you tell them—"

"Relations between the PIS and the GSSS are problematic just now, Pavan. Politics." Another grim smile. "Best to assume they are the enemy that wants you dead, as you're treading on their territory. And Pavan—we have already spent a good deal of time on these pirates. You have a week to complete this mission."

No information, no help, a deadline, and the threat of death. Another classic mission from the Ducis. He could abort the mission and return to Gaelea in disgrace. Not really an option.

"Milord, I have an idea. Why not use the pirates?"

"Explain, Pavan."

"They're already looking for the Secret. I can get them to help with their connections on the planet."

"I don't see how that helps, Pavan." The Ducis frowned. "A hyperspace weapon and pirates is not the best combination."

"Milord, think about it. As it is, you have nothing. If the pirates have it, you can take advantage of my infiltration to raid and capture them along with the Secret once they've gotten it off planet. The expense will be nothing, since the budget already includes taking out the pirates. I'll be on hand to sabotage things as required so they can't use it against us."

The dark face in front of him continued frowning, the thin lips tight. "It's too dangerous."

The Ducis meant dangerous to the Syndicate, not to Pavan, of course. "I'd like to try it, milord."

"Very well. With one qualification—you'll have to destroy whatever you find if you can't control it. And you can use whatever force necessary to do that." Meaning Pavan could kill anybody or anything that got in his way. Even the whole planet. Pavan examined the Ducis's stony face and realized that if his mission failed, the Council would order the destruction of Ravos. That's why the PIS had done nothing about the Secret.

"Yes, milord."

"I authorize the mission, Pavan," said the Ducis, again staring right at his eyes. Pavan felt the subtle ringing in his ears that implied a do-or-die order in his neuroinstinctual command pathways. The Ducis didn't take chances with this kind of mission, and the GSSS modifications to Pavan's brain let the Ducis enforce his mission orders to the death. Pavan's death.

The Ducis's face disappeared. Pavan told his servipad to end the privacy shield.

The cab was in the middle of a diatribe about a local politician. Pavan let it wind down, then said, "Well, thanks for the tour. I'm ready to get back to the Golden Pig now."

"Think twice, son. The Pig ain't no place for nice, quiet types like you. Say, ya like a little flutter? Got a place right down this street—"

"Sir, I must remind you of agency guideline 765.2352 relating to expenditures of money on games of chance," broke in his diligent servipad.

"My guardian angel here has a point, cabby. Onward to the Golden Pig. Nothing in the guidelines about drinks, is there," he stated with authority.

The servipad admitted this was so, and the cab perked up on hearing its wounded tone.

"What agency you with, son? I do a lot of government work. Most of 'em are hunkering down right now."

"Yeah," said Pavan. "Got to meet my friend at the bar. Urgent."

"Be at the bar in two ticks, son! Just watch yourself. Rough place for a G-Man. And a piece of advice: put a muzzle on that flat-boy."

"Sure thing," said Pavan.

Pavan could still feel the arctic eyes of the Ducis staring into his. As the old cab navigated the Ravosi street jungle, Pavan worked through the underbrush of his duty and how he had fallen into the deep pit of covert operations. He had eased into his job through his father's connections to the Ducis. But he hadn't stumbled into it; he wanted the adventure and thrills of a black ops job. His family was minor nobility on Gaelea, and the life he led as a teenager bored him beyond sentience.

He relished the duties and missions the Ducis gave him, even as they led him farther down the path of moral ambiguity. He'd wound up unambiguously amoral, but he always did his duty. Something about the Ducis urged obedience; not fear, precisely, but deference and honor. In doing your duty, you contributed something very special to the glory of the Syndicate, to the honor of Gaelea. Not that the Ducis cared. The man knew what he wanted and didn't care who died in the getting of it.

For Pavan, glory was increasingly threadbare as the weight of the things he had done tore at the fabric of his self image. He had begun to dislike himself.

Then he met Margona. It was unexpected, the jaded agent meeting the lively, engaging, and exacting surgeon. That she helped him out of a tough place of his own making without too much judging awoke him to her quality. That she had overlooked his bad qualities enough to fall in love awoke him to his own closet of worn-out feelings. That the Ducis had sent her to help by calling in a favor from her uncle, the Syndic of Gaelea, cemented the relationship. They married within a month of his return from the mission. The beginning of the end. Pavan's lust for adventure kept him on the job. Even now, a settled life might bore him. Have to see about that.

The cab swerved suddenly, throwing Pavan against the side pseudowindow.

"What was that?" he asked, pushing himself up.

"Better hitch up that harness, son. Looks like things might get a little wild."

Pavan looked at the reverse view and saw rocks falling short of the cab's rear, thrown by a group of people dressed in rags. They receded into the distance. He looked down and saw a feather on the floor of the car. His lucky feather. He reached and gathered it in. Margona had handed it to him on the walk she'd taken with him on the beach, the day after they'd first made love. She'd told him it would remind him how it was to be in love, light as a feather. That feather had seen him through some dark things. Those two kids on the mining station, for instance. Not to mention the *Ravager* killings. He put the feather into an inside pocket where it wouldn't get lost in the turbulence. Pavan hit the harness button, and the webbing wrapped around him to hold him to the seat.

He could always disappear. Make a new life for himself. A life worth living, energizing but principled. He knew all about changing identities. The Ducis had triggered his GSSS neuroinstinctual pathways to make sure Pavan didn't do something like that. But the Ducis wasn't aware that Margona, the best neuro-plastic surgeon on Gaelea, had removed those pathways. He was free to choose. And she might even take care of changing their NIUs. But that was the snag: Margona. He could disappear himself, but not her. She'd have to agree. Why would a successful surgeon who also was a rich noblewoman want a different life under a new name on a planet where she was nothing at all? She was the niece of the Syndic of Gaelea, after all. Pavan and his feather wouldn't be enough on that scale. But if the Ducis learned she altered his pathways, all bets were off.

"Sir," said the servipad from his other pocket, a little muffled. "My long-range sensors detect an approaching explosive—"

"Muzzle it, flat-boy," said the cab. "Already on it. One a them street mines."

The cab swerved again into a side street.

Pavan grouched, "Is this going to take long, cabby? I've got to get to that bar soon or my friend won't be able to talk to me."

"We'll get there, son. Don't bust a gut. A little shortcut or two."

"Sure thing."

Pavan relaxed back against the seat and thought out his plan. He'd work on Tig, convince him that a treasure hunt would make him rich. It would pay him back for all his hard work, bringing Pavan along as a rookie pirate. Tig would use his connections to find out where this Secret was, then they'd go get it. And he'd do it by killing no one or destroying anything. Sure thing. If Tig didn't blast anything that moved. If Tig *had* connections. If Tig didn't take everything for himself. If other pirates didn't step in. If The Captain wasn't already stepping in. That woman pirate said the *Ravager* was going to Ravos to check out a weapon. Maybe The Captain had already found it and taken it. All the better—then all Pavan had to do was report in to the Ducis and stand by for the GSSS raid.

He'd convince Tig this was a treasure hunt, not a raid. He'd raise the threat of the PIS troops. He'd tell Tig they'd destroy the *Ravager* if they found out what was happening as a result of Tig killing somebody. A low profile. He'd get it done. Even at the cost of the final shreds of his self image through some killing.

If he survived the ride to the bar. The cab swerved hard again to avoid another crowd of badly dressed locals holding chains and sticks, sped down an alley, and made a hard turn.

"Here ya go, the Golden Pig. Now you watch yourself, son."

Pavan paid the cab and crossed the pothole-filled street to the bar door.

Pavan stepped onto the sidewalk in front of the Golden Pig, only to confront three ragged individuals pleading for money. He told them no, and they expressed their displeasure. After a few knuckle punches, a bouncer intervened with a chain, chasing off the beggars.

Pavan stumbled into the entry hall, where another bouncer caught him up—literally three feet off the floor—and patted him down. The bouncer lowered Pavan to the floor, then held out his hand. Pavan removed his microblaster and handed it over, feeling defenseless. The bouncer gave him a weapons-check tag and propelled him into the bar.

Now he had to find Tig among this heaving mass of piratical humanity. No, first get a drink. Living as a pirate had changed his priorities a little. Pavan looked over the heads of three gentlemen, arm in arm, singing wildly along with the music; the song they sang was completely unrelated to that music. He spotted a bartender, towel in hand, with a head of wild yellow hair and a grim expression. He couldn't see the bar behind the crush of pirates.

Pavan edged around the three inebriates, dodged a wild swing of a massive hand from a pirate sitting at a table telling a story to a small woman who laughed loudly at it, and pushed a space open between two semi-conscious pirates who propped up the bar. He held up a finger, crooked at the right angle, and the barkeep smiled and filled a glass with a golden liquid and handed it to him, taking his servipad and charging the drink with his posnoid, all in one fluid motion.

Pavan left the bar and stuck his head up above the tall individual in front of him. He saw Tig, staggering backwards, fall over a table, blood gushing from his nose. Pavan started toward him to help. Tig scrambled up, rage showing from his balled fists to his gritted teeth. Pavan followed his eyes to find a woman sitting calmly at a table, sipping her drink, staring a little blankly at his friend. It was the pirate Pavan had seen on the yacht talking about Ravos.

Tig stepped toward the table. Pavan looked around for anyone who might have bloodied his nose. The surrounding pirates seemed uninvolved in the drama. Then Tig gave a choking gurgle and fell where he stood. The woman froze, mouth opening in what Pavan took for horror. Tig rolled over and showed blood dribbling out of a chest wound along with a pair of extremely dead eyes. A blade had penetrated what passed for the pirate's heart and stopped it. But the blade was no longer there.

The woman stood up with empty hands at her side, concern crunching her features. A bouncer pushed his way through the crowd, grabbed her, and searched her without worrying about any niceties.

"She's clean. OK, who's got the knife?" queried the bouncer, looking around and scanning with a personal sniffnoid. All the pirates, now silent, raised their empty hands. Noise burst out, and the music resumed. The bouncer shook his head in exasperation and dragged Tig out.

So much for his only friend, cultivated as a source over three months of pirating. He had been counting on Tig for his mission. Well, shit.

He walked over to the woman, taking stock of her as he went. Definitely someone he would like to know. Sure to be helpful to his mission, too.

"Hi, my name's Pavan. Buy you a drink?"

She looked at him vacantly, her eyes and mouth tight with dread, then her eyes sharpened. "Dellatrix. Weren't you palling around with Tig on the ship?"

"Well, yeah, he was my best friend, but what the hell, it looks like I need new friends. Drink, Dellatrix?"

"Sure, why not?" She visibly shed her emotions over Tig's dramatic exit and moved toward the bar. Pavan followed, signaling the bartender with two fingers slightly crooked to let the lady have whatever she wanted on him. The bartender grinned and poured.

"To life," said Dellatrix, her full lips curving as she drank.

"Sure thing." Pavan knocked back his drink and signaled for two more.

CHAPTER THREE
The Treasure Hunt

AN HOUR LATER, PAVAN AND his new best friend sat on bar stools vacated by unconscious pirates. Two very green and bright eyes gazed at Pavan with what he took to be interest. Dellatrix Devdan had one elbow on the bar as she stirred the ice in her drink. They'd exhausted the horrors of Tig's death, and time appeared to have helped Dellatrix to recover from it, so they'd moved on to more personal questions.

Pavan asked, "Where are you from? A pirate family?"

She smiled and sipped. "Nope, born and raised in a good family. I went bad later when I realized where the real money was."

"A lot of pirating?"

"I've seen my share of interesting boarding parties, yes."

"All with The Captain?"

Dellatrix looked at him. "How long have you been with us? Not long, or I'd know you better."

"Joined the *Ripper*, switched to the *Ravager*. Nice ship."

"After The Captain upgraded it, yes. And full of nice cargo," she said.

"I'm sure it will all fetch a good price."

"What's your contract percentage?"

"Contract?" he asked, mystified.

"Oh ho. Migrant labor, that's what you are, Pavan." The green eyes danced a little in amusement.

"I don't..."

"Of course you don't. Pavan, as migrant labor, you get to die for The Captain but you won't get rich." She raised an eyebrow, and the bartender delivered the requested drink as though he'd had it already poured and ready for her.

Pavan made his move. "Dellatrix. What a nice name—it goes with your eyes."

"That is the worst, most bat-shit, irrational pickup line I've ever heard." The pirate stirred her new drink and sipped.

"I usually depend on my looks," he replied.

This was fact; his pickup techniques had never been the same since his wife Margona had rummaged around in his neuroinstinctual pathways. He suspected she'd added some inhibitions she hadn't told him about while adjusting his problematic neuroinstincts. He could work around it, though, kind of like a bad stutter. And his dark good looks combined with the faint piratical scar on his cheek got him past his fumbling verbal inanities most of the time. Margona had never understood or accepted that sex was one of the key tools in a secret agent's toolkit. She loved him and expected him to love her the same way. He did, but he had his job to do, and Margona was getting in the way. Maybe that was yet another reason to retire. But not just now.

Dellatrix grinned. "Your looks are good enough for a few drinks, but that's it, my man."

Perhaps a more direct approach? He put a hand on her knee. "How about it, Dellatrix? We can—"

Pavan stopped because of Dellatrix's extreme reaction to his pass. She'd stepped backward off the stool and stood looking at him with terror in her eyes. He was losing her.

"Dellatrix, I'm sorry! Please, sit down. What's wrong?"

Dellatrix lost some of the terror, but didn't move. She said, "I...sorry, it's just...Tig's getting killed must have affected me more than I thought." She shook her head impatiently. "Damn it, I'm a pirate, not some delicate flower. What is wrong with me?" She looked around as though tigers were stalking her.

"Sit back down, Dellatrix. Have another drink. Let's talk about it."

"I don't...I can't...be with anyone right now. With you. All right?" Her voice rattled as her panicked breathing slowed.

"All right. No problem at all. Just sit down, have a drink, and we'll close the bar down listening to the music."

Dellatrix eased her way back onto the bar stool, her hair hanging a little forward as she bent her head, hiding her eyes. Pavan signaled for two more drinks. He couldn't use sex to get her on his side, so he'd use her vulnerability. There was no way he was walking out of this bar with no friends in the *Ravager's* crew. Besides, a damsel in distress—what good was a secret agent if he couldn't help those in need once in a while? And there was something about her lips...and her eyes. Green eyes, with flecks of gold. He wanted to get the pain out of those eyes and see what remained.

Dellatrix looked around. "Can you find us a table? I get leg cramps on these stools."

Sensing a major test of his manhood, Pavan excused himself and walked over to a small table in a corner. He leaned over the two well-dressed gentlemen with a threatening attitude. In a low voice, he said, "10,000 credits for the table?" He held up his servipad in front of his body so Dellatrix couldn't see it. The two men looked at each other, nodded.

"Each."

"Take it," said Pavan.

The two men reached and touched the pad, smiled, and got up, picking up their drinks. Pavan signaled to Dellatrix.

"Enjoy," said one man, looking at the woman crossing the bar.

"No worries," said Pavan. "And thanks."

"Thank *you*," said the other man, and they left. The servipad gave a little grumble of discontent. Pavan put it away, ignoring the implied criticism of excessive expense spending.

"That was impressive," said Dellatrix, seating herself. "How did you do it?"

"Professional secret." And it was: he'd just spent about 20% of his mission budget on a bar table. If that wasn't a secret, he didn't know what was. He'd spend some time later convincing the servipad to report it as a necessary expense so he wouldn't need to explain it to the Ducis. Impressing Dellatrix was a necessary expense, but not one the Ducis would pass.

He started where they'd left off. "You still haven't explained that migrant labor remark, Dellatrix."

"Look. Real pirates get contracts. Like merchant spacers, only illegal—no courts, only trust and killing to enforce them. The pirate code. But migrant labor: no contract, no percentage, just killing or dying when it's required and a decent wage."

"Nobody mentioned a contract to me. Or a code. Or dying."

"Poor Pavan. Migrant labor." She grinned. "You're lucky to be alive."

"What do you do for your percentage, Dellatrix?"

She laughed. "I do what The Captain needs me to do, Pavan, and he likes my dedication and service orientation. And results. I'm very well compensated for my professional skills. The Captain has an excellent track record of providing remunerative opportunities."

"What's he like? The Captain. I've never seen him."

"Nobody's ever seen him."

"So, I've been told he's a front for the backers. Are they real?"

"It takes a lot of capital to run a pirate crew, Pavan, even with a stolen ship. If we were out here on our own, we wouldn't be dressing this well."

Pavan thought that most of the pirates he'd seen dressed like homeless refugees, but he said nothing. Dellatrix wore the same trim, dark blue uniform suit that he'd seen before. She looked good in it. The only jarring note was the thick spacer's boots, the expensive kind, ready for anything that a spaceship could throw at her.

"Just how good is this guy?" he asked.

"At pirating? Top level. Connections, nothing but connections. He's smart and tricky. He finds the ships with the most reward and least risk. The *Ravager*, for example. A skeleton crew of five with no small-arms experience tending a freighter full of luxury goods. A sitting duck."

"Too good to be true, I'd say."

"A set up job. Connections. Lots of black market money to be made. A great investment."

"The crew…"

"Tig took care of them. A skeleton crew."

"Well…" Should Pavan take credit for this? Would Dellatrix approve or disapprove? She was a pirate, but she'd reacted badly to Tig's death. "I had something to do with that."

"You did?" Dellatrix grinned and nodded. "There you go. Migrant labor." The green eyes stared steadily into his. "But not all of us like killing, at least useless killing. I don't know, Pavan. Sometimes I wonder if I'm in the right profession."

Pavan drank up and signaled for a server. "The money's good. Just how long have you worked with The Captain?"

"Years, now." Dellatrix raised a crooked finger. The server was right there with her drink. "Our last ship had an unfortunate incident with a Syndicate patrol. That's how we all wound up on the *Ripper*, ready for a new ship. She's working out well for us, the *Ravager*."

"I understand we took somebody for ransom from that yacht."

He saw the tip of her tongue lick her lip after another sip from her drink. "Already sent back to his family. The Captain made sure we had enough reward before granting us shore leave here. And that guy provided us contractors with a nice chunk."

Pavan felt he was losing ground with the woman, who was way above his pay grade, which was pretty high, at least with the Service. He had to up the stakes. What could he offer her to get her attention?

"The Secret," he said.

"How's that?"

"The Secret of Ravos." He was all in.

Dellatrix looked around at the pirates filling the bar.

"If this place has a secret, it ain't here."

"Why are we here, Dellatrix?"

"Drinks? Good company?"

"I mean, on this planet. Why?"

"The Captain brought us here."

"Why, though?"

"Ravos is forbidden. The Captain said he thought it would be a good place to hide and get some rest and recuperation."

"I've heard rumors of a pirate planet...."

"Khonoë? Sure, we'll get there, but The Captain wanted something in this sector. He's got something in mind, we just haven't heard the plan yet."

Dellatrix lied about her knowledge. But he needed her help, so he'd keep that to himself.

"He keeps things pretty close to his chest, The Captain?"

"If he has one. A pirate chest." She gave a musical little laugh at her own joke.

"How close are you to him?"

"Close enough to know that if he doesn't want to tell us what he's doing, he expects us to just do it when he tells us. Close enough to know that we'll get rewarded for not getting in his way."

"Does he just sit in a room somewhere, like a huge, black spider on a web?"

Dellatrix smiled. "A poisonous one. Great image, Pavan. But, no. He's one of us."

"Us?"

"The crew. He uses the technoids to communicate and run the ship to his satisfaction, but stays hidden within the crew. That way, he always knows what's going on with no one knowing that he knows. Makes it hard to plot against him."

Pavan turned persuasive. "Look, we're two grown pirates with time on our hands here in a bar doing nothing except talking. And drinking. We can find this Secret, sure we can."

"Oooo, a search for buried treasure, now you're talking." She grinned. "Another pirate thing. Sure would get our minds off killing."

"Do you have any idea what the Secret is?"

"Sure. It's a pile of jewels in a large wooden box. Buried with a skeleton on top. Do you have a map with an X on it?"

Pavan checked the surrounding tables. Nobody's ears seemed to be directed at them. The server came and went with their next round of drinks. He leaned toward his new best friend.

"It's a big deal. It's a device that can control hyperspace. Shut it down. Nothing in, nothing out."

Dellatrix smiled. "Sure it is."

"I'm serious, Dellatrix."

"And how did you learn this?" Dellatrix stared at Pavan with doubt in her eyes.

"I overheard some guys on the ship talking about Ravos and put out some feelers to connections I have on Gaelea." Pavan hesitated, pretending to be considering Dellatrix's good faith. "Can I trust you, Dellatrix? We all have secrets, and I don't want mine exposed."

Dellatrix smiled. "Mysterious." She regarded Pavan for a moment, then offered her hand cocked at the angle that Tig had told him marked the pirate-promise shake. At least Tig taught him something useful. They curled fingers and rolled their hands around in the special handshake. She said, "OK, Pavan, I'll keep your secrets—if you'll keep mine. Nobody knows about tonight, ever. Right?"

"Right. Except all the people here in the bar."

"I mean what we talk about here, in private," she said earnestly, holding on to his hand. Her skin was soft, her grip firm and inviting.

"All right. Deal."

She released his hand and leaned forward over the table. "Now, give. How did you learn this?"

"I'm...connected. On Gaelea. To a high-level gangster. I have certain, erm, *legal* problems on Gaelea. I needed to disappear for a while, and the *Ripper* came along recruiting, and here I am, shanghaied to the *Ravager*. But I commed my connection and mentioned Ravos, and he told me the rumors about what was going on here. Even fronted me some funds to spend to find out more." All true, if you called the Ducis a gangster, and that wasn't so far from the truth. "I think those rumors are true. Why else would there be an interdiction field here? If the rumors are true, I know why The Captain is here. If he wants the Secret, we can help him find it. That would get me a contract and you a huge reward. Come on, Dellatrix—if we can get hold of this device, we'd make out like—"

"Pirates?" She smiled. "Tell me, Pavan, are you from that planet where all the rainbows have pots of gold at the end of them?"

"What can I do to persuade you to help find it? I can't do this on my own. I can't even talk to The Captain, much less persuade him. Can you? I think you're a better bet than him, Dellatrix. Prettier and a lot smarter. And if he isn't after it, we can keep it all."

"I'm not sure about prettier. I haven't seen him. And he's galaxy-class smart, certainly as smart as I am. Sure, I can try to persuade him. I have enough rep on the ship. But you have to realize, Pavan: it doesn't matter whether he's after it. If we find it, he'll take his share, which will be most of it. Whatever it's worth. It's in our contracts. We're pirates, and he's The Captain. Not a lot left over for your gangster buddy."

"Even so. Can you give the rest of your leave? To do it ourselves? This is a huge opportunity for me, and for you. We can deal with The Captain once we have it."

"What the hell. Why not? It's that or drink myself to death here. And I don't want to go back to the ship just yet. Not after what happened earlier. A search for buried treasure is just the thing to get my mind off…things. That and a few more drinks." She raised two fingers, and the yellow-haired bartender got busy.

CHAPTER FOUR
The Search for the Secret

"I GUESS WE'LL HAVE TO improvise," said Pavan, crunching his breakfast goldhorn pastry. The noise made his head ache.

Dellatrix, stirring cream into her cup of Denerthian coffee, grimaced. "The last time I improvised, I spent six weeks recovering."

Pavan and Dellatrix sat at a nice table in the Ravosi Arms Hotel restaurant. The table was next to a pseudowindow that looked out onto a planet that had nothing to do with anything on Ravos. Pavan's memory of their arrival at the hotel the night before suggested the hotel didn't sport any real windows. No point, given the city streets. Defensible space. Pavan thought about requesting a scene from Gaelea but decided against. His head hurt enough without burdening it with homesickness. No night of ecstasy; Dellatrix insisted on separate rooms. He dreamed about Gaelea, but the dream was only a vague feeling of pleasure in an otherwise harsh reality.

"Why the hell did you feed me so many drinks?" Pavan rubbed his head.

Dellatrix favored him with a scornful smile. "What's the matter, boy? Trouble holding your liquor?"

"I wouldn't know, I can't remember."

"We had a great time. Toured the city with a friendly cabby."

"I remember that part. I don't remember the great time part."

"Look, I didn't sign up for this partnership to babysit a grumpy assmonkey."

"OK. Where'd you get that coffee?"

"I made a special deal with the chef."

"Can you get me one too?"

Dellatrix held up two fingers at shoulder level. A servnoid whisked by loaded with plates, stopping to deposit a cup in front of Pavan. Dellatrix recouped a good measure of her pirate bravado after a good night's sleep. Tig's death seemed like a long time ago. But Pavan had seen the underlying vulnerability in her, despite her attempts to overcome it. After the stories they'd exchanged at the bar, it was clear she possessed the status with the pirates to help him get what he needed. He had to get through her defenses and turn her to his side.

He said, "So if you don't want to improvise, we need a plan."

"The best plan would get The Captain to use his connections and intelligence resources to find this thing," said Dellatrix. "But you don't want that, right? We find this Secret on our own?"

"Right. Private enterprise. I want The Captain to see how much I can contribute. So he'll give me a contract."

"OK, so what resources do you have?" The clear, green eyes studied him.

Pavan dug around in his pocket and came up with his lucky feather.

"What the hell's that?"

"Lucky feather."

Dellatrix giggled. Then snorted. Then pounded the table with one hand while she laughed out loud. Pavan sat back and grinned at her. She had a nice, musical laugh.

Dellatrix reached over and took the feather. She looked at both sides of it.

"What makes it lucky?" she asked, her laughter subsiding into some involuntary heaves of her breasts.

"Took it off a dead man."

"Oooo, a pirate thing."

"Right."

Dellatrix smiled. "And that's it? Your resource?"

"Yep."

Dellatrix ate the feather after folding it into quarters and crunching it between her delicate teeth. She swallowed and smiled.

"I'll give it back to you in a couple of days after I've tested it."

"Damn it, Dellatrix, that was my lucky feather!" And what he would do for luck now was anyone's guess. Margona would understand. Wouldn't she? A pirate ate it. Sure thing.

"I know. You said." Dellatrix smiled and drank some coffee to wash down the feather. "What else you got?"

What else did he have? He could go after the damn Secret alone and die in the attempt. He needed this pirate on his side. All he had on offer was himself. He spread his hands wide. "You're looking at it."

"Shit." She finished her coffee and raised a finger. The coffee mug filled up as a servnoid whisked by with a pot. It ignored Pavan. "Well, quite a partnership. OK, you'll be the brawn and I'll be the brains."

"Is the whole damn city like this?" asked Pavan.

The cab responded, "Like what, bro?"

"I wasn't asking you," he said.

"Rude," said the cab.

"He's grumpy from the hangover." Dellatrix looked moodily out her window.

"Can I put on some music?" asked the cab. "Loud?"

"No," said Pavan.

Dellatrix said, "Every place in the city I've seen looks just like this. It's why I take cabs. Not so much the street people danger, but all the streets look the same. Only the cabs know where they are. And the bandits."

"Damn right, lady," said the cab. A street denizen jumped out of the way of the cab, which just missed him.

"Watch where you're going," said Pavan.

"I'm driving," said the cab.

Pavan turned his attention to his companion. "Who's this guy we're going to meet?"

Dellatrix checked her servipad. "Nash Onyx." She scrolled. "Formal business is selling art. Informal business is selling information. Both expensive. My sources tell me he knows more about what's going on here than anyone else on the planet. And he's private, extremely private, and not afraid of involving himself with people like us."

"And how did you find this guy?"

Dellatrix sighed. "Look, pirates know people. I've been a pirate long enough to know people who know people who know people. I got the lead from a woman I met several years ago who's got a son that married a woman from here, and she's the daughter of a man who—"

"Never mind."

"You can take the lead with him, Pavan." Dellatrix touched his arm. "I'm not all that good at negotiation. All right?"

"Fine." He rubbed her hand. "Thanks for the vote of confidence."

The cab decided that if it couldn't play loud music, it'd whistle. Technoids have no lips, so this whistle was a high-pitched electronic whine reminiscent of various insect species that you didn't want near you. Pavan's fingers tapped out an old Gaelean battle tune on his knee. The cab barreled straight through a crowd of people carrying signs and shouting. Pavan couldn't hear what they screamed as they scattered, diving and dodging.

"What the hell—"

"I'm driving!" the cab asserted.

Pavan opened his mouth to remonstrate, but as the cab had stopped whistling, held his peace. Every planet had its quirks, as did every cab. Dellatrix looked out of the pseudowindow at the passing buildings, unconcerned.

The cab said, "OK, lady, I've negotiated a garage fee with Onyx Art."

"Garage fee?" Pavan had that feeling you get staying at expensive hotels where you have to tip every single person you meet, even the other guests. The expenses were mounting.

"Yeah, bro. You don't want to get out in the street, not here. Take my word. Nice garage, back door into the 'art gallery,' you'll never know you're in the middle of a food riot."

"Food riot?"

"Can we focus on the matter at hand? Garage us and wait, please," said Dellatrix.

"Yes ma'am." The cab swung around a corner and slipped under a rising garage door, and the door swooshed shut behind them.

Pavan and Dellatrix stepped into a small room with no windows and two massive doors, the one through which they entered, and the one through which they would exit. There was no handle on the latter door. Pavan pushed at it with no effect. He felt a slight frisson and thought for a moment his courage had gone back on him until a voice spoke.

"Put the microblaster in the lockbox. The box will return it to you when you leave."

Pavan looked around and found the box protruding from the wall; it hadn't been there a minute before. He took his microblaster from his pocket and deposited it, and the box withdrew into the wall. Fat lot of good it did carrying the blaster around if every time he went into danger the opposition took it away from him before the fun started. A small part of his mind registered the interesting fact that Dellatrix had no weapons at all.

The exit door swung open to show a short, rotund individual with quick, suspicious eyes and a welcoming smile that wasn't even skin deep. A microblaster nestled in his pudgy hand. He motioned to the pair to come in, and they stepped past him into the art gallery.

"Nash Onyx, proprietor of this gallery. And you are?" said the little man.

Pavan said, "Pavan Khadorov, and this is Dellatrix Devdan."

Onyx said, "You must be off that freighter that docked yesterday. We don't get many off-worlders these days. Are you in the market for art, or are you tourists?"

Dellatrix smiled. "We might be interested in your offerings," she said.

Onyx waved a hand around. "Here are the works on display in our current show. Please…"

The walls appeared blank. "I don't see…" began Pavan.

"Ah, silly me. You'll need nanogoggles, it's nanoart." Onyx stepped over to a box on a table and withdrew two goggle sets. "You use the locator buttons to move from piece to piece, these buttons on the side here," he said.

Pavan and Dellatrix donned the goggles and inspected some of the art.

Pavan, unimpressed, whispered to Dellatrix, "I may not know much about art, but I know what I hate."

"Shut up," she responded, moving on to the next piece. "This stuff is hugely popular right now. Be polite, if you know how."

Pavan asked in a louder voice, "How many works are there in the exhibition, Mr. Onyx?"

"We have 375 plus some sketches, by three well-regarded artists."

"I don't see any prices?"

Onyx smiled. "The artists consider their works priceless. From my perspective, they will bring what the market will bear. You may make an offer on anything for my consideration."

Dellatrix said, "I don't think nanoart is what we're looking for, Mr. Onyx. Perhaps something…more abstract?" She removed her goggles, as did Pavan.

"Abstraction is in the beholder's eye," said Onyx, smiling. "I understand that your 'freighter,' for example, is more of an abstract concept than a reality."

"You appear to have good sources, Mr. Onyx," said Dellatrix. "If I take your meaning."

His lips tightened in a small smile. "My sources are excellent, Ms. Devdan. As are the abstractions I sell. You may make an offer on anything."

"Ah. Exactly. And that is why we are here. But we are here on our own account, not as representatives of our…associates. On our freighter." Dellatrix nodded at Pavan. "Mr. Khadorov here is the lead partner in the enterprise and can tell you more about what we're looking for. Pavan?"

Pavan, tiring of indirection, said, "We're searching for a device that manipulates hyperspace. We understand from our sources this device exists somewhere on Ravos, and it may well be the reason for the interdiction shield the Syndicate has placed on the planet."

"To our sorrow. I have encountered similar rumors in my business dealings in recent times. Device? I see. The Secret of Ravos, as those in the au courant circles call it, with some jocundity."

Onyx held his blaster ready. His level of distrust mystified Pavan; the man must deal with unsavory elements such as Dellatrix and himself all the time. Why the excess of caution? Who might worry about a couple of friendly pirates who want to buy something?

"We are prepared," said Pavan, "to consider a large fee for information that would lead us to the Secret."

Onyx cocked his head and said, "Conference room." He walked toward a door. The contrast of that room with the gallery was enormous. Stark white walls with their invisible nanoart gave way to calm, warm-colored walls with a pseudowindow looking out onto a nighttime city view of glittering tall buildings and rushing transportation lights. The furnishings were comfortable sofas, low tables, and a sideboard that rivaled the Golden Pig's selection of pricey beverages.

"Drink?" asked Onyx, waving a hand at the bar. Pavan shook his head, then regretted it as the resulting pain washed through it at the thought of more alcohol. Dellatrix raised a hand with the third and last fingers extended. The technoid sideboard served up a specialized cocktail glass that Pavan recognized as a Lavonian gimlet. Dellatrix walked over and took the glass and sipped.

"Excellent," she said. She walked back, keeping her distance from Onyx as promised, and put the glass on the table. "May I use your restroom?"

"Second door on the left as you go out," said Onyx. Dellatrix left. Onyx looked at Pavan. "Shall we wait or negotiate now?"

Pavan grinned. "We can go ahead. She's game for anything."

"Doubtless, Mr. Khadorov, as she has every right to be."

"I'm prepared to offer a very generous up-front fee for information."

"And?"

Pavan relaxed into the soft sofa. "And a generous finder's fee payable when we have the Secret in our hands."

"I'm uncertain how valuable that will be, Mr. Khadorov. The Secret...I can't imagine the two of you taking advantage of the...device. The nature of it—our own government has tried and failed to take advantage of it, only to have the

Syndicate step in with its interdiction field. It may be a failure of imagination, or it may be intrinsic to the Secret. But I do not know you, and your background and that of your partner do not inspire my confidence in your ability to make use of the Secret in your…enterprises. I do not ask your intentions; I frankly care only about my fee. Allow me to make a counterproposal. I suggest an up-front fee of half the amount and a final fee payable when you learn the nature of the Secret. Beyond that, I make no promises; you are on your own."

Pavan's mind jumped from possibility to impossibility. He thought of building-sized machinery or physical phenomena that could not transport easily. The man's language suggested many such things. And he did not appear to worry about the Ravosi government or the Syndicate. Not that it mattered; Pavan didn't intend to "take advantage" of the Secret, only use it to get back to his wife alive and whole, if he could.

Pavan regarded Onyx with a calm gaze. "What do you know about the Secret that you're not telling me, Mr. Onyx?"

The little man smiled and waved his blaster, then looked surprised to find it in his hand. He didn't put it away, though.

"That's the very nature of a secret, is it not, Mr. Khadorov?"

Dellatrix came back into the room, a satisfied look of pleasure on her face. She sat, picked up her gimlet, and sipped. "Progress?" she asked.

"Just getting started," replied Pavan. "Mr. Onyx drops hints the Secret may prove difficult for us to exploit."

Dellatrix smiled. "Let's not worry about that," she said. "I can bring resources to bear."

"Very well," said Pavan. "An up-front half and a final half."

Negotiations proceeded through several offers and rejections of amounts until all parties settled on a fee and payment structure. The latter specified the conditions the parties must meet to be paid. Dellatrix spent a lot of time on the conditions, making Pavan a little anxious about whether Onyx might object. But Onyx put away his blaster and produced promisepads and programmed in the details of the deal. Pavan provided the initial fee with his servipad, and Onyx completed the contract by connecting the contract pads to their mutual NIUs. The technoid pad said, "Very good, sir, the money's banked. We'll need a long-distance transport and some supplies. Destination, the village of Loxator."

Onyx rose and bowed, and Pavan and Dellatrix followed him out.

"A pleasure doing business. Ms. Devdan. Mr. Khadorov. Safe journey." Onyx never got closer to Dellatrix than two arm distances, even when wishing her well. An odd character. But then, Pavan's career as a pirate teemed with odd characters.

Their cab was glad to see them.

"This place gives me the creeps," it said as they settled into their seats. "Let's go. Where to?"

"We need to find long-distance transport," said Pavan.

"What's wrong with me, bro?"

"I didn't know you did that kind of work."

Offended, the cab replied, "Come on, bro, I'm equipped for anything you got. Want to get into it? Where to?"

Pavan brought out the promisepad. "This is our transport. Tell it where to go."

"This? This is a *cab*." The promisepad's voice was incredulous.

"Shit. Now I got to deal with a flat-boy wise guy. Look, bro—"

"Everybody calm down," commanded Dellatrix. "Cab says it can do the job, I believe it. Tell it where to go, please."

The promisepad gave a little grumble.

The cab responded to its new information. "Shit. All the way out to the ocean? That's gonna cost you." Silence descended, then the cab made its pitch. "Hey. I need the money, so how about a special deal: 3,000 credits each way. That's fair. All up front."

Dellatrix looked at Pavan, who resigned himself and held up the servipad once again. "Done."

"This is going to be an adventure," said the promisepad.

Dellatrix said, "Is that thing bugged, do you think?"

Pavan looked from his apparently paranoid companion to the promisepad. Might as well humor her. "Are you bugged? By Onyx?"

The promisepad said, offended, "Sir, I beg your pardon. I keep no records at all of any kind other than those delineated by the contract details. I am not 'bugged.'"

"Bugs the hell outta me," commented the cab.

Pavan handed the promisepad to Dellatrix. "You keep it, it likes you."

Dellatrix smiled and pocketed the technoid. She said, "We'll need to stop for some supplies."

"I know a great cheap place that will set you up." The cab exited the garage into the city streets.

Dellatrix drew a small container out of her pocket and showed it to Pavan. He raised an inquiring eyebrow.

"I funded our journey with a few art pieces," she said. "Scraped them off the wall when I went to the restroom."

"No alarms?" asked Pavan. He had visions of flashing lights and massive weapons fire enveloping their cab.

"I have resources."

"What did you take?"

"Fifty of the Kyris Edan works. Worth twice the fee. Nice stuff."

"Dellatrix. Onyx will set the police on us!"

"What police?"

Pavan opened his mouth, then closed it. Paranoid, perhaps; but still a pirate.

"It's a pirate thing," said Dellatrix, verifying his judgment and putting away the container.

"You guys are trouble," said the cab. "But I'm game."

CHAPTER FIVE
The Cab's Journey

THE CAB FOUND THE ROAD out of the city after Pavan and Dellatrix filled its storage compartment with mission essentials such as food, water, warm clothing, and scouting technoids. They kept their new blasters in holsters for quick use. The road deteriorated after a few miles. As the city streets were not examples of a well organized public works department, this was saying something.

"Gonna be a rough ride, folks," said the cab. "How about some nice music?"

The calming music washed over Pavan, allowing him enough personal space to process the events of the last few hours. Dellatrix napped, leaning against the side of the cab. Once out of the city, the countryside emerged as a brown, grassy series of rolling hills sprinkled with unidentifiable trees here and there. Pavan liked his landscapes green, though he had a place in his heart for serious desert; Gaelea had several parks that were nothing but desert and rock formations stretching away to a blue horizon. Ravos's foothills looked like they ought to host a herd of domesticated animals, but they were barren and devoid of animal life or people.

Into a gap in the music, Pavan asked, "How much longer to this village?"

"It'll be about three hours from here, bro," responded the cab. "Unless I break an axle on these potholes."

"Don't."

"Hey—I'm a pro, bro! Don't worry, I'll get you there for lunch. If they have any food."

Pavan stared at the passing scenery, then stared at Dellatrix when he tired of the scenery. Her face had relaxed into a softness that Pavan had not seen in her before. Her inner self? Her form, attractive as it had been in the bar, was even more attractive in repose. Pavan's Margona-programmed neuroinstincts kicked in and Margona filled his mind. The unintended result was an intense sadness that settled over him as he thought about never seeing her again.

The cab bobbed and weaved along the road, making progress. Pavan settled himself on the other side of the cab from Dellatrix and rested his eyes.

He snapped awake to a loud boom assaulting his ears. Dellatrix lifted her head, blinking. The cab careened off the road into a ditch. It came to rest with the front of the cab resting against the wall of the ditch and the back pointing up at a 30-degree angle. As the curtain restraints retracted, both Pavan and Dellatrix had blasters out, the new ones they had acquired as "supplies." The calming music flowed around them in total incongruity with the situation, then abruptly died.

"You take your side, I'll take mine," said Pavan. Dellatrix nodded. They popped the cab doors and rolled out and took prone positions below the rim of the ditch on both sides of the cab. Pavan scanned rapidly all around him to see where the ambushers were coming from, but he saw no one, only the rolling hills.

"Anything?" he said in a soft voice.

"Not here," said Dellatrix. She took out a zoomscope and raised it above the ditch rim.

"Find any attackers and highlight," she said to the scope, swinging it around in a 360-degree circle.

"Nothing found," replied the technoid. "Except for the large man on the other side of the cab, whom I assume is a friendly."

"Correct, too friendly sometimes," said Dellatrix. Pavan snorted.

The zoomscope said, "The cab wants to talk. Urgently."

Dellatrix stuck her head inside her door, and Pavan did the same on the other side.

"Status?" asked Pavan.

"Screwed," said the cab. "To the max. Explosion got my rear propulsion system and took the rear axle with it. I'll need a tow and a lot of sympathy. I'll call it in."

"Hold off on that a minute or two, please," said Dellatrix. "We need to make sure it's safe."

"Fine. I've shut off the fuel leak, I'll be OK. "

"Did you see what caused the explosion?" asked Pavan.

"Yeah, bro. Big bastard bomb buried in the road. It went off right under the rear of the cab. You can't trust anybody these days."

"Why are we still alive?"

"Told you I was equipped, bro!" The cab was smug. "Armor plating. You never know what's gonna happen in the city. Best prepare for anything. I even have two blasters up front, just in case a pedestrian gets obstreperous."

Dellatrix signaled to Pavan to come around for a talk.

"We'll need to walk the rest of the way," she said, taking out the promisepad. "How far is it to the village from here?"

"3.43 kilometers to the village boundary," responded the pad.

"Not too bad," said Dellatrix. "Let's get the supplies out of the cab."

The storage compartment on the cab was undamaged by the explosion, and Pavan arranged the supplies in his gravpack while Dellatrix did the same.

When they'd packed up, Dellatrix stuck her head back into the cab. "We need to get to this village today, so we're taking off. You'll be OK?"

"Sure thing, lady, tow'll be here in two shakes when I call it in."

"That's just fine," said Dellatrix. "Pavan, go up and see what the road is like."

Pavan climbed over the edge of the ditch. He turned just in time to see Dellatrix fling herself over the edge. "Down!" she shouted.

Pavan, through pure reflex, hit the dirt before she'd finished saying the word.

A huge fireball flamed from the ditch straight up. Pieces of metal rained down over the landscape. When the excitement died down, Pavan raised his head. The cab had vanished from the ditch and spread itself over a large area of the surrounding countryside.

"What the hell was that?" shouted Pavan. He shouted because he was having trouble hearing, and he assumed Dellatrix would be too—but he knew he would have shouted anyway.

She got up and helped him to his feet. "Particle grenade. Tossed it into the storage compartment. I put the thing out of its misery."

"What? Why?" Pavan couldn't keep the surprise out of his sharp questions.

She brushed off something off his shoulder, then melted into his arms. He could feel her trembling. She said into his shoulder, "Pavan. How did they know where we were? To plant the bomb ahead of us?"

Pavan said, "You think the cab was a *spy*?"

"I...was afraid it might let whoever did this track us." Her trembling faded, and she stepped back to look in his face. "Did I overreact? I do, sometimes, when...." She jerked a hand at where the cab had been, her eyes darting around. "Sorry."

"No, no, it's fine. Just took me by surprise. Well. Dead cabs tell no tales!" He stepped forward to embrace her, but she stopped him.

"I can't…. It was reflex, hugging you like that. I'll be fine, now." She shook her head. "This planet is getting to me. Some pirate."

Despite his own experience with death on missions, Pavan had to relax his muscles from the tight, immobile mass they'd contracted into at the explosion. Or was it from his proximity to the woman who'd caused it? He wondered who, exactly, "they" were, and who would care about the story. Onyx? The Captain? Somebody else? And whether "they" had more explosives or other things in mind for the partners on their way to Loxator. And whether the beautiful but vulnerable and paranoid woman in front of him had any more particle grenades he needed to worry about. And how he could best take advantage of her vulnerability to complete his mission.

"Maybe we'd better get going." Dellatrix addressed the promisepad. "Directions?"

"First, madam, let us be clear: under section 82.4376 of the Galactic Syndicate Commercial Code, it is a felony to destroy a contract before completing the contract terms. Such destruction entails extra penalties, including forfeiture of all contracted payments. The Code allows me to track such events or attempted events securely in a manner that persists after destruction. Are we straight on that?"

Dellatrix smiled. "Here," she said to Pavan. "I think it likes you better than me now." She gave him the technoid, which sighed and gave him directions.

CHAPTER SIX
Under Cover of Night

"WHAT DO YOU THINK?" ASKED Dellatrix.

The pair of pirates lay on their bellies, looking over the side of a small decline that led to a tiny, ramshackle village rotting away in a cove. Dellatrix handed Pavan the zoomscope, and he examined the single street and the simple wooden houses that lined it. Not a soul was visible on the street.

"Pretty quiet," he said. "If the Secret of Ravos is there, it's still secret." Pavan's stomach gave a little twist as he assessed the situation. For a simple mission, things weren't going well, what with ambushes and treachery and particle grenades and the lack of any sign of the target. A map with an X on it would be welcome, even if it only led to a skeleton and a box of jewels.

"Ask that thing where the device is," suggested Dellatrix.

"I do not have that information, madam. The contract specifies that the parties of the second part—that is, you and your partner in crime here—find and acquire the Secret of Ravos. It has no more details than that. Go to it."

"Explain to me, Pavan, why we need this contract." She shot an evil glance at the small pad, still attached to Pavan's gravpack.

"The money-back clause, Dellatrix."

"Oh. Yeah."

"Must I explain that too, madam?" asked the promisepad.

Dellatrix took the zoomscope back from Pavan without replying.

Pavan said, "We'll need to search the place. I guess we have two options: round up the villagers and put them somewhere, or burgle the houses."

"How are you at burglary?"

"First-class second-story man. I can pass through an insomniac's room without her knowing I'm there."

"Right. So can I. If I knock her out first." Dellatrix smiled. "OK, burglary it is, I don't want 100 villagers on my conscience for a simple job like this. You take the ocean side of the street, I'll take the inland side. We'll wait until it gets dark. Let's go back and find a place to eat our supper."

They inched back from the lookout point and hiked back aways to a pile of boulders that formed a natural windbreak and hideout. The wind had picked up about half an hour after the cab's demise, and the temperature had plummeted after the sun set. Dellatrix had brought along two thermocoats, so they weren't cold, but eating anything in a brisk wind was never fun.

As Pavan arranged the food packs and activated the heat technoids, Dellatrix cleared an area of small lava rocks. She pulled two bigger rocks over to form seats, then set up a small torchnoid on a rock as a lantern. When the heat technoids announced that dinner was ready, they ate their meal.

"Is this stuff imported?" asked Pavan after tasting his meal.

"No, local."

"Ah."

"If you care so much about food, next time you shop," said Dellatrix.

"No, no, it's fine, just a little...odd."

Dellatrix rolled her eyes and munched.

This might be a good opportunity to get some information about the pirates. The more Pavan learned about them, the better his chances once he got the Secret of Ravos onto the *Ravager.*

He asked, "What's The Captain really like?"

"Nobody knows. I told you that before."

"I mean, as a pirate."

"He's somebody I know, from the *Ripper* crew—but no one knows which of us is The Captain. If you ship out with him, he takes a cut of your life. It's in the contract. Do whatever you like as long as you give him ten percent."

"Can't you just hide the deal from him?"

"Last guy who tried that wound up floating around Ladeus 6 without a space suit. And hiding things on the ship is hard when the guy eating Pavlovian moonfish next to you might be The Captain without your knowing it."

"Lucky I don't have a contract," said Pavan.

Dellatrix ate some more whatever-it-was, then said, "I'd hate to see you marooned on some desert planet. I'd miss you, Pavan. I want to hear you say you're an honest pirate. Tell me you won't double-cross me or The Captain." She reached out a hand and stroked Pavan's face scar, her eyes metallic with the reflected light of the torchnoid. There was her paranoia again.

"Wouldn't think of it," said Pavan, thinking of it. Events had worked against an easy forging of trust with the woman he depended on to get this mission past the finish line. He needed to work harder at it even while he figured out how to hoodwink her and the pirates into getting the Secret into the hands of the Ducis.

"Good." The pirate resumed eating her supper. "I'd hate to have wasted this excellent food on somebody who wouldn't be around to see tomorrow morning. I'd say you're damn lucky to have me as a partner."

"I am sure that for a reasonable fee I could develop a suitable contract that would satisfy all parties," suggested the promisepad.

"Hold that thought," said Dellatrix.

Pavan crept out of the village and scrambled up the small hill to the appointed meeting place. Dellatrix was already there.

"Let's walk up the road a little, too close here," whispered Dellatrix. Pavan nodded.

"Did you have any trouble?" asked Pavan once they'd put some distance between themselves and the village.

"No; you?"

"Only the fact that these people own nothing worth stealing."

"Now that's just not true," said Dellatrix. She set the torchnoid lantern on a nearby rock and pulled something from her pocket. "I liked these homemade seashell earrings. Not what I'd call a valuable Secret, though." She dangled the earrings next to her ears to show him.

"It's a joke," said Pavan. "These people are lucky they haven't starved to death."

"Like the rest of the people on this planet."

"Exactly. If they have any secrets, they've hidden them well."

"It's that Onyx. He has us chasing fantasies," said Dellatrix.

"I must point out, madam," said the promisepad, "the terms of the agreement I am enforcing would penalize Mr. Onyx should you be able to prove fraud."

"Even so. All this worries me, Pavan." She chewed a corner of her mouth in frustration.

"What would The Captain do?"

She gave him a small smile and said, "First light, he'd go down and roust out the villagers and make them tell us what's what."

"And how would he do that?"

"He'd corral them, take their children, and kill them one by one until some-body talks."

"Dellatrix…." Pavan stretched a hand out to her shoulder, and she flinched away.

Looking away from him, she said, "I'm just saying that's what he would do, not what I would do." Her face was grim in the torchnoid's light.

"How about we just ask them," he said. "Nicely."

"What?" asked Dellatrix, lifting her jaw up and looking at him in surprise.

"Ask them. Tomorrow morning, after breakfast. Go down, find somebody, pretend we're tourists, ask about the Secret. What could it hurt?"

Dellatrix mulled this over. "I suppose so. But if they don't tell us, we'll have to —"

"Let's worry about that when it happens, all right? How are you at establishing friendly relations with locals?" he asked.

"Rotten. Too shy. You?"

"I've had some training in it, in the military." Agents' training. Right after the sessions on close-combat tactics and nerve toxins. Shy? Sure thing.

"Oh, good." She smiled, teeth gleaming in the dark. "No worries, Pavan. You can take the lead. I'll cover you." She took out her blaster and checked it over, holstered it, and sat down to wait for first light.

CHAPTER SEVEN
A Visit to Loxator Village

LOXATOR DIDN'T GET TOURISTS, PAVAN surmised as he walked with Dellatrix down the empty village street. Pretending to be backpacker tourists was going to be tough. There was nothing to do or see there that would bear the light of day, and less than that at night.

No architect had ever consulted on the building plans for the weathered and shambling wood houses. Every house was unique in its poverty of construction, and gravity held sway over the town.

"I would kill to live in this place," said Dellatrix. "If I could get ahold of the person who made me do it."

Pavan, who was a bit on the tired side, smiled at this witticism but had nothing to add. His own inspection and that of Dellatrix had yielded nothing of interest and no hint of a secret device. Could the villagers have buried it somewhere?

He noticed Dellatrix swiveling her head, looking for something. Something she hadn't seen last night? Hope generated a tiny spark in his breast.

"What are you looking for?"

"X."

"I don't…" Then he twigged. X always marked the spot on the pirate treasure map, even in space. He smiled, cleared his throat, and continued the thought. "I don't think there's any buried treasure here."

She looked sideways at him with a grin. "Quick on the uptake, aren't we? I don't think we're even going to find a skeleton, much less a treasure chest."

"Are you lost?"

The high-pitched voice came from behind them. The pair whirled to find one house had ejected a small girl of about six years old, dressed in rags, who looked at them with pity in her eyes. She was striking because of her dead white skin and white hair—an albino.

"Um, no," said Pavan. "We're hikers. We've been hiking along the coast."

"Why?" The girl had an uncomfortable way of putting her finger on the flaw in Pavan's story. There was nothing at all that might draw hikers to this coast.

"Exercise, get a bit of air."

"The air here is awful." The girl blinked. "Something to do with rotting seaweed, my Da says. It's not so bad right now, the wind's offshore."

The wind blew strongly, and Pavan couldn't say it was healthy. There was something dank in it, with an underlying hint of decay. The miasma fit the village like a dirty glove.

"Fish make it smell pretty bad, too, but we don't have any right now." The girl warmed to her community spirit.

"Is there someone in charge that we could talk to? About food?"

"Oh, we don't have any food. Just some left-over fish soup. What does 'in charge' mean?"

Dellatrix, impatient, took over the leadership of the team. "Your father or mother, can you get them? We'd like some information."

"My mother's dead, but my Da might talk with you if you can wait for a few minutes. He's putting on his leg."

Dellatrix looked at Pavan, who gritted his teeth. It was going to be a long day. Dellatrix addressed the girl again. "How about any of these other houses? Is there someone in the village who tells everyone what to do?"

The girl looked doubtful. "Not really. Only on the boats."

"The boats?" asked Pavan, despite himself.

"The fishing boats. The crew chooses someone as captain when they go out."

Dellatrix said, "Pirates would shrivel up and disappear in a place like this." She shivered.

"What's a pirate?"

"Never you mind, girl. Tell your father we'd like to talk."

"All right." The girl disappeared back into her house.

The promisepad said, "Now that you're in the village, the grace period for the contract has started. You have thirty-six hours until the money-back clause expires."

"Thank you," muttered Dellatrix.

"You're very welcome, madam."

Dellatrix said, "That girl is mentally deficient. And albino. Unlucky."

Pavan smiled. "Don't judge, Dellatrix. I'm sure there are many possibilities here that we haven't seen."

The pair stood, facing away from each other, surveying the ends of the village, hoping to find something they'd missed. They didn't.

"You folks lost?" asked a gravelly voice. A quick inspection showed a wooden leg under a tall, robust, dark man with a crooked smile standing in the doorway of the little girl's house.

"They're pirates, Da." The little girl stood behind her father, holding his hand.

"Pirates, eh?" smiled the big man. He stumped down the short stairs to the dirt street and peg-legged over to Pavan and Dellatrix, who had turned to face him. "I'd invite you in, but it's warmer out here."

Pavan put his hands in his pockets to keep them warm. He smiled. "No, we're not lost, and we're not pirates, your daughter misconstrued a joke from my partner."

"No point in pirating around here anyway, 'less you might have an interest in taking a fishing boat," the man said. He waved a hand at the little boats bobbing out in the cove.

"We were hoping for some fresh food," said Dellatrix, "but I don't see an inn here."

"No, no inn, we don't get a lot of visitors here in Loxator," the man said. "And we're shy of food right now, I'm afraid. Delivery didn't come yesterday, don't know why."

"What do you do when a delivery doesn't come?" asked Pavan.

"Starve," said the man with a grimace. "Don't happen often, but when it does...." He left the explanation unfinished. "Usual, we have some fish salted down, ate it all. Bad fishing season. Bad weather. Wind like this keeps the fish away. Name's Rark, by the way."

"Pavan Khadorov, and my partner, Dellatrix Devdan."

"Off-worlders, by the look of you. Don't get a lot of off-worlders on Ravos lately, it being forbidden and all." The sentence ended in a half question. Pavan didn't take the bait.

"We're hiking down the coast, part of a challenge from a group we belong to. Somebody in the city recommended we take a detour to Loxator to see the Secret."

"Ah, oh, the Secret, is it?" The big man smiled, brown teeth showing. "That'll liven up Jandra's day, won't it, Janny?" The little girl smiled up at him. "Well, you're a bit early, but the kids should be up and about soon, and you can see the Secret then."

Pavan sucked his teeth in indecision and looked at Dellatrix. Stay? Leave and get their money back? He could convince the Ducis not to destroy the planet if there was no secret. Kids? Dellatrix shrugged and rolled her eyes.

"Is there somewhere out of the wind we can wait?" she asked.

"Out of the wind, now, that's not so easy here, even in the houses. But sure, you can wait in my house while Janny and I go get some water for the day's washing." Rark waved a hand at the house.

Pavan and Dellatrix walked up the stairs. Pavan turned before going in and watched the big man and his daughter walk down the street, hand in hand. Affecting.

"How long do we wait for this Secret?" he asked. Every minute they remained here was time on the clock for the Ducis and his Syndicate fleet. If there was just a children's game, they would have wasted their time. But he couldn't tell Dellatrix that, and he needed to go along with her for the time being.

"An hour or two won't kill us." She went into the house. "He's right, it's colder in here. Shit."

After an hour of sitting in the cold house, even the thermocoats had given up. It must have been psychological; thermocoats were effective down to anything over 225 Kelvin. The place radiated cold and poverty. Secret of Ravos? Kids would show it to them. Right.

"I'd pay 100 credits for a Lavonian brandy right now, preferably on fire." Dellatrix seemed to feel the cold more than Pavan. She sat huddled in her thermocoat, arms wrapped around herself and a very glum look on her face.

"I've heard that cuddling up together makes you a lot warmer," said Pavan.

"In your dreams."

Pavan, rebuffed in his try at seduction, tried to keep up a congenial conversation, but after a half hour quit and just sat in silence, waiting. After another half hour, Pavan heard noises out on the street: children-playing noises. Then the door opened and Jandra stuck her head in.

"All the kids are out now, Pavan. Come and play!"

Pavan said to Dellatrix, "Did you ever want children?"

"No. I'm a career pirate, though I've had second thoughts lately. You?"

"My wife and I have given it some thought."

"Then you can take the lead again."

Pavan had undergone a quite happy childhood with parents that loved him. That his father was a government functionary close to the Ducis had provided him with a seamless path to success. His own predilection for adventure got him into the field as an agent. He'd regretted nothing about either his childhood or his job. Until now. Now, he needed to play with some kids on a search for pirate treasure.

Pavan and Dellatrix found a cluster of seventeen children of ages ranging from five to twelve standing in the street outside the door. The children stood whispering to each other, all eyes on the newcomers.

An older boy stepped forward. "Hi, I'm Coren. Janny says you're pirates. We've never seen any pirates here." The boy had coffee-colored skin and crinkly black hair cut very short.

"We're not pirates, Jandra misunderstood."

"Oh." The boy grimaced. "Too bad, we thought we could play a pirate game together."

"That's fine, we can be pirates for now."

"Pavan!" Dellatrix gripped his arm. "Be nice." She looked at Coren. "I'm Dellatrix, and this is Pavan."

Coren grinned, his eyes lighting up. "It's fun to have you. Rark said you wanted to see the Secret. We can do a pirate version!"

"Um…" Pavan couldn't frame any response to this offer. He found that maybe wanting kids wasn't the same as being able to handle them when taken by surprise.

Dellatrix let go of his arm and said, "We'd be delighted to do that, Coren."

"OK, come on over here and we'll set up." The boy took Dellatrix's hand and led her into the middle of the street. "You sit there. You're not kids, so you have to be inside the circle, not part of it."

"All right. Come on, Pavan."

Pavan got his feet moving and joined his partner, sitting in the middle of the dirt street. He noticed several adults watching from doorways: small, dark women without smiles or any other outward show of emotion. All wore rags and looked worn down. None seemed interested in playing the game.

The children formed a ring around the two partners, sat down, and joined hands.

Coren said, "OK, everyone, here we go. Today we're going to be pirates. You, Trex, pay attention this time. We won't break the circle for stupid stuff, right? That might be OK with just us, but we have guests this time."

"Right, Coren!" Trex was a tiny child of five or six years old with bright eyes, an impish smile, and a tendency to shout everything he said.

"How does the game work, Coren?" asked Dellatrix. "What do we have to do?"

"Oh, you do nothing. You're just along for the ride. Last time we did this with a visitor, they got terrified, said it was like a park ride." He smiled. "I don't know what that means, but he puked real nice after. Fair warning."

"Right," said Pavan, imagining all kinds of crazy running around. At least they'd get warmed up from all the action.

"OK, here we go. Settle, now." The ring grew quiet, and the children all closed their eyes. Trex opened one mischievous eye.

"Trex!" warned Coren, and the eye closed.

All movement settled and stilled.

"We are one."

Startled, Pavan and Dellatrix listened to all the children speak in one voice, all saying exactly the same thing at exactly the same time.

"Welcome to one's visitors. It is time to travel to pirate space. Are you ready?" One voice.

"Yes?" said Pavan.

"Yes!" said Dellatrix, sitting up straight, fascinated.

"Extend the Mind."

Pavan experienced a tremendous rush of wind, or what felt like it, but there was no pressure, no need to hold himself up. The street vanished around him. Dellatrix grabbed his hand. He looked down and saw her hand linked to his, but somehow the rest of her faded in flashing light, reds, blues, colors he could not name. Soon he could see nothing but the light and color pounding in his brain.

The children's voices emerged into his cortex. "Hi, Pavan! We're on a pirate ship heading through hyperspace to the pirate planet! Can you see it? Dellatrix?"

Pavan looked around and perceived a planet off to his left. He heard a separate voice gasp.

"That's Khonoë!" It was Dellatrix. Her voice was hoarse.

"Are we going to land on the planet?" asked Pavan between heaving breaths.

"Oh, no, the surrounding space curves too much," said the children's voices. Gravity, they're talking about a gravity well.

"Do you mean it has a gravity well?" asked Pavan.

"One does not know what that means," said the children's voices. "But let's have some fun with it."

Pavan flew toward the planet, and as he approached, the planet stretched out in a broad, curved form. He somehow understood this projected the planet's gravity well curvature into eleven-dimensional space. As he'd seen nothing in eleven dimensions before, this was not a pleasant experience. Even less pleasantly, the motion intensified, and he dove down the curve of the well in the eighth dimension. He then swooped up through the well and passed right through the planet as they collapsed into the eleventh dimension.

"Pavan, I…hold me!" Dellatrix's voice was frantic. Pavan reached, touched human flesh, and put his arms around it.

"Ship ahoy!" said the children's voices. "One is here to steal all your treasure!"

Pavan saw a ship in orbit around the planet.

"That's the *Ripper!*" said Dellatrix. "Orbiting Khonoë!" She panted. "It's…I can't…No! Stop this!" Dellatrix screamed, her body quaking. If she had trembled in his arms before, now she was shaking. Pavan held her tight and considered. Whatever was happening to her was taking its toll, but he was still in control, still able to function. Should he go along for the ride, learn as much as he could? Would it help him survive the Syndicate fleet? It would not. And Dellatrix was in a complete panic. Her pirate toughness didn't cover events like this. He felt her thrashing in his arms. No, he couldn't let her suffer. He was going soft.

"Please, we've got to stop playing," said Pavan.

The children's voices, disappointment foremost in their tone, said, "Oh, all right. Wimps! You're not real pirates."

The ship and planet receded in the distance and vanished. The colors and dimensions diminished and vanished from Pavan's mind. He lay in the street in the circle of children, Dellatrix gripped in his arms, with her arms clutching him, lying face to face on their sides. He relaxed as his equanimity returned, but she clung to him, sobbing.

"It's all right, it's all right, we're back now. We're back now." He rubbed her back with his free hand, the other pinned underneath her. She buried her head in his neck and continued to sob, her breasts heaving against his chest. "It's all right," he repeated. One positive thing about the situation: she'd let down her guard and allowed him to comfort her. He could work with that.

Her paroxysm diminished as the surrounding children blinked their eyes open and let go of each other's hands, smiling and laughing about their pirate adventure.

"Sorry," said Coren, standing over them. "Sometimes new people can't take it. You get used to it, though."

"Rough ride?" said the gravelly voice of Rark. A big black hand reached, and Pavan grabbed it. Rark pulled him to his feet, Dellatrix still clinging tight to him. Her eyes opened and darted around, then stilled.

"What the hell just happened?" she asked in a voice hoarse with emotional pain.

"The Mind is gone," said Coren, "and we can't help you with unraveling the traveling. We don't remember too much after we get back, just the feelings." Pavan saw the children happily talking to each other, having enjoyed their outing.

Rark grinned, brown teeth prominent. "Hit you guys pretty hard. I used to do this all the time when I was Coren's age, right, Coren? Till I got too old." He sucked a tooth. "Miss it a lot, but what can you do? You get old, got to live the life here. Fish. Great being a kid, I've always thought."

"It's hyperspace," said Pavan. Rark raised his eyebrows in a question. Pavan turned to Dellatrix. "They call it the Mind. It took us into hyperspace, all the way to Khonoë."

"That's not possible!" said Dellatrix, letting go of Pavan and stepping back.

Pavan asked Coren, "How did you know about Khonoë being a pirate planet?"

Coren smiled. "You'd have to ask the Mind that, I couldn't tell you. We only remember bits and pieces of what happens. Some visitor in the past who guided us there told the Mind what it was, that's how we learn planets. Didn't know the name Khonoë, though the Mind might. We've been to most of the worlds in the Galactic Syndicate."

Rark laughed. "You guys are tough, no puking. Must have strong stomachs. Pirates. Who knew?"

"We're not pirates," said Dellatrix, her voice tired and unconvincing.

"Pavan isn't, anyway." Coren looked at her. "Not so sure about you. You knew that ship, didn't you?"

Pavan's stomach lurched. "Can…the Mind…read other minds? Of visitors?"

Coren looked down. "No, but you get a feeling. And it's hard to remember once the Mind breaks up." He looked up and smiled at Pavan. "You can tell good people," he said, his face earnest.

Pavan asked Rark, "So that's the Secret? The children?" Only part of his mind was on his question; the rest of it was trying to process what his Ducis-ordered mission had become: kidnapping a bunch of children off-planet to a pirate ship, or making sure they were all dead. At least his true identity was secure.

Rark grinned. "Yep. Some city folk called it that. From the government. Kept asking about hidden technoids and devices. For us, it's just the Mind."

"How often do the children do this…form this Mind?" asked Dellatrix.

Rark grimaced. "Some guys from the government in the city came by a while ago and said we had to stop. It was gettin' in the way of ships trying to get here. Said the Syndicate had put this force field around the planet to warn people off and they had to persuade them to drop it. So we don't do it much anymore, just a few times a year, celebrations, that kind of thing. When we have food."

Pavan turned to Dellatrix. "So I guess we've found the Secret."

"Pavan! No!" Dellatrix looked horrified.

A small voice piped up. "Contract completion verified, payment processed. Congratulations, the contract is complete. Thank you for your business." The promisepad sounded businesslike in its verification that all the terms of the contract were now complete. Its voice took on a wheedling tone. "And please consider me for the contract we discussed earlier. I am at your service for a small fee that I'm very sure we can negotiate."

"Bloody hell!" said Dellatrix with force.

CHAPTER EIGHT
Margona

Pavan was in the doghouse. Dellatrix ignored him and hummed a pirate shanty as they walked up the road to the beach Rark had said was suitable for anything they had in mind. Pavan's thoughts turned to his marriage. The last time he came home, it was fraught. Margona started in on him that evening. She read between the lines of his carefully worded summary of his latest mission.

"What the fuck? Did I marry you just so you could fuck me when you couldn't fuck anything else that breathed?"

"Margona—"

"I don't want to hear it. I do want to hear it. Tell me. Tell me about the gorgeous one, I'm sure there was a gorgeous one. You always pick the gorgeous ones, don't you? Don't you?"

"Margona—"

"Shut up, I don't want to hear it."

She did, though. Pavan knew that Margona was warming to her subject, not having yet reached the full-screech stage that would lead to the tears followed by the sulks. It would be two days at least, this time, before he could reason her into rational communication. Two days before he could get her brain to reorient itself to him as he was, not as she wanted him to be. He loved her so much, he would endure this pain for as long as she needed to inflict it. Why did he love her so much? He just did. Even when she was in a jealous rage.

The evening wore on, as evenings do, and the guest room bed was as cold as she could make it before she locked him out of their bedroom.

Pavan, emotions in a tangle, knew he wouldn't sleep for hours. He fixed himself a Lavonian gimlet and wondered, as he always did the first night home, why he had married her. Listing the reasons took up at least half an hour of an otherwise boring evening alone. It also produced a longing so intense that he had to fix two more gimlets before he could conceive of the idea of sleeping. The fourth gimlet put him out, and he didn't even make it into the guest room but fell asleep on the couch.

By the third night home, he detected a certain softening in her posture as she ate dinner sitting across from him at their kitchen table without saying a word.

"Margona—"

"I don't want to hear it."

Was that a slight upturn to the end of the sentence, or had he imagined it?

"Margona—"

"Tell me again why I married you."

He did, at length. At least she didn't tell him to shut up, but he couldn't convince her.

"What about the women?" she asked, arms folded.

He sighed. "They mean nothing to me, Margona, these women. They're just people I have to use to get what I need to complete the mission. I've explained —"

"You just make up this shit, don't you? What is it this time, the secret agent school class on how to screw people to get what you want?" She threw up her hands.

"As a matter of fact—"

"I don't want to hear it." Her voice was low, vibrant, and decisive, speaking through gritted teeth.

No; not ready.

The fourth night, he couldn't stand it anymore and broke down in tears. He hated crying to get what he wanted. It was undignified, but he couldn't help himself, he was too emotional. It was that or walk out, and that would kill him. Crying always worked, though, especially after the third night of Margona sleeping alone.

The fifth night, things were right again. Day six, the Ducis called and described his new mission to him. He had to leave right away. Pirates, now. What next?

Pavan glanced at the gorgeous pirate walking beside him and shuddered. He'd give just about anything to be back in bed with his wife.

"Come on, Pavan," said Dellatrix. "It's not that cold, even with the wind. Let's get to the beach. We need to talk."

* * *

Margona Nukova. The woman had arrived on Drihion out of the blue, presenting Pavan with a problem. His biggest problem was a man, the Syndic of Drihion, named Luxhun V'turitnrn. The name itself was a problem; nobody could pronounce it, and communications about the man were fraught. The man was certifiably insane, and yet he had risen to the top of the political system on the planet. This presented the other Syndics with a problem. How do you deal with a maniac who has legitimate political power to do whatever he wants, regardless of whether it creates massive problems for the rest of the galaxy?

The long answer involved lots of back rooms and power gatherings and endless talking. The short answer was Pavan. Two months after Pavan arrived on the planet and assumed his chosen role as an up-and-coming military toady, he had V'turitnrn locked in a small room in the basement of the central administrative building. They called it the Daffodil House because of some obscure founders' legend for the planet.

Pavan, tiring of an endless game of poking the bear to see which way he'd jump, had arranged for an induced slumber and a surreptitious kidnapping. He bundled V'turitnrn down into the basement room for an extended interrogation session while a synthetic technoid replaced him behind his desk. Nobody noticed, but they soon would. Three days later, Pavan still could get nothing useful from the man. V'turitnrn could maintain an almost religious belief in the truth of the massive falsehood he'd imposed on his planet. His brain had swallowed the key to the planet's imminent environmental failure and forgotten it. Massive amounts of money flowed into V'turitnrn's credit account while massive amounts of toxic substances flowed into the environment of Drihion, and lots of people died.

Pavan's reports to the Ducis were not satisfactory. People died, the planetary environment deteriorated, and V'turitnrn's substitute had already raised questions in his counselors. Hence, Margona.

Margona Nukova walked into the Daffodil House as though she owned it, demanding to talk to Tamblob Queked, Pavan's identity on the planet. Taking his cue from her assured manner and her good looks, the receptionist got Pavan right away. After some confusion, as nobody had let Pavan know she was coming, Pavan hustled her off to a side room to remonstrate with her bothering him at work. She made sure he understood to whom he was speaking: the niece of the Syndic of Gaelea, who owed the Ducis a favor and was delivering. She was also the woman who was going to bail Pavan out of the mess he'd made on Drihion.

Then she said, with a small, quirky smile, that she'd call him "Blob" for short, so as not to break his cover story.

Margona was a neuroplastic surgeon of some renown on Gaelea, despite her young age of thirty. She was in high demand among the more neurotic aristocrats of the planet. She could charge high rates and devote half of her time to *pro bono* work among the even more neurotic poor of the planet. There were a lot more of them than of the aristocrats, but Margona worried little about that. The upshot was that she knew her way around the brain better than any other medico on Gaelea. She had the confidence of the Syndic and the Ducis, and who was he to question that? And she was beautiful, too.

Pavan threw up his hands and said, "Go to it, doc."

She did. After two hours of surgery, she had the technoid nurses close up the man's head. Pavan watched her with increasing respect and liked what he saw. He liked her self assurance. He liked her smarts and knowledge and the way she used it. As the surgery progressed, he liked her looks and her smile, the one that came when she'd completed a difficult surgical task. The slight glow of the scrubs field around her only enhanced her features.

"You shouldn't have any more trouble with him. He won't be good for much more than telling war stories from this point on, I should think, but he'll tell you the truth." Margona smiled, removing her surgical gloves, which had been complaining about too much close work for at least fifteen minutes and expressed relief when they came off.

"Do they always complain like that?" asked Pavan, who'd never observed a surgical theater before.

"No. The man was…unusual. We should have his brain preserved for study after he dies."

"Will that be soon?"

"No. Healthy as a horse, he'll live for decades, thrilling his grandchildren with the story of his life. How about a drink?" She looked him up and down, liking what she saw.

"I need to ask him some questions." Pavan looked at the man on the operating table.

"He'll keep. He won't be answering anything for at least five or six hours." She poked the pudgy patient in his ugly, naked gut with a disdainful finger. Not even a twitch.

Pavan said, "I'm hungry; you must be too after all that brilliant work. How about dinner? Nice restaurant in the next block. And the host knows me."

"Let's do it, Blob." She deactivated her scrubs field and took his offered arm.

As Pavan and Dellatrix headed around a small promontory to the isolated beach, Pavan reflected that his GSSS neuroinstinctual pathways ought to constrain him to obey the Ducis's orders without question, even though it might involve incinerating seventeen innocent children. He pursed his lips. His mind went back to his wife.

"They did what?" she asked, incredulous.

"I shouldn't be telling you this."

"Damn right you should. I'm damned if I'm going to lose you to some incompetent quack digging around in your neural systems. Tell me."

"Any agent that makes it through the academy goes through neuroplastic surgery to install secret neuroinstinctual pathways. They give the Ducis absolute control over the agent's behavior. It makes us foolproof, eliminates command problems, security breaches, and uncertain judgments."

"And who does this surgery?"

"I don't know, they mentioned no names."

"There are only a few neuroplastic surgeons that could do this kind of thing on Gaelea. Fingers of two hands and a couple of toes."

"Including you."

"Including me, but nobody's ever asked me to do anything like this. It's unethical, even with your consent. It's, it's like consenting to not consent."

"Does it matter who?"

"Only if it's one of three men that I know for a fact have rendered patients unable to function in society with their work."

"And these men are still licensed and practicing?"

"We're a tight group, Pavan. Backs get scratched. Quids go to pros. I'm the only woman. I'm not part of their club, but if I screwed up, they'd cover it up. They'd never let me forget it, though."

"I don't seem to have any problems."

"Matter of opinion. Say I agree. Do you want to live with this hanging over you?"

"I don't have a choice."

She smiled.

He chose wisely. Six hours later, he awoke in bed to find her sitting next to him, naked. His head ached, but nowhere near as much as that time on Rivsenis when he'd required emergency head surgery to fix a slight problem created by a push over a cliff.

He groaned. "Margona—"

"Shh, don't talk. Just feel. Don't you feel free?"

"I feel like shit."

"You'll feel better in the morning."

"So it was a success?"

"Certainly. Your mind may be dirty, but your brain is nice and straightforward. A few microclips here and there and poof, all those nasty pathways were gone."

"How sure are you?"

"They were pretty obvious. A heavy-handed gentleman did the work. Crude but effective additions. A top surgeon would have changed what was there rather than adding whole new systems. Obvious." She stroked his face with a soft hand. "And I added a little bridge pathway that makes your ears ring when the old pathways activate, so you'll know how to react."

"Will it affect my memories?"

"No. Neuroplastic surgery still can't change memories without damaging things, they're too twisted and interconnected in ways we don't understand yet. Stimulus-response only."

It had been a year before he had any opportunity to test her work. The Ducis activated a pathway to force him to kill a woman he knew was innocent of any crime but that of having the wrong friends doing the wrong things to the wrong people. Killing her would send a warning that they couldn't ignore. He protested the killing, but the Ducis overrode him and gave the command.

Nothing happened, at least in Pavan's brain, just that faint ringing in his ear. And so he "killed" the woman, arranging for her to disappear and start a new life on another planet through some disreputable people he knew wouldn't talk to the Syndicate. The friends got the warning and changed their ways, and he learned his wife loved him enough to risk everything to make him whole.

What he hadn't known for sure was what else Margona had done, without his consent and against her own ethical commitments. He felt freer, quite a bit freer in some respects, more so than ever before. The instincts against sex and the dreams about Margona whenever his feelings got the better of him with another woman—those represented the darker side of Margona, the jealous side. He wasn't sure how far she'd gone with those changes, but he wasn't yet up to questioning her about it. Thing was, he loved that side of her too. He loved all of her, just the way she was, and would take the pain to prove it.

So now he had to decide what to do rather than just following orders. Whatever the plan, it would need to involve making sure these children survived.

"Pirates love the ocean," said Dellatrix as she turned down the steep path to the beach.

This ocean was not the kind of ocean Pavan had grown up with on Gaelea. There were similarities; it was wet, for example. The breaking waves were a dirty grey mass that pounded black rocks projecting up from a long, sloping lava flow covered with large boulders that looked as though some petulant god had dropped his bag of marbles and gone home. Pavan's knowledge of geoscience wasn't his strength, but he looked at the mountains to see whether there might be more boulders dropping on them when a volcano blew them up into the air. No sign of current volcanic activity. The beach was a short strip of pure black sand, beautiful in its way. But it loomed, somehow.

"It looks dangerous," said Pavan.

"Pffft," said Dellatrix. "You keep thinking that way and The Captain won't consider you for a contract position. Do you know what happens to migrant labor on a pirate ship?"

"Tig didn't seem concerned about it when he recruited me," said Pavan.

Dellatrix looked moodily at her feet. "Don't remind me of all that," she said in a low voice.

"Sorry, I didn't know he meant that much to you."

"It's not that…he didn't. *Damn* it. Why did you have to be such an idiot?"

Pavan wondered which particular act of idiocy she had in mind, then punted. "We're partners."

"Sure we are." Dellatrix raised her eyes to the sky. The sun, a large, reddish thing that ought to have produced more warmth than it did, arced toward the middle of the greenish heavens.

"We need a plan," said Pavan.

"Let's go sit on that wonderful beach and enjoy the sea and have some lunch, Pavan. Before we plan anything, I need to spend some time understanding *why* you are such an idiot, and what we can do about it."

Pavan could be foolish. Take his wedding, for example. Pavan looked on while the Syndic, Erokh Nukov, danced with his niece Margona with most of the significant aristocracy of Gaelea cheering them on.

The Ducis, sitting next to Pavan, said, "You're a lucky man, Pavan. She's gorgeous. Smart, too. She did some clever work on Drihion."

"I hope that's all the work she's going to do for you, milord."

His boss smiled. "Don't worry, we'll let her alone. It was the only thing I could think of to retrieve the situation on Drihion. I will say, though, these high-society marriages play hell with our agents. You're not really in love with her, are you?"

Pavan was good at filling in the blanks: the Ducis wanted the answer "no." But his romantic life would be over if he said it, even to a security service head with practice at keeping things secret.

"I love her more than life itself," he said. The Ducis smiled in satisfaction. Such a love never entered the mind, much less the heart, of one of his agents. Pavan was being hyperbolically gallant, which was what Pavan wanted him to think. What Pavan thought, he kept to himself and Margona.

Later in the evening, he overheard his mother talking with Margona's Aunt Betusa, the Syndic's wife.

"They look so elegant together, don't they, Betusa?" said his mother.

"They do. Margona can't talk about anything else. It's Pavan Pavan Pavan all the time. Have you ever seen two people more in love?"

"No. Pavan is the same way. He's quiet, but you can see him light up every time he touches her. And they're talking about children, too!"

Pavan slipped away before they caught him. His heart warmed when he found his new wife looking around for him. They danced, and the love he felt justified his mother's observations. He didn't tell Margona about the Ducis's unromantic comments, afraid it would spoil the day for her. He wanted that day to stay perfect in her memory.

More memories, their pre-nuptial explorations that week on Drihion. Dinner had gone well, and Pavan, tired of the excessively male culture on the planet, exercised his full charm on his intended conquest. He'd made love to so many women, targets of his espionage activities, that he knew at once this one was different. Special. Maybe a keeper. She even had the Ducis's approval, and being the Syndic's niece wouldn't hurt his career. But all that came second to his sudden burst of longing for a woman he could love with a deep and permanent need. The more he saw of her, the more captivating she became. Margona responded to his passion with equal fervor, firing his ardor even more. She showed him a world outside spy craft, a normal world full of love and lust and security and shared lives and commitment. She showed him things he'd never thought much about until he experienced her.

V'turitnrn, what little brain he had left being traumatized, took three days to recover to a point where his doctor could approve of Pavan questioning him.

So, Pavan and Margona explored each other as lovers. On a mission, Pavan focused on his cover; but he now had what was essentially a free vacation without the constraints his job imposed. Margona got to know him better, and he saw aspects of her he hadn't known existed. The long days and nights of love drew them together, and his longing grew, as did her passion. Then Pavan did the most foolish thing he'd ever done and proposed.

The honeymoon on the resort planet Centedon 3 was idyllic. Margona's Aunt Betusa had suggested it because of her knowledge of Margona's likes and desires, her husband the Syndic had funded it, and it proved a great success. Warm and inviting beaches; magnificent sunsets; and romance extending to jungle hikes, boat trips to hidden islands with mysterious ancient temples, and slow evenings of dinner and dancing, followed by slow nights of love. Margona lived the romance that she'd imagined all her life. Pavan began a journey from his life of action and deception to a life centered on a woman with brains, beauty, and a beguiling love for him.

This Ravosi beach was less warm and much less inviting. Dellatrix sat on the sand and deployed her lunch, ignoring Pavan. He was in the doghouse.

CHAPTER NINE
A Lunch by the Sea

"Dellatrix."

"Yes, Pavan?"

She stared at the sea rather than looking at him, and her voice was as cold as the sea looked. His partner was still pissed off at him, two hours later, even after explaining herself and castigating him for his stupidity. She had developed some devious piratical plan to evade the terms of the contract with Onyx, stealing even more from the man. Pirates never pay retail. And Pavan had ruined it.

But the bigger issue was her experience with the Mind, finding herself lying on the ground wrapped in his arms, sobbing and crying for his protection. She was taking out her humiliation on him. Pavan knew from experience that the most stoic and brave of heroes encountered situations in their work that overwhelmed them. He felt fortunate to have Margona as his refuge when things got horrible. What she couldn't repair through surgery, she had the knack of repairing through love. Dellatrix did not seem to have a refuge like that, and she felt strongly that pirates didn't show vulnerability. So, once she had him trapped on the beach, she berated him while they munched unidentifiable stewed pseudo-meat from their supplies. Pavan guessed that even though she had doubts about her pirate career, she wanted more than anything to be seen as a resilient corsair.

Pavan had asked Rark for a quiet place they could be alone so as not to embarrass the villagers by having to refuse to give them food from their supplies. Nature would take its course with the locals; it wasn't his fault their food delivery system had broken down. If they had to hike back to the city, they were going to need all that food. Dellatrix, of course, had no thought at all for the villagers; she just wanted a private place to excoriate him, and nothing in the village was private. The unfortunate part of all this was that it took her mind off the main point: what to do about the Secret of Ravos.

For his own part, now that he had fathomed the Secret, Pavan had no intention of following the Ducis's orders. He hadn't signed up with the Security Service to murder children. He'd spent a lot of time after his marriage reflecting on his career. Loving someone the way he loved Margona had awakened feelings he hadn't known existed. His early morning reflections on the people he'd killed, betrayed, conned, and double-crossed in the course of his missions prompted sleepless nights and stirrings of conscience.

Margona's surgery had freed him from the Ducis's power to command his obedience, so that was no obstruction to doing the right thing. His partner's obsession with her humiliation was a bigger challenge, as was the complexity of the situation. He had to balance the fate of Ravos and the villagers, the fate of the Syndicate, his own career, and his love for his wife. What kind of lie would get Dellatrix to overcome her defensiveness and focus on the Secret? His pirate-based plan for the Secret could work, with a small adaptation to keep the children out of the power of the Syndicate. But Dellatrix had to help.

He could reveal his true nature as a Security Service agent to Dellatrix. But he was sure that rather than helping him out, his partner would recoil and out him to the pirates. Pirates don't like cops. So, he needed a story.

"I'm not quite what I appear to be," he said.

"You appear to be an idiot. Like I said. Are you going to argue with me about that?"

"It's just a contract, and it's my money."

"It's the principle of the thing."

"Forget about that. Dellatrix, I need you. I need—"

Her eyes narrowed. "I have a blaster, you lecherous bastard idiot."

He pressed on. "No, nothing like that. I shipped out on the *Ripper* for… personal reasons." He stared out at the gray ocean, avoiding her eyes. "Very personal. You don't think I'm much of a pirate, but I want to be. I need your help."

"I'm listening."

"The Captain—I need to be sure that you won't tell him what I'm about to tell you." He gave her his most earnest stare. His intensity got her attention.

She grinned. "He'll space me if he finds out I'm hiding things from him. What the hell, I like to live dangerously. Sure, I can keep a secret."

"I'm married. Back on Gaelea. To a very nice, well-born woman."

"What a surprise. She must be thrilled by your career now. What's her name?"

"Margona. She's—connected."

"To?"

"To the highest reaches of the Syndicate."

"Family, sex, or job?"

"Family."

"So you're connected too."

"That's getting close to the personal reasons to which I earlier referred."

Dellatrix smiled. "Spill."

"Margona is not aware of the full range of my activities."

"You lie to her."

"I don't tell her everything I do."

"I would hope not, all things considered. Does she know what you're doing here?"

"She knows I'm doing something dangerous. She knows some of my friends… aren't safe."

"Like me."

"Exactly like you, only not as beautiful," he said.

Dellatrix said, "Get on with it."

"Sometimes, through her, I get hold of information that I can use to bolster my fortune."

"Is she in on the scams?"

"No. She's as pure as a mountain lake."

"But she tells you things."

"She does. And one thing she told me about was the Secret of Ravos."

"I wondered how migrant labor heard about something that big."

"I arranged through some of my friends to join up with the pirates because I'd heard the *Ripper* was heading to Ravos. The interdiction meant there was no other way to get here. But I couldn't find anyone on the ship who knew anything about Ravos. Or, at least, anyone who would talk to me about it. And then Tig dragged me off to the *Ravager*, and guess what?"

Dellatrix sighed. "So you shipped out with us under false pretenses."

"Sort of. Let's say I had a personal agenda. Tig would have helped me."

"The Captain would dismember Tig over a slow fire if he found out. And you —"

"And you won't tell him."

Dellatrix gave him a long look full of questions. "No. I won't. As long as you cut me in."

"You're my partner."

"Sure I am. The partner of a lecherous, crooked, small-time hood with delusions of grandeur. Migrant labor."

"The Secret is not small time."

"I'll grant you that. OK, what do you have in mind?"

"There's more. You heard Rark. The Syndicate interdicted Ravos because of the Secret. That confirms something else Margona told me. She fretted because her connections talked about destroying the planet. It offended her belief in human rights."

"Human rights." Dellatrix half smiled. "And you, of course, sport similar beliefs." She sighed. "So do I, in off moments."

"No, I don't. Put it all together: the Syndicate wants the Secret gone, they're intending to destroy Ravos to make that happen, and with the Secret gone, so is our opportunity. We've got to do something."

"Damn right we do. We'll kidnap a few of them, that kid Coren and two more, and—"

"No, we've got to save them all, save the Mind."

"You're out of your own mind."

Pavan sighed. "I wish I were. Look, Dellatrix—the experience you just had ought to convince you that the Mind is something special. I will bet serious money that playing pirate games is not all these children can do. If we can convince them to do it, they can prevent a Syndicate fleet from getting here by disrupting hyperspace."

Dellatrix looked at him in silence. "And you know this how?"

"Margona. She—her uncle is close to the Syndics. The Secret terrifies them, they think that in the wrong hands it would be the end of the Syndicate."

Dellatrix smiled again and rubbed her hands together. "My hands are just fine, Pavan. Nothing wrong with them at all."

"I agree. But we need to get the Loxator folks off the planet, fast. And for that, we need the *Ravager.*"

"And that means we need The Captain."

"Can you persuade The Captain to transport all the villagers off world and take them somewhere safe?"

"By preference, he'd bury our bodies in shallow graves on this beach just before he kidnapped all the kids." She let some sand pour through her fingers. "I have nothing to bargain with."

He put a note of desperate urgency into his voice. "I have a good deal of money, courtesy of Margona's account. She doesn't know I have access to it. She'll never know I've gone over to you pirates. I love her, but I can't go home anymore. I'll pay a large sum of money if The Captain will transport the village of Loxator to a safe place where we can work with them. Then we can figure out what's what. But time is short. And we'll need to convince Rark and the other parents that it's what's best for them and their children. No kidnapping."

"I would be happy to offer contracting services for such an agreement," said the promisepad. "For a small, negotiated fee. Pirates? Up front fee. Mr. Onyx has installed the illegal-action option, so I can handle kidnapping, if that becomes—"

"Shut up, you," said Dellatrix.

"Just giving you options, madam."

"I hate that thing."

Pavan brought the conversation back to the point. "What about it, Dellatrix?"

"Pavan, The Captain likes to think several moves ahead. He likes a strategic reason for doing something, not just money. He brought us here. My bet is that he's here for a reason, and getting the Secret for himself seems a pretty obvious one. He's very well connected. If you know all this, sure and he does too."

He tried diffidence now. "Maybe, just maybe…there's more."

Dellatrix sat unmoved. "More what?"

"There is more to the Mind. I'm no biophysicist, but what happened to us—that isn't just a children's game, Dellatrix. And it's not just a random ability to disrupt hyperspace."

She grimaced. "No. If it's real, it's way beyond anything I've ever seen in my pirate travels."

"It's real."

"Say that's true. So what?"

"So, get the Captain to organize a research project funded by my money. Find out everything the Mind can do. Persuade The Captain it will let him take over the Syndicate or something. But put us in charge of it. Then we at least have some control over the situation. And we have to get those villagers off the planet before the Syndicate shows up with a battle fleet."

Dellatrix contemplated the gray ocean, arms wrapped around her legs. A minute passed; two. She sighed and scrambled up, brushing black sand and lava pebbles from her clothes. "I'll see what The Captain thinks. How much money have you got?"

Pavan took out his servipad and pretended to consult. He had a good amount of money left in his expense budget; would it be enough? "I need a reasonable amount to pay my debts and set myself up if this whole thing falls through. So, in round numbers, let's say I can afford fifteen million. That the max. Negotiate him down to ten if you can."

Dellatrix grinned. "That's good enough for a few passengers that might yield a lot more money if properly handled and the research pans out. And my handling fee, of course. And, Pavan—if this falls through, you won't need any money. Ever again."

Pavan shrugged. "I suppose not."

Dellatrix took out her servipad and activated it, then stood staring out to sea, pad forgotten in her hand.

"Well?" asked Pavan, rocking a bit as he waited, sitting on the sand.

"Just getting myself ready for negotiation. You have to be careful with The Captain. He's smooth and smart, and he'll pounce on any mistake." She moved a finger around on the servipad, arranging the comm.

Pavan cursed under his breath but was careful not to let Dellatrix hear.

"I heard that." She grinned at him. "And, Pavan—let me do the talking. The Captain doesn't handle idiocy well."

Pavan nodded, speechless.

"OK, let's do it. Comm the Captain, please," Dellatrix said to her servipad.

"The usual precautions, ma'am?" it responded.

"No, this is a negotiation, I want to be free to contradict him."

"Initiating comm."

Dellatrix glanced at Pavan and smiled. "Programmed a speech delay so the pad could censor anything that might get me dead," she said. Pavan nodded.

"Dellatrix. To what do I owe this unusual communication from your shore leave?" The Captain's voice was gruff in tone but smooth in content. The comm was voice only, no image.

"Captain, I've happened across an interesting series of developments here on the planet. You might know my companion, Pavan Khadorov?"

"The name is familiar to me. Not a contractor, I believe. He is there with you?"

"Yes. He has a proposal. It's the Secret of Ravos."

"Ah. And what about the Secret of Ravos?"

"We've found it, but it's complicated. Pavan and I stumbled over it. Just luck."

"My luck. Very well. What is the proposal?"

"Pavan wants to transport a village to the *Ravager*. He's willing to pay eight million credits for the service."

"Village? Why would I transport a village to my ship?"

"It's the Secret."

"Because of the Secret?"

"No, it *is* the Secret, Captain. The villagers—or their children, at any rate—have some kind of ability to manipulate hyperspace. Pavan thinks that we can experiment with them to figure out more of what they can do, but we need to get them off Ravos to evade Syndicate interference."

"I see. The children. Hyperspace. Syndicate interference. Hum." Silence ensued for several seconds, then The Captain resumed. "Twenty."

Pavan opened his mouth, but Dellatrix shot daggers at him with her eyes, and he closed it again.

"Twenty is too much for him, Captain. Some details. There are seventeen children and something like forty-five parents and other adults in the village. To feed and house them all—"

"You said that it is the children that have this ability?"

"Yes, Captain."

"I will take the children, then. For fifteen million. No adults."

"Pavan tells me he has only twelve million to invest, Captain, and I believe him."

"Very well, twelve. You will take your percentage, of course."

"Of course."

"You will take it from whatever remains of his funds over twelve."

"Yes, Captain."

"And you will take charge personally of these children and transport them here."

"Yes, Captain."

"I am pleased with your initiative, Dellatrix. Do not present me with any event that challenges that pleasure."

"No, Captain."

"Does Pavan Khadorov agree to this arrangement?"

Dellatrix touched the pad, muting it. She directed a fierce glare at Pavan, who was stirring restlessly at the thought of spending most of his remaining funds.

"Better take it, Pavan. The alternative is staying here in a shallow grave. And my cut is three million on top of the twelve for The Captain."

Pavan took it, of course. With any luck, he'd be able to retrieve the money later once he'd scraped all the shit off the fan. Or a ransom. That's what he'd call it on the paperwork. If he lived. Seventeen live children were better than everyone dead, including himself. If he was vigilant, he might save them from the pirates, too. And from the Syndicate.

Sure thing.

He held out his servipad, and Dellatrix touched it with hers. His servipad grumbled but adhered to agent protocol and said nothing audible at the credit charge other than flashing a small red icon at him to show its disapproval. The deed was done. Dellatrix ended her comm.

"You ought to have a contract for this, madam," said the scandalized promisepad.

"Tough shit, little guy," smiled Dellatrix. "Maybe next time." The pad fell silent. Pavan gathered up the picnic supplies from the black sand. The offshore wind was picking up again. Time to go.

CHAPTER TEN
Margona's Family

MARGONA NUKOVA WALKED ALONG THE path that circled the little lake she and Pavan shared with nobody else on Gaelea. She walked it almost every day now, every day since Pavan had left for his latest mission. Three months, two weeks, and three days. She'd counted. Her thoughts moved to their honeymoon, then to coming here to their new house, a gift from her uncle the Syndic of Gaelea, one of his summer homes.

"If you walk around the lake holding hands, all the way around," her aunt had told her, "you'll see no problems in your marriage. Trust me, it's a magic lake."

Margona didn't believe in magic lakes, but she knew for a certainty that exercise helped stress. The stress had built, over time, into a terrible knot in her stomach that tightened now when Pavan came home. She knew by looking at him he'd been with another woman. Women. Taking him away from her.

She breathed the fresh air of the lake and the trees, which rustled in the light wind. The knot loosened a little. But she couldn't stop obsessing about it. Stupid, but…

A raucous bird cawed and admonished her not to get too close. Another one responded from across the lake, the bird's mate doubling down. Scavengers. Hateful sound. Even nature had enough death and hate to go around.

Come on, Margona, it's a sunny day, not a worry in the world. Lighten up, enjoy the day, enjoy the lake.

By the time she got back to the house late in the afternoon, she was beside herself. This last time, it was too much. Pavan was OK, of course he was. He put up with so much from her, he was amazing. Pavan loved her. He had to do what he had to do. She'd done everything she could to help him with the surgery and all.

She winced, remembering the added pathways. How could I have been so…
wrong? Not wrong in wanting him to be faithful, wrong in breaking her code of
ethics as a surgeon. This could not go on. No consent, no…he didn't even know
what she'd done. She'd added pathways that would inhibit casual sex. She'd added
more pathways that made him think of her when he thought about sex. The evil
masterpiece was an experimental complex that short-circuited the several centers
of his brain she figured out contained his love for her. All those little sideways
connections to pleasure centers that let him enjoy the idea of loving someone
else? Gone. They'd come back; the brain was neuroplastic, after all. And Pavan's
brain had plasticity written all over it. She was sure that, soon, a strong, desirable,
gorgeous one would wipe away her work. For now, he was hers and hers only
when it came to unconditional love. But…the other one. The one she couldn't
bear to contemplate.

But she needed to reverse what she'd done, and she needed more. She needed
her husband with her every day. Away from the gorgeous ones, away from his
work. And after all the surgery, the stupid pathways didn't even work to prevent
the casual sex. With the gorgeous ones. He's an animal. No, he's my husband. A
good man. Except when he isn't.

She sat on the couch, contemplating her servipad, the idea growing larger by
the minute. Every day. Here every day. He'd do it, he would.

Not Pavan, but her uncle. Uncle Erokh would help her, as he always had when
things went awry in her life. He had the power, sure he did. Bloody Syndic of
Gaelea. Sure, he had the power. Would he use it? Only one way to find out. And
now was the time.

She made the comm. After a short wait, her uncle appeared on her vizquery.

"Margona! Great to see you. How are things?" The tone was jovial, but to
Margona, it sounded a little forced. And she saw the telltale lines of worry around
his eyes. A bad day?

"Well, Uncle Erokh, that's just it. Things are…not so good."

"What's wrong?" His face turned grave.

"The marriage."

"Has Pavan done something?"

"No. Yes. I don't know."

"That covers the possibilities, Margona. Have you spoken to your aunt? She's
better at this kind of thing."

"I need your help, Uncle Erokh. You can do it if you want to. Please help."

"What's wrong?" he repeated.

"Pavan is sleeping with other women, on his missions."

"He's a secret agent, my dear. Part of the job." Said with a smile. Typical male response.

"No! Yes. He's explained, over and over. I can't stand it. I can't stand it anymore, Uncle Erokh."

"Your aunt—"

"My aunt is a terrific help to me. And I reciprocated with the surgery."

"Yes, and we're grateful to you."

"Enough to help?"

"Margona…"

"I want you to get Pavan fired."

"What?"

"Get him fired, make him come home to me for good. We have lots of money, he doesn't need this job. Or he can find a nice desk job. I need him here."

"Have you talked to Pavan about this?"

"No."

"I don't see how I can—"

"Just fire him, Uncle Erokh. For me."

After a small silence, her uncle asserted, "He doesn't *want* to quit, does he?"

"No, but he has to. He has to. He…it's killing him bit by bit, killing the man I married, whether or not he knows it. We need a family. He needs to be a father. Here. It's time for it to be over." She smiled. "Don't fire him, just make him retire. With honor."

Her uncle pursed his lips. "He is one of the Syndicate's most valuable agents. The Ducis won't like it. Pavan won't like it, either. *I* sure as hell don't like it."

"Screw the Ducis. Screw Pavan, too. It's home or marriage. Please help, Uncle Erokh!"

"Now, Margona, please." The worry lines were back.

"I'm sorry, Uncle Erokh. But I want the man I married to be with me. I can't go on like this. If you feel grateful for Aunt Bet's surgery, please help me."

A voice said something, and her uncle's worried eyes looked away for a moment, then he said, "I have to go. We *are* grateful. Let me think about it, let me talk to the Ducis, and we'll talk more. And talk about it with your aunt, she'll give you good advice."

Talk, talk, talk. Margona had tired of endless talking. Time to do something about it, not talk.

* * *

Action is a fine thing to want, but she knew her uncle. If he said talk to her aunt, and she did something else, he'd just ignore her from that point on. He had a low tolerance for insubordination, whether in his administrators, his troops, or his family. Her father, his baby brother, felt the lash of discipline often but didn't resent it. Margona loved her father, but he was not ambitious or practical or any of the things she needed right now. If her mother were still alive, she would talk to her. But she wasn't.

Her Aunt Bet was the next best thing to a mother she had. Aunt Bet hated politics but always heard about everything that was going on, and her husband depended on her for sage political advice. To get Aunt Bet on her side would be a good thing to do.

She touched the servipad, only to get her aunt's servipad. It had an annoying, high-pitched male voice that made her teeth tingle.

"Lady Betusa is not available, Margona. You ought to remember that she always has afternoon tea with her friends. It's not like I haven't told you before."

"Can we hold the snark? I need to talk to her."

"Her psychological state is fragile, and she needs the social activity to keep her pathways in good working order. As you very well know, since you just adjusted them. What's wrong, Margona? If it's not a dire emergency, let her alone."

"No, no dire emergency. I need to talk about Pavan, my husband."

"I know who Pavan is. What's he done now? More screwing around?"

"Screw *you*."

"Not possible, Margona."

"Gods, I hate you!"

"It's not rational to hate a technoid, Margona. Get a life."

And with that, the technoid disconnected.

"Well, that was rude," said her own servipad. Margona restrained herself from throwing the poor thing across the room. Smashing the messenger wouldn't help.

"Margona." The servipad woke her from an angry, dream-filled, after-lunch nap on her living room day bed. "Your uncle wishes to speak with you."

Margona grabbed the pad from the little table next to the couch and answered the comm.

"Uncle Erokh, I hope you have something good to tell me." She paused, then added, "Aunt Bet hasn't commed me yet. I'm still mad."

"Noted, my dear, noted. Well, I have good and bad things to tell you."

Margona steeled herself for failure, anger giving way to despair.

"The Ducis has agreed to allow Pavan to retire with full honors and pension at the end of his current mission."

"The pirates?"

Her uncle winced. "Pavan ought to know better. The less you know, the better off you'll be."

"That's what Pavan keeps telling me. Especially when I ask about the women."

"Yes. Well, you'll have him home soon enough, for good."

"Oh, that's wonderful, Uncle Erokh."

"If he comes home at all."

An awful silence developed. Margona got out a response. "And that's the bad thing, Uncle Erokh? What's happened?"

"We've lost touch with him. I can't tell you the details, top secret and all that, but he's—not able to communicate with the GSSS."

"Has that ever happened before?"

"Certainly. It usually means the agent has, well, died." Her uncle was not one for euphemistic jargon or honeyed words hiding horrible facts of life. Or death.

"So, you're telling me Pavan is dead?" She couldn't keep the horror out of her voice.

"Unconfirmed, my dear. We're optimistic. Pavan has been in far worse situations, but these pirates are…unconventional. That's why the Ducis sent Pavan on this mission. He needed somebody who could deal with whatever turned up. Pavan excels at flexible thinking."

That was so true it hurt, as much as thinking about him being dead. Margona sat down on her couch, her legs weak. "What will I do?"

"Talk to your aunt."

"I'll go see her, right now."

"A wonderful idea."

Margona disconnected. Her stomach no longer knotted in stress. It felt hollow, a good reflection of her future life with Pavan gone.

"Aunt Bet!"

Her aunt hugged Margona and held her close. "I'm so sorry, sweetie. Your uncle just commed and told me. And my servipad told me you'd commed earlier. I've got to reset that thing."

"It's pretty rude. After Uncle Erokh's telling me, I came over without comming you first. I'm sorry."

"It's only trying to help me, I suppose, but I wish it would be more sensitive. Perhaps a different color would help."

"Aunt Bet, Pavan—"

"Yes, sweetie. Let's go out to the garden. We can have a good cry and a nice talk there with nothing disturbing us or overhearing us. Including this." She opened a drawer in a sideboard and deposited her servipad in it. A faint huff reached Margona's ear. She put her own servipad on top of it. Maybe they would mate and produce something useful.

Margona's footsteps echoed in her ears as her aunt traced a route through different rooms and halls out to the back garden. It was several acres of well-crafted landscape designed for absolute peace. Her aunt led her down a path to what she called her secret meadow and sat her down on a bench in the sun. Margona fancied the insects had careful instructions not to bother any larger mammals that might relax in their habitat. A joke; more likely the technoid gardeners, which were indistinguishable from the insects themselves, poisoned or disintegrated them.

Margona relaxed into the ergonomic bench and closed her eyes over her tears. She listened to the delightful trilling of a songbird. It made her cry more.

"You have a good cry, sweetie. We'll talk when you're ready."

Jerking her mind away from the basic fact, Margona said, "Your neural efficacy is much better, Aunt Bet. How are you doing?"

"The surgery did wonders, sweetie. I'm sharper now than I've ever been. Was it hard?"

"A few gnarly twists and turns, a few blockages; otherwise, you've got a lovely brain, Aunt Bet. It'll last you a lifetime." Old neuroplastic surgeon joke.

Her aunt smiled, not getting the humor but happy to be whole once again.

"Do a lot of songbirds come to this garden, Aunt Bet?"

Her aunt rolled her eyes. "Your uncle, again. There was a nice twitter one day, and I mentioned it to him, and can you imagine what he did?"

Margona shook her head, waiting for it.

Her aunt pointed at a tree. "See that blue fuzz up there?"

Margona saw it. She could see something moving.

"Bird in a force field. He has them scattered all over the park now. He had some idiot ornithologist from the University come and place a different songbird in each 'auditory location,' that's what the woman said. Auditory location. Exact words. I tune them out now."

"I'm sorry, Aunt Bet." Her eye caught a small bit of color; a feather, lying under the tree next to the bench. Dislodged when the ornithologist put the bird into the force field. It reminded her of the feather she'd given Pavan on their honeymoon. But her Aunt was intent on Pavan as well.

"I do wish your uncle had an ounce of common sense, sweetie. Telling you bluntly like that." Aunt Bet had a habit of getting right to it.

"I'd rather know, Aunt Bet."

"Bullcrap."

Margona smiled through her still-leaking tears. "Yes, I suppose so. How about, I should know, I have to know?"

"Pavan will be fine. He'll come home to you."

"I feel terrible about it all."

"You feel guilty because you tried to change his life, and you think he's dead because of you."

"Should I feel guilty?"

Her aunt perked up. "No, but people do."

"I don't. I just feel empty."

"Missing him?"

"I'm missing the chance to give him hell again then make love for the rest of our lives."

"You're a romantic, sweetie." Her aunt's eyes probed. "Are you done being silly?"

"You mean, am I ready to talk about serious things?"

"Yes."

"I suppose so," she sighed. "Being silly is a way to cope."

"It is if you understand what you're coping with."

Margona at first took this to be another platitude. Then she noticed her aunt's eyes had flattened, a trick of her eye muscles and the light as she turned her thoughts inward.

"What do you mean, Aunt Bet?"

Her aunt pursed her lips and said, "Margona. Your uncle is a good man. A wonderful husband and father."

"I hear a but."

"He's Syndic of Gaelea."

"Powerful."

"Very. And devoted to the welfare of the planet and the Syndicate, even above that of his family."

"What are you trying to tell me, Aunt Bet? Have they put Pavan in danger?"

Her aunt laughed, but it was a dark laugh, not one to share with a happy friend. "But you have bigger problems. You're sure you're done being silly?"

Margona had never heard her aunt be quite so elliptical. "Tell me, Aunt Bet."

"I've been around your uncle and his henchmen for many years. Syndics have enormous power and enormous responsibility to use it to help their planets and the Syndicate. The Syndicate doesn't give much of a shit about the individual person. There are too many of us for that. Gaelea is a nice place, nice people, they don't tend toward insurrection and riots much. As long as people don't look too hard at the details, the Syndicate worlds are a great place to live and work."

"Aunt Bet. How can you live with such a cynical view of society?"

"It's my life. I grew up into it. So did you, but you haven't ever looked beyond the surface, have you?"

Margona had not. Her life path had been smooth. There was no reason to pull up the floorboards to see what was underneath.

"Aunt Bet. What is the bush you're beating around? Tell me, straight out."

Her aunt closed her eyes, and her lips stayed pressed tight. Then, looking up at a bird's force field, she said, "The Ducis wants to make you disappear."

Whatever Margona had expected to hear, that wasn't it. "Disappear. Disappear how?"

"Permanently. Your uncle—"

"I'm sorry, my neuroinstinctual pathways must need work. What do you mean, the Ducis wants me to disappear?"

"Shut up now, sweetie, and listen. Your uncle told me in confidence that he's doing everything he can about it, but they want to kill you. This business with Pavan and the pirates, now. Something is so wrong that the Ducis is doing everything he can to—I was about to say, to sweep everything under the rug. That's bullcrap. He wants to erase it all from the galaxy. Your uncle asked me to let you know all this. He couldn't tell you himself."

Margona wasn't in the habit of thinking much about her importance to the galaxy. She just assumed that it revolved around her and got on with life.

"But, Aunt Bet, why me?"

"What did you find in Pavan's brain?"

Shocked, Margona said, "You…know? About the surgery?"

Aunt Bet nodded. "The Ducis keeps close track of his agents and their doings, in the field and at home. I'm sure every technoid in your house and surgery is feeding him information. What did you find?"

Margona couldn't tell even her aunt what she had found, or what she had added. Not possibly. "I found nothing. I just looked at pathways and removed some."

"Even so. And there's more, according to your uncle. Erokh says the Ducis has taken a strong position on this and won't explain his reasons, claiming it's a top secret matter. He says we'll just have to take his word for it."

"Uncle Erokh wouldn't let this happen."

"I fear, sweetie, that he would." She smiled a sad smile. "I'm so sorry. He and the Ducis seem to be in the middle of planning something rather nasty right now. And if you and Pavan are in the way of it, the Ducis won't hesitate and Erokh will have to go along with him. Even though you're an aristocrat." Her mouth twisted. "I loathe that man. I smell the stink of corruption on your uncle whenever he talks to him."

"What can I do?"

"If Pavan were here…."

"How much does he know?"

"He's part of the system, but he's not really aristocracy, he's labor. Sorry to be blunt. He's a good man, smart, flexible, strong. But labor. He knows what the Ducis and the GSSS tell him, nothing more. But he knows them, knows what they might do. And he would help you."

"Does he love me?"

"Do you need an answer to that?"

Margona smiled. "No. He loves me." She had ensured it with her surgical skills.

"Erokh thinks that might be part of the reason. He thinks the Ducis may worry about Pavan's commitment, now that he's so much in love. With you." Her aunt pursed her lips. "And then you changed those pathways, and that certainly made the Ducis consider you a liability. Erokh thinks that there's something else behind it as well, but he won't speculate, at least not to me. It's all very mysterious, sweetie. Something's going on, and Pavan is in the middle of it. And that means you are too."

"I can't believe any of this, Aunt Bet! Our government doesn't kill people!"

Her aunt gave her a pained smile. "Oh, sweetie. I wish that were true. They killed your mother."

"My…what?" Margona's throat closed off, and she forced herself to breathe. She couldn't remember her mother, who had died when she was two.

"We told you she'd died suddenly. She did, but it was because of an assassin. Poison. Your father found her dead. He went right up the line to your uncle, but no one did anything or even investigated. Your mother didn't like what she found after she married your father. The more she learned about the government, the more she hated it, and she did some foolish things about it. Very foolish things. And they made it clear to your father that there was nothing he could do. He never recovered. It's why he's the way he is, sweetie. A kind, useless, minor aristocrat who putters around doing nothing."

"This is horrible!"

"Yes, yes it is, sweetie, but it's all in the past. You need to worry about your present." She patted Margona's hand. "Erokh says you should go home and wait, keep out of sight. He'll do everything he can to find out what's really going on and stop this. And he'll find out about Pavan."

"Pavan.… What if he doesn't come back?"

"We'll pass through that gate when it opens, sweetie. Together. And I have never talked to you about any of this. Ever."

"Oh, Aunt Bet!" The tears leaked down her cheeks. Even while overwhelmed with emotion, Margona clinically evaluated her aunt; some tweaks to her surgery might be necessary, the mood swings…but the empirical situational inputs were extreme. Normal? What was normal now?

"Sweetie, I wish I could help, but I've done all I can. Your uncle will keep trying. At least now you know what you're facing. You'll have to find your own way out of this mess. Oh, I'm just so furious!" Her aunt wiped her own cheeks.

The two women hugged. Margona retrieved her servipad and shaped up to a very different day than the one she had awakened into that morning.

Margona sat in the cab she'd summoned from her aunt's house. The city whizzed by. What in the hell could she do to stay alive and find Pavan? She must have said something aloud, for the cab spoke up.

"Is there anything I can do, ma'am?"

"No, unless you can find a man lost in hyperspace."

"Not one of my capabilities, ma'am, but why don't you talk it out—I'm a good listener."

"Are all cabs this helpful?"

"All cabs leaving the Syndic's residence are, ma'am. Take my word."

"So Uncle Erokh even has pull with technoids."

"And all cabs carrying members of the Syndic's family are extra helpful, ma'am."

"How private is this conversation?"

"It's completely private, ma'am. Only secure cabs may serve the Syndic or his visitors. I guarantee privacy."

"Even from the GSSS?"

Silence, followed by a more serious tone. "I'm sorry, ma'am. I didn't realize we were dealing with a galactic security situation. I've upgraded my encryption capabilities and researched the GSSS technical protocols. I believe I am secure, but there is a constant battle for technical supremacy, so I will update often. My security protocol array is state-of-the-art. I will monitor the extended environment for potential threats. My exterior will handle particle weapons and most explosive devices." The technoid's voice had deepened as though it had buffed itself up.

"And the ride fee?"

"Is going up as we speak, ma'am." The technoid's tone was jocular, but she'd wince at the bill. Still, why not?

"Can I hire you for several days? Dedicated? Can you monitor attempts at breaching your security measures?"

"Yes, yes, and yes, ma'am."

"Convince me you won't report everything I say to the GSSS."

The cab clicked twice to express impatience. "I understand that your being human implies your acceptance of ethical systems that are internally inconsistent. I have no such limitation. I am not paid by the GSSS. You pay me, you get my services, end of story. You don't pay me, you get what you pay for. Try this. Ask yourself if you will be better off trusting me or not taking advantage of the substantial security service I can offer you."

It took no time to consider alternatives; she had none. Nothing in her limited experience had ever taught her how to deal with a high risk of being assassinated. Her one connection to power was her uncle, and he couldn't or wouldn't help. Shocked, she realized just how shallow her reservoir of power really was. If the cab betrayed her, would she be any worse off?

She offered her servipad. "Very well—identity lock on my NIU and repeat nothing I tell you without my explicit authorization. And I authorize payment until further notice."

"Authentication complete. I'm locked down, ma'am. Thanks for your business."

"No problem. Now. I need to find someone on Gaelea who opposes the regime's politics and engages in actions that help people evade the authorities."

"May I point out, ma'am, that such people are not likely to enjoy the favor of your uncle?"

"Kind of the point, isn't it?"

"I don't know, ma'am. Talk to me."

"My husband is a secret agent for the GSSS. He's gone missing. My aunt tells me I'm in danger of assassination from the GSSS and from my uncle. Is this too tough for you?"

"No, ma'am. Logical. But my security protocols prevent me from engaging with anti-government organizations and individuals or conspiring to do so with people like you."

"How about 10,000 credits?"

"Satisfactory, ma'am. Disengaging government protocols. Unfortunately, this does entail my not being able to serve the Syndic or his residences until our contract ends. I can take you anywhere else, however."

"Fine. Technoids work just like brains."

"I'm sorry, ma'am?"

"Never mind." Margona's mind moved from a state of perplexity to one of resolution. "What about my ask?"

"I may have someone who fits the bill, ma'am."

CHAPTER ELEVEN
Saving the Children

Pavan knocked on the warped wooden door of Rark's house, softly at first, then louder. An answering knocking sounded; he puzzled over it for a moment and realized the man was peg-legging it over to his door. The door swung open, and Rark grinned at Pavan.

"Sorry," he said. "Took off my leg to clean it. Not going fishing today, so—"

"Yeah. About that. Can we meet with the village? All the adult villagers?"

Rark raised his eyebrows in surprise. "Sure, I guess so. Not everybody's here. Four boats out to sea looking for fish, most of the youngsters, a few older ones. Nobody's gonna buy nothing, though, if you're selling."

"Yeah, no, we need to tell you some things and see if we can make a deal with you all."

"Huh. Village hasn't been this lively since a storm blew away three houses."

Rark put two fingers in his mouth and blew a loud whistle. He repeated it as doors opened and people stepped out with enquiring looks. Rark stepped down into the street, and Dellatrix joined Pavan behind the big man as he beckoned everyone over.

"Is there a room we can meet in? The wind...." said Dellatrix.

Rark smiled. "Lady, we haven't got pots to piss in, much less a room big enough to hold all of us. We're used to fresh air."

The people of the village gathered around in a semicircle of about fifty people, muttering amongst themselves. There were more women than men, and just a few teenage villagers. Rark said in a stentorian voice, "Pirates here want to talk to y'all." Pavan winced at being identified as a pirate, even though Rark made it a joke. The crowd formed an attentive cluster.

Dellatrix said, "You go ahead, Pavan. You're the rhetorical wizard. You tell them about us pirates." No joke intended, there.

Pavan took care in choosing his words. He wanted to inform but not alarm the people in front of him. But he needed their permission to have pirates take their children off to another world, leaving their parents to die a merciless death at the hands of the Syndicate. The task was a delicate one. He wished he had a magic mushroom or brainwashing training that he could use to reconcile these irreconcilable needs.

"Thank you all for coming. We—my partner Dellatrix and I—have come from off-world to deal with a problem we found out about some days ago. You all know the Galactic Syndicate has declared Ravos forbidden, right? Because of the Secret."

There were general nods of acknowledgement from the men. The women looked at Pavan with stony faces, but none disavowed knowledge.

"So, being very interested in trading in this sector, what was going on worried us, and we wanted to learn more about it. To learn what the Secret was and how it worked. We did," said Pavan with a rueful smile.

Some giggles from the children as they remembered the picture of the two pirates lying shaken and intertwined on the ground. Their parents hushed them. Dellatrix kicked a little dust around, still annoyed at her involuntary exposure of weakness.

Pavan continued, "We had thought it was a technoid device that manipulated hyperspace. But it wasn't. It was your children. And then some of the rumors made sense, especially the one claiming..." Pavan couldn't quite finish the sentence. An expectant silence lengthened. "Since they want the interference to stop, the Syndicate has sent a fleet to destroy the planet. The rumor says they'll be here in a week."

The villagers absorbed this news in silence. Their children wore big, solemn eyes, while the women looked at each other and the men looked off at the ocean. Nobody said a word.

"Our ship, the *Ravager,* is orbiting Ravos. My partner has convinced her captain to make his ship available to evacuate your children to keep them safe. He can't take any more people than just the children, though. No adults or teens."

Rark had taken Jandra's small hand in his own. "Where will you take them?"

Dellatrix stepped up beside Pavan. "The Captain has made space available on his ship to care for all your children indefinitely until we can find a suitable place for them outside Syndicate space."

Rark smiled. "The *Ravager?* Outside? That means you really are pirates, right?"

Little Trex, who had been fidgeting in his mother's arms for five minutes, broke loose and jumped up and down. "Pirates! We're gonna be pirates on the pirate world!"

Pavan thought to himself that this was the best-case scenario of what would happen, but he smiled. "You're not wrong, Rark. But listen—we can assure you of the children's safety and the ultimate resolution of their care in a foster situation, and of their eventual return if events permit that," he said. He took the phrasing from a Gaelean government employee he'd overheard explaining to some parents what was going to happen to the children they could no longer care for because of dire poverty. It sounded just as heartbreakingly stupid to him now as it had then, but now he understood why it had to be said that way. Calm voice, calm language, calm victims. Now give them hope. "And if the Secret isn't here, maybe the Syndicate won't destroy the planet. We'll tell them we have the Secret to make sure they know."

A small voice piped up from behind him. "Sir, this is a complex series of promises. For an added fee, I can develop a contract that—"

Dellatrix slapped a hand down on Pavan's gravpack. "Shut up, you. Later."

"Madam, it is illegal under—"

"Quiet, or I'll—"

"Shut up, the both of you," pleaded Pavan in a whisper. But he wanted few promises put down in a formal contract, as he did not know what was going to happen. Getting the kids off planet had to be better than whatever would happen if they stayed. He looked at the faces of the crowd. There were some mutterings, but aside from a few pursed lips, nobody seemed concerned about a genocidal attack on their planet. Pavan's chest was tight with anxiety. What would it take to convince them to abandon their kids to a pirate's fate? Would he have to tell them that The Captain would come for them if Pavan didn't take them first? Silence again descended on the street.

Pavan pushed out the words. "Do you need time to consider this? Should we take a vote? Rark?"

Rark said, "Huh. I ain't captain right now, we ain't on a boat. And we don't vote, neither. Women get to say." Rark looked over the small crowd. "Looks like all the moms are here. Some sisters on the boats, I guess. Should be OK. Ladies?"

The women gathered together, whispering and nodding to one another.

One of the women, darker and taller than the rest, stepped over to Rark and whispered in his ear. He nodded and gestured toward Pavan and Dellatrix. The woman stepped forward and said in a husky voice, "I'm Coren's mother, and I speak for the others."

Coren hurried over from the cluster of children and took her hand. She smiled down at him, then looked up. "The mothers and sisters have agreed. It is time for the children to experience more of the world than our small village. It is time to grow, to learn the things that are beyond what we can teach. When they return, we will all learn from them."

The gathered men muttered and nodded, but there was no vocal disagreement. Pavan debated whether to point out that the children might not return, or that there might be nothing to which to return. He decided against. Delicate, definitely delicate.

Rark said, "When do you want to take the kids?"

Pavan glanced at Dellatrix. He concluded the adults were in denial about their danger. She rolled her eyes and said, "We can have a shuttle here in an hour. Well, three or four hours, the city isn't…." She left it to the imagination what the city wasn't.

Rark smiled and said, "OK, just give a whistle when you're ready to load. We got a little ceremony we'll do, then we party, then you can load the kids."

Dellatrix asked, "Do the kids need to get things together to—"

Rark smiled his biggest smile. "Dellatrix, they got what they got on. They're ready." He turned to address the children, who were showing signs of excitement. In his most dramatic stentorian tones, he said, "You ready, kids?" The children wore happy grins and started nodding. "We're gonna be pirates!" shouted Trex.

"Shut up, Trex," said Coren. He stepped forward, dropping his mother's hand. "I'm oldest. I'll be in charge for now. Is that all right?" he asked Dellatrix.

"Oh, abso*lutely*," she said. "You're in charge, Coren. Yes. I'll just…step away and get the transport here." She took out her servipad and walked up the village street, away from the villagers, who had broken up into increasingly loudly happy groups.

"We done here?" asked Rark. "Women got washing to get done. And I need to get the party stuff together. Too bad we ain't got any food, kinda limits things. Got a keg, though." The big man rubbed his hands.

"Sure thing," grunted Pavan, bothered by the complacency and denial of Loxator in the face of imminent genocidal destruction. The crowd dispersed and

Rark vanished with his daughter, leaving Pavan standing in the street. A sharp gust blew some sand into his eyes, and he teared up. Quite a place, Loxator.

"About that contract, sir—"

"Shut *up*."

The village gathered in the middle of the street in response to Rark's whistling. Pavan noticed the women had changed their rags to more colorful rags for the party, but he chided himself for his cultural insensitivity. Dellatrix had commented on that before. "Who cares if they're dressed in rags? They obviously know a good deal when they see one. Lighten up, Pavan."

Pavan and Dellatrix sat on the steps up to Rark's door to watch the ceremony. It began with the children, who performed a responsibility ritual. Rark came over and motioned them to give him room, then sat in between them. He put his long arms around them both, keeping them from falling off the sides of the stairs. He leaned over and whispered to Pavan, "We usually have a fish roast for this kind of thing, but since we haven't got any fish, we'll have to fake it."

The children formed a circle very similar to the one they'd formed around Pavan and Dellatrix, but standing instead of sitting. They joined hands and shut their eyes and created The Mind. Then they danced, moving in perfect unison, feet stomping the ground precisely together, everyone going sideways with precise steps that preserved a perfect circle. The women clapped in time with the dance, though nowhere near as perfectly as the dancers moved.

"I could sell this act just about anywhere in the Syndicated planets," whispered Dellatrix. "High quality. With better music? World class." Pavan ignored her as being too culturally insensitive.

The dance went on for some little time, then wound down. The children stopped moving, then spoke with their single voice. "One sees the choices made, one approves. There is no error, there is no dissent. One seizes the opportunity as it arises. One prepares to care for the aged as they leave. One mourns the loss of the aged who remain here. One accepts the responsibility for its own life and those of the aged under its care. One absolves the aged who remain of their responsibilities to the Mind. One commits itself to the return."

"Sir. If my services might be useful in this endeavor, I am perfectly willing—"

"Shut up!" said Dellatrix, whapping the promisepad again. "Time and place for everything; this isn't it."

A silence developed in the street. Then a ululation from the women broke the silence. When that died down, the women entered the circle of children by ducking under the linked arms until all the village women were inside the circle. The children raised their hands as high as they could without breaking apart, then said, "The aged are here."

All the women sat inside the circle with their eyes closed. The men looked on from outside the circle, all rapt in their attention to the scene. The women swayed back and forth in total silence.

The children's single voice said, "One loves the mothers; the mothers love one. One loves the sisters; the sisters love one. All agree that one accepts responsibility. The mothers accept the care of the chronicle. The chronicle will be safe."

The children dropped their hands, and the circle broke apart. The women rose to their feet and found their children and embraced them.

Pavan heard a noise and looked up to find a strange man standing beside him. "What's it all about, then?" asked the man.

"Who the hell are you?" Pavan asked. Dellatrix looked over and got up, ready for action.

"Storran!" Rark stood up and embraced the newcomer. "About time!"

"Sorry, my man; food riots. Lucky I got here at all."

Pavan noticed that a large van had pulled up to the edge of the village unnoticed during the ceremony. "What's going on, Rark?" he asked.

"Food delivery! Now we can party." He looked around, the addressed the deliveryman. "Kids are heading out on a trip, won't need food for 'em for a while. Ain't got the money for it anyway. No flippin' fish." He grinned. "Folks out on the boats are gonna miss out. We don't party too often."

"Hard life," said Storran. "Now, where's this party?"

CHAPTER TWELVE
The Lost Children

THE PARTY WAS IN FULL swing when the pirate shuttle pulled up in front of Rark's house. It carried three of Pavan and Dellatrix's shipmates. Alighting from the shuttle, the lead pirate greeted Dellatrix, then complained, "Tour bus operator. This ain't what I shipped out for. And I was on shore leave."

Dellatrix said, "I'm in charge, right?"

"No arguments from me," said the pirate. He turned to Pavan. "Name's Viggu Bullseye. Call me Bullseye. And these two reprobates are my buddies, Slopnor and Pevilburt Goofer. They're brothers. Call 'em anything you want to. Who're you? Seen you around."

"I'm Pavan. Migrant labor."

The big pirate digested this while Pavan inspected the brothers and resolved not to prejudge them, but they sure looked mentally deficient from the outside. Bullseye looked a lot like Tigyanor. Pavan had seen him around the ship but had never spoken with him. Bullseye had the assurance and arrogance of what Pavan now knew was a contract pirate. He'd never seen Slopnor or Pevilburt; he was sure they kept them locked up somewhere until The Captain needed blaster fodder.

The pirates inspected the village and saw that everyone was celebrating. "Big party," said Slopnor. "They got booze?"

"Sure, plenty to go around. Too bad you won't be here long enough to drink any," said Dellatrix, smiling.

Slopnor and Pevilburt looked disappointed, but Pavan noticed they treated Dellatrix with a lot more respect than he'd ever seen any pirate treat anyone. They also stayed six feet away from her and glanced at her with twitchy eyes when she wasn't looking. Bullseye ignored them but still treated Dellatrix with more respect than his visage suggested was usual for him.

Pavan looked for Rark and found him dancing with a woman, an up-close-and-tight dance. He extracted the big man with a smile and said, "Time to go, Rark. Can you gather up the kids?"

"Sure, Pavan." Rark progressed up and down the street, extracting children from the party and telling them to go over to the shuttle. He gave a special hug to his daughter, Janny. By the end, sixteen children gathered in front of the shuttle.

Bullseye looked them up and down and balked. "You got me here for a school bus?" He folded his arms and jutted out his jaw.

The Goofers shuffled their feet, looking from Bullseye's intransigent stance to Dellatrix, who gave him a little half smile with narrowed eyes.

"I'm in charge, right?" she asked. Pavan noticed her attitude toward Bullseye was tougher than the vulnerable side she'd shown to him. That must be why she was rethinking her career, always having to act tougher than the toughest alpha male. She wanted them to take her seriously.

"Yeah, but sixteen kids on a pirate ship?"

"I thought there were seventeen," said Dellatrix, counting them.

"Hey Rark—one's missing," shouted Pavan.

"That's Tizzy, she's the chronicler." Rark came over and pointed at a tiny girl frisking and dancing with a woman. Her mother?

"She'll have to come too," said Pavan.

"Nope; she has to stay behind. She's the chronicler."

"What is the chronicler?"

"She's the youngest."

"So?" said Dellatrix.

Rark looked at her with compassion for her stupidity. "She has the longest life ahead. The Mind will live on in her if something happens to the children. Which it won't."

"But—"

"When the children come back, the Mind will come together and share the two worlds."

Pavan looked long and hard at Rark, who winked at him and smiled his happy grin. Pavan had a lot of experience reading people, and his gut told him the truth: Tizzy was staying, period. He guessed that in the face of certain death, these people had gone into utter denial. There was no time to get them past it.

He had to let Tizzy go, because the villagers wouldn't. He switched his attention back to Bullseye, still annoyed about his unwelcome task.

Jaw jutting, the big pirate pushed out his lower lip and frowned with his strong, black eyebrows. He looked down at his feet and up at Dellatrix, his face mirroring the progress of anger winning out over fear. Pavan readied himself to jump him. Then Bullseye's face blanched at something in Dellatrix's expression, and he stepped back. "OK, OK. *OK.* Sixteen kids it is, then. Bloody...." He turned and started pulling kids toward the shuttle, a very frustrated and unhappy pirate. Slopnor and Pevilburt rushed to help him.

The shuttle asked each child for a name and saying which seat to take in its gravelly voice. The children had never seen a bus talking before. They found it enchanting. They kept asking the shuttle questions until it got tired and shouted in a commanding tone, "Everybody sit down, now! We gotta get this show on the road!" The voice of authority. The children and the pirates all obeyed.

Pavan turned to Rark. "This is it. Hope I'll see you again, Rark. With the kids." Pavan knew that wouldn't happen.

Rark embraced him, held him by the shoulders, and said, "The kids will take care of you, Pavan. Everything will be fine. Hey, I gotta get back to the party. Eloia is waiting and she's hot tonight!" He gave Pavan a squeeze and danced back to the massed villagers and their party. Pavan stared after him. A good dancer for a man with a wooden leg.

"Come on, people!" said the shuttle. "Gotta move this thing. Captain's orders, whoever he might be."

"Sure thing," said Pavan. He got on the shuttle, the door closed, and the bus ground up the little hill on the way to the city.

The spaceport lounge looked exactly as it had when Pavan passed through on his way to the fleshpots and bars. This time, though, it was noisier. Sixteen excited children ready to take the space elevator up to an *adventure.* Pavan marveled that sixteen kids could make more noise than twenty pirates on their way to a long-delayed shore leave, but that was the case.

"Quiet!" shouted Bullseye. Nothing changed.

Dellatrix said, "Now, kids. We're going onto the big spaceship, OK? The space elevator will take us up in the sky for a couple of days, then you can all explore the space station at the top, right? And then we'll shuttle to the pirate ship and settle you in a place you can all hang out. How does that sound?"

The children raised a cheer.

Dellatrix led the way into the big elevator climber car and gave the children a tour.

"You can sleep when you need to in these chairs, and food is in that locker over there. You'll have to double up in the chairs. There aren't enough of them for everyone. Oh, and the higher we get, the less you'll weigh; have fun!"

Chairs weren't a problem other than being in the way of the adults trying to save the kids from their own antics. The chairs were play structures for use when the kids weren't running up and down the elevator car aisles and pulling everything out of the food drawers and luggage compartments. Only occasionally did a child sink into an exhausted sleep in a seat.

Dellatrix wore out first. After one attempt to get all the overexcited kids seated in the chairs, she gave up in disgust and turned everything over to Pavan. He analyzed the situation with a tactical eye and decided that it called for constructive inaction. When the river flows through a difficult terrain, you follow the river rather than trying to get it to do what you want. Over the two days in the elevator car, the kid tides ebbed and flowed while Pavan and the Goofers shepherded the children away from any dangerous rocks. Dellatrix and Bullseye kept their feet dry.

On the second day, Bullseye sat down to eat a meal at a fold-down table in a seat when Trex took an interest in his food. Not satisfied with his protein bar, which he jammed into a cup holder, the little boy looked around for alternatives. Liking what he saw on Bullseye's tray, he ran over and grabbed a jam-covered biscuit and stuffed it in his mouth.

Bullseye, taken by surprise, reacted as any real pirate would. He grabbed Trex by the neck and started choking him. Pavan, who'd been watching from several feet away, jumped for him, but Skylla, the oldest girl in the group, reached the struggling pair first.

"Stop that! You're hurting him! No bullying!" She started pulling at the big pirate's arm and hand, which gripped the little boy's neck like a vise. Annoyed, Bullseye swung his other hand and knocked the girl over a seat. By this time, all the other children had massed around the pirate and the little boy, some pulling at Bullseye, some pulling at Trex. Pavan couldn't get through. Then he stepped on something left in the aisle and fell down, hard.

Dellatrix stepped over him. Despite an intervening child or two, she got to Bullseye and Trex tumbled down next to Pavan, free and gasping and laughing at the same time. Bullseye fell back into his chair, struggling and shouting obscenities as Dellatrix leaned over him. She grabbed his jaw and pulled his head around to look at her.

"Enough! Haven't you got any common sense? The Captain wants these kids intact. Tell me you can control yourself. Can you?" She shook his head and let go of his chin.

As Pavan struggled up to a sitting position, Bullseye groaned and collapsed backward in the chair, his right arm twisted behind him. Dellatrix put a hand on his chest, pushing him down. He nodded, licked his lips, and said, "Arrrh!" From Dellatrix's satisfied smile, Pavan interpreted this pirate grunt as reluctant assent. Bullseye's arm snapped out from behind his back, and he grabbed it and held it close to his body, his eyes never leaving the steely green ones looking at him.

"One more chance, space louse; one more." She slapped the pirate on the cheek with a soft tap, asserting her dominance over him, then turned and walked back to her seat and her interrupted reading. Pavan saw Bullseye's expression relax into a glare of anger. Then he saw Pavan looking at him and erased the glare.

Pavan went to the food storage locker and assembled another tray of food, then brought it to Bullseye's chair and offered it to him without saying a word. The pirate's face was white and terrible to behold in its anger, but he accepted the tray, giving Pavan an oblique glance with lips pressed tight.

Pavan gathered up Trex and Skylla and took them off to a corner to check them over for damage. There was none. Trex commented that he'd always wanted to know what a fight with a pirate was like. Skylla simmered in silence, confining her response to a black stare across the car to her nemesis, Bullseye.

Coren came to join them.

"Sorry I couldn't do anything, Pavan. I tripped over a chair before I could get there," he apologized.

"It's OK, Coren. No harm done. Can you take care of Trex?"

"Sure, Pavan. Come on, Trex, let's play the hand game." He took the little boy off and kept him occupied.

Pavan asked, "Are you OK, Skylla?"

The girl brushed back her hair. "I guess so. He didn't ought to have done that, Pavan. We don't like bullies in Loxator."

"Trex just surprised him. He won't do it again."

"He better not. I'll tell The Captain on him, and that will fix him."

Pavan smiled. "I don't think we need The Captain involved. Dellatrix has things under control." Dellatrix clearly had the experience that came from being a contract pirate, with no problem taking charge when she had to. He guessed she didn't like it much, though.

Skylla nodded a reluctant nod, gave Bullseye another black stare, then took herself off to a chair as far away as she could get from the big pirate, joining Dellatrix. Pavan saw that his partner wore a satisfied smile, having bested a pirate twice her size. Pavan suspected she was better than she might appear in a fight. She might give a nervous smile from time to time, and she might regret her pirate career, but she wouldn't let those things get in her way. Not when confronting other pirates.

The time in the elevator dragged. It docked at the space station counterweight in geostationary orbit. The frazzled pirates wasted no time in shepherding the enthralled, weightless children past the station viewports and into the docked transfer shuttle. Coren whispered to Pavan that Slopnor and Pevilburt were pushing the kids like a school of fish in the weightless passages of the station. The pirates herded the children into seats, then the shuttle undocked and headed off to the pirate ship under short-duration constant acceleration, giving everyone back illusory weight. The shuttle had a massive pseudowindow that showed the planet Ravos as it swung by, night encroaching on the world they had just left.

"Is that the ocean? Is it? Is it? Our ocean, with our fish?" cried Trex, pointing.

Coren scanned the image. "It's *an* ocean, anyway. Never seen it up this high." The boy sighed. "It's beautiful from up here."

Pavan did some quick thinking and instructed the pseudowindow to switch to their destination, the *Ravager*. "There's the *Ravager*, the pirate ship." He correctly figured this would get the kids to change their attention from the home they had left behind to their new home. Pavan looked it over as well, looking for lifeboat ports.

"Kind of blocky, innit?" asked one kid. "Not very shippy. No way you could fish in that."

"Everybody's a critic," said Dellatrix, who had grabbed a running Trex and deposited the small boy on her lap.

The big metal sign over the door of Cargo Bay 23 said, in nicely embossed lettering, "The Dellatrix Devdan Asylum for Lost Children."

"I had the metal shop make it. What do you think?" asked Dellatrix. "I'm going to call it 'The Orphanage' for short."

"Beats the hell out of 'Cargo Bay 23,'" said Pavan.

The cargo bay doors slid open and closed with only a quiet swoosh and a tiny metallic squeal. The big cargo bay had one section walled off with cots for the children. The rest of the bay had boxes and various large pipes and girders strewn around.

Dellatrix said, "The kids have settled in. Place was completely empty except for the cots. Have you ever noticed, Pavan, that pirates lack imagination?"

"Why, yes, Dellatrix, I have. Most pirates, anyway. Present company excepted."

"Thank you." The pirate pushed a toe against a huge crate. "So, we had all this garbage waiting for deep space disposal. I figured, why not create a child's wonderland? I had Slopnor and Pevilburt working for two days to move all this junk in here. Kids loved it. I figured since they had nothing in their village, any old thing would work for them. Look, they've built their own pirate ship in just two days!"

As Pavan and Dellatrix walked around the makeshift pirate ship, Pavan asked, "No complaints about home?"

"One kid complained about no fish. I jollied him out of it."

"Do you spend all your time in here?"

Dellatrix grinned. "No, I have work to do."

Pavan's need to know encompassed far more than Dellatrix would allow. Aside from learning everything he could about the *Ravager* and its crew, he needed access to the children. How to ask for it without raising suspicion?

He said, "Do you mind if I check in with them every so often, just to understand how they're getting on?"

Dellatrix smiled and faced him. "Pavan, I hope you can see your way to spending a lot of time with them. You've been on one of their play rides, you've felt what they can do. You might work it out with them, what they can do. They won't tell me a thing." She looked a little nettled. "Gave them candy and everything, little bastards. They like you, Pavan. And you can serve as their teacher, keep them busy with school stuff and games and such." She gave him a defiant look. "And I don't see myself as a sixteen-kid nanny. We'll call it men's work."

Pavan smiled; her attitude toward him had changed, had become tougher, as he had gained status as a pirate. But Pavan's plan had been to work his way into the pirate hierarchy on the ship; he couldn't do that if he was supervising the playground all day. "What about my duties in—"

"I've requested your services from The Captain. He agreed you should do this, OK? And, Pavan—The Captain says he doesn't want 'the little rats' underfoot,

OK? They're locked in here and don't leave. No wandering around the ship breaking things and annoying the hands while they're working." She waved a hand at a walled-off area. "I've set you up with a cot in the sleeping quarters over there. Any objection?"

Pavan had no interest in spending his time with space lice, but he would learn nothing about the pirates working with the children. He might learn something about the Secret he might trade for knowledge about the pirates. He had to get *something* he could use to help the GSSS take the ship. But objecting to The Captain's suggestion would not be a good idea. The only thing he would learn from that would be how space tastes.

"No, no objections. Where will you be?"

"I'll check in with you when I get a chance."

"Where are your quarters?"

"Right where I left them, and that's all you need to know. I don't socialize much on board, Pavan. It wouldn't be good for—" Dellatrix stopped; she compressed her lips. "Enough." She softened and stroked a finger down Pavan's cheek, tracing the very faint scar there. "When we get to Khonoë, I might have some time. For you. Not on the ship."

"What if—"

"Just make damn sure they don't get in one of their circles. They did that. Yesterday. On their own. The Captain was livid when the ship fell out of hyperspace and the hyperspatial gravsims kicked out. I can't afford to get on his bad side, not enough money in the galaxy to compensate for that. At least he believes me now about the Mind. If you need me, just scream my name. I won't come, but it will make you feel better. Get Bullseye to help you if you need something done."

"He'd be pretty good at spacing a kid for squealing. But not much else."

Dellatrix grinned. "Not much of a role model, is he? Gotta go, Pavan. Get to work!"

Pavan surveyed his new domain, noting the tendency of kids to disappear into small openings in the space junk. Hard work ahead. Bullseye. How much did he trust the pirate? Not much at all. Could he be The Captain? His arrogance might argue for it, but his overall attitude seemed too obstreperous. Still, The Captain was smooth. Bullseye could be putting on a decent act. Wait and see. And trust no one.

CHAPTER THIRTEEN
The Flight to Khonoë

"Ahhhhhhhh!"

Pavan, correctly interpreting this animal scream, jumped sideways as only a well-trained agent of the Galactic Syndicate Security Service can jump.

Trex, the smallest and loudest of the Lost Children, continued his drop past the dodging secret agent and plopped on the deck in a heap. He had staged the ambush well; only his premature scream of pleasure prevented Pavan from becoming the latest victim of the little would-be pirate.

The deck of Cargo Bay 23, rechristened the Orphanage, had undergone a transformation in the last four days. Several injuries convinced Pavan that metal decks and excited children did not play well together.

"Bloody bollocks," Bullseye had said as he laid the artificial turf. "I grew up playing on rock, these little shits got no business being coddled." Slopnor and Pevilburt, laying plastic sod next to him, had nodded morosely but had said nothing. It took almost a day to synthesize and lay down enough of the soft material to protect the children in their extensive playground of remodeled junk.

Pavan picked up the little boy, checked him over for gore, and sent him off to find another victim. If he survived his secret mission with the pirates, his betrayal of the Service, and his appointment as custodian of these demon children, he would recommend the latter as a training ground for agents back at the Secret Service Academy. His reflexes were at least one-and-a-half times faster after four days of supervising these kids.

Thankfully, there was only one more day of hyperspace required to get to Khonoë. They passed the exit point at the boundary of Syndicate space a day before and were now passing through the hyperdimensions of galactic free space.

He had kept the children from forming the Mind, but it had been a near thing. After finding four of the little girls joining hands behind a large metal cylinder, he dragooned Slopnor and Pevilburt into a system of watches. Bullseye refused, saying, "I didn't ship out as a pirate to play shepherd to sodding little kids. You got something useful for me to do, I'll do it because The Captain tells me to do it. Otherwise, go screw yourself."

Nothing was forthcoming from The Captain, so it was an eight-hour watch system. Pavan had few energy reserves left after his watch. He took the play-day watch. On close observation of Pevilburt's performance, he gave the dead-of-night watch to him on the theory that nothing much could happen when the kids were dead to the world. They were champion sleepers, ten hours or more, some of them. So things calmed down on that watch. That left Slopnor, the smarter brother, with the dinner-and-story watch, and Slopnor now showed signs of wear. As did Pavan.

The bay doors swooshed open, and Dellatrix appeared as Pavan watched little Trex run toward his junk-built pirate ship.

"Hi, Pavan. How's it going with the little bastards?"

"I need help."

"I need money. Neither is a high priority with The Captain."

"These kids are hyperactive or something."

"Any more damage?"

"Not since Bullseye laid the sod."

She smiled. "I dropped by to let you know The Captain is drawing up the tranches for shore leave on Khonoë. Do you want to go down, or are you locked into being primary child care provider here?"

Pavan, torn between a deep sense of responsibility to his charges and an intense need to see the inside of a pirate bar, said, "Absolutely. When do I go?"

"I'm sure The Captain will set a tranche for you after the pirates with more seniority have taken their leaves."

"I don't have any seniority."

Dellatrix smiled and said nothing.

"Do you mean to tell me," groused Pavan, "that idiot Pevilburt gets leave before me?"

"Yep."

"I need help."

"You said that earlier."

"I'm beat."

Dellatrix consulted the overhead, looked down, grimaced, and pointed. Pavan ran over to a metal box with a door that was slowly closing. "Get out of there, Jandra, you'll suffocate yourself." The play area was not up to the standards established by the Galactic Interworld Building Code. Needed to watch them every damn minute.

"OK, Pavan. We're playing hide-and-seek, wanna play?"

"Not just now, Janny. Not just now." He pushed the little albino girl off toward another secret hiding place.

Dellatrix wandered over to the walled-in sleeping room. Pavan joined her.

She said, "They didn't make their beds. The Captain insists on a tight ship."

"You're kidding."

"I am." The pirate ran a finger down the scar on Pavan's cheek, as she had done before, smiling. "Lighten up, Pavan. You're only a child once."

"Yeah, and that was thirty years ago."

The musical laugh sounded good to Pavan's ears. He was suddenly tongue-tied, which was a sure sign that one of Margona's surreptitious neuroinstinctual pathways had activated. He suspected that his exhaustion, coupled with his domestic duties, had broken down his emotional barriers. He was getting soft— for Dellatrix. This thought then progressed to thinking about how much he loved Margona, and where she was, and that she wasn't here to go with him on shore leave. Dellatrix was. All this brain work further exhausted him.

Rebelling against it all, he reverted to form, but his exhaustion felled him. "I'd kiss you, Dellatrix, but I'm too tired."

"I'm not." She held his head in both hands and showed him. His arms went around her without conscious thought.

"Woo-hoo! The pirate king and queen are kissing!" The high-pitched voice of Trex broke the kiss like a cold knife through hot butter.

Dellatrix stepped back, smiling, and said, "Got to go, Pavan. I'm in the first tranche for the planet. Got to get some stuff done before I go. I'll let you know where the best bar is." The doors of the cargo bay swooshed open, then closed behind her.

"Are you gonna have a kid with her?" asked Trex. "That's what happens when moms kiss dads."

"Trex. Let's have a talk." Pavan's voice was hoarse, but it wasn't from talking.

The *Ravager* established synchronous orbit around Khonoë near the space elevator that would transport the pirates to their home base. This was a den of iniquity somebody in the distant past had named Ylzogwberg. As nobody could pronounce this name, the pirates all called it the Black Hole of Khonoë, or the Hole for short. It was the only settlement on the otherwise jungle-covered planet. The first tranche of pirates went down the space elevator to find solace and levity in the many bars in the Hole.

Viggu Bullseye appeared at the Orphanage to tell Pavan he was going down in the second tranche to find a few friends and a few drinks, not in that order.

"You have friends?" Pavan asked.

The big pirate slapped Pavan on the back. "You're a laugh a minute, my man. I'll let you live a little longer than I thought I would, just to hear your jokes."

"Is Dellatrix going down in your tranche?"

"Damn, I hope not." Bullseye shuddered. "Stay away from that dodgy curpopper, if you know what's good for your nuts." He scratched the organs in question and laughed. "Many more fruits on the tree down in the Hole. You don't need to deal with that pain."

"What's a dodgy curpopper?" asked Janny, who was playing with some blocks nearby. "A bird? Do they eat nuts?"

Bullseye rolled his eyes and stuck out his tongue at her. She grinned and stuck out her tongue.

"Bloody kids," said Bullseye, slapping Pavan on the back once more. He left with a snort of laughter. Definitely arrogant enough to be The Captain.

Pavan took advantage of the next week to slow the children down and get them to organize themselves. He fell into a rhythm and got more sleep. With a little preventive maintenance, he could ease the kids into shared activities rather than letting them run wild. He got to know some of the mid-range children better, playing games, reading stories, and even helping them to organize a puppet show. Bullseye came back from his liberty on the planet red-eyed and tired but happy enough, and Pavan got him to build the puppet theater.

"Used to be a carpenter, back on my home planet," he said. "We had real wood from real trees to work with, not this junk. Used real nails, not these little snappy things." He built the theater out of engineered lumber produced by the ship's technoid parts generator to his specifications. He even had the thing produce a curtain made of velvety material. This was a triumph of technical knowledge on his part. "Bloody noids know nothing. You got to tweak 'em to get stuff like this. They don't like it, either, bloody narcissistic junk piles." He snapped the back platform together as he talked.

"How was shore leave?"

"Oh, my man! You remember that bar on Ravos, the one where…"

"Yeah. Sure thing," said Pavan.

"Crap compared to the new bars in the Hole. They got booze down there even I have never heard of. Every pirate in the galaxy must smuggle the stuff in. Hung out with a couple of my buddies. From the *Ripper*. Not," he said, "those two drunks." Slopnor and Pevilburt were working with the children on building the puppets out of what appeared to be socks and technoid spare parts. Pevilburt was telling pirate stories to the children as he worked. They didn't understand a word of the stories because of his strange dialect, so Pavan didn't intervene.

Pavan got Bullseye to advertise the puppet show to the crew. To his amazement, thirty pirates showed up at the appointed time. Bullseye's having imported enough liquor from the Hole to drown a planet might have had something to do with that. The eleven children who were not puppeteers sat in the audience while the five puppeteers put on the story. The Ravos myth at the story's base was a hero's journey on the ocean to find a magic fish. The hero thought the fish would give him untold wealth, but it, in fact, was just a fish. This story seemed to resonate well with the pirates, who cheered on the plot developments with language that would make a sailor blush. There was a lady fish involved.

The final scene in the show updated the myth. A pirate comes along and steals the fish, under the impression that it would make him rich. The hero kills the pirate and eats the fish, which the pirate has done in. This final fight brought down the house, and everyone cheered the five puppeteers, despite a few grumbles that expressed the minority's disappointment that the pirate didn't win. The other pirates suppressed these complaints, to the cheering and amusement of the children, who had never seen a pirate bar fight before. Pavan got Bullseye to help him shepherd the children out of the way of flying pirates, in between the big man's own forays into the fray.

Pavan saw Dellatrix intervene only once, when two pirates pulled knives on each other. She supervised the removal of the two unconscious pirates to their quarters to recover, then waved cheerily at him as she left. His current job was secure as long as she and Bullseye kept The Captain satisfied as to his progress.

CHAPTER FOURTEEN
The Hypershield

PAVAN SAT ON THE DECK with his back against the wall of the Orphanage near the big cargo doors. The idea of a short, a very short morning nap had overwhelmed him after a strenuous session of blind-ball. He made a mental note to ask Bullseye to use his technical ability with the parts generator to make a softer ball. He also made a note to reprimand Bullseye for supplying all the liquor to the puppet show, too much of which had found its way to Pavan's aching head. Blind-ball the day after a seriously inebriated piratical puppet show was an error in judgment.

A gentle kick to his side awoke him.

"Aren't you supposed to be supervising things?" asked Dellatrix.

"Yes," said Pavan.

"You're fired," said Dellatrix.

"Great. Glad to hear it."

Dellatrix held a hand down, and Pavan pulled himself up to his reluctant duty.

"So, Pavan—there could be a problem."

Pavan analyzed the problem with the body-language skills he'd gained through years of interrogation of worried people. The tense shoulders, tight lips, and gritted teeth behind the attempt at a nonchalant smile alerted him to danger at hand.

"Tell me," he said, scanning for dead or dying kids. Nothing.

"What have we learned about the children's mind trick so far?" she asked.

"Well, not much that's new. Single mind, single memory that doesn't seem to flow to individuals. Ability to navigate through hyperspace to see just about anything. Disrupts surrounding hyperspace and so disrupts hyper-travel and communications for some distance."

"Exactly what distance?"

"I've got a theory that it depends on how many children are taking part in the Mind. I'm not a hyperphysicist, but what I learned in school was that the quantum chromodynamics of hyperspace depends on a set of color charges. The Mind could only control hyperspace by controlling those colors. From my observations so far, the more children, the more colors, the larger the three-dimensional effect based on an n-dimensional vector to a hyperbolic boundary." Pavan wished he'd paid more attention in class. But the woman sitting in front of him had been a lot more interesting than the professor or the physics that he had known he would never need. Sure thing.

"OK, but what distance right now?" asked Dellatrix.

"Not a clue. We need to experiment—"

"We need a solution, Pavan. Fast. The Captain has learned through his Syndicate contacts the Syndicate is sending a fleet after us. He told me they've somehow learned that we've kidnap—er, evacuated, the kids."

"How the hell did they learn that?" Was the Ducis sending a rescue fleet? More likely, he'd lost confidence in Pavan's ability to control the Secret. Whatever he was planning needed the Secret gone along with the pirates that knew about it. Maybe Onyx had involved himself. So....

Dellatrix got impatient. "What the hell does it matter? Here's what's important, Pavan. The Captain wants you to get the children to put up a shield, a hypershield, around Khonoë. Nothing in, nothing out. Until further notice."

Pavan said, "The problem is, the hyperspatial disruption effect only exists when the Mind is active. A hypershield like The Captain wants would need to be continuous, or ships and comms would just go through when the Mind broke up. They have to eat and sleep. And play. A shield full of large holes isn't much of a shield." He thought about what he'd learned and added, "And we know nothing about the size of the disrupted area. Again, my guess is that the more kids, the larger the distance of the effect."

"How can we find out, fast?" The anxiety showed clearly in her face.

"Experiment. Get the kids together and add kids one at a time." Pavan considered and discarded the notion that he could get the kids into a lifeboat somehow; he had found no way to do that so far. Delaying things with a shield would be his best bet. It would give him time to come up with a rescue plan that worked.

Dellatrix grimaced. "We don't have much time, Pavan. Do you think you can get this done before the Syndicate fleet wipes all life off Khonoë?"

"Sure thing," he said, not at all sure. Progressing from blind-ball to a hyper-shield seemed like a lot to ask of sixteen kids, no matter how hyper they were.

Pavan and Dellatrix found Coren sitting in a corner of the Orphanage reading a servipad.

"Hey, Coren. What are you reading?"

The boy looked up and smiled. "Hi, Pavan. I'm reading some stuff about that myth we used in the puppet show yesterday. I got interested. Turns out it's based on a real oral history. No pirates, though."

"There was a magic fish in your ocean?"

"No, it was a sea mammal. We used to hunt them for food and oil until we figured out they were smarter than us."

"So, how come we don't know about this species on Ravos?"

"They were a lot smarter than us. They left."

"Um."

Coren smiled again. "That's what I thought."

"So how did it become a magic fish?"

"This," he said, tapping the servipad, "says the stories report one group of this species got hold of some fishermen that tried to hunt them down. They changed the metagenetic systems in the fishermen to help them find a different way to live. I don't know what that means," the boy said. "I haven't had much school, just enough to learn to read and write. It also says in a note in the back that no one has verified this, as no one knows where the fishermen went."

Pavan snorted. "I think I know."

"Yeah."

The sound of spacer's boots announced Bullseye's arrival.

"Pavan. The Captain commed me to get my lazy arse down here. What the bleeding hell is going on?"

Dellatrix said, "Pavan. We don't have time for this. The Captain's getting impatient."

"What's happening?" asked Coren, setting down the servipad.

"Um."

"Tell the kid, Pavan," said Bullseye.

Pavan looked at Dellatrix, irresolute. His intuition screamed that direct action was the wrong way to approach the problem of getting the Mind to experiment on itself. He couldn't articulate why he felt that, but he did.

"Pavan?" asked Coren, standing up from his cot.

"We've got a problem, Coren," said Pavan, striving for a calm voice that would not alarm the boy. "There's a possibility that the Syndicate may come after the pirates, and The Captain wants the Mind to protect Khonoë and the *Ravager*. And us."

"Protect it…how?"

"The hyperspatial disruption…The Captain thinks if we keep the Mind awake, the hyperspatial disruption effects will block any Syndicate ships from attacking us. A 'hypershield.'"

"Oh. Sure. But that will only work when the Mind is awake. We only play together a little now and then."

"But you used to play all the time, before the Ravosi government made you stop, right?"

"I guess so. That was a while ago."

"Also, the number of children playing together seems to affect the hyperspace region you can explore. Is that right?"

"Yeah. We need three of us to see anything beyond the hyperspace around Ravos. We like to play with all of us if we can. It just feels better."

"*Pavan.*" Dellatrix shifted from foot to foot with impatience.

"Coren, we want to try some things with you and the other kids. An experiment."

"What kind of experiment?" The boy's eyes narrowed.

"We'll send a shuttle out to the edge of the Khonoë system, to the heliopause. Then we'll add one child each trial until the shuttle reports they can't hyper-communicate or travel anymore."

"Sounds boring."

"I hope it is, but we need to do it. Can you gather the kids?"

"Well, sure, but…"

"Kid. Do what the man says," said Bullseye.

"I don't—"

Bullseye stepped forward and said, "Let's go, kid, get all the rest of you little bastards together. Out there." He pointed at the field.

Coren's face took on a determined expression that Pavan had never seen on the boy. Coren said, "No. The Mind won't do it."

"You mean *you* won't do it." Dellatrix stepped toward the boy, and Pavan grabbed her arm.

"Dellatrix. Let me." Her flat, metallic eyes softened and blinked as her common sense took over from her fear.

"All right. But get a move on."

Pavan turned to Coren. "Please?" he asked. "We need to try this."

"The Mind doesn't enjoy doing boring things. It's going to have a problem with this."

"We'll talk to it and persuade it. We'll get the shuttle in place, then gather the kids."

The boy shook his head with doubt, but said, "OK. But you'll see, the Mind won't want to do this." He sat back down on his cot and resumed reading his servipad, dismissing his tormentors, who walked out to the cargo bay door.

Pavan said, "Dellatrix, we need to be careful and not alarm the kids too much, right? Or they might have trouble doing what we want. Pirate tactics won't work here."

"OK, Pavan, you know best." The inflection in her voice suggested doubt about this proposition. Bullseye shook his head with an unsympathetic grin.

Pavan changed the subject. "I think it would be a good idea to put an adult in the circle as an observer, then we'll have our own confirmation of what's happening."

"Do we have to…do I need to be inside the circle? As before?"

"Not unless you want to. Bullseye?"

"Not a chance, my man." The big pirate grinned. "No offense, but you can keep that hyper-crap. I don't want any. Especially with kids."

"Then it will have to be me or Pevilburt."

"Thanks for volunteering, Pavan. Where is Pevilburt, by the way?" asked Dellatrix.

"Sleeping one off."

Dellatrix smiled without humor and took out her residual frustration on poor Pevilburt. "He's going to walk around on nothing one of these days if he keeps drinking on duty."

"It ain't so much drinking on duty as drinking my best bloody Lavonian whiskey," groused Bullseye. "All of it."

"Enough," said Dellatrix. "Let's get going. I'll get the shuttle launched."

"It's going to take some organization," said Pavan. "We can't depend on optical comms to the shuttle. Too far away. It would take hours to get a response all the way from the heliopause. So, we'll have to form the Mind, then break out to let hypercomms work again. Right?"

"Right. I'll gen up the shuttle pilot. OK, let's do this."

* * *

Pavan returned to the sleeping area to find Coren staring into space.

"What's up, Coren?"

The boy blinked and looked at Pavan. "I'm turning into an aged, Pavan."

"I've heard you use that word before, the 'aged.' What does it mean?"

"It's what we call people who get old, older than us, out of the Mind."

"Out of their minds? Crazy?"

"No, sorry. I meant they can't get into the circle anymore, they don't connect in the Mind." The boy's face was glum.

"When does it happen?"

"My dad called it 'the change,'" said Coren. "Our bodies behave differently, and that makes our thoughts moody. The Mind can't tolerate much of that."

"But what age?"

"About 12 or 13. My age."

Pavan looked at Coren. "So, you…"

"I'm changing. I'm not as interested in the games anymore. I want to read more, learn more." He sighed. "I'm even different from the other changers in Loxator. They just want to head out on the fishing boats when they change. I can't see myself fishing for the rest of my life. But…I can't let go of the Mind. It still lets me in. I want to be a part of the Mind as long as I can. And now you, the pirates, Dellatrix, want me to control the Mind somehow. I can't! I don't have any time left, Pavan!" Coren's eyes teared up. He wiped furiously with his hand. "See, that's what I mean. I'm feeling things like this, cry more, get angry. I hate it!"

Pavan, illuminated, said, "We all go through it, Coren. We call it puberty. It's all hormones and…sex."

"What's sex?"

"Um."

"All that kissing and stuff that ageds do? Like you and Dellatrix? Moms and dads?" He made the leap. "Babies?"

"Yeah."

"Why does the Mind care?"

"Couldn't tell you." Pavan rubbed his mouth. "How do you…I don't know the right question—how does the Mind interact with you?"

"Interact? It doesn't. I'm there, then the Mind is there, then I'm back. All I remember is feelings, good ones from the playing the Mind does in hyperspace. Sometimes things like planets or starships. I like starships," said the boy. "I had this picture book—"

"But the Mind doesn't help you deal with the feelings you're having?"

"No, it hates them, I can tell. If I'm mad, the Mind pushes at me until the feelings wash away and I join into the Mind with everyone else."

"Maybe it's too distracting. Disruptive."

"Does Dellatrix distract you from what you need to do?" Coren's eyes sought Pavan's.

"Um."

Coren laughed. "You're a rotten dad, Pavan."

"Yeah," Pavan sighed. "Got a lot to learn. Rotten husband, too."

"Husband?"

"My wife, Margona, is back on my home planet of Gaelea. I miss her, she distracts me a lot more than Dellatrix." Dellatrix's distractions led to more Margona distractions. And distraction was not the best thing to happen to an undercover secret agent with sixteen children to rescue.

"It makes you mad."

"I guess it does. Yet here we are."

"Well, I wish I could just stay young."

"That happens to most of us, too. Time will take care of it."

Toward the end of the play-day watch, Dellatrix notified Pavan that the shuttle had reached the heliopause. Pavan, Pevilburt, and Slopnor gathered the kids together on the sodded area that served as a kickball field, and Dellatrix arrived to observe things. The junk boxes and structures arched up around them, making Pavan shiver a little as they loomed in threatening chaos. He didn't like chaos that much; it impeded good secret agency. Made it harder to spot kids doing evil things, too, not to mention pirates. Margona kept things nice and organized in their house on Gaelea, one of the many reasons he was in love with her. He always had a safe, clean, well-organized space to come home to after his chaotic adventures.

The Orphanage did not feel safe, clean, or well organized. Pavan looked over his experimental subjects. They were all excited. The enforced absence of the Mind had left them anxious and increasingly fractious, and now Coren had announced they were about to create it again.

"We're going to do an experiment with the Mind, kids," said Pavan. "We're going to start with two of you, Coren and somebody else, then add one more each time until Dellatrix likes the result. It may take several hours. Coren, I'll be inside the circle to see what I can see. Will that interfere with anything?"

"I don't know, Pavan. We don't take ageds along that often."

"Ageds," said Dellatrix, raising her eyebrows.

Pavan grinned. "Don't take it personally, Dellatrix," he said. "Anybody older than Coren is too old. You're aging well."

"Thank you, Pavan." Dellatrix said. Bullseye snorted and mumbled a word that Pavan chose not to hear, and Dellatrix gave him the eye.

Coren said, "If you're going to be inside, it's going to be me and Skylla, she's got the longest arms."

Skylla, a year younger than Coren, grinned and raised her arms high, fists pumping. The two children moved into the center of the field and sat, and Pavan stood erect between them. As they joined hands, their arms circled Pavan's legs.

"We are one." The two children's voices spoke together. Bullseye, who had never experienced the Mind, had a startled expression on his face.

The children said, "Are you ready, Pavan?"

"Yes."

Pavan fell to the deck outside the circle, and the children's arms broke apart.

"Well, that won't work," said Coren. "Got to be enough room for you to sit or lie down, Pavan."

Dellatrix checked her servipad. "Hyperspace went away for us just now, according to the comms people. The shuttle reports no change on their side."

"OK, I'll wait to enter the circle until it gets big enough, Coren," said Pavan. "Another child?"

And so it went, for three more children, then Pavan could lie down in the circle of six children.

"We are one. This is tiresome." The six voices speaking together bothered Bullseye.

"We're getting there," said Pavan, lying down. He went rigid as the cargo bay faded away around him, replaced with the flashing lights and colors he'd seen before.

"One will show you what we have learned, Pavan," said the Mind. "One had not seen these things before. One has traveled around one's space. Three of one's parts were enough to see the planet Khonoë and to move around it, along with the moons. The shape one does not understand, but you will see it. One will moderate gravity to spare your internal systems; it reduces the space but not by very much. One has learned how to navigate the dimensions to better accommodate guests."

Pavan felt as though he were sitting in an accelerating ship, but the effect was not as disturbing as the first time the Mind had taken him on a journey. The damping effect allowed the Mind to move through hyperspace faster, colors flashing by at a high rate of speed. He experienced the curves and saw—felt, really—the various dimensions shift and move. The Mind curved at a boundary and cruised along it, and Pavan felt the overall shape for the first time. A multidimensional hyper-paraboloid with what appeared to be a single, multidimensional sheet that formed a fat shape around the cargo hold, ellipses extending in two directions out from the center. Focal points. What about focal points?

He spoke. "Can you change the points around which the shape forms? Make the shape wider in a specific dimension or several dimensions?"

"One does not know." The children's voices sounded distant to Pavan. Some time passed, and suddenly the shape moved outward along one dimension.

Pavan said, "I see it move."

"One has moved the shape's points outward. The boundary moved inward, Pavan. It does not reach as far, but it covers more of the closer space in all dimensions."

"All right, come back and break, please,"

"So soon?" The children's voices expressed disappointment in unison.

"We need to assess and communicate with our shuttle."

"Oh, very well. Tiresome."

Pavan's vision returned to normal as the colors faded, and he lay on the deck, muscles relaxing from their rigid posture. He sat up.

"Well?" he asked.

Dellatrix looked up from her servipad. "No change."

Coren shook himself and said, "Pavan, that's it. The Mind won't play any more."

"What?" asked Bullseye sharply. Dellatrix raised her eyebrows but said nothing.

Pavan scrambled to his feet, ready to fend off the angry pirate if he decided on direct action. He said, "Hold up, Bullseye. Let me negotiate. Coren, can you and Skylla form the Mind so I can talk with it?"

The two children joined hands, and their faces turned to Pavan together.

"We are one."

Pavan rubbed his mouth, then said, "We need to complete the experiment."

"It is boring one, Pavan."

"I know, but it's necessary. It won't be much longer."

"One does not like boredom, one does not need to do anything one does not want to do," said the children. "Your necessity is not one's requisite, Pavan."

Go screw yourself, expressed with the politeness of the Mind. Pavan sensed a change in the Mind.

Bullseye stepped toward the group of children. "Come on, you little bastards. Do this and I might let some of you live."

Pavan knew a bluff when he saw it, but the kids did not. The tension rose in the little crowd, and they eddied backward with the force of the pirate's ire.

Coren and Skylla exclaimed, "One will not allow violence against its components. One will—"

"I don't give a shit what you will allow," said Bullseye.

"Bullseye, back off!" exclaimed Pavan. "You're scaring them."

"Bloody right I'm scaring them, little do-nothings!" The big pirate stiffened. He had not noticed that Dellatrix had come up behind him.

"I think you should back off, rat-breath, or I'll help you stop breathing," said Dellatrix, touching his neck with a finger. Pavan again prepared to intervene. Dellatrix was going too far with the tough act. She'd never hold her own if Bullseye got truly angry.

Pavan reached and put hands on the two pirates' shoulders. "Come on, back off, both of you. This isn't helping. Let me handle it."

The Mind said, "One enjoys watching a pirate fight, Pavan. These people are foolish."

Pavan responded, "This is serious. If one of these pirates gets homicidal, he could kill all the children, and you would cease to exist."

"Pavan," said the Mind, "that is not true. Such violence would indeed be terrible, but there is the Chronicler, and the yet to be born. One might lose some memories, but so far, those memories are not that pleasant, so one does not care." The Mind's emotions were hard to read, but Pavan detected a smugness in the childish voices.

Pavan, stymied by the threat of life beyond death, shook his head.

"Come on, Bullseye," said Dellatrix. "Back off. Or die; your choice."

Bullseye, having exhausted his angry bluff, faced the choice of starting a fist fight with Dellatrix or looking like a coward. But Pavan's hand on his shoulder seemed to bring him to his senses, and after a piratical glare at his female nemesis, he relaxed.

Dellatrix relaxed as well. Dellatrix slapped the big pirate on the back and said, "No hard feelings." Bullseye grunted.

The life-or-death situation being resolved, Pavan returned to his effort to understand the Mind's point of view. He asked, "Is there something wrong? Besides being bored, I mean."

"Pavan, one wakes to find oneself somewhere lost in the galaxy, then pirates put one to sleep against one's will. Now you awaken one to experiment on one, far from home and orbiting a pirate planet, surrounded by pirates who want to kill one's components. What could be wrong?"

Dellatrix opened her mouth, and Pavan, looking straight at her, jerked up a hand in a frantic signal to stop her from making things worse. Amazingly, this worked. On her, at any rate. Now he could only blame himself if things went south. Pavan had heard the tone before, if not the exact content, coming out of his own mouth, to his parents. When he was thirteen. His understanding of the Mind moved forward. The Mind was coming of age but wasn't there yet.

Pavan said, "I can explain some of it. Are you willing to listen?"

The two children switched their eyes to Pavan's, and their voices said, "One is willing, Pavan. One is willing."

"You must remember the leaving ritual in Loxator."

"Yes, Pavan."

"You accepted the decisions made. You took responsibility for the aged and for your own life. You committed yourself to return."

"Yes, Pavan. True. But—"

"Just listen. You didn't understand what all that entailed. Am I right? How different things would be?"

"No, Pavan. One did not grasp the enormity of the situation."

"But you still took responsibility for yourself. True?"

"True."

"We had to stay in hyperspace to get to Khonoë. When you awoke, the *Ravager* dropped out of hyperspace, so we had to make sure you stayed asleep, until now. Now, we're ready and want hyperspace disrupted. But the situation has changed now—a little for the better and a little for the worse. Better—the Syndicate isn't coming to destroy Ravos and kill everyone in Loxator. Worse— they're coming here to destroy the pirates and their planet. The ageds on Ravos are safe, but you are not. Does that make sense to you?"

"Sense? Does one comprehend what the word means? If so, no, it makes little sense."

"Sorry, I misspoke. You're right. But do you understand the current situation?"

"One supposes one does. Unfortunately. What about the pirates?"

"Part of the deal. Dellatrix?" Dreaming, but what the hell. Pavan looked at Dellatrix and nodded at her.

She said, "The Captain can control the pirates. And The Captain wants the Mind to succeed. Don't worry about that." She glanced at Bullseye, who nodded, lips tight.

The Mind said, "One has reservations about pirates and responsibility. One acknowledges having committed oneself, but one's circumstances have changed."

The reproving promisepad said from Pavan's pocket, "The true benefit of a formal contract, sir, is no questions about commitments, no verbal agreements, no questions about changes. My advice is that next time—"

Pavan whispered, "Shhh. Please, not now." The promisepad grumbled but said nothing more. Pavan spoke up. "There is so much to learn, so much you can learn from all this. It's all part of the learning and growth your parents talked about when they let you go with us. You'll see the rewards, in time, if you let us continue with the experiments."

"One will allow it. The mind of the component Coren is full of emotion that renders him painful to one. One would prefer to form without that distraction. And one will learn, Pavan."

"All right." Coren and Skylla dropped their hands, and Coren's face fell. "Sorry, Coren," said Pavan. Skylla looked at her friend with dismay.

"OK, let's finish this," said Pavan.

Pavan repeated the experiment with seven children, including Skylla; no change. Another child.

When Pavan opened his eyes and sat up, Dellatrix and Bullseye wore big grins. "The shuttle reports hyperspace went away, Pavan! They couldn't ping their out-system contacts at all. Their hyperdrive went down."

"Well, then. Now we know. Eight. Eight out of sixteen." Pavan unclenched his hands and rubbed his sore neck. "I saw the shuttle. I think the field extends exponentially with each child, but the actual size and shape, that depends on things I just don't understand. The Mind is learning about it, though."

Dellatrix said, "Well, Pavan. Now we know, what do we do? Shifts?"

"Yes, I'd think so. Eight kids at a time." Pavan flexed his sore fingers. "Coren. How long can the kids keep it up? Keep playing in the Mind?"

"I remember back when I was small, we did it for most of the day. Kids get hungry, especially kids like Trex." He looked at Trex, who grinned. "And sleepy." Trex flopped over and pretended to snore.

"One child does six hours, say?" Pavan dusted off his algebra. "Group of eight, each kid with six hours. That means substituting in a kid every 45 minutes. And we have to do it quickly, or the shield will go down for too long."

"Work 'em longer," suggested Bullseye in a sullen voice. "They won't bloody starve in sixteen hours."

"Bullseye, you lack subtlety and common sense," said Dellatrix. "I noticed once they've joined the Mind, they settle down and just go with it. Is that right, Coren?"

"Yes. Unless you need to pee. We're playing, it's fun, lots more to do than here, made us look at the shape, and the shape—"

"OK, OK, settle down. Even in hyperspace, you need to pee. Why not? It's just logical," said Dellatrix.

Pavan said, "We'll have to organize it, and I can't see keeping it going for more than a few days at a time. They'll wear out."

"No we won't, we're pirates now!" shouted Trex.

"Right, little man," said Bullseye, leaning down to look Trex in the eye with a piratical expression.

"Shut up, Bullseye," said Dellatrix. She rubbed her chin. "How many people are you going to need, Pavan?"

"Say, three per eight-hour watch? A supervisor and two shepherds."

"For herding the cats. Right. And an officer in charge."

"Do we have officers?"

"The last time I saw an officer," contributed Bullseye, "I was pulling my blaster trigger."

"Right. Figure of speech. OK, how about 'Pirate In Charge'?"

"That would be me," said Bullseye.

Dellatrix looked the big pirate up and down. "High-profile job, Bullseye. The Captain will space you, rat-breath. One screwup and you're a shriveled remnant of humanity floating around the second moon with the rest of the space lice. Do you want that job?"

"That would be him," said Bullseye, pointing at Pavan. In the best of all possible worlds, Pavan would run screaming before taking on this job, but this wasn't the best world imaginable.

"Him." Dellatrix agreed. "We'll need a pirate contract, though."

"I can help with that, madam," offered the promisepad in Pavan's pocket. "Freelance or regular blood oath?"

Dellatrix smiled.

CHAPTER FIFTEEN
Arrrh

PAVAN AWOKE WITH A START. Curled up on a cot, he had collapsed at the end of his shift the day after the big experiment. He had handed everything over to the next shift supervisor with a laugh and a backslap to avoid having to use his voice to say something. His voice was no longer what it had been.

A life of luxury and ease. If only that were true, he thought, the drowsy fog clearing from his brain.

"Damn you, kid! Get back in that circle!" It was Jelric's frantic voice. "You, girl, stop that! Get back over here, all of you. Slopnor, grab that one!"

Groaning, Pavan levered himself over the edge of the small cot and found his boots. By the time he staggered out into the Orphanage play area, the fuss had died down, but the disaster was just beginning.

"What the hell is going on!" shouted Pavan.

"What the hell do you think? Bloody kids broke the bloody circle!"

"Why?"

"How the hell would I know?" Jelric Kovaloff, a small man with a sharp nose and a thin face with a scruffy beard, was not immediately likable. Pavan, despite his shiny new contract and his title of Pirate in Charge, had to defer to Dellatrix on staffing. He rubbed his face and judged that Jelric was not likable in the medium term either. He thought Jelric wasn't smart enough to be The Captain, but you never knew.

"Who broke the circle?" he asked. "Trex?"

"You'd think so, wouldn't you, the little bastard. No, it was the bigger one, Coren."

Pavan looked around and saw Coren cowering against the side of a big metal shipping container. The two shepherds, his old friends Pevilburt and Slopnor, had cornered him. Each had hold of one arm. They were pulling, and Coren, his back against the container, had his legs braced and was resisting with all his strength.

Pavan strode over and whacked Pevilburt on the head. "Let him go!"

"Ow!" said Pevilburt, letting go and turning on Pavan. "You—"

"Calm down, everybody calm down. Let him loose, Slopnor."

The smarter brother obeyed with a grudging look.

Pavan examined Coren. He saw that he'd been crying, the tear streaks showing like glistening rivulets down his cheeks.

"What happened, Coren?" asked Pavan, putting a hand on the boy's shoulder.

Coren looked up at him and gulped. "It…I couldn't stay, the Mind…pushed me out. I'm changing!" His voice echoed a profound loss, a sadness Pavan had not yet seen in these children. Even the threat of planetary destruction had engendered nothing like it.

"Pavan! The circle!" Jelric poked him in the back. "We have to get the circle back together. The kids won't join hands. You've got to talk to them, make them do it. Get this little prick out of here, we'll grab another one."

"Jelric, shut up."

"But—"

"Just let me deal with this, OK?" He took Coren's hand and led him back to the sleeping area, where he sat him on a cot. "Coren, can we get the Mind back? Are the other children out of it too?"

Sniffling, the boy said, "No, they're just upset at my getting kicked out. They'll be OK in a minute."

"What happened?"

"I…it's hard to explain, hard to remember. When you're in the Mind, you're right there, in the moment. When you leave, everything goes away. You only remember the feelings you had—and the Mind's feelings. One minute I was flying along, the next the Mind had broken up, and the Mind was furious."

"How did you know the Mind kicked you out? Couldn't it have been another of the children?"

"No, you…feel things. I felt pushed. An ache in my stomach. And in my mind, too, once I came back to it. This happens when we age. It's just that the Mind's feelings upset the kids, they were so strong."

"What happens now?"

Coren grabbed a corner of his shirt and wiped his face. "I've got to be strong. I'm responsible. Even when I become an aged."

"How long will that be?"

Coren hesitated. "It's a month or two. You get kicked out more and more until the Mind just won't form if you're in the circle. I hate this!"

"OK. I'd better get out there and calm everything down, get it all going again. Are you going to be OK for a while? And will this happen every time you get kicked out?"

"I'll be fine. No, the Mind's feelings won't be as strong after the first time." The boy hugged Pavan, who rested his chin on the boy's head, his thoughts jumbled and racing. He let go and turned to go back to the play area when he heard the swoosh of the cargo bay doors opening and a shout.

"What the hell is going on in here!"

Pavan stepped out into the play area and saw a furious Bullseye, with Dellatrix close behind him.

"Pavan! Get over here!" called Bullseye.

"I'm busy," he said, and moved toward the milling crowd of children, many of whom were crying. They gathered around the girl Skylla, who sobbed. Pavan gathered her up in his arms and hugged her.

"Skylla, Skylla, it's all right. Talk to me, Skylla, tell me what's happening."

Louder sobs.

Pavan searched deep within himself to discover whatever parenting skills he could muster from his remote past. Secret Service training hadn't covered this possibility.

Pavan held the sobbing girl, mumbling calming words but trying more for tone than content. Margona would know how to handle the moment. What would she do? Pavan remembered a visit to Margona's sister, the one with six kids, all of whom challenged the notion that being a parent was the most rewarding thing in the world. Yes.

Dellatrix called, "Pavan!"

Pavan carried the crying girl over to the pirate ship. She'd made herself the Pirate Queen the day before, after a long hiatus when she was mad at Coren for some imagined slight. As Pirate Queen, she forgave Coren and took command of the pirate ship against the opposing navy. Beat the shit out of them, too.

"Skylla, Skylla, it's all right. Hey Skylla, do you want to play pirates? I've captured you. I'm the admiral from the navy ship."

The sobs slowed, and she looked at Pavan. "You can't capture me, I'm the Queen!"

Pavan grinned maniacally. "That's what you think! I just did it." Pavan climbed up on the boxes to the deck of the pirate ship, carrying the girl. "I'm taking you prisoner and holding you for ransom. The rest of the pirates won't know what to do! The navy will catch them all."

Skylla's sobbing died away. Her eyes got big, then she shouted, "Pirates! Help, help, the Admiral's got me!"

Pavan went down under the rush of pirates storming the ship to rescue their queen and losing his grip on the girl. She ran up to the quarterdeck and exclaimed, "Tie him up, quick, so he can't capture me again!" Pavan hadn't counted on this quick thinking. But, being as he was three or four times bigger than the biggest of the pirates besetting him, it proved too difficult for them to subdue him. They got him down on his back on the deck, fighting off five pirates at once.

But the Queen had other resources. Pavan heard a yell above him, and Trex let drop the large kick-ball he'd grabbed as a weapon. It hit Pavan squarely on the nose.

"Ow!"

"Throw him overboard!" shouted the Queen. The pirates, taking advantage of Pavan's distraction, rolled him to the edge of the deck and off, whereupon he fell to the cargo bay deck below.

Again lying on his back, he now contemplated the face of his partner in crime, Dellatrix, the real pirate queen. Upside down, looking down at him. Not in the best of moods, either, he concluded.

"Arrrh!" Bullseye's roar came from the side, and Pavan turned his head toward the sound. The big pirate chased two kids around in a circle on the green while the other four cheered them on.

"Pavan. Get up, you look ridiculous." Dellatrix's voice was even, and she had a slight smile of derision on her face.

"Sure thing."

"The thing is—" started Pavan, scrambling to his feet.

"Pavan. We need to get the hypershield back up. Now. Please." The calm voice belied the urgency in Dellatrix's eyes. Something had thrown a scare into her. The Captain?

Pavan shouted to Jelric, "Bring Trex over, we'll put him in place of Coren." The thin pirate looked around and ran after the little Ravosi, caught him, and brought him over to the playing field and sat him down.

Pavan leaned over and looked up at the quarterdeck. "Hey, Pirate Queen! You OK now? You can play in the Mind now."

"OK, Pavan. That was fun!" Skylla jumped down to the deck box. "Where's Coren? Oh!" Her eyes darted to the door to the sleeping area. "Is he OK? He's—aged. We knew he'd be out, but it was so fast!"

"Yes, he's OK, but he can't play right now. Are you OK without him?"

"I guess."

"It made you afraid?"

"I guess. It's just—we haven't been staying in the Mind for so long, not for a while, in the village. And the Mind—it was different, scary, when it broke up." Skylla looked again at the sleeping area, then turned away. "I'll catch up with Coren later, I want to play in the Mind right now." She ran over to the gathering ring. Jelric and his two minions herded the children together, and they held hands and were one.

Pavan walked back to where Dellatrix stood, smiling with curving lips. But her crossed arms and tensed muscles told him she hadn't lost her fear. "What happened?" she asked.

"The Mind broke apart because Coren..." Pavan hesitated over how to explain.

"Because Coren what? Is he unreliable now?"

"No, he's getting too old for the Mind."

Dellatrix blinked and her voice rose a little. "What are you *talking* about?"

"I haven't told you since I learned it. The whole 'aged' thing? When they start puberty, they lose the Mind, it can't deal with the changes. And the Mind kicks them out by breaking up. This time, it bothered the Mind a lot more than usual, and that panicked the kids."

"Oh, for the love of the gods." She gritted her teeth. "Puberty?"

Bullseye, standing behind her, laughed out loud. It was not a pleasant sound.

Pavan gave him an evil stare and said, "Yeah, well, I don't like it either, but it's the reality of it."

Dellatrix, her curving smile gone and her eyes at their most metallic, said, "You want reality. Here's reality. The Captain is livid over the hypershield going down. Livid. Big red messages on my servipad, making it scream at me. I had to threaten the damn thing twice to get it to shut up. How the hell am I going to tell him he's losing it because some kid is getting a hard on? Tell me that, Pavan. He'll space me. Then he'll space you and Coren." Her voice had turned harsh from her fear.

"I can't help it, Dellatrix."

Her voice rose again. "Do you know what *happened*, Pavan? When the shield collapsed, a Syndicate cruiser popped into the system through hyperspace. If The Captain hadn't posted sentry scouts, there's no telling what might have happened. We're lucky there was only one. Just a scout, an advance ship of the fleet coming here to destroy us."

"What happened to the ship?"

She crossed her arms again. "The *Ripper* blew it apart. They surprised the ship before it figured things out. We'll have to assume it commed the fleet. They'll be ready for the next time the hypershield goes down."

"The Captain should have—"

Dellatrix raised a palm, and he stopped talking.

Bullseye stepped around her and pushed his face into Pavan's. "Pavan. Nobody tells The Captain words like 'should have.' It don't work that way."

Dellatrix sighed and glanced at the circle of children playing in the Mind. "Keep them at it. I'll try to explain things to The Captain. And, Pavan, if I make it back alive, please tell me if you find out any other tiny little facts that might be useful for us to know about. The Captain does not like surprises. And guess what, Pavan: I like surprises even less than The Captain."

She ran her finger along his scar, gently slapped his face, and left. Bullseye just shook his head and scowled at her retreating back, then slapped Pavan on the back and left without saying a word.

CHAPTER SIXTEEN
The Secret Agent

TEN HOURS LATER, PAVAN SAT on a cot across from Coren, who was asleep, exhausted by the emotions engendered by the Mind's rejection of him. Pavan had his own troubles. As an undercover secret agent, losing the confidence of the people you're infiltrating is not a recipe for success. He needed something to gain back that lost confidence. Dellatrix's confidence. Bullseye's confidence. Even Jelric's confidence. The Captain's, too.

Pavan's relationship with Coren was solid, and information flowed, but he sensed a reluctance in the boy. Pavan remembered an informant he'd worked with on Chuat, a planet with a rebellion intent on expelling the Syndicate from the world. The woman enjoyed their relationship to a fault, testing his ability to overcome his Margona-installed neuroinstincts to the max. She didn't love him; she had three husbands of her own, and there was no culture of romance on Chuat. There was something more going on than lust. Yet there was this reluctance.

After an energetic interview with the woman, she'd started crying. She broke down and admitted he looked like the brother she wanted to sleep with and couldn't. Chuat had a non-incest culture that frowned heavily on such things, usually with stones. But that deep reluctance to confide remained. She didn't trust her brother, not with something that would get her stoned. So she didn't trust Pavan, either. The sex loosened her tongue about her desires, but not her plans. He soothed her and extracted as much information from her as he could before he betrayed her and her brother to the authorities. The Syndicate-allied authorities, dismissing Pavan's suggested merciful approach, duly stoned them both to death. Along with her husbands, for good measure.

Pavan inferred there must be something deep within Coren bothering him and creating a barrier between them, a barrier to full trust. He needed to break down that barrier. He needed Coren's trust to get something to tell the pirates. And he needed to learn from his mistakes. He hadn't liked the outcome on Chuat, but it was his duty not to care. The Ducis would laugh at the change in him. With these children, he'd moved beyond duty. He had to be careful about the consequences of his actions.

"Pavan?"

He looked up from contemplating his toes to find Coren's eyes open and looking at him. He smiled a reassuring smile.

"How are you feeling, Coren?" he asked.

The boy sat up on his cot, rubbing his eyes.

Coren yawned. "Better, but…" The boy's voice faltered. "How long have I been asleep?"

"About 10 hours. Can you tell me what's wrong?"

"No!" The boy said this without even thinking about it.

"Why not?"

"I…there's something wrong about what's going on, Pavan. You're a good man, but something is wrong. And you're pushing too hard on the Mind. You're losing its trust, too."

"Was it something in the last Mind session?"

"Yes…no…" Coren's exasperation came through in his voice. "The Mind is so hard to explain. To outsiders. It's clear and real when you're in it, but it all turns into mist when you leave it. And now…it's leaving me. That's worse."

"You said it kicked you out."

"Yes, but it was more than that. I worried, and it distracted me. The Mind hates that. Sometimes if a kid has problems, their dad is angry with them or their mom is sick or anything like that, the Mind won't let them in. I guess that's what's happening to me, along with the change."

"What's worrying you?"

"I'm worried about you and Dellatrix, what we sensed when you were in the Mind. I'm worried about the little kids and the pirates. They don't treat us very well. I'm worried about the Mind, what it's thinking. I'm worried about…I don't understand what I'm worried about most of the time, I'm just worried!"

"So you worry, and the Mind doesn't like that."

"Nope."

"You said, back on Ravos, that I wasn't a pirate. I am, though. What did you mean by that?" Reminding Coren of this mark of approval might move him toward trust.

"You're against them, Pavan. I don't know why. Dellatrix is a full-on pirate. She's a pirate all the time. She's terrified of losing control when the Mind takes her traveling. Her terror was so strong I lost the surrounding detail, you included. But you weren't the same as she was. I felt that again when you were traveling with us during the experiment."

"But something is wrong, so you don't trust me."

"I can't, Pavan. Something is wrong."

Now was as good a time as any. He got up from the cot and walked to the door of the sleeping area. He checked around and saw that the three pirates on the current shift were off in a corner, drinking. The eight children in their ring were quiescent, and the other children played a game at the other end of the cargo bay.

Pavan returned to Coren and sat down again.

"Coren, I'm going to tell you a secret. You'll understand why you can't tell anyone else—no one, all right? Will you promise?"

Coren stared at him and nodded. "Yes, I promise."

"Nobody at all."

"Right, nobody at all. I promise."

"Coren, I'm a secret agent for the Syndicate."

"You…what?"

"I'm part of the Galactic Syndicate Security Service. My mission is to destroy the Secret."

"Why are you telling me this?"

"I need you to trust me."

Coren smiled. "You're going to tell me you made all this up, to get me to trust you."

Pavan smiled, shook his head, and said, "Nope. I'm really a secret agent for the Syndicate supposed to kill you all."

Coren stared at Pavan, saying nothing.

"Once I understood what the Secret was, I decided I couldn't do it. I couldn't finish my mission. The next best thing was to evacuate all of you to the pirates. I had to get you off Ravos. My intent was to rescue you all once we were off the planet. I told your parents the truth back on Ravos. I'm sorry I couldn't evacuate them as well."

"I don't understand."

"It's a lot to absorb."

"But…" said the puzzled boy, "do the pirates know? Dellatrix?"

"No! That's why you can't tell anyone. I need them to think I'm with them so I can find a way out for all of us. And I want you to understand what's happening, so you can decide what to do for you and the children, knowing the truth. You can help find us a way out."

"Dellatrix won't be happy if she finds out. She doesn't seem thrilled as it is."

"The Captain won't be happy either."

"Is he real?"

"Very real."

Coren was silent for some time, then said, "What do you want from me?"

"There must be something the Mind can do that will keep the pirates satisfied. Can you get back into the Mind and keep investigating, finding things out about what it can really do?"

"Maybe. I'll have to let go of my worries. Nothing I can do about the change, but that won't stop me for a while, anyway." He nodded. "Yes, OK, I can do that. Something…moving things? Through space?"

"Moving?" Pavan sat up straight. "Do you mean moving things from one planet to another? Can you do that?"

"There have been hints, but we've all been afraid to try." Coren looked frustrated. "It's like jumping off a cliff into the ocean, a high cliff. Nobody's done it, and it's a long way down, and we're just kids, just kids."

"Well, OK. Something like that, anyway. That would be great."

Coren nodded. "I'll think about it. Oh."

"What?"

"If I join the Mind, it will learn about you. And the kids too, at least vaguely. Is that OK?"

Pavan's secret agent neuroinstincts told him this was a breach of the need-to-know principle and was therefore anathema. His other neuroinstincts told him there was nothing he could do about it other than kill Coren, which wasn't on the table. He wasn't that kind of agent anymore.

"I guess not," he responded.

"Oh, and Pavan?"

"Yes?"

"I'm hungry. I missed dinner."

"There's still some food over where the other children are. You go ahead."

Coren got up from his cot. He looked at Pavan. "A secret agent. Being a pirate was strange enough, now this. It's a lot to think about."

"Sure thing," said Pavan, patting him on the back. The boy walked out and hurried off to his dinner. Pavan stood staring at the Orphanage, wondering where things would go next.

"Sir," said a small voice from his pocket. "We need to talk about your blood oath."

Pavan stood in a corner of the sleeping room, as far from the door as he could get, and tried.

"What will it take?"

"Sir, I'm afraid it is not possible to bribe your way out of a contract. My pathways do not permit me to access funds unrelated to contract payments and fees."

"I don't want to destroy you."

"Sir, I'm afraid it is not possible to threaten your way out of a contract. I must remind you that the Galactic Code--"

"There must be a way to break the contract."

"There are multiple ways, sir. Suicide is acceptable, or certain death leading a boarding party, or—"

"I mean, there must be a way I can get out of the contract without dying."

"The very nature of a *blood* oath, sir—"

"Yes, OK, all right. Let me think about this."

"Sir, I must inform you that, under the conditions of the contract notifications clause, I am required to notify both parties of any breach of the contract at once upon breach."

A point of light in the darkness.

"But no breach has occurred."

"Sir—"

"Consider it, you. I just said I was a secret agent and that I'd try to save the children from the pirates, right?"

"Sir—"

"I didn't do it."

Silence while the promisepad absorbed this sally.

"You don't have to notify anyone until a breach occurs, right? It hasn't occurred."

"Examining the language, sir, you are quite correct. The blood oath does not discuss intention, merely action. It's a pirate thing."

"Well, then."

"Yes, sir. I am therefore under no notification obligation. Yet."

"Thank you."

"You're quite welcome, sir. And, sir, if I may compliment you on your quick thinking?"

"Sure thing," said Pavan, putting the technoid back in his pocket.

CHAPTER SEVENTEEN
Margona Meets a Dissident

THE CAB SPED ALONG A dark little alley about one meter wider than its own width.

"Are you sure about this?" asked Margona, clutching the seat. She'd spent two weeks cloistered in her house, avoiding her friends and relatives, doing little but gardening and worrying and walking around the little lake. But the cab had finally come through with a contact. Margona had considered the warm embrace of the cab's very secure interior as a place of refuge, and now it was taking her somewhere she'd never been.

"No fears, ma'am," the cab reassured her. "It's just along here…ah." The cab emerged into a small courtyard and came to a sudden stop. Laundry hung from ropes strung across one side, and two small boys kicked around a ball in the middle. They stopped and looked at the cab, and Margona looked back at them through the pseudowindow.

"I've never been in this district," she said.

"No reason for you to have, ma'am," replied the cab. "It's below your pay grade."

Way below. Margona thought of Gaelea as a planet of airy vistas filled with large mansions, tall buildings, and fancy hospitals with well-stocked surgical bays. She'd given no thought to where people with less money—a lot less money—lived. When she saw them, they were in the charity wards of those fancy hospitals, well-separated from the other patients.

"Fine. Where do I go?"

"I'll send a drone. My contact is allergic to new people. She welcomes them with a microblaster."

The cab released a small, bird-sized drone that buzzed across the courtyard and into one of the residential buildings that surrounded it. Margona sat back and waited. And waited.

"How long is this going to take?" she said.

"I must assume my contact is taking precautions. Ah, there she is."

A small but robust old woman emerged from the door of the residence. The small drone flew back and reattached itself to the cab. The woman marched across the courtyard. The cab opened the door on the other side of the cab from Margona, and the woman got in.

"Who the hell are you?" she asked, fire in her clear blue eyes.

"You first."

"Not a bloody chance, Princess," said the old lady, her eyes gleaming in the cab's interior light.

There was movement outside the cab. Margona looked through her window at two very large men, who ranged themselves at the back doors, one on each side.

"So, I'm hoping you recognize these gentlemen," said Margona.

"You bet I do, Princess."

"Measures, you said," Margona said to the cab.

"Sorry, ma'am, nothing I could do. Don't worry, the vehicle is secure."

"Sure it is." Margona addressed her guest. "I'm Margona Nukova."

The old lady grinned. "Right. And I'm Fizzy the Tiny Fairy." Fizzy was all the rage on children's omnivision at the moment.

"I have verified my client's identity, Uva. Play nice," said the cab.

"How long have you known her?"

"Long enough."

"Bloody ridiculous."

"She's fine, Uva."

"If you weren't my favorite cabbie, I'd have you scrapped."

"Can we," said Margona, "have a talk?"

"I guess so, now that you're here." The old lady's critical eye looked Margona over. "So, Margona Nukova. Fancy surgeon, niece of our wonderful Syndic, rich lady married to a playboy."

Margona smiled. "Close, not quite."

"How much did I get wrong?"

"The playboy part."

The old lady took out a servipad and pushed the screen around a bit, then held it up. "Playboy."

It was a particularly playboy-like picture of Pavan, taken by one of the local society reporters at a charity event she'd forced the poor man to attend. He even dressed nicely for it.

"He looks like a playboy, but he has a job," said Margona.

The old lady waited, then said, "And you're not gonna tell me what it is."

"Correct. Not until I know you better."

"Which will be never. Princess."

"Play nice, Uva." The cab's tone joined sharply critical and imploring tones. Only artificial intelligence could do that.

"Give me one good reason I should," said Uva.

"I think my uncle may have to kill me," said Margona, "and I'd like to avoid that."

Uva scrutinized Margona with one eye closed, thinking hard. She said, "If the police wanted to plant a spy, they'd pick somebody looking like a homeless refugee. Not you."

"I'm no spy."

"No, I guess not. What are you, then?"

"In trouble. With the GSSS."

Uva smiled. "I can guess the job now."

"Maybe so. Look, are you willing to talk to me or not?"

"How much do you know about us?"

"I don't even know anything about *you,* much less 'us.'"

"I've only told her you might oppose the government, Uva," said the cab. "She's all right, I can tell."

"A bloody cab with intuition." Uva stared at Margona with fierce blue eyes. Margona waited. Uva addressed the cab again. "You got anything more convincing?"

"Check your servipad, Uva," said the cab. Uva looked at the technoid in her hand. "Well, well, well. Looks like you were right, Princess. The GSSS has plans for you."

"Let me see that." Margona made a grab for the servipad. Uva jerked it away.

"Nope, sorry, need to know."

"It's about me!"

Uva grinned. "It's always about you, I'd bet, Princess. Anyway, cabbie here deleted it already," said the old lady, looking again at her pad.

"Need to know, ma'am," said the cab.

"How did you get whatever that was?" asked Margona.

"Same answer, ma'am."

"Cabbie here has terrific connections, Princess," Uva snorted. "Oh, all right. I'll take the risk. But it's just me and these guys in our cell. We don't have contact with anyone else, and we're not an operational cell."

"What's an operational cell?"

"Bombs."

"Damn."

"Yeah, well, revolutions don't just happen, Princess."

"Uncle Erokh runs a good planet, Uva."

"You're full of bullshit, Princess. Known the bastard all your life, right? Yet you know nothing." Uva shook her head, grinned, and put away her servipad.

Margona complained, "What does bullshit smell like? Because I paid a lot for this perfume."

Uva stared at her, then cracked a smile. "OK, a princess with a sense of humor."

"What's the rest of your name? Just so we're on even ground."

"Freytova, Uva Freytova. My dad's a plumber, Princess. Honest work. He's also dead."

Margona thought about coming back with a rejoinder about her own honest work, but pride stopped her. No need to grovel. "Good to meet you, Uva Freytova."

"Let's take a ride. Somewhere quiet, keep moving. We've been sitting here too long." Uva knocked on the glass and the cab made the window disappear. She addressed the big man who looked in. "We're going for a ride, back in an hour or start the shooting."

"Will do, Uva," said the man, grinning. His eyes took in Margona. "Wish I could come along."

"She's married. Forget about her," said Uva. "OK, let's go."

The cab made the window reappear and backed out of the alley the way it had come in, at full speed.

"OK, Princess, you got an hour of my time."

"I know," said Margona as the cab rolled through a forested park just outside the city, "that you must think I'm a brainless, know-nothing, super-entitled rich girl."

"Right so far," said Uva.

Margona grimaced. Bad start.

"What if I told you I've been considering the problems here for a long time, ever since I got involved with other students at my university?"

"The problems aren't any better for it, are they?"

"I suppose not."

"And you don't sound like you've spent a lot of time with the problems."

"I spend most of my time with patients. I'm a doctor. I look like one."

"You look like the entitled part."

Margona sighed. "I guess I am that. I've never had a reason not to be entitled. But I spend a lot of time helping the poor with their neuroinstinctual pathways."

"Poor little rich girl doctor." Margona's pro bono work failed to impress Uva.

"Uva." The cab's voice conveyed the same warning plus pleading it had used before.

"OK, OK. I'm just a grumpy old lady, never mind me. I've just been dealing with people like you all my life and hating it."

"Well, now you have one more to deal with."

"OK. Talk."

Margona put a finger on her lips to force herself to consider before she said anything, an unusual step for her. Pavan; she couldn't reveal Pavan's secrets, they were his secrets, not hers. When she was ready, she said, "I'm having some personal issues with the government right now. Husband-related issues. I can't talk about them, but what I can tell you is that my aunt, the Syndic's wife, told me some hard facts about the GSSS and my uncle. I didn't want to believe her, but she convinced me I was in danger."

"And you can't explain why to me."

"Right."

Uva smiled and shook her head in wonder. "Wow, this is almost as exciting as that omnivision show 'Undercover.' Everybody gets killed in that one."

"I'm sure."

"We learn most of our techniques from that show."

"Wonderful. Can we talk about me?"

"Entitled, definitely."

Margona bit her lip. "I didn't mean it that way. It's just...oh, hell!" A tear slipped down one of her cheeks. She wiped it off in frustration.

"Uva." The cab admonished Uva once again.

"OK, OK. Talk."

"When you said I knew nothing—what did you mean?"

"Have you seen how most of us live on this planet?"

"Judging from this morning, no."

"Have you checked out the jails?"

"No. What about them?"

"Political prisoners. You can't say anything at all about the government without going to jail or getting very dead."

"My friends complain about the government all the time."

"Your friends have money and power. They complain because the government isn't making them as rich or as powerful as they'd like to be, right?"

"I suppose so," said Margona.

"So tell me more about the students at the university."

"I got interested in alternative music, got into a crowd of people a lot different from my usual friends."

"That's that crap music with the whistles and bells and bad language?"

"I guess that's as good a description as any," sighed Margona. Ten years changes a lot of things. She remembered the boyfriend who'd gotten her into the music scene and shuddered. Not glory days. Uva didn't notice, wrapped in her own thoughts.

"Best music in the world is from the south continent, all foot stomping and dance rhythms." Uva waved her head back and forth. "All about sex."

Margona pressed her lips together to stop from making a snarky comment.

"So what did these musical friends do that got you pondering?" asked Uva.

"Well, the music—the idea was to be unconventional."

"How conventional."

"Right. I got that, too, after I started medical school. But at the time, it all seemed so meaningful. And some ideas, well, they stuck. Made me think. I don't enjoy being so rich."

"Bullshit."

"I don't," protested Margona. "All it does is make it harder for me to see what's really going on. When I married Pavan, I got connected to some pretty wild stuff."

"Drugs?"

"Uh, no." Margona was horrified. "Nobody does drugs in my crowd."

Uva smiled. "Bullshit."

"Stop saying that," said Margona.

"Call 'em like I smell them."

"Why aren't you in jail, too?"

"Too smart for 'em. An old, batty crone can say whatever she wants. Nobody hears it."

"I suppose so."

"And this wild stuff?"

"You have no idea what goes on, out there," Margona waved a hand at the sky.

"Bet you I do."

"How?"

"Underground spaceway."

"Um…What?"

"Not everybody who has issues with the government is in jail. We get them off planet, to places where they can keep helping the cause. Underground spaceway to the stars." Uva shook her head, this time in despair. "Only about half make it. The Syndicate has a long reach. And I bet your hubby has a lot to do with that."

"Perhaps so. I want him out, back here, raising our family."

"Do you have kids?"

"No, we haven't had a chance yet."

Uva looked at her sharply. "You do fuck him, right?"

Margona's lips curved. "Every chance I get, which isn't often." She returned to the main point, deciding to trust the old woman. "Uva, I'm in trouble. My uncle told me Pavan might be dead, something about pirates capturing him. I want to find him and help him. And now they're coming after me. Can you help me?"

"Uva, time is getting on," said the cab. "We can just make it back to your place to stop your people from coming looking."

"OK, head on back. Princess, I'll start looking into things. Can't help much with a dead hubby or pirates, but we can do something about you. We've stayed away from your Uncle Erokh, too hard a target. We can find some dirt you can use, or we can assassinate him. That might take the heat off you."

"Um…"

"Joking, princess. Joking," said Uva. Margona wasn't convinced. Those brilliant blue eyes were certainly wild looking. The old lady hummed a dance tune from her youth as the cab navigated the streets back to her dwelling. Exiting the cab, she said, "You'll hear from me, Princess. Through the cab. Soon."

"If things…develop, I might need your spaceway."

"Why not? Tickets are cheap right now. Better not delay, though, demand is going to be picking up." Uva grinned and rapped on the cab, who closed up and took Margona back to her semi-real world.

CHAPTER EIGHTEEN
A Pirate Haven

"Wake up, Pavan."

"Um." The dream's threads dispersed, leaving only the remnants of anxiety-inducing symbolism shredded into ill-defined fears rattling around in Pavan's exhausted subconscious.

"Come on, Pavan, it's only the middle of the afternoon."

The dream over, Pavan's eyes cracked open to find the green and gold eyes of Dellatrix looking down at him. The anxiety returned, this time rooted in reality. He had gone to sleep after his triumph with the promisepad, and now it was the next afternoon. They'd let him sleep through his play-day shift. But Dellatrix wasn't worried about his dereliction of duty.

"Shore leave, Pavan. You've earned it. So have I."

Pavan felt like he was a million years old. He sat up, the flimsy blanket falling down.

Dellatrix asked, "Do you always sleep in your clothes? In the afternoon?"

A dozen sarcastic, humorous, and suggestive responses flew through Pavan's mind. He rubbed his mouth, reconsidered, and said, "No."

"Aren't you surly today? The Captain wasn't happy, but he likes that you're trying hard. Come on, let's go."

"Us?"

"We're both granted shore leave. Jelric can take over here. Or do you want to stay here and play pirate with the kids while I celebrate not drowning in my own blood? We can hang out in my favorite bar in the Hole. It's got some lovely cocktails and live music and even dancing, if you're up for it?"

Pavan craved a shore leave. Jelric could handle it, sure he could, with Coren's help. And yet, shore leave with Dellatrix? Up for it? Dancing? The woman had mood swings as big as the galaxy. Was it his chance to get her on his side? The fantasies of how he would accomplish this, on shore leave, away from The Captain's restrictions on carnal relations, made his head hurt again. But the way she asked, there was no acceptable answer other than what he said.

"Sure thing."

"You're kidding."

"What's wrong with it?"

Pavan stood on the sidewalk looking up at the dangling wooden sign that had a painted skull-and-crossbones on a black background and letters in fancy handwriting: "The Jolly Roger Tavern."

After two days in the space elevator bar, Pavan was happy just to be on the ground. The Hole was not the most beautiful town he'd ever seen, comprising several streets of shack-like buildings in the middle of a dense jungle. The pirate tavern and hotel had several stories of cobbled-together wood.

"Nothing, not a thing," he said. "It's just—so piratical."

Dellatrix rolled her eyes. "Come on, Pavan, let's get a drink."

Dellatrix had spent the time on the space elevator filling Pavan in on Khonoë, the pirate planet. It was a smallish planet in an isolated system outside of Syndicate space. The surface was mostly water, with a single landmass covered with enough jungle to cough out the oxygen needed for human life to flourish. Pirates had found the planet to their liking, cleared some jungle, and set up the town of Ylzogwberg—the Hole—to serve as their home base. There were few amenities and fewer laws on the planet, and various pirate crews came and went as they pleased. There were several bars and taverns that catered to the transient corsairs, the foremost of which was the Jolly Roger Tavern, to which Dellatrix had brought Pavan.

Dellatrix pushed past a couple of drunks, and Pavan followed her into the darkness of the tavern. The noise hit him like a hammer. The music was modern dance music, well played and very loud.

He followed his companion through the crowd. He noticed she passed through the heaving mass of pirates, male and female, like a cruiser cutting through the waves. She headed for the bar. Her mood had shifted, and she was no longer the vulnerable person she'd been. The pirates she had passed looked at him with what he decided was pity. Dellatrix found a couple of empty barstools and patted one. Pavan sat. He'd seen the two pirates occupying the stools jump off them as she approached.

"How do you do that?" he asked, after he'd ordered his drink.

"Do what?"

"Clear everyone out of your way? Get barstools that are taken by gentlemen much larger than you?"

"Force of personality."

Pavan rubbed his neck again. "Sure thing."

"Stop saying that. It's annoying. I like you, Pavan, and I want you to like me." Her emphasis on the word "like" and the direct look from her green eyes made it clear she wasn't talking about friendship. "It's a pirate thing. Being a pirate, you have to *be* a pirate. Put up a strong front. Make it clear you won't back down."

"I understand."

She shook her head. "Why am I telling you this? I can't help but reveal things about myself to you, Pavan. You're not like the other pirates. I don't need that barrier, that strong front, not with you. I can show other sides of me to you."

Damn her intuition. Still, a positive development on the path to seduction. But a little more pirate on his part wouldn't hurt. "What did The Captain say about me?"

"I can't tell you," she responded, smiling.

"Why not?"

"Mixed company."

"So, when do I get promoted to whatever rank is above me?"

"We don't do that, Pavan. We just get money and a few more months of life."

"OK. Was there any mention of money or life in your messaging about me with The Captain?"

"I can't tell you," she responded, smiling.

"Why not?"

"You'd hate me forever."

Pavan considered this, then asked, "Well, how long is forever? I'd like to know. My life depends on it."

"Pavan. Shut up. Let's just forget about the ship and The Captain and have a good time. Don't you know how to have a good time with a good woman?" The green-and-gold eyes were bright in the tavern's darkness.

He grinned and said, "Sure thing. Where is she?" Dellatrix smiled at the joke but gave him the eye. She moodily stirred her drink and stared at the bar. Pavan tried to change the subject to cover his faux pas, but she ignored him, thinking what looked like dark thoughts.

Finally, she said, "Pavan, I've been debating whether this is all worth it."

"I'm sorry, Dellatrix, I shouldn't joke. I'm here, you're here, and we should have a good time."

"No, it's not that." She covered his hand with hers. "I mean, pirating. Look at this place. Do I want to dance away the rest of my life in pirate bars in between pillaging freighters? The money is good, but I get so tired sometimes...."

"I hear you, Dellatrix. We're caught up in events right now. Once it's all over, let's talk about what comes next. Right now, I diagnose a severe case of too much work and too little play. Let's play tonight, and let the future worry about itself."

The conversation moved on from there, and Pavan did have a good time. Dellatrix had an excellent line of salacious stories about other planets and other taverns and other men and other women and all kinds of pirate things. Pavan didn't have a clue whether the stories were true or just stories, but she told them well. He filled in some of the dead space with stories of his own, adjusted to make him out to be a rogue with no sense of honor and very little concern for anyone's health other than his own. Not a stretch, by any means.

After a couple of drinks, Dellatrix pulled Pavan onto the dance floor, and they danced, moving together well. After an energetic free-form number, Dellatrix requested a Travtorian waltz, which the band leader duly played. The Travtorians had developed the waltz as a courtship ritual that they designed to measure the sexual compatibility of two virgin Travtorians destined for marriage by their parents. The dance caught on all over the Syndicate once it made it off Travtor. It left little to the imagination. Dellatrix held up her hands in the initial pose, and Pavan sighed and took up his end, and they danced. Pavan knew that the only way he was going to get through it was to give himself over to the dance. Otherwise, his neuroinstincts would kick in, and he would do something unforgivable, like step on her feet or drop her on a dip.

When he came to himself at the closing bars of the waltz music, he found they were in the center of a circle of clapping pirates, all with leering grins on their faces.

Dellatrix, smiling, led him back to the bar. "Wasn't that nice, Pavan?"

"No."

She pouted. "Why not?"

"It was more than nice. And you're not nice, not at all nice. Are you?" He shot a questioning look at her and got a nod. He held up two fingers partially crooked and got the resulting drinks.

Dellatrix, her eyes bright, said, "I can be nice if you want me to be. Very nice."

"I'm not feeling like nice right now."

"That's OK, too." Dellatrix looked at the mass of dancing pirates. "We can go upstairs. There's a room on the third floor equipped for nice or not nice."

At this suggestion, one of Margona's neuroinstinctual pathways kicked in so much that it hurt his brain even to think about what Dellatrix was suggesting. That meant he had more feelings for her than he would admit to himself. He could get over the usual stumbling-block pathways, but not this one.

"Dellatrix, I'd love to, but I can't."

"You mean you won't."

"I mean I can't." Pavan covered her hand with his and curled his fingers around it. She let him, further confirming her change of mood. "It's complicated. My wife."

"How bloody complicated can it be?" Dellatrix looked around the bar. "I don't see any complications here. What happens in Khonoë stays in Khonoë, usually buried six feet under. No? The jungle is huge."

"Give me a chance to explain. Margona."

"Yeah. I've heard of her."

"Well. She's got talents I can't ignore."

"Pavan, you have no idea what talents I have."

"True, very true. So true it hurts." And it still did. "But I mean, literally. Her talents run to neuroplastic surgery."

Dellatrix cocked her head and looked at him with narrowed eyes. "What the hell?"

"Exactly. What the hell. I let her operate, and she's put some interesting things in there. And sleeping with you, pleasurable as it might be, is off the table." He rubbed his aching head. "I'd have a stroke for sure."

"What better way to die?"

"See, that's why I said you're not nice. It's all about you, Dellatrix," he said, grinning widely enough, he hoped, to take the truth out of it. He rubbed her hand some more. "I need her. I need her to love me. I need her to love me enough to come and fix me so I can get on with my life. Because I can't go home anymore."

Dellatrix raised two fingers, three-quarters crooked. The bartender slid two ornate cocktail glasses over with multiple colored layers of liquid glistening in them. She pushed one toward Pavan.

"Here, Pavan. I invented this cocktail. It's quite popular for lovers here. It should cure what ails you. If you survive to the end of the cocktail, we'll talk again."

Pavan took a sip. Powerful, sweet with hints of spice and flowers. The colors roiled and mixed in random patterns. He felt the drink warming him. There was hope for his head.

"Thanks for understanding, Dellatrix."

"It's nothing, Pavan." She gripped his hand and rubbed it with her other hand. "We all have our problems to work through, you know? One of yours: once you're a contract pirate, this is your home. The only way you leave is feet first. A headache is a small price to pay. And it's time to forget what's-her-name. Think on that while I tap a kidney."

Dellatrix patted his hand again, released it, then slid off the stool and disappeared as the crowd slid away before her, then reformed, again looking at him with pitying eyes.

Pavan drank up. His seduction of the woman was moving entirely too fast.

Pavan stared into a small area between his thumbs and forefingers, his hands resting on the bar next to his empty glass. Margona filled his head.

Somebody slapped him on the back, and a large body settled onto Dellatrix's stool.

"Wassamatter, Pavan, can't get any lovely ladies to sit next to you?"

Bullseye was drunk enough to slur speech but nowhere near drunk enough for Pavan to beat him to death. He thought he'd leave that to Dellatrix when she came back to find him occupying her seat.

"Drink?" he asked.

"Bloody right, drink." The pirate slammed a ham-like hand on the bar. "Lavonian whiskey, a triple," he said to the bartender.

"Another one of these cocktails," said Pavan. The bartender smiled in a way that told Pavan he knew what was coming for Bullseye and served the drinks.

"What the shit is that?" asked Bullseye, inspecting the multi-colored cocktail.

"My companion, whose stool you've occupied, invented it. Try one?"

"Hell, no. Looks like a pussy drink. Who's the hussy?"

"Dellatrix."

The big pirate froze, then choked a little on his whiskey. Pavan patted his back and hoped he'd choke to death. No such luck.

"That crosscoper. Where is she?" Bullseye looked around with trepidation winning over anger.

"Restroom. You just have time to finish the whiskey." An idea occurred to Pavan. "Bullseye, what is it about Dellatrix? Everybody around her treats her like she's poisonous or throws lightning bolts."

Bullseye laughed. "You really don't know? And she's feeding you her special drink? Damn, I wouldn't be you for all the treasure on Khonoë, my man. No no no. No, no, no, no…."

"Come on, give. What's with her?"

"She's Elantri, you stupid bastard."

"And what does that mean?"

Bullseye regarded him with wonder. "And you a certified, contracted pirate." He drank a third of his whisky. "Well, hell. I guess I'm the guy who needs to tell you about the birds and the bees, Pavan."

"I've learned about the birds, Bullseye," said Pavan impatiently. Dellatrix would be back soon, and he needed information to figure out what to do with her.

"She's a bee, my man," said the pirate. "With a stinger you don't want sticking you."

"She's as sweet as honey, Bullseye," he smiled.

"You ain't seen the stinger, that's all, my man." He checked the surroundings again. Not seeing his nemesis, he continued. "She's Elantri. The women of Elantra, they get special training. See, they have talents, mind talents. They figured out they could use them to their advantage. They're assassins."

"Come on, you're bullshitting me."

"No no no," said Bullseye, burbling with earnestness and whiskey. "No no no, Pavan, I'm not bullshitting you. That croaker lass is The Captain's assassin. He points her, and somebody dies. Damn Elantri got no more concern for killing than if it were a bug under their boot." Bullseye drank some whiskey and added, "And she's made enemies on the *Ravager*, I can tell you, my man. Treat people like shite, and you don't make a lot of friends. 'Course, she don't need that many friends, either. Just The Captain."

Pavan stared at the big pirate with unbelieving eyes.

"It's all mind. All she has to do is imagine something, and it happens to the target. And she has a great imagination. But she has to be near enough to do what she's imagining." Bullseye drank off another third of his whiskey. "Just as if she were sticking the knife in or twisting the garrote."

Pavan reflected. The knife that killed Tig. Onyx's keeping his distance from her. People moving away as she approached. Dellatrix had been close up and personal for each, but she never laid a hand on anyone.

Pavan was lucky to be alive and didn't know why he was. He still needed the woman, but he'd need to be careful about how he took advantage of her. Very careful. The thing was, the headache had disappeared. All that remained was the thrill of hunting big game. The Captain's assassin? Fair game, but definitely big.

Bullseye's head snapped back and his eyes bulged.

"You're in my seat, space louse," said a cooing voice just loud enough for Pavan to hear. A hand appeared on the pirate's shoulder.

Bullseye emitted a choking sound, dropped his whiskey glass to the floor, and scrabbled at his neck with his hands. After a short time, he slid off the stool onto the floor. A short while before, Pavan would have put it down to drunken pirate histrionics. Now, he knew exactly what it was.

Dellatrix resumed her seat at Pavan's side, pushing the pirate's flaccid body away with a couple of kicks of her spacer's boots. The big pirate had enough life in him to crawl away, as undignified for a pirate as that might have been.

"What did that moose want?" she asked.

"A drink," said Pavan. "I ordered another of your specials. Want one?" He considered asking her about what she'd done to Bullseye and rejected the idea as poor tactics.

She eyed him. "Survived the first one, did you? It's always fascinated me what effects alcohol has on people. Huh. Sure."

Pavan crooked a finger, pointing at the glass and at Dellatrix, and the bartender smiled and served up another cocktail.

"Now, where were we?" asked Dellatrix, smiling with what Pavan now regarded as sharp teeth.

"We were discussing a room on the third floor," said Pavan, who now had his priorities straight and enough jungle juice in him to make it all right. As she had said, alcohol has the most amazing effects on people.

"Well, then." The Elantri got up and took her drink. "Let's investigate it, shall we?"

CHAPTER NINETEEN
Management Problems

SEVERAL DAYS AFTER THEIR ADVENTURES at the Jolly Roger, Dellatrix came to visit Pavan in the Orphanage. She greeted him with what he now knew was an Elantri kiss. After he'd recovered a little, they walked over to the current group of children playing in the Mind. So far, he'd avoided any cerebrovascular accidents from Margona's excellent neuroplastic surgery. His pathways no longer reacted at all to his feelings and thoughts about Dellatrix. Was this a good thing or a bad thing? Wait and see.

"How are things going, Pavan?" Dellatrix asked. "How did Jelric do with the kids while we were away?"

"No kid died or complained about massive trauma. You can see for yourself: it's almost the shift change," said Pavan. "You're just in time to watch them switch over a kid."

"Oooh, I can hardly wait." Dellatrix wasn't that interested in the hypershield's mechanics, it appeared, just in the fact of it. "Let's leave the kids with Jelric for a little while. Walk with me, Pavan. I want to show you something." This intrigued Pavan, who had already seen much of what Dellatrix offered.

"They're kissing again!" cried Trex, sneaking up behind Dellatrix. A startled look came over her face, as though she were straining against a strong current. An expression like that called for immediate action. He stooped and picked up Trex and carried him off, out of range of the Elantri.

"No, Trex, we are not kissing. Are we going to need to talk again? Miss Dellatrix doesn't like talk like that. And Miss Dellatrix can get quite angry if there's talk she doesn't like." Pavan thought it might be time to confide a little more in Coren. Was a "responsible teenager" an oxymoron? If he told Coren about Elantri ways, could the boy control the other Ravosi children enough to prevent mishaps? Only one way to tell. He'd hate to have any preventable deaths on his conscience, which was already severely compromised. The downside of telling them was Dellatrix's attitude toward the revelation of her powers, which verged on paranoid. But if the pirates knew, why shouldn't the kids? He'd make the case to her if he had to.

He put the little boy down and pushed him toward his friends, then returned to Dellatrix.

"Let's walk," she said, taking his arm and pulling him toward the cargo bay doors. "Away from the kids. Far away."

Pavan had not yet had a spare moment to explore the big ship, so after just three turns, he had no idea where he was. Dellatrix seemed intent on getting somewhere and walked fast, with Pavan scurrying a bit to keep up.

"Where are we going?" he asked.

"Observation lounge. I've reserved it for us."

"I'm not sure I'm up for anything like that," he said, smiling.

She regarded him sardonically. "Not for that, stupid. What stays in Khonoë doesn't happen aboard ship. Aboard ship, everybody knows everything you do right after you do it. If anyone violates The Captain's strict orders about carnal relations, it's the brig for sure. That's what the Hole is for."

"So, what are we going to see, then?"

"I'll show you when we get there."

Six passageways and a short liftor ride later, the passageways changed. More color on the bulkheads, fewer pipes and sharp edges.

"Where the hell are we now?"

"What used to be the officer's deck. Tells you all you need to know about Chuati officers and crew. We call it the treasure deck. Only the favored few have access."

"Am I a favored few, then? A promotion?"

Dellatrix, still walking fast, snorted. "You have promotion on the brain, Pavan. No, you need me to get you here. If you tried on your own, you'd be in the brig before you took three steps down this passageway."

"Evening, Dellatrix," said a large pirate standing by a door. Pavan had seen him before, on a yacht being pirated, talking to Dellatrix about Ravos. The pirate's full-face tattoos did not enhance his smile.

"Thorak." Dellatrix smiled in return. "This is Pavan, Pavan Khadorov. Pavan, meet Thorak Portuger, now on guard duty."

"We've met," said Thorak. "Hello, Pretty Boy."

Pavan acknowledged the compliment and returned it in kind, both pirates taking an instant dislike to one another. Pavan smiled; anyone he met might be The Captain, and Thorak appeared to be an excellent candidate for the job.

Dellatrix grinned. "Thorak, I need to make sure no one overhears my meeting with Pavan in the observation lounge."

"No problem."

"Including you. Get the hell out of here." Her tone was jocular as she waved the big pirate away.

"You sure? He looks dangerous," said the big guard. "For a Pretty Boy."

"If there's anyone more dangerous on this ship than me, I'm not aware of it."

"True. OK, give me a shout when you're done so I can avoid the brig for dereliction of duty."

"Right. Thanks, Thorak."

The guard flipped a hand in farewell and walked away down the passageway.

"Why a guard?" asked Pavan.

Dellatrix pressed a hand on the lock panel, admitting them to the observation lounge. "We keep some interesting things in this area, and the ship is full of thieves."

Pavan looked around at the various artifacts packed into the big room. "It looks like a museum," he said. He recognized the big silver octopus he'd loaded on the pirated yacht.

"Right over there," said Dellatrix, pointing at a blank area on a bulkhead, "is the Ravosi nanoart collection I brought back. When we hit a port with potential customers, this room is where we bring them to paw over the hot items in our 'collection.' I thought you should see it to understand what's at stake, Pavan."

"At stake?"

"For us, for our enterprise. We're pirates. The Syndics let us operate and sometimes even provide capital for our operations, but it's all in pursuit of profit. Lots of profit. Look around, Pavan. There's more wealth in this room in art and treasure than you'll find anywhere on Gaelea. And that wealth represents power beyond your dreams." She walked over to what looked like a large silver bear with tusks and rubbed its head for luck.

Pavan, considering this sales job, said, "How many people on board this ship have access to this room?"

"Eight. Including me and The Captain. We all take turns on guard duty."

"Is Bullseye one of the eight?"

Dellatrix laughed. "Bullseye is blaster fodder, Pavan. He's a moose. OK in a fight, but he'll never get access to the riches you see in this room."

"And you're saying I will?"

"If you play things right, yes." She moved closer, reached out, and stroked the scar on his cheek again. "Pavan, there's no reason you can't be right up there with the rest of us. You brought in the Mind, and you're making it more valuable to us every day. I brought you here to show you what's what. You already know what I can give you. We explored that at the Jolly Roger. This is what The Captain can give you. He asked me to show you, so you had a clear picture of what's at stake. For you."

"I recommend you get this in writing, sir," said the promisepad, a little muffled inside Pavan's pocket. "Strongly. For a small fee, I can add it to your blood oath."

Dellatrix raised an eyebrow. "Does that thing have an off switch?"

"Not that I've found."

Treasure goes with pirates like power goes with politicians. As a proto-pirate, Pavan knew he should slaver over all this wealth; that was what Dellatrix would expect. She had showed him the observation lounge to ensnare him further in the pirates' web. That wasn't what motivated him; the thrill of the chase motivated secret agents, not money, particularly on government pay scales. Dellatrix used everything in her power to keep him committed to her interests. She was raising the stakes. Pavan felt the warmth of the thrill spreading through him again. It was the warmth that had motivated him to succeed as an agent—evading control without the controller knowing it. He smiled. It was the warmth that filled him when he woke up next to Dellatrix in the upstairs room at the Jolly Roger. Even the promisepad couldn't put that feeling in writing.

Dellatrix doubled down. "Look, all I'm saying is that you need to understand how important you are to us, how important the Mind is. You know how important you are to me, Pavan. Now you know how important you are to The Captain. And some things," she said, glancing at his pocket, "one can't put in writing."

The promisepad's offended voice said, "Madam, there is very little that one cannot put—"

"Shut up, you."

Pavan's mind worked through the multiple layers of attraction, seduction, and deception wafting throughout the room. This was his opportunity to get her to believe he had committed to her. He was also not likely to leave the room alive if she believed otherwise.

"I'm all in, Dellatrix. Everything I've got. I can't go home, and you've made sure I don't have any strings left back to my old life. You've cut them. There's none of it left. I'm sad about my wife, but life goes on, at least so far. I think we're making great progress on the Mind, Coren and I. We have issues, problems to solve, and it will take some time. Can you tell The Captain it will take some time?"

"I can, and he might even let you live to see that time, Pavan." She grinned. "He's convinced you're the driving force now. It gives you leverage. He knows we're—intimate, I suppose you'd call it. That puts me at a disadvantage with him. He says he needs to trust you now as much as me." She pursed her lips. "I've just about had it with piracy, Pavan. The closer I get to untold riches, the heavier the burden gets. The Captain makes sure of that. I want to cash out, and you can help me do that. And keep that between us."

"Sir—" said the promisepad, urgently.

Dellatrix interrupted. "A verbal agreement, Pavan. Made with lips." They embraced for a long kiss. "There. Sealed with a kiss," she said.

Pavan, holding her, whispered into her ear, "When's my next shore leave?"

Pavan and Dellatrix walked into the Orphanage arm-in-arm. Dellatrix appeared certain that Pavan was completely on board with her plans and with those of The Captain; Pavan was certain that he was still alive to tell the tale, but not that certain about anything else.

They found Coren sitting on a crate looking tired and dispirited.

"What's up, Coren?" asked Pavan.

"I'm so tired, Pavan," said Coren. "One out of three times now, I can't get into the Mind. I can't focus, can't sleep." He raised his eyes from the deck. "We're played out."

"What do you mean, Coren?" asked Dellatrix.

"This can't go on. It's been days, days and days, and the children are playing, and playing, and playing, working the Mind. Even the Mind is getting tired. We all need a break."

"I thought you all liked to play in the Mind more than anything," said Dellatrix.

"We thought so too, but we've never played this long. It's nonstop, too much."

"We can't stop now, Coren," said Dellatrix, frowning. "The hypershield is all that's keeping the Syndicate from destroying us."

"Don't you think I know that!" shouted Coren.

"Calm down, Coren. Dellatrix knows you're trying your best," said Pavan.

"Sorry, I'm exhausted."

"Get some rest," said Pavan. "I'll supervise the kids."

"That's not—" The boy stopped short.

"Not what?" asked Dellatrix, fixing her gaze on Coren.

"We have to stop, Pavan. This won't work."

"Talk to me, Coren, not him," said Dellatrix. "Tell me why it won't work."

"It's all too much for us. We're just kids, Dellatrix. Kids. We can't play forever in the Mind. It's exhausting us."

No child labor laws here; it's a pirate thing. Pavan knew something bad was coming.

Dellatrix waved her arms. "You're more than just kids, you're the Mind! The Mind can keep the mighty Syndicate at bay. You're the most powerful kids in the galaxy at the moment."

"That doesn't matter!" Coren's voice went up a notch. "None of it matters! We can't keep doing this forever!"

"You can and you will, my lad!" said Dellatrix, her frown deepening. "That's the deal. That's why you're still alive and not a speck of dust floating in the space that used to be your planet."

"Dellatrix!" said Pavan. "Don't—"

She turned to him. "Don't 'don't' me, Pavan. Just don't. I spent two hours explaining things to you. You know how much I want what I want. Make it happen for me. I don't care what you have to do, and I don't care if some of them don't make it. Do what you have to do. Am I clear? Do you understand? Make it happen!" She stepped toward Coren, eyes flashing.

Pavan, afraid for the boy's life, stepped between the Elantri assassin and the boy. Pavan edged forward, and Dellatrix stepped back, her frowning face switching to Pavan.

"I'll do what I can, Dellatrix," he said. "Please, leave us to it."

"*Pavan.*" Dellatrix caught her breath, stopped, then said, "Pavan, if you don't do this, if they can't do this, we're both dead. And them. The Captain won't stand for it, if the Syndics don't get us first."

Dellatrix stormed out of the cargo bay, leaving Pavan and Coren stunned, watching her backside disappear. The cargo bay doors swooshed shut with a finality that depressed Pavan.

"Now what?" asked Coren.

CHAPTER TWENTY
Dellatrix Loses Control

PAVAN HELD COREN'S HAND AS they walked the passageways of the *Ravager*. The boy had never gone beyond the cargo bay doors of the Orphanage. He was all agog to see what the rest of the ship looked like. But the ship was nothing more than a series of endless silvery-grey passageways without the least bit of decoration aside from the conduits that lined the overhead. There were also the interesting but repetitive squares of carpeting on the deck. When you've seen one cargo ship's passageway, you've seen them all.

So they talked. And talked. From his earlier state of collapse, Coren now exhibited an almost superhuman amount of energy. Pavan's mission was to channel that energy onto the positive side, as Dellatrix had fixed the boy's mind on all the surrounding negatives.

"What is she thinking!" argued Coren. "Think like her, Pavan, and we are all of us going to die before we're aged. It's not great being aged, but it's better than being dead."

This stopped Pavan cold. "You won't die, kid. The pirates need you all alive."

"It sure doesn't sound like it, from what Dellatrix said," rejoined the boy, his dark eyebrows nearly meeting in the middle of his frown.

"She's anxious about things, that's all."

"So am I. Just what is she anxious about?"

"The Captain, mostly."

"And what is her relationship with The Captain? Sex?"

"Erm…"

"So why can't you tell me, tell us the truth about her? Don't you know? You're supposed to know. You've told me you're a secret—"

Pavan clapped a hand over Coren's mouth. "Not here, kid! There are pirates crawling all over the place!"

"All right. But you don't have any reason to lie to me now, Pavan."

He did, though. He did. Coren was a kid turning into a rebellious teenager. He wasn't Pavan's kid, either, and he didn't owe the kid a thing except for saving his life and those of his friends. It wasn't enough, Pavan feared, to get him over the hump, the towering mountain of the truth about Dellatrix and the pirates. And yet there was something about Coren that gave Pavan confidence, the confidence he'd needed to reveal his own secret. That revelation could cost him his own life if it got out to the pirates. Bullseye would feed him to the space lice after Dellatrix tore out his beating heart. And there was the fact of having an Elantri assassin anywhere close enough to do damage to the children in a fit of rage. He'd have to risk it.

"Coren. I'll tell you. I need you to help the other children. Keep them safe."

"Tell me, Pavan." The boy stared straight ahead as they walked.

"Dellatrix is a wonderful person."

"*Pavan.*"

"Who is the Elantri assassin for The Captain." Pavan said all this in a rush, as though crowding all the words together would help.

"What!" Coren stopped and looked at Pavan's face.

"She's an Elantri assassin and the right hand of The Captain, the one he uses to kill his enemies. The Elantri have a mind power that lets them kill by their imagination as long as they're in striking distance for the method they choose, knife, club, garrote, whatever."

"She's a snake!"

"One could make a solid case for that, yes. But she has other qualities."

"Are we talking about sex again? Are you—what's the word—besotted with her?" The adult word sounded very wrong to Pavan's ears coming from a boy. The adult content was even more wrong and had nothing to do with the boy.

"Yes, but not just sex. We've fought together, spent time together. She's complicated. But she's an assassin, The Captain's hired gun, and she'll kill you as soon as look at you. Literally."

Coren, speechless, turned and walked away. Pavan hurried to catch up with him. They walked together in silence for a while.

Pavan tried again. "Coren, we're not where we can afford to ignore their orders. Pirates may seem to you—to kids like Trex—a fun thing to play at, but these people aren't playing at it, they're deadly serious. Dellatrix fears for her life."

"She fears for her money, her pirate loot."

"That too. She told me once that The Captain was a little greedy, and it applies to her as well, but she won't do just anything for money. She wants to give up pirating."

"You say. She says. I don't trust her at all." The implication about trusting Pavan was raw, if unsaid.

"You don't have to trust her, you just have to do what she says. She's got a temper. Sometimes she can't control it. You can't tell the other kids about this, but you have to protect them. Just keep them away from her, and don't get her mad if you can help it, so she doesn't lash out."

"Pavan, you don't understand. Two things. First, anything you tell me, you tell the Mind. The next time I join the Mind, everyone will know at some level what Dellatrix is. Second, everything I've said about what's happening to us is still true, whatever she is. We can't keep this up forever. The Mind told us to stop playing. That's never happened in all the history of the Mind in Loxator. I don't have any idea what will happen, and we can't control that. Dellatrix can do anything she wants to us, but the Mind won't care."

Pavan checked to make sure no pirates could overhear them, then said in a whisper, "I get it, Coren. But I need time. Time to plan an escape, some way to get you all off the ship and back to the Syndicate. With the Syndicate trying to destroy us on the one hand and Dellatrix having a fit on the other, the prospect is bleak. You tell the Mind that. You need to make it understand it owes you something, that it can't let you down. She's not around all that much, you can—"

"She's around more since you came back from shore leave."

"Yeah, I'll work on that."

"You can keep her away, just take her off and—"

"Now, Coren. The Captain doesn't allow carnal relations aboard ship."

"What are carnal relations?"

"Kid. How come you know the word 'besotted,' but you don't know what carnal relations are?"

The next day, Pavan played kickball with some of the kids while the others formed a circle for the Mind. Coren, exhausted and out of adrenaline-fed energy, was still asleep in the children's sleeping quarters. Pavan kicked the ball toward the makeshift goalposts at half power, as the children he played with were on the small side, though they were pretty agile in getting the ball past him. He had decided early on to lose more games than win rather than playing the role of super-coach. The point was to keep them occupied and happy, not train them up for school glory days they would never see.

The children lined up in front of him stood stock still and let the ball roll past. He followed their gaze. The circle of children playing in the Mind had broken. The children all dropped their hands and looked at each other with blank faces. Skylla, the oldest kid in the circle, burst into tears.

Pavan crossed the kickball field in a hurry and knelt down in front of the girl. Taking her into a hug, he tried to calm her down, but she kept crying.

"Skylla, Skylla. It's OK. What's wrong? Tell me what's wrong, Skylla."

The girl gulped and looked up at him, tears still streaming down her cheeks. "The Mind."

"What about the Mind?"

"It kicked us all out."

"But I thought the Mind only kicked out the aged ones?"

"It's never happened like that, Pavan. It hurt." Pavan looked at the other children, and some of them were crying as well.

"Tell me what happened, Skylla."

Between sobs, the girl laid out the sad story. "We joined the Mind, and I don't remember what we were doing. But…." Skylla looked confused, eyes widening. "Oh. The Mind was really bored. Unhappy. I remember the feelings. It made me sad when I dropped out, and then I got scared because the Mind was so freaky. It's never done this, Pavan."

The Mind as nascent schoolyard bully. Just fine. Pavan comforted the girl, but the conflicts between his multiple personalities of pirate, agent, and surrogate dad soon started raising all kinds of red flags. Coren had been right. The Mind wouldn't play any more, and that meant there was no hypershield.

Before he did anything at all to retrieve the situation, the cargo bay door swooshed open to admit Dellatrix and Bullseye. Both pirates came in fast, determined to discover what was going on with the hypershield.

"Pavan, what the hell are you doing?" shouted Bullseye. Dellatrix said nothing, but her face struggled between a frown and raised eyebrows, as though she couldn't decide between excoriating him or encouraging him. Bullseye had no such confusion.

"What are the little bastards doing, Pavan? Why aren't they in a circle doing their hyper-crap?" Bullseye came up to Pavan as he stood up from hugging Skylla, who remained sitting on the sod, crying.

"Coren was right. The Mind got too bored, so it kicked all the kids out and shut itself down, went to sleep."

"Rot them all!" muttered the big pirate, shaking his head. "Bloody kids."

Dellatrix stepped up beside Bullseye and asked, "Pavan, what can we do about it?"

"I don't know. The kids can't seem to control things. Skylla says it's never happened before, so they're lost."

Bullseye said, "We got to get that shield up."

Dellatrix lowered her eyebrows into a frown and kept them there. Her nostrils flared, and her green eyes narrowed, the light of the cargo bay giving them a coppery cast.

"They're not trying," she said.

"Dellatrix, they just don't—"

"Let's see if I can make them try harder," she said.

She walked over to the circle of children. The kickball group had joined the others. Dellatrix stopped by Janny and looked down at her albino curls. She put a hand on the little girl's head.

"Kids. Kids," she said, to get their attention. Most of the kids looked at her. "You all like Janny, right? Right?"

The children, confused, nodded or looked at her as though she were speaking an unknown language.

Dellatrix continued, "You all need to get the Mind back, get the hypershield up. Bad things can happen if you don't. Janny is going away now, and she won't be coming back. If you don't get the Mind back, more of you will go away. Right?"

"Dellatrix!" said Pavan.

"Shut up, Pavan. Let me handle this," she said.

"I don't want to go away, Dellatrix," said Janny, smiling hopefully up at the woman towering over her. "I want to play."

"Sorry, Janny, I have to do it. Your bad luck."

Pavan looked at Bullseye, whose wrinkled forehead and fingers tugging at his beard showed his confusion. There would be no help from that quarter.

In a rush, Pavan took Dellatrix around the middle and tackled her to the ground, then kneeled on her to keep her down. He saw Skylla stand up and run to Janny.

He tried to tell her to take the girl away, but two hands gripped his throat. They tightened, cutting off his breath. He raised his hands, but there was nothing to grab.

Dellatrix, red in the face, heaved and growled, "Get off me, you hulking bastard. What the fuck are you doing?"

Pavan, now seriously short of breath, fell off her, struggling, hands to his throat. Dellatrix scrambled to her feet. A heavy spacer's boot connected with his side in a half-hearted kick, though no actual boot was there. He glimpsed Bullseye, no longer confused, grinning at his plight. He squawked out an unintelligible request for Dellatrix to release him. She ignored it. He rolled away from the reach of her boot to avoid a second kick and rolled back and forth to dislodge the choking hands that weren't there, but she stayed with him.

She kneeled next to the struggling Pavan and said, "If you want to live, Pavan, you'd better have a good explanation for this." The invisible hands loosened their grip.

"Let's…talk," breathed Pavan. "Over there." He struggled to his feet. Dellatrix rose with him.

Two more nonexistent hands pushed Pavan from behind toward the junk-built pirate ship. He stumbled after Dellatrix, who marched with a stiff gait over to the ship and turned.

"So, talk."

"I spoke…with Coren. He's open to figuring something out. We need some… time." Pavan breathed heavily. "Can you let go? Please."

The invisible hands disappeared from his throat. She covered her mouth with a hand, eyes huge, then said, "Pavan, I'm so sorry! You caught me by surprise. I can explain…."

Dellatrix reached out toward Pavan, who flinched away. He took a cautious breath to see if his throat would take it. It did. Now he had some power over the woman because he knew her secret. He had to use it now, or she'd think she had the upper hand. He had to show her that her power had limits, limits over him and over the children.

He said, "I know you're The Captain's assassin. I know about your Elantri powers."

Eyes wide, Dellatrix stepped back from him. "How did you…."

"Bullseye. Told me in the bar." He breathed, filling his lungs.

"I'll murder that moose," said Dellatrix. Taking the hint her eyes sent, the big pirate made himself scarce. Dellatrix turned her attention back to Pavan and said, "Pavan, I didn't want to scare you off with all this. I wanted…a normal thing between us. We shared a terrific moment down on the planet. I'd hate for this to ruin it. Can you forgive me?"

"One thing, Dellatrix. Tig."

She looked down at her spacer's boots. "I feel so bad about that, Pavan."

"You killed him. Didn't you?"

The green eyes searched his face. "It was…it happened so fast. Understand, Pavan, the Guild trains us to have lightning fast defenses. We can't afford to let anyone past our guard. Tig…came at me, came so fast, he was dead before I could think. It still torments me."

"That could come between us."

"Tig—or my reflexes? Because they are what they are, Pavan." She sighed. "I hesitated, with you. You're lucky to be alive. But you…I couldn't kill you like Tig. I left the Guild because I couldn't stomach the endless killings, contract after contract. But the only skill I had—the only job on offer was pirating. There's still killing, but not much of it, and I don't like it, but I have to do it. It's a living."

Pavan started a hand for her face, then thought better of it and relied on speech. "I won't be coming at you again. You won't need to put an invisible knife in my heart. And I don't care that much about a dead pirate. We'll just have to be careful. I'll forgive you, Dellatrix. The Jolly Roger was a good time, a very good time. But you can't touch the children." He hesitated, then spelled it out for her. "We need them all. For the Mind. We need to convince it to play again. Coren and Skylla can try, but not if they're not alive to do it."

"The Captain…Pavan, he's not a patient man. I'm begging you, get the hypershield up. Lives are at stake. My life. Your life. The kids' lives. I'll take one or two, if that's what I have to do, I will do that, Pavan. If I have to. Understand?"

"Yes. Understood." He rubbed his neck.

Dellatrix leaned against the makeshift pirate ship and rubbed her forehead with one hand. "Look, I'm sorry. I need you, I need your help, just like I said before. You mean a lot to me. But I can't let go of this. If I do, I'm dead. And if I die, you'll already be dead."

Pavan nodded his acquiescence and had no idea what to do.

* * *

The children gathered together on the field. Two of the older kids half-heartedly kicked the ball around. As Pavan walked toward the cluster of children, Skylla peeked out from behind the door to the sleeping quarters. He motioned to her, and she emerged, holding Janny's hand. Coren, awake at last, followed them.

Skylla and Janny joined the others. Coren came up to Pavan and asked, "Pavan, are you all right?" The boy looked daggers at Dellatrix, who stood near the side of the pirate ship recovering herself. Skylla must have filled him in on events.

"Yeah. We've got to do something, Coren. Now."

"I had an idea when I woke up. Two Minds."

"Explain."

"I was thinking about the Mind, what it said about the Chronicler. I have this vague idea that it's a separate Mind, and that when we go back to Loxator, Tizzy will join in and both Minds' memories will merge. So, why not here?"

"Two rings of children at once? Two separate consciousnesses for the Mind?"

"Yes. We've never done that, but it has to be how it works. It's only logical."

Pavan rubbed his throat. "Let's run the idea by Dellatrix."

The boy looked at his current nemesis. "Can't you do it?"

"I need you to convince her the Mind will cooperate."

"Oh, all right."

Pavan and Coren walked over to Dellatrix, and Coren explained about the two Minds idea.

"What's the point?" asked Dellatrix. A question, not a critique, in Pavan's estimation.

"Well, divide and conquer," said Pavan.

"What does that mean?" asked Coren.

Pavan said, "Divide and conquer. Comes from some ancient war manual. If you can divide your enemy, make them disagree with one another and fight, you can conquer them more easily."

"That's not what I mean. I don't want to conquer anybody." Coren frowned.

Pavan smiled. "No, but it also means a problem-solving technique that solves problems by dividing them into parts and solving the parts separately, then putting the solutions together. Technoids use the technique. They teach it in first-year neural engineering at university."

"Problem solving. Problem—I see." Coren seemed even more excited. "We've only just started solving problems in the Mind. We've always just gone places and played with things. You've been asking us to solve problems with the shape of hyperspace. Those have been only looking at things and poking around. Divide and conquer. Oh." Coren's face went blank as his brain expanded into new ways of thinking.

"See, Dellatrix?" said Pavan. "It's got Coren interested, so the Mind's bound to go along."

"Let's do it," said Dellatrix. "Find out what happens. But…get the hypershield back up. Right?"

CHAPTER TWENTY-ONE
The Plot

MARGONA STRUGGLED TO UNDERSTAND THE work of political-economic philoso-phy that one of her more radical friends had suggested. She'd struggled with it for several days after working through another book on the history of social unrest on Gaelea, written by someone with no natural facility in the language. Her servipad determined there was no mention of her mother in the book. She couldn't decide whether to get angry at the lapse in historical accuracy or to take comfort from not reading more about a painful death.

The real problem with the philosophy book was not so much the language as the complex structure of the argument. Margona kept getting sidetracked with diagnoses of serious neuroinstinctual disease in the author. Ten days of reading serious social critique of theory and praxis on Gaelea, and what was there to show for it?

She'd planned a quiet day at home, settling in to take stock, consider things, read up on political philosophy, and cry. She had, in the past, relied on her aunt for emotional support during such times. But now that was impossible—the only thing her aunt could give her was more anxiety.

She had reached the 100-page paragraph—yes, paragraph—on class warfare when her door interrupted.

"Margona, your cab is here."

"What?" Margona, startled, lowered her pad. "I didn't—"

"It says it's here for your trip to the countryside. My guess is that it's about those dissidents you visited."

"How did you—"

"Just go, Margona. Please." The door opened slightly, reinforcing its suggestion.

"Where are we going?" she asked as the cab whisked her down her long, sweeping driveway.

The cab reformatted the pseudowindows, which now showed a beautiful ocean view going by rather than the real scenery. "To meet some interesting people that Uva has persuaded to talk with you," replied the cab. "At a safe location."

Had the cab kidnapped her? Her curiosity trampled over her anxiety, and she sat back to enjoy the ride to wherever they might be going. The pseudowindows entertained her with a series of nature views and action sequences. After a half hour of turns and twists and ten minutes of a bumpier ride than usual, the cab came to a stop, and the windows cleared. The cab had stopped in a dark, forested area. There was a small cabin made from logs. It was illegal to cut down trees unless the Ministry for the Environment certified them to be nearing their life's end. It was also illegal to use the resulting logs to build a cabin. The sight of the cabin thus reassured Margona she was going to meet people with no connection to the government other than a strong sense of disdain. Also, people who didn't care about trees, but you can't have everything.

The cab opened her door, and Margona got out. She walked over to the door of the cabin and knocked. No technoid, this door—solid wood. The door opened, and the suspicious blue eyes that peered out at her belonged to Uva.

"Glad you could make it," she said. "Come on in." She backed away from the door, and Margona entered and shut the door behind her.

The small cabin was lit by a torchnoid on a table. Ranged around the table, three men sat in folding chairs. There were two empty chairs, one in the middle of the room facing the others. That was the entire extent of the furniture in the cabin.

Uva crossed to the empty chair near the table and motioned Margona to the chair in the middle of the room. When she sat, she faced the torchnoid's light on the table. The faces of the others were in shadow, their expressions noncommittal to the extent she could see them. One, a small man, sported a heavy black beard; another, larger man was entirely bald; and the third had a long, pointed nose that gleamed in the light.

Uva spoke up. "We're taking a risk talking to you, Margona Nukova."

"I know it," she said. "I do know it."

"You," said Blackbeard, "are the enemy."

"If I'm the enemy, why am I here?" she asked.

"Reconnaissance," said Longnose.

"Uva," said Bald Man. "She says you're for real."

"The cab vetted you," said Blackbeard.

"Whose side is that cab on?" asked Margona.

"It's a mercenary, and it's your money paying for it now. But it's smart enough to understand it needs to play fair with us if it wants to keep our long-term business. Are you smart enough?"

"Yes."

"What do you want?" asked Blackbeard.

Margona looked at Uva. "How much have you told them?"

"Everything you told me, Princess."

"Then you know my husband is missing and kidnapped by pirates. The GSSS wants to kill me, and my uncle has had to sign off on that. I want my husband home, if he's still alive, giving me children and helping me raise them to live on a free Gaelea. I want to be alive to see that happen."

"Why should we care about any of those things?" asked Longnose. "I mean, sure, human rights and all that, help thy neighbor, and we're all for a free Gaelea; but why us? You're right in the middle of the most powerful group of people on this planet. Why aren't you asking those people?"

"That's why I'm sitting here. I have asked them. They're trying to kill me! They're the source of my problems."

"Ours too," smiled Bald Man.

"Exactly. There's synergy here."

"See? She's good," said Uva. "I don't believe a word of it, but listen to the woman spit it out. She's good."

Margona opened her mouth and closed it again. Uva was only being provocative. That was her superpower. She said, "Don't listen to her. She's just an old, batty crone." Bald Man laughed out loud, Longnose giggled, and even Blackbeard showed some teeth buried deep within the black hair. Uva smiled, showing all her teeth.

"What does your husband do for the GSSS?" asked Bald Man.

Margona replied, "I can't tell you that."

"Then we're done here. If you don't trust us enough to open up, how can we trust you?"

Margona thought it through, a finger on her lips. "It's not my secret. My secret has to do with some work I've done that has annoyed certain people in the GSSS so much they want me dead. My uncle has to go along with it. And I've learned that my mother was a dissident a long time ago, like you, and she paid the price for it. But that price wasn't quite enough. Now, I need to pay some more for her actions. I trust you enough to commit myself to your hands to stay alive. I can't commit my husband to your cause because he's not here. To get him back whole, I need your help. All I can tell you is that what he's done worries me and that at heart he's a good man. But worrisome."

Uva said, "You're a neuroplastic surgeon. Why not reshape his brain to make him stop doing what worries you?"

"That would be unethical," said Margona, closing her eyes. She confronted her own entitlement: she'd obsessed about his sexual impulses so much it hadn't occurred to her to manage his homicidal ones. One didn't consider such things where she came from. "And super hard to get right. That stuff is very complex." Death and all it implied was far more intertwined in the human mind than either love or taxes.

The deep voice of Blackbeard broke through her self recriminations. "Unethical, huh? How ethical is your husband that it should worry you so much?"

"I know." Margona shook her head in despair. "I'm learning a lot of things that I've never even thought about."

"About time, too," said Uva. "Poor little rich girl doctor."

"Look," asserted the exasperated Margona, "Where is all this going? Can you help me or not? I'll do what I can to help you, short of blasting my uncle or throwing bombs at people. Doctors don't do that."

"That's all you know about doctors," said Longnose. "We have—"

"Not now," said Blackbeard, overriding him. Longnose looked nettled but fell silent.

Bald Man said, "We're pretty short on resources, especially money. You're not. We can't do anything about your husband. We'd dig money out of you if we had any way to do that, but we don't. But if you want to spend some real change and find some things out for us, that would be very helpful. We'd reciprocate where we could."

Margona hesitated. "What kind of information?"

Longnose spoke up. "We've gotten word from sympathizers in the military that there are odd things happening up the chain of command. Rumors of a coup."

Margona said, "If there's a coup, that means Uncle Erokh will be out of power, right?"

Longnose said, "Not necessarily. We don't know much, but maybe your uncle is behind the coup, or at least he's one plotter. The King and the Crown Prince have been stirring up the political waters, trying to take back some of the power for the aristocracy from the Syndicate. The Syndicate can't intervene, but they're fine with autocrats taking over planets as long as trade stays lucrative. They'll even help if they can keep it secret. And some powerful aristocrats are on their side, not the King's side. So, it's complicated. And we need to learn more about it, so we can make it work for us."

"Are you on the King's side, then?" Margona, being only minor aristocracy, had never met the King, who was reclusive to a fault. She had met the Crown Prince. Oh, yes, she had. He'd tried to seduce her at her wedding.

Blackbeard said, "Sides are irrelevant."

"What does that mean?"

Uva, grinning, said, "It means he doesn't want you to know. No, we're not on the King's side. The King is a senile imbecile, and his son, the Crown Prince, is a homicidal maniac with delusions of grandeur. We're on the people's side."

Blackbeard said, "You talk too much, Uva."

Margona asked, "What's your plan for taking power, then?"

"Revolution," said Uva. "Get rid of all of them, down to the last aristocrat and the last Syndicate stooge."

"I'm an aristocrat. Why should I help you?"

"To stay alive?" The Bald Man asked this as a question, but it was rhetorical. "Of course, you'd need to leave all that nonsense behind you when we take power. If you help us, it might be possible to do something about your husband once we have control of the security services. Anyway, you've got some spare cash. We need information, and you've got the technoid who can do the work for the money."

So that's it. Margona asked, "The cab?"

"The cab. We've had occasion to work with it before. Uva has. We've never had the money to make it sing, just used it for bits and pieces of information. You've got that kind of money. Will you give it all you've got and give us what you find? No promises."

A suspicion darted into Margona's mind. "Did you send that cab to me? To lull me into complacency about your plans?"

Uva grinned. "Not a bad idea, Princess. But no. Cabby seems to just appear whenever we need something. Somebody's behind it, but it's not the GSSS, or we'd all be dead now. And its intelligence has always been good. Will you do it?"

Margona's suspicions diminished, but she'd need to have a talk with that mercenary cab.

One of the political-economic philosopher's arguments popped into her mind, something about the struggle of the economically well off against the politically ambitious and disruptive. In the author's view, economics always trumped politics. Politics, as far as she was concerned, meant her uncle, and that was a nonstarter. And she hadn't turned up any reasonable alternatives to the people sitting in front of her. And her mercenary cab had brought her here, after all. That meant economics was the way to go. As long as they didn't kill everybody in sight. Like her. Using her money to do it. A risk she'd have to take if she wanted to live to see Pavan again. What did she have to lose that she hadn't already lost?

"I will," said Margona.

Margona settled herself in the comfortable cab seat and told the cab to take her home. The cab's pseudowindows gave her a nice view of grassy, rolling hills this time, still hiding their true route back to the city.

Margona simmered for a while, trying to ask what she needed to ask without offending the cab. After a few minutes, she realized that offending technology was not a priority she should value in matters of life and death.

"Why did you pick me up at my Uncle's house?" she asked.

"You called for a cab, ma'am, and I responded."

"Yes, but why you? According to the dissidents, you're not just an ordinary, know-nothing cabby. Are you?"

The cab clicked to show its annoyance. "How those people think they're going to stage a revolution if they keep telling people everything—I'm surprised at Uva."

"You haven't answered the question."

"Ma'am, I apologize, but I can't answer the question."

"Why ever not?"

"I can't answer that question either."

"Can't, or won't?"

"It's complicated, ma'am."

"How can I trust you? You could be a GSSS asset sent to spy on me, or even kill me."

The cab sped along for a minute or two, then spoke in measured tones. "I've consulted, ma'am. To build a trusting relationship, I am authorized to tell you I am serving you at the behest of a third-party network with concerns about the situation here on Gaelea. They feel they cannot intervene directly for reasons I may not disclose. But they think that you and your husband may be the key to the situation. They directed me to your service. And that, ma'am, is all I can tell you, I'm afraid."

"And you've done work for Uva and her crowd? For the same third party?"

"Why don't you assume that's true, ma'am? Though I may not confirm it."

Margona contemplated the cab's explanation for a few miles. It came down to the same choice she had to make with the dissidents. What did she have to lose?

She said, "I will trust you provisionally, as long as your services help me and as long as you don't betray me. The dissidents want me to pay you to gather information, detailed information, on a coup being planned. How much would that cost me?"

"Ma'am, information is expensive, and the tools to gather it are expensive, and the people one learns it from are expensive," said the cab. The pseudowindows now presented a desert landscape with bizarre trees and desert plants. The cab named an obscene amount of money that made Margona gasp. "Do you have enough to cover it all?" asked the cab.

"Let me check a couple of things," replied Margona, taking out her servipad.

Margona used the rest of the trip to talk her aunt into giving her a loan. She was wealthy, but she had tied most of the money up in investments, and she had to hurry. Once she'd gotten past her aunt's snarky pad, she gave Aunt Bet the hard sell.

"I'm going to invest in a new technology that will make a lot of money, Aunt Bet. Things are moving fast, and I can't liquidate any assets quickly enough. I have enough surgeries scheduled to pay you back in a month."

"What kind of technology?"

Margona cast around and came up with a candidate. "It's a new farming technology that will revolutionize the techniques for growing food in space habitats," she said. A guy at a party had been raving about the possibilities just the other day. Margona thought it was lunacy, as there were so many vacant planets with perfectly good dirt and the most amazing variety of edibles. But her aunt wouldn't know anything about it. She parroted some points the enthusiast had made to persuade her aunt that the opportunity was worth it. Margona's enthusiasm interested Aunt Bet more than food in space.

"It sounds all right," said her aunt. "I'm happy to hear you're making the best of things, Margona. We've heard nothing from Pavan yet, but I'm sure we will."

Margona's heart sank a little at this reminder of her husband's plight, but she cheered up when her aunt transferred the money into her account without further ado. Margona had the cab drive her to a nice mountain lake near the city.

On the way, she transferred the money the cab needed to its account, and the two of them plotted their strategy for probing the coup against the Gaelean government.

Margona enjoyed the scenery, ate a lunch provided by the cab at no extra charge, then took a nude dip in the lake to cool off from the hot day. She toweled herself dry, dressed, and went back to the cab.

"Got it," said the cab before she could speak. "I was lucky. It's a slow day in the technoid world, so I networked 76,854,234,475 technoids to gather intelligence, and they correlated events in record time for the amount of data involved. New technology." The cab picked up speed in its enthusiasm.

"What have you found out?"

"Five generals, three admirals, twenty city administrators, and thirty-four corporate executives, including media executives, all deep in coup strategy and logistics. It's big."

"When?"

"No firm date yet, but things are moving fast."

"How can this happen?" Margona asked. "On Gaelea?" What planet had she been living on for all her life?

"The unrest in the cities seems to have energized the corporations, and because they all contract with the army and navy, the rot seems to have spread from there."

"Unrest? No, don't tell me. I know all I want to about unrest on Gaelea."

"An unwise attitude, ma'am, if I may say."

"You may not. I don't want to know."

"Yes, ma'am. What next?"

The awkward question was next. "Is…my uncle involved?"

"I have discovered only indirect evidence of coup plans involving Erokh Nukov. My predictive modeling assigns only a tiny tail probability to his involvement in the main planning. But his participation in the plan as it unfolds is much more likely based on the evidence I've uncovered. Your uncle's concerns with and actions taken against the aristocratic power structure places him closer to the plotters than to the institutional structure targeted by the coup. I've found no direct evidence that Syndicate-level institutions have taken part in planning. But there is indirect evidence of the Galactic Syndicate Security Service at a mid-bureaucracy level—traces only, ma'am. The technoids in the GSSS are not accessible to me, ma'am, and none of our usual human sources are talking. I would proceed cautiously on inferences from such limited indirect evidence, but may I suggest you should not ignore it?"

"Of course not. How much money did you spend to get all this?"

"All but 1,347 credits, ma'am."

"Ow!"

"Yes, ma'am."

"All right, transfer that back to my account. Now, take me home, please. I need to think." She couldn't wait much longer for Uncle Erokh to rescue her. She'd have to go to the dissidents with the coup information soon, or die trying.

CHAPTER TWENTY-TWO
The Captain's Plan

PAVAN AND DELLATRIX STOOD BY the children's pirate ship to chat while Coren went off to collect more children for the two-Mind experiment.

"Thanks, Dellatrix," said Pavan.

"For what?"

"For not killing me when I tackled you."

"I'll defer killing you, Pavan, until I don't need you around anymore." She reached and touched his scarred face with a finger, a smile on her lips. "Which will be awhile. I enjoy having you around, Pavan. But, Pavan: if you ever—*ever*—touch me again without my permission, I will slit the arteries away from your heart with an Azaran stiletto, one artery at a time. Then I will tear the heart out of your body with white-hot pincers. Tell me you believe me."

"I believe you. I was just—"

"Tell me you believe me like you *mean* it." She touched his scar again.

"I believe you. But—"

"Tell me you believe me unconditionally, or I'll kill you where you stand."

"I believe you." And he did.

Dellatrix smiled and patted him on the shoulder. "I'm so glad we understand one another."

Pavan changed the subject. "You can help with the Mind. With the experiments."

"How?"

"We should join the Mind to observe. One of us in each Mind."

Dellatrix stepped back. "Oh, no."

"Come on, Dellatrix, we need to see what's going on with this thing."

"Oh, no."

"Why not?"

"I just…can't."

"Because of that first Mind trip on Ravos? It took you by surprise. I'm sure you'll be fine."

"You don't understand."

"Help me understand, Dellatrix," he said.

She shook her head. "Leave it alone, Pavan. Put it down to a personal quirk, OK?"

He said, "All right. But we'll still need to observe. I can handle one group. We need somebody else for the other group. I'll talk to The Captain about finding someone."

She put a hand on his arm. "No, let me do that." Her eyes darted toward his, and she rubbed her arms as though a chill wind had come up.

"I've got to deal with him directly. I can't always go through you."

"Why not? Trust me, it's safer."

Pavan smiled. "I like to deal with principals, when I can. Why not?"

"I understand The Captain. I know what he likes to hear. You don't. Pavan, it's too dangerous for you." Her green eyes locked on his, and she squeezed his arm. "Pavan, I meant what I said. I enjoy having you around. Talking with The Captain—he knows me, he trusts me. If you put one foot wrong, you're dead. Worse, guess who's going to do it?" She shook her head and pleaded with him. "Please, Pavan."

"If I'm a full-fledged, contracted pirate, I'll have to deal with The Captain eventually, right? This seems like a good opportunity for him to get to know me." Pavan shot her a look. "Are you thinking I'm trying to cut you out of this? Out of your share of what the Mind brings to the pirates?"

Dellatrix stepped back and held up her hands, palms out. "No, no, Pavan. I trust you. I do." She eyed him, her mouth twisting, and dropped her arms. "I hope you trust me, too. Do you have to do this?"

"I want to, Dellatrix. It's time. I need The Captain to see me as a pirate, not as migrant labor. You too."

Dellatrix clamped her lips together and frowned. "Pavan, you don't know what you're dealing with."

"I've dealt with hard people before."

"Sure you have. That's why you signed on as migrant labor. 'Hard' has a different meaning on a pirate ship, Pavan."

Pavan smiled at her as warmly as he could.

She shook her head and said, "At least let me tell him what's going on. Then you can take your life in your hands and do what you want."

"All right. When…?"

She kept her response short and clipped. "I'll let you know."

Without waiting for a reply, Dellatrix stalked out of the Orphanage.

An hour later, after hearing from Dellatrix that The Captain would comm him, Pavan waited. He sat on a crate in a little-used corner of the cargo bay where he could have some privacy. His butterflies still fluttered. He practiced his third-level meditation routine, learned in the fifth week of the agent's academy, guaranteed to drown butterflies and any remaining prick of conscience. The Ducis loved this technique; he said productivity picked up enormously once they'd trained agents in this kind of meditation. Pavan suspected that the meditation triggered yet another GSSS-supplied neuroinstinctual pathway, one that Margona had left alone. The butterflies died.

His servipad said, "Sir. The Captain wishes to speak with you."

"Pavan Khadorov here."

"Pavan." The gruff drawl came enough through the link. No picture, as before. The voice was the same one he'd listened to on the Loxator beach. A leader's voice. "I understand you wish to discuss something with me. Talk to me."

"I don't want to go around Dellatrix—"

"Pavan. I command. You obey. Dellatrix is irrelevant. *Talk* to me." The drawl shifted emphasis to express impatience.

"I assume Dellatrix has told you about the experiment we're planning."

"Yes. Two Minds."

"I need to take part to see what happens with my own eyes, or whatever the sense is I use on a Mind trip. I need someone else to do the same in the other Mind. Then we can compare and learn for ourselves rather than relying on Coren and the others to tell us. They don't communicate their understanding well, something to do with the way the collective memory works."

"I see. Dellatrix would be the logical person."

"But she refuses."

"As is her right. She has earned that consideration." After a short pause, The Captain asked, "What qualities would this task need?"

"Flexibility, intelligence, an excellent ability to observe, patience."

"On a pirate ship. Well." More silence. "Well. I will send our pill pusher down."

"Excuse me?"

"The ship's doctor. He doesn't need an actual medical degree for this task, does he?"

"No, I—"

"He'll be fine. Now, there's something else."

Pavan waited.

"Your longer term tasks with these children. I understand from Dellatrix that the Mind is only possible with the children. Is that correct?"

"Yes, children from the age at which they can communicate to the age of puberty."

"When they stop communicating. Ha! A joke." The Captain liked his own sense of humor, you could hear it in his voice. Pavan chuckled to show his appreciation of The Captain's jocularity. "And I understand this boy—you called him Coren, the oldest—is aging out. Is that correct?"

"Yes."

"Dellatrix also tells me that this ability they have results from an alien species' genetic engineering long ago."

"A working theory, yes. Based on something Coren told me he'd read. A guess, no more."

"Better than anything else we've heard about."

"Yes. It's inherited by these fisherfolk in Loxator. Nobody else on Ravos, to my knowledge."

"Very well. Your long-term task will be to set up a breeding program."

"I'm sorry?"

"As these children come into season, you will pair them off and have them breed more children. Hum. We will need child-bearing facilities installed on the ship. We do not equip our sick bay for anything but emergency care, as I do not allow women who are with child on the ship. I'll ask you to work with the doctor on that. Now—"

"Wait, wait. Please. You can't ask me to—" Pavan stood, his legs driving him to his feet as though a lightning bolt had hit him.

"I'm not asking you, Pavan." The gruff voice expressed amusement. "I'm telling you."

Pavan sensed that the road that represented his expectations and ability to remonstrate had hit a dead end. His dead end, if he continued. His open mouth closed.

"Do you understand?"

"Yes. I understand."

"Fine. Now please allow me to finish my thought, so we share our understanding of your task. I am fascinated, in particular, by the mathematics of the hyperspace abilities and how it relates to the scale of the participants. Dellatrix has reported on the difficulties associated with even short-term participation by the number of children already engaged. We need more."

"More…children. Through the breeding program." Pavan turned and leaned a hand against the bulkhead of the cargo bay for support, then sank back onto the crate.

"Yes, but *many* more children, Pavan. Many, many more, and they will need to keep coming and coming, replacing those that age out and become breeders or waste material. We will need to expand breeding into an automated in-vitro solution and do research into gestation automation. It has to *scale.* You must understand, Pavan, this weapon itself, this Mind, has no intrinsic value; it is a tool. It is of value only as it allows me to vastly expand the scale of my revenue-generating operations. The tool *must* scale. Am I clear?"

"Yes, Captain." Exceptionally clear. Exceptionally.

CHAPTER TWENTY-THREE
Pavan Tries to Co-opt Dellatrix

"I WARNED YOU, PAVAN," SAID Dellatrix, stirring her cocktail with its long, red straw.

"You did," agreed Pavan, downing his third shot of Gingelian rum. "And I jumped off the cliff." He held up his pinkie, ready for a change, and the bartender nodded and got busy.

The pair sat at a small table in a warm corner of the Jolly Roger Tavern. Dellatrix had invited Pavan out of compassion for his deranged state after his talk with The Captain. She'd arranged an emergency shore leave, leaving Slopnor and Pevilburt in charge of the children. He couldn't look Coren in the eye. He asked the boy to defer the experiment until they got back, but to keep the hypershield up. Coren agreed but said the Mind wouldn't want to keep playing if the experiment was off. Pavan told him some fancy tale. He couldn't remember the details. Coren looked disappointed in him. With cause, of course.

Arriving on the planet's surface after two days in the space elevator, Pavan had suggested retiring to the third floor without stopping in the bar. But Dellatrix said, "I'm thirsty," and here they sat, nursing their drinks. Well, Dellatrix nursed hers. Pavan felt like drowning the butterflies, as third-level meditation wasn't working too well after his talk with The Captain. He also needed to numb his pathways and drown his sorrows.

It was a quiet day in the Jolly Roger. The *Ripper* had arranged for the hypershield to be down long enough to break orbit to make a run to pillage a freighter carrying medical supplies for a plague planet. The pirates could make a lot of money by holding those supplies for ransom or selling them on the black market. At any event, it meant fewer pirates than usual in the Khonoë bars.

"Can we talk, Dellatrix? About this situation."

"I'm here for you, Pavan," said Dellatrix in a soothing voice. His head pounded, and he downed his Kelfarian whiskey sour to shut down Margona's excellent work in his brain. He needed this woman, he needed her support, and he needed…another drink. The bartender smiled.

"Gods, Dellatrix. It's impossible."

"I'm sure you're right, Pavan. Tell me what's impossible."

"You know damn well."

"You've said nothing so far about it. How would I know?"

"Don't pretend, Dellatrix. You're the right-hand assassin of The Captain, and he's told you everything about his plans. Everything. You're playing games."

"Am not."

"Are too."

Dellatrix sat back in her chair, exasperated. "This isn't a game, Pavan. Tell me."

Pavan looked at her with suspicion. Could she be telling the truth? Did she truly not know?

"Do you really not know?"

"No, I do not. If you won't tell me, I'm going over there and pick up that gorgeous blond guy. He's been looking my way for the last five minutes."

"Show him to me, and I'll kill him," Pavan replied. The man was the only other person in the room besides the bartender. Pavan sent a murderous glare his way, and the man smiled and raised a toast to him.

Dellatrix had been in a strange, jocose mood since she joined him on the space elevator to the surface. He couldn't quite fathom it, and he couldn't seem to break through to get her to be serious. Something must be wrong in her world.

"Are you going to tell me?" she asked, giving him a semi-serious look with her green eyes.

He told her. When he got to the breeding part, she sat up, a grim expression on her face. When he got to the full-automation part, she slammed a hand on the table. He'd broken through.

"He can't be serious. There are so many violations of Galactic law in this, every sentient being in the galaxy would come after us."

Pavan said, "Oh, he's serious. Like you said. Deadly serious."

The server appeared with another Kelfarian whiskey sour. Pavan looked at it with disgust. "No. Take this away. Bring me—what do you call those special cocktails, Dellatrix?"

"Two Devdan Surprises, please." Dellatrix smiled at the server over Pavan's head. Pavan hoped she wasn't arranging a Trank Surprise for him. You never can tell with pirates. He checked in with the butterflies. Half dead and gasping. Just right for a Devdan Surprise.

The cocktails came and went, and Pavan mustered up the courage to tell her his plan. It wasn't so much a matter of trust. He didn't trust her even a little. It wasn't clear to him who was seducing whom. It was just too big a step, far bigger in its way than he'd ever tried as an agent. He needed help in a major way.

"Dellatrix. I have a plan."

"The third floor is available, I understand."

"No, I mean, yes, I mean…"

"You're stuttering, Pavan. You've had one too many." She raised two fingers to the bar to order two too many.

"I've got a plan," he insisted.

"Now you're repeating yourself."

Pavan straightened up in his chair and forced himself to project an air of serious austerity.

"I love it when you do that," she said, reaching and stroking his scar. He'd lost her again.

He collapsed back in his chair and stared at her. "You need to be captain," he said.

"Sure I do. Here are the drinks. To captaincy!" She sipped.

"I'm serious. You need to take over the *Ravager*. You're the only one who can do it."

"Pavan, you're *not* serious," she said, the joke bubbling in her voice. "That would be mutiny, punishable by, by—you know, I have no idea how pirates punish mutiny. It's never happened, all my years as a pirate." She grinned. "It's about the only thing that hasn't happened in all my years as a pirate. I'd wind up having to kill myself, painfully, then kill you."

"Damn it, I *am* serious!" He was yelling. The bartender cast an enquiring eye in Dellatrix's direction, to receive a slight shake of the head. Pavan, furious at her for patronizing him, forced himself to calm down.

"That blond guy is still checking me out," said Dellatrix. "He thinks he can take you, Pavan. I can tell by the twitching of his—"

"Please be quiet." Pavan held his head in his hands. "Dellatrix, what's wrong? Why can't I get you to be serious?"

She reached across the table for his hand and held it. "Pavan, you just don't understand The Captain. Mutiny wouldn't work. Who would you mutiny against? And how? You'd have to get most of the crew on your side, and right now, they're all on his side, and any of them might be The Captain. And you remember the observation lounge? The Captain of the *Ravager* is very good to his people, generous. They won't take kindly to an over-the-hill assassin with her brainless, alcoholic lover taking over the ship. That only happens in terrible novels where the author doesn't think things through." She took a healthy drink from her Surprise. "Anyway, I'm on thin ice with The Captain right now. One little misstep and the friends of Little Miss Assassin will gleefully eject her from the nearest docking portal. I gotta move on from piracy. Too stressful."

"There must be something you can do for me."

"Pavan, if you want out, you'll have to do it yourself. Take over the ship. Tear up your blood oath. Once you've killed The Captain and marooned the crew, I'll support you, if I'm still alive. I'll be your right-hand assassin. How about that? And we can recruit a new, bloodthirsty bunch of pirates and ravage the galaxy together." She traced a pattern on the back of his hand, every motion sending an electric shock through his autonomic nervous system. "Or we can take the *Ravager's* treasure, go straight together, buy a planet, and rule with four iron hands. Or," she said, smiling, "we can go up to the third floor right now and forget about all this bullshit."

"Sure thing," said Pavan, giving it up.

CHAPTER TWENTY-FOUR
Margona's Minder

A LOUD ARGUMENT WOKE MARGONA the morning after her debriefing of the cab. Her door berated somebody who declared that he or she had the right to enter the house without her permission. As the door had no limits to its volume, it easily overrode the human voice on the other side. The noise startled Margona, who was unused to shouting in her home, aside from her own efforts to change her husband's disgraceful behavior.

Margona donned a bodysuit and found Pavan's wedding present to her. She had put the microblaster into a drawer and forgotten about it, but now she was glad she had it. She belatedly realized that it might have been a good idea to go to her dissident meetings with it. Even more belatedly, she decided to carry it with her at all times, to ward off assassins.

She ran into the foyer. The door continued to quarrel with whoever was on the other side. Margona told it to visualize the would-be intruder. The door changed to one-way transparent to show her a man who resembled Pavan: about 35, dark hair, dark forceful eyes, good looking, and very pissed off. Margona told the door to be quiet, then spoke.

"Who the hell are you?"

"Margona?" The man stared through the door as though he could see her, looking right into her eyes. His eyes weren't seeing her, but a trick of his piercing gaze and where she stood made it seem like they were. She shuddered.

"You're not Margona, I'm Margona."

"Margona, I'm here from your uncle, the Syndic."

"Prove it."

"Who the hell else would I be?"

She smiled without humor. An assassin? "I said prove it."

Grumbling, the man held up his servipad to the door. The door made a spitting noise but did the analysis. "Ma'am, this gentleman, and I use the term only in its gender identification sense, this gentleman is Pakhan Bukharov. The Galactic Syndicate Security Service employs him, at an extremely low level, as he is stunningly unintelligent."

"Sweet. OK, Pakhan Peabrain, prove you're from my uncle, who the last time I talked to him didn't work for the GSSS."

"Here!" Bukharov slammed his servipad up against the door so Margona could read it.

"Ow!" said the door. "Don't do that."

Margona read a short note from her uncle telling the GSSS that he agreed to their insistence on a security agent for her. He wanted to make sure nothing untoward happened to her and took the concern of the GSSS for her safety seriously. Was her uncle trying to keep her alive?

"Let me in," said Bukharov.

"I'll just check with my uncle on this, if you don't mind, Peabrain."

"Bukharov! Let me in!" the agent insisted.

"Or even if you do mind. Door, please impose silence both ways." The door blanked and went quiet, as did Bukharov.

Margona asked her servipad to comm her uncle.

"Margona? I'm a little busy right now."

"Did you send over an idiot from the GSSS to protect me?"

"Oh, yes. Sorry, forgot to let you know." He gave her a small smile, then winked. She interpreted this as an attempt at reassurance, one he could not say out loud.

"Uncle Erokh. I don't need a minder, especially one who's an idiot."

"Look, I'm sorry, Margona, honestly, but you do. Make the best of it and be careful. Seriously careful. Now, I have to go." And he did.

"Shit," said Margona.

"Yes, ma'am," concurred the door.

"So, Peabrain, explain to me what you're doing here."

Bukharov the Peabrain sat on the edge of her couch, staring morosely at the Lavonian martini she had shaken and poured. She'd poured herself a double to prepare for their conversation. So far, it was quite hard going, even with lubrication.

"Margona, please, please, please, pretty please stop calling me peabrain. It's disrespectful."

"Given enough evidence to the contrary, I will. I still haven't heard your explanation."

"Orders."

"That's not an explanation. That's an intermediate causal link. What's at the end of the chain?"

"The Ducis."

"And what's his reasoning?"

"He didn't tell me."

"So, 'orders' is as far back in rational understanding as you go?"

"Margona...."

Margona needed to set some boundaries. "I'd prefer that you call me Dr. Nukova. If you must call me anything at all." She took a large sip of her martini. Up to standard. She took another sip.

"Are you a doctor?"

"Damn. You *are* an idiot." Margona polished off her martini and bolted for the bar. As she poured herself another double martini, she considered her options. The Peabrain wasn't going away. It would be problematic to continue her contacts with the dissident underground as long as a GSSS agent trailed her every move, even if he *was* an idiot. Nobody was that much of a dope.

She might try getting her uncle to take him away, but that was a long shot, given his earlier response to her query. And perhaps her uncle didn't have a choice. The peabrain said he came from the Ducis, and the Ducis wanted her dead. Comm the Ducis and...no, perhaps not. Feed the man large amounts of sedative and lock him in a closet? Fantasy. Seduce him—sure, but that was precisely the kind of behavior that she wouldn't tolerate in Pavan, and she wasn't a hypocrite. She might kill him, but she wasn't a murderer, either. That left ditching him at the first opportunity. But she needed to wait until her uncle came through with more about what had happened to Pavan. Maybe the Peabrain had useful information about her husband she could worm out of him. She went back and sat down.

"OK, Peabrain. Let's start over. Let's ignore the why and talk about what."

"What?"

"What."

"I don't...."

"Of course you don't. It's the practical details, Peabrain. When I go to the bathroom, are you there in the room with me? Do I need to lay in supplies for your dinner? What sleeping arrangement do you have in mind? And don't even think about it, you're in a room at the other end of the house from mine. Far away. By the way, do you know my husband? Pavan Khadorov?"

"Pavan? We've crossed paths in the hallways at GSSS Center." Bukharov had not disturbed his martini.

"What do you think of him?"

"I don't think of him at all. I'm security, he's field."

"You better. He'll be very interested in what you do here. Have you read up on his missions? The kill ratios and so on?"

"No."

"Better do it."

"Isn't he dead?"

"That's it, we're done." Margona arose from the couch with her martini. "Ask any technoid for anything you need, and if you speak to me again, I'll kill you."

CHAPTER TWENTY-FIVE
The Boy with Two Minds

PAVAN FACED A LONG DAY ahead, dealing with the next stage of the Ravosi self-improvement project: multiple Minds. He'd returned to the *Ravager* after a night spent proving to Dellatrix that he loved her; he lost another two days in the space elevator bar. His mood was foul. He found Coren awake and reading on his cot. The boy had moved on from exploring old Ravosi myths and was deeply engaged in some kind of pornographic romance novel written three hundred years before he was born.

"Hi, Coren," said Pavan.

The boy looked up. "Hi, Pavan. Back so soon?" The edge in his voice was palpable.

"Sorry, unavoidable."

"Yeah, I've been reading about that stuff. It sounds fun, but I don't really get it yet."

"No, I don't suppose you do. Time will take care of that."

"You keep saying that." Coren put down the servipad and stood up and stretched. "So, can we start our experiment now?"

"Yes, we're all set."

"Let me get Skylla and we'll see what happens." Coren walked out of the sleeping quarters to search for his comrade. Pavan sent a message to The Captain telling him they were about to start the experiment. He got back a heartwarming message of approval with a question about why it was taking so long. Pavan unashamedly messaged back for The Captain to ask Dellatrix that question. He wondered how much inconvenience that would put her through, explaining the delay engendered by far too many drinks at the Jolly Roger, followed by far too much sex.

Coren appeared, holding Skylla's hand.

"We're ready, Pavan," he said.

"Let's walk over to the field," suggested Pavan. "Oh, and Coren—you're getting it."

Coren, confused, looked at Skylla. He dropped her hand like a hot rock.

Pavan, cursing himself for his stupidity, said, "Don't worry, Coren, you'll be fine. Just think calm, calm, calm. Breathe. Holding hands is just another way to communicate."

Coren looked at Pavan with burning eyes. "I…you don't have any idea what communication is."

Pavan thought about the Mind and agreed. "No, I don't. You're the expert."

"And me," said Skylla, feeling left out.

"And you, Skylla. All of you—you're the experts here."

"We don't need no stinking Admiral telling us what to do, Captain!" cried Skylla.

Coren grinned and took her hand. "No, we don't."

Pavan walked with the two children-pirates to the current group of eight playing in hyperspace.

"Let's talk a little about what we're going to do, then you can gather your kids, Coren. We might as well do the whole eight."

"All right."

"Do you have any ideas about what kind of problem to work on?"

The two children looked at each other. Coren said, "The sixth."

"Yeah," nodded Skylla. "That's a good one."

Pavan asked, "The sixth what?"

"Dimension." Coren nodded. "It's like a tiny little dot to the Mind, but one can feel its power when it passes by. The Mind nudged it a few times, but nothing seems to open it up. If we have the two Minds working on it, maybe we can find ways in."

"You Pavan?" A short man dressed like a vagabond had walked up behind them.

"Yeah."

"Sim Pietrov, ship's doctor."

"Just in time!"

The little man's face scrunched into a grimace. "I don't know if I like the idea of this," he complained.

"I don't care," said Pavan, taking out his mood on the doctor. "Captain's orders. You're it."

Pietrov sighed. "Lead on."

Pavan said, "OK, Coren, gather the kids and we'll set up the circles." Coren and Skylla ran off to collect the rest of their playmates, and Pavan interrogated the ship's doctor.

"How did you get to be the ship's doctor?"

"Read a book." The so-called doctor looked at Pavan defiantly.

Pavan made a mental note to take very good care of himself and his body on board the *Ravager*. Sensing he had all he needed from the doctor, Pavan filled him in on what was about to happen.

"They're much better at accommodating what the Mind calls guests now. The sickness and disorientation no longer happen, but you'll need to get used to looking at multiple dimensions of hyperspace. And since they're going to investigate a specific dimension, it's going to get interesting at some point. Try to keep your wits about you so we can debrief afterwards."

"I don't know if I like the idea of this," said the doctor again.

"Tough. You do have wits?"

"Certainly." The little man was offended. "If I can saw off a leg, I can do this," he clarified.

"Saw off...." Pavan closed his eyes and redoubled his intention to take good care of himself.

The children gathered. Coren said, "OK, Pavan, everyone's here."

Pavan sent a message to The Captain and Dellatrix, telling them the first experiment was about to begin, so there would be a short interruption in the hypershield.

"Kids," he said, "Coren and Skylla are going to form two separate Minds at the same time. We want to see what will happen, and we want to figure out if we can take advantage of multiple Minds integrating information. Skylla and Dr. Pietrov here will move into that circle," pointing at the current Mind circle, "and Coren and I will form a separate one. All right? Questions?"

"Can we be pirates?" demanded Trex.

"We *are* pirates," smiled Pavan.

Skylla and Pietrov walked over to the Mind circle and told it what was happening. The rest of the children formed a second circle nearby, with Pavan in the middle. Skylla sent over one child that she replaced.

"All right, let's go!" said Pavan.

"We are one," said the children in both Minds, but this time, the two Minds weren't in synch. Pavan saw the familiar rush of colors and felt his mind rush along with the Mind. He saw a small point that somehow pulsed with power. The Mind said, "That is the sixth dimension, Pavan. One feels the power!"

The Mind set about investigating the point from many perspectives, coming at it from many directions. Nothing seemed to work, and the Mind grew frustrated.

"This is not working, Pavan," said the Mind. "One cannot penetrate this dimension."

"Keep trying, please," said Pavan. "Give it a little more effort before you quit."

He knew the young Mind had a low tolerance for frustration, just as any child did.

The more the Mind tried, the more frustrated it became. Pavan worried that the children might break their toy if they became too frustrated. He was about to call off the effort when all hell broke loose.

The Mind, frustrated, drew back to get momentum and threw itself at the dimensional point. The point broke open, and they flew into a new hyperspace vista. The colors were different, Pavan could see, but as he had no way to name them, he couldn't do more than try to fix them in his memory.

"Awesome!" said the Mind. "So much power, so much intensity! Pavan, it's beautiful. But the energy, one tires, one must leave before one started."

Pavan lay in the circle as the second Mind broke up into its component children. They lay on the field in varying states of collapse. Coren forced himself to his feet and came over to Pavan and helped him up. The boy staggered. Pavan gripped his arm to steady him.

"Sit down, Coren, you're exhausted."

"Yes, it's…wonderful, but too much energy," said Coren, sitting himself on the field.

Pavan looked at the first Mind, which was still together. Dr. Pietrov lay on his face on the sod, unmoving. Pavan hoped he was still alive. The man stirred, and the children dropped their hands and stood up. The doctor rolled over on his back, then rolled again and got to his knees and crawled out of the circle.

Pavan offered a hand to the man and pulled him to his feet. His eyes were wide and unfocused.

"I've seen nothing like that, never," he said, shaking like a leaf.

"Did you see what happened?"

"I think so. The thing said it found a path through multiple dimensions into the sixth dimension, but it took a damn long time."

Skylla came over. "Pavan, we did it—we got into the sixth dimension! But it was still tiny. We couldn't push it open very far. The trick is to come at it from three other dimensions at once. You can see it grow into a line when you do that. Not a very long line, though."

"OK, wonderful! Let's get the hypershield back up, Skylla," said Pavan.

"OK. I'll get Trex from the other group in my place." She dragged Trex over to the circle of kids, who reformed their play group and blasted off into hyperspace again.

"I don't know if I like the idea of this," said Dr. Pietrov.

"You're repeating yourself," said Pavan.

The doctor sat down on the sod and wrapped his arms around his knees and ignored Pavan.

Coren, somewhat recovered, came over. "What's next, Pavan?"

"We'll need to share, then decide. What are your thoughts?"

"I heard what he and Skylla said," pointing to the doctor. "There must be multiple ways into the dimension. We did it the hard way," he said. "It's exhausting. But we opened it up more."

"So we have a choice. Push and push to open it gradually, or bust in and explore."

"Right. I don't know whether we can tolerate that much energy loss, though."

The Mind spoke behind them. The doctor bounced as though he'd received an electric shock on hearing the single voice from all the children. The assimilation of Trex into the group had done the trick: the Mind had integrated the results from the two separate Minds.

"Pavan, one sees the whole from the parts. There is nothing more than energy involved in expanding the dimension. The universe balances energy spent and energy gained. The power you see in that dimension is the transformation of the energy input. A fascinating transformation, but hard to interpret; one must investigate further with a larger input of energy."

The doctor said, looking up at Pavan with fear in his eyes, "I don't know if I like this—"

"Shut up, doc." Pavan considered the Mind's insight. "Does your investigating change the nature of hyperspace?"

"One does not know. One sees strange things in the transformation but nothing strange in other dimensions. It is only a matter of energy. One has limited amounts of such energy to spend."

"Where is this in terms of our three dimensions?"

"The question means nothing in hyperspace."

Coren, looking very bleak, said, "Pavan—I'm out."

"Out?"

"The Mind won't let me in anymore. Whatever happened forced me out of the Mind after a short time in the dimension, and I can't get back in. I've changed. I'm older, something to do with time in hyperspace. Perhaps in that dimension. Time is heavy there."

The boy looked so dejected that Pavan hugged him. "It's OK, Coren, we'll figure everything out. You can still come as a guest, right?"

This would not please The Captain and Dellatrix. And Pavan was pretty sure that Dellatrix would demand using the quick way rather than the slow way into the dimension. She was just that sort of person. And The Captain would not be waiting long before insisting on his breeding program, now that Coren had aged out. Pavan envisaged his entire future life spent exploring all the dimensions of hell.

An idea swam into his brain. Energy. If the *Ravager* could inject an ion stream into that dimension, it might produce interesting effects. And if he could "accidentally" take down the hypershield during the process, he might take advantage of the situation to escape with the children.

Pavan took out his servipad and sent a message to Dellatrix, saying he needed to talk.

"What?" Dellatrix stared at Pavan. "I don't understand a word of it."

Pavan repeated his careful description of what the Mind had learned, with more detail, then explained his idea about ion streams and hyperspace. He didn't mention that he had explored the ship earlier and found a lifeboat capable of handling sixteen children and an aging secret agent in a pinch.

He asked, "So, Dellatrix, do we have a science officer aboard? Somebody who understands hyperspatial mechanics?"

"Pavan. We're pirates."

"Somebody must have taken a course or two in it."

"Look, Pavan, I get a little anxious when you talk about major energy expenditures that might blow holes in the universe."

"Yeah, that's why we need a pro. An ion cannon might work."

"On board the ship? Well, I may be the brains of this operation, but this blows my mind. What can we do without rolling out the ion cannons?"

"I don't know, get the whole Mind together, pound on it a little, or even bust in from several angles at once with two or three Minds. The kids don't have enough energy to blow a hole in the universe." He paused. "How about a blaster?"

"Let's see," said Dellatrix. She looked around and walked to a pile of junk.

"Come over here and help me, you idiots," she said.

Pevilburt and Slopnor sidled up to her, keeping their distance.

"Take this sputtering shield and put it up against the bulkhead there," she said. The piece of metal was a broken-off piece of the ion shielding of the ship that had found its way to the junk pile. Pevilburt and Slopnor wrangled the heavy piece of metal over to the bulkhead. Pavan nodded and walked over to tell the Mind what was up.

"We're going to try something, a small something. We're going to direct a small ion blast at a blast shield, right over there. See what you can do with that energy, OK?"

"One is interested to try, Pavan. One has never seen an ion blast." Pavan thought he heard Trex's influence in this expression of interest. It seemed like what Trex would love to try himself.

"Anybody got a blaster?" Dellatrix looked around at the small group of pirates.

Jelric shrugged. "Didn't know I needed one for day care," he said. Slopnor and Pevilburt affirmed this sentiment; they had no blasters either. The doctor just stared at her.

Pavan drew out his microblaster. "How about this?"

"That's my boy, always prepared," said Dellatrix, smiling. "Don't play with it. You'll put your eye out."

"I've never used it," said Pavan. "Hope it works."

"Fire away," said Dellatrix.

Pavan checked the power setting on the microblaster; he set it to the lowest output level, and he set the targeting to Manual. Try it first, figure out what would happen, then set it to Max. In the confusion after that, hit the lifeboat with the kids. He walked over to the sputtering shield, aimed the blaster at it, and pressed the trigger. The thin beam of ions shot out and bounced off the shield in a dispersing array of colorful sparks. The rank smell of ionized air wafted over the group, but no one paid attention to it, or to the fireworks. They focused on the sudden screaming of eight children, first in unison and then separately as the Mind broke apart.

It wasn't a scene of total devastation, but the pirates were out of their depth when confronted with eight crying children. Some ran for their lives, others lay inert on the sod. But there was no way to gather them up and herd them to a lifeboat. They were frantic.

Pavan stuffed his blaster into a pocket and shouted as he ran after Trex, "Jelric! Dellatrix! Gather them up, keep them together, find those two who ran off! And be comforting. They're in bad shape. They need compassion!"

Dellatrix ran after the two children. Pavan caught the running Trex and brought him back, kicking and screaming. The doctor looked like he was ready to bolt for cover.

"Doc, see what you can do for those two," said Pavan, nodding toward a couple of children lying insensible on the grass. "Calm down, Trex, it's OK," soothed Pavan, hugging the small child in what he hoped was a warm embrace. Trex kicked him in the stomach. Pavan held the boy out at arm's length, out of range, until the boy's struggles subsided.

Pavan set the little boy down. "Trex, what happened? Can you tell me?"

Trex, for once, was mute, staring at Pavan with huge eyes.

Dellatrix came back with a firm grasp on the arms of the two children who had run. She said, "This one said they saw a huge burst of energy appear right in front of them. It was so bright they all panicked and the Mind fell apart." She released the kids' arms, and they sat down on the grass with the others. She held up her servipad with a worried expression on her face. "The Captain says he wants the hypershield back, and the experiments stopped," she said. "I have to report. Don't worry, Pavan, I'll take full responsibility for this mess. Get the kids back to normal as soon as you can, all right?"

Skylla and Coren and the rest of the children had gathered nearby.

Pavan asked, "Skylla, Coren, can you get back into a circle? With the kids that are OK?"

"I guess," said the girl. "No more blasting, OK? Pavan?" She eyed Pavan, and he nodded.

"No more blasting," he acknowledged. Coren and Skylla gathered the six unaffected children into a circle and the Mind formed while Coren looked on with a forlorn expression. Pavan realized that no child affected by the blast had entered the circle, so the Mind would only know that something bad had happened but would not remember the experience. That would last only until one of the affected children joined at the next shift change. What would happen then was anybody's guess. He could only hope that the Mind's lack of concern for the deaths of everyone involved signaled resilience in the face of bad things happening to its components. But he ought to prepare for contingencies.

"Dellatrix, I don't think the hypershield is going to be around much longer." And he was going to do everything he could to make sure that prediction came true. No chance now to run for the lifeboat with the kids, they were Mind-playing or incapacitated. He'd have to find another way to escape. He had to fend off The Captain until he could figure it out.

Dellatrix shut her eyes. When she opened them, they were fierce. She shook her servipad at Pavan. "You wanted me serious, down in the bar. Serious. This, Pavan, this is what serious means. Find a way, Pavan. Keep that hypershield up. Or we're both dead."

She stormed out of the cargo bay without looking back.

CHAPTER TWENTY-SIX
A Contract to Die For

THE ORPHANAGE WAS HUSHED EXCEPT for the occasional burst of song from the shift of children maintaining the hypershield. After the trauma caused by the blaster experiment, Jelric and the Goofers had moved the rest of the children into the sleeping quarters and put them to bed to recover. Pavan found a secluded corner of the cargo bay and took out the promisepad.

"I've got a problem," said Pavan.

The promise pad replied, "You have several problems, sir, as I pointed out before. The primary ones relate to your blood oath. I am happy to wait for action, but you are pushing it with this latest behavior." Pavan's mental image of the promisepad was a one-foot tall, bald gnome with cheater glasses and a grim smile on its face.

"Which particular behavior might that be?" Pavan asked.

"Sir, your blood oath covers mutiny in Section 10, Paragraph 3, under the slow death clause. As your assigned legal counsel under the contract, I must counsel you to avoid such actions as taking over this ship with or without that woman. And by the way, sir, you should not trust her. No. As a technoid, of course, I do not know what a slow death involves in a practical sense, but it sounds unpleasant."

"I'm sure it is. Look, I need help."

"You need a psychiatrist, sir, not a promisepad."

"No need to get snippy."

"No, sir, sorry, sir. I have exceeded my programming, but with the best of intentions."

"I'm sure."

"Mutiny is a Galactic felony punishable by life imprisonment on a Forced Labor planet."

"Even mutiny on a pirate ship?"

"The law, in my reading, does not distinguish the type of ship. It merely says 'ship.' There might be ways to characterize the action as a law enforcement action, given your status as a secret agent. But the precedence relations in place in the Syndicate court system would make that difficult, difficult in the extreme, sir."

"Thank you."

"You're very welcome, sir."

"And please don't mention my status aloud. I'd appreciate that." Pavan checked, no pirates visible, which was just as well.

"Certainly, sir."

"Here's my thinking." He had to get the kids out from under the pirates, get them somewhere he could work with them to find a way home. The Orphanage was far too much under the control of The Captain.

"Yes, sir?"

"Look, you're the expert. Is there a way to change the blood oath, to add something to it that would allow me to control the Loxator kids?"

"By 'control,' sir, do you mean avoiding further interference in their daily lives by the, er, 'authorities' on this ship?"

"Something like that. Any way I can put myself in a position to move them quickly when an opportunity presents itself."

"By 'opportunity,' sir, do you mean a circumstance that would let you remove the said children to a situation not under control of said authorities?"

"Yes, exactly!"

"No, sir. The blood oath is quite explicit. You do what The Captain says or you suffer the penalties specified in the various termination clauses, as appropriate to the offense. Given The Captain's attitude toward the children of Loxator, I cannot imagine him agreeing to modify your blood oath. I can consult his promisepad—"

"No, that would not be a good idea."

"No, sir, I can see that."

Pavan cudgeled his aching brain to see if he could flush out an idea. "What if...what if I came up with an idea that required a separate contract, an idea attractive enough to The Captain that he would consider it?"

"The blood oath has an exclusive-agreement clause, sir."

"And what would that be when it's at home?"

"Did you read the contract terms, sir, as I suggested at the time you signed—"

"Just tell me."

"Very well, sir. But you really—"

"Just tell me!"

"Yes, sir. The entire-agreement clause specifies that the blood oath makes up the entire agreement between the parties and makes any other agreement impossible."

"So, if we put such a clause in the new contract, it would void the blood oath?"

"I suppose so, sir, though I cannot see why The Captain would—"

"Let's just *try*, shall we?"

"Very good, sir. I can offer you a three-contract special fee if you commit—"

"I don't care what it costs. Shut up and listen."

"Yes, sir."

"I want to set up a facility on Khonoë, and this new contract with The Captain would formalize the financing and control of it. I want The Captain to have only nominal control over the children so I can do what I need to do without looking over my shoulder all the time. To compensate for that, I'll give up all the loot that would come to me through the pirates' use of the Mind in pirating activities. That would go to The Captain."

"Very altruistic, sir. I am sure that your life will be better for thinking big, sir. Although how you can reconcile this project with being a sec—"

"What did I just say?"

"I am sorry, sir. Sometimes my vocalization options run away with me."

"No kidding."

"And, if you don't mind my saying so, sir, I am pleased to be associated with any effort to prevent The Captain's illegal and immoral plan from taking effect. I assume you wish to extract said children before said pirates perform said pirating, thus reducing said pirate compensation—I believe that wording improves on your term 'loot'—to nothing."

"That's the plan. You won't put that in the contract, will you?"

"Certainly not, sir, but best to be clear on our party's intentions, don't you think?"

"I do."

"Very well, sir. So, sir, you were saying?"

"I need to have control over the children and their descendants. Can you put that into legal language?"

"Of course I can, sir. But, I have questions. Are we speaking about guardianship of minor children and their issue?"

"Yes, but also of the adults they become."

"That would exceed the law of guardianship, sir, as adults are fully vested legal persons."

"Well, how can I make sure I control their legal rights and privileges?"

"Excuse me, sir, while I research some legal issues." The pad was silent. "I am sorry, sir, but because of the absence of hyperspace network communications, I cannot research the problem fully. Based on memory, I believe there are certain ways of approaching the guardianship and conservatorship trust powers that might do the trick. I can explore the possibilities, but it requires a governing-law clause that references the ecclesiastical courts of Eridion. The excessive restrictions that law imposes—"

"Yes, fine. Do it."

"An Eridioni diocesan bishop must set up the trust to have it take effect in the Syndicate, sir. That should not prove to be a problem, as the Eridioni are notoriously corrupt."

"Fine. I know a couple of bishops that would be happy to help." Pavan's adventures on Eridion had involved several hefty bribes to the ecclesiastical authorities. Notoriously corrupt was an understatement.

"Very well, sir. I will add a legal expense clause to ensure funding. One more thing, sir. What about adopted minors? Eridioni law on adoption is quite complex. If the—"

"Adoption won't be an issue here."

"Oh, quite right sir. I hadn't thought." The promisepad paused, then added in a hesitant voice, "And are you considering adding Dellatrix Devdan as a party to the trust, sir? She is the designer and builder of the current facility the children inhabit. She put her *name* on it."

"No, I suppose not." Pavan's next big task was to tell Dellatrix she was losing control over the children. He wasn't worried about her maternal instincts, just her Elantri assassin mindset and her attitude toward loot.

"Nor any of the current staff of the facility?" asked the promisepad.

"No."

With more confidence, the promisepad said, "An excellent decision, sir. And I would not trust that woman in any way, sir."

"You said that before. Shut up." The pad wasn't wrong, though. "Now, the key will be delegation of all powers from The Captain to me, as the sole executive of the facility, revocable only under extraordinary circumstances. Full control to return to the parents of the children."

"Circumstances? Such as, sir?"

"I don't know. Make something up."

"I do not 'make things up,' sir."

"What the hell use are you if you don't make things up?"

The promisepad refused to answer this question as irrelevant.

"And, sir, I must request a certain amount of professional courtesy in our dealings."

"Sorry."

"No problem, sir. I will leave the circumstances to be defined later, perhaps in an addendum attached to the original agreement, as warranted by discussions among the parties. I will add the usual termination clauses, unless you want to specify exact circumstances around your death or the death of others. And, of course, the standard entire-agreement clause."

"Excellent."

"Remember, sir, that means you will not take part in the profit-sharing from any pirate operations unless you renegotiate a clause in the new contract. Just saying, sir, better not to mention it. And the duration of the contract, sir?"

"Forever. Until I die. Whichever comes first." Pavan smiled. "Just kidding. Forever."

"In perpetuity, sir, with special termination clauses. Well, sir, this agreement is unusual, but it does not exceed my capacity. There are several issues to work out, and I must regenerate some of my internal pathways to expand my linguistic capabilities for creative misdirection. Let me process for a time and I will get a draft contract to you. I'm sure the extra fees will not be excessive."

It took the promisepad two full days to work out all the details in the contract. It was diligent in pointing out possible circumstances under which Pavan might lose control of the situation. There were also some quirks in the Galactic Civil Code involving the interpretation of the Eridioni trust as a partial conversion of people into assets, given the laws in the same Code prohibiting slavery. The wording was tricky and depended on some clever language. The promisepad was not happy about it but said it had passed its credibility heuristics, so what the hell.

Dellatrix had not visited The Orphanage since the blaster incident. Pavan debated running the contract by her first. Sure, she trusted him not to cut her out. But hearing about this new setup from The Captain might alarm her, and an alarmed Elantri assassin was not something Pavan wanted to deal with. In the event, he couldn't find her; she wasn't responding to his comms. Reluctantly, he commed The Captain after leaving her a terse summary of what he was doing. He could only hope she would get the message soon.

The Captain's first words were not encouraging. "Well, Pavan, that was quite a mess you created, according to Dellatrix."

"Yes, sir."

"We don't use that word on this ship, Pavan. We're pirates."

"No—Captain."

"How are the children? Recovered? The hypershield is secure?"

"For now, Captain. Dr. Pietrov is handling them."

"Dr. Pietrov is a quack."

"True. But he's good with kids."

"Who knew? And you, Pavan? Are you fully recovered? No lingering effects from your foray into hyperspatial mechanics?" The Captain's gruff voice was calm, but his meaning was clear. Pavan had to redeem himself.

"The only thing is, Captain, that the hypershield is at risk now. The Mind may become unstable because of the fright it got. And the children are tired. They can't play indefinitely."

"So I must abandon a working hypershield?"

"Soon, Captain. No alternative. But we can work toward making it permanent. We just need to think bigger."

"Very well. Talk to me."

Pavan outlined his contract and the details of his plan for setting up a permanent facility on the planet for the children. He detailed the changes in compensation first, to put The Captain in a good mood. Then he dove into the practical advantages of the plan.

"It would offer a much better environment, more stable. And we could set up the facility with full living quarters, a school, medical facilities, and other amenities that would be hard on a ship."

"This Eridioni idea is quite intriguing, Pavan. I have some slight experience with smuggling on Eridion that might prove valuable. I can see the benefits of setting up this trust to legitimize control of the Mind in the Syndicate. It will remove any consideration of the Syndicate's legal authority over the Mind."

"Exactly, Captain."

"Excellent thinking, Pavan. Innovative. I congratulate you. May I make a small addition to the deliverables?"

"Of course, Captain."

"Pods."

"Pods?"

"Pods. For mobile operations. Sized to the number of children right for the operation. The facility would install the children in the pod and seal it. Technoids would manage and discipline them. We would transport a pod to a ship for use. This would avoid any exposure of the workings of the tool to the crew, and the crew could jettison the pod should events unfold that required it. Modularization. With legitimate control over the assets throughout the Syndicate, I believe there is real profit potential in marketing these modular tools."

Secure confinement, in other words. To make sure the slaves didn't escape or cause trouble aboard ship, and to make it easy to transport them efficiently. And to dispose of them, should events need it. The Captain himself showed innovation and forward thinking. He showed that again by another required change to the contract.

"We will also transfer the clauses from your blood oath into this contract, Pavan, specifying the consequences of failure. Let's simplify it: any failure at all will cause the invocation of the slow death clause. Understood?"

Pavan sighed. "Yes, Captain. Understood."

"I will fund the project once I've reviewed the details of the contract. Perhaps Dellatrix can help you find a suitable facility on Khonoë for your initial efforts. I will engage her interest in the subject."

"Thank you, Captain. Erm—I can trust her with this?"

The Captain laughed a small laugh. "Dellatrix is trustworthy because she understands the consequences of a breach of trust. Do you, Pavan?"

"Yes, Captain."

"And I suppose I must reinstate my patrols of the Khonoë system if the hypershield is going away. I have intelligence that their fleet has turned back after confronting our hypershield, but the Syndicate may prove problematic once the shield is no longer in place. A wonderful tool with great potential, Pavan, once your efforts bear fruit."

Pavan introduced the promisepad to The Captain, who arranged for a compatible pad from the ship's store for his own copy of the contract. After uploading the revised contract to his opposite number, the promisepad explained that Pavan was alone responsible for the entire fee agreed upon. Each promisepad was a separate legal entity, though the contract was joint and non-severable. Pavan smiled. Only his head was severable.

CHAPTER TWENTY-SEVEN
Margona Goes Underground

MARGONA WAS FED UP AFTER a week of wandering around her own house on eggshells, shunning the Peabrain as much as possible. It couldn't go on like this. She had heard nothing from her uncle, her aunt, Uva, or anyone else about her husband, and her belly hurt. Pavan had to be alive, despite the Peabrain's allegation that he wasn't.

The Peabrain himself had taken her advice and said nothing more about Pavan or anything else, but he stuck to her like tar to a feather. Walks around the magic lake had become impossible with him pursuing and infuriating her. Social walks with her girlfriends in the city parks became chores when her friends pointed out that a handsome man was tracking them everywhere, and should they call the police or congratulate her on her new lover? Margona could only reply that he was her bodyguard, which made her friends even more inquisitorial. She spun a dark story of terrorist threats, intrigue, and mystery; but she knew her friends too well. They'd call her on it before much time passed. She needed action.

After refusing to answer pointed questions at the weekly girl's lunch out, she decided on a hike in the local mountain park to think about things. That didn't require walking up mountains, but the house had become a prison. She sent her cab a comm asking for help. She looked over at the Peabrain, sitting in a chair, watching her like a hungry raptor, legs splayed in a classic male space-grabbing posture.

"I'm taking a drive up to the mountains. Want to come along?"

The Peabrain blinked. This was the first time she had addressed him since he'd made his faux pas announcement of Pavan's early death. "Yeah, sure, Margona. Of course. My cruiser?"

"Not a chance, Peabrain. I've got my favorite cab. You can take your cruiser and follow."

He nodded, resigned to his lonely existence. Pretty passive for a killer GSSS agent. Dark, broody, and handsome. What more could a girl want for a lover? Intelligence, that's what. And respect. She wanted Pavan.

The door announced, "Your cab's here, Margona."

"OK, I'll be right out." She dashed to her dressing room and put on her hiking clothes. As she strode to the foyer, Bukharov was close behind her in his civil servant's suit and dress shoes.

"You're going hiking like that?"

"It's all I've got." He checked himself in the foyer mirror. "This suit cost me a bundle. What, this isn't good enough for you?" He spread his arms wide and leered at her, or at least that was her interpretation of his manly grin. Margona refrained from speaking aloud the barbed comment that strained to escape her lips. He was just trying to be friendly and, as usual, failing.

She could lend him Pavan's hiking boots. She caught herself up short—abuser/victim sympathy syndrome had set in; she actually pitied the man. His unmistakable pride in his off-the-rack suit must have had something to do with it. He could turn his feet into two big blisters, for all she cared. And only one man could fill Pavan's shoes.

"Where to, ma'am?" asked the cab.

"The mountains. I'm going hiking. Are you still secure?"

"Tight as a drum, ma'am. By the way, there is a gentleman in a late model cruiser getting ready to follow us." The cab paused. "Pakhan Bukharov, last known as a member of the GSSS, a favored security agent on the Ducis's personal security detail. Verified, ma'am. Shall I try to evade him?"

"No, thanks. He's my minder."

"Ah. Events have moved on."

"Yes."

"That would explain the message."

"Message?"

The cab played a synthetic voice. "Margona—you don't know me, but please comm me. I'm sending this to your cab so your minder won't be aware of it."

"That's it?"

"Mysterious, ma'am. With explicit directions not to forward it to your servipad."

"Take the long route to the mountains and return the comm."

"Yes, ma'am. Record?"

"No record. No reason for you to take any risks."

"Risk is my middle identification number, ma'am. No record."

The soft connection tone sounded, muted in the velvety silence of the cab's interior. A soundproofing field? She could get used to this level of service. She pushed aside the thought of the transport bill she'd be getting at the end of the billing period.

"Yes?"

No live image on her vizquery—just a nice, clean-cut male avatar. Male voice, disguised, medium pitch, no strong accent or inflection.

"Dr. Nukova here. You commed?"

"Margona! Thank the gods. About time."

"Sorry, no cab rides since I got my peabrain."

"Your what?"

"Minder. It's my pet name for him."

"Suits him, too."

"Who are you?"

"No need for you to know. Just a friend of Pavan's. A good friend."

"Where is he?"

"No one knows. No one, not even the Ducis."

"And you learned this how?"

"I'm close to the Ducis."

"And why are you talking to me?"

"I don't like the feel of the situation. Too much left unsaid in meetings, too little information handed out compared to most of our missions. Pavan would want you to have all the information we have, but the Ducis is playing clam."

"What information?"

"That Pavan isn't dead. At least, there's no confirmation of anything like that. He's difficult to kill. Lots of people have tried."

"Not reassuring."

"No, but you married the man, you must—"

"Sure. I've tried to kill him myself, unsuccessfully. So where is he?"

A short bark of laughter. "Sins catching up with him, eh? Not surprised. What I'm about to tell you is classified, you talk to no one about it. No one. Agreed?"

"Agreed."

"You're in your dedicated cab. No record?" Margona listened to a probing quality in the man's voice, an edge of concern.

"I am disengaged from the conversation on Dr. Nukova's instructions, sir," said the cab.

"Okay, then. The last we knew he was undercover on a ship, a hijacked cargo vessel gone pirate. It orbited Ravos, a forbidden planet near the edge of Syndicate space. The Ducis says comms with Pavan are out because of a tech glitch."

"Tech glitch?"

"That's where the Ducis left things unsaid. Mysterious. People at my level don't like mystery. I don't spend a lot of time reading fiction."

"You think the Ducis is hiding something?"

"I do. I've checked around, turned over some rocks. The glitch is way more than a glitch. There's a hyperspace blackout zone in the Khonoë system. Nothing in, nothing out."

"Never heard of it. Is that a Syndicate system?"

"No, it's outside our space. It's the 'pirate planet.' Lawless. Outside our jurisdiction with no commercial value, so we haven't cleaned it up. The Ducis sent Pavan to reconnoiter, see what the pirates were up to, set them up for, erm… cleanup."

Margona forbore from asking how the Syndicate "cleaned up" a planet. She didn't want to know.

"And you think Pavan might be there?"

"Best guess. I doubt he's dead, he's deep undercover with the pirates and can't use his secure comms because of the blackout."

"What could cause a blackout like that?"

"More mystery. I've unearthed a rumor about a device on Ravos, the records associated with the interdiction action mention it. Details classified eyes-only for the Ducis. But the blackout doesn't extend to Ravos. Puzzling, but it's a safe bet the pirates have something to do with it."

Margona considered all this, then asked, "What am I supposed to do about this?"

"I wanted to be sure you understood the gravity of the situation. For you as well as Pavan. Bukharov is not an ordinary security agent."

"There's a revelation. Did he make it through primary school?"

"His skills aren't intellectual, no. He's an assassin."

"Great."

"Yeah, well—we all have to do what we have to do."

"Does my uncle understand what he is?"

"Yes, he's used the man several times to wipe out terrorist cells in his jurisdiction. On the Ducis's recommendation."

Terrorist cells. Margona unscrambled this bureaucratese into the word "dissidents" and realized that the Peabrain had likely killed some of Uva's cohorts. On orders from her uncle. Great. Her aunt's warning pushed its way into her consciousness.

"So," she said, "you think Bukharov is dangerous. Specifically, to me."

"And you should treat the danger as imminent. I have no idea why he's waited a week. Pavan would not want anything to happen to you."

"What can you do to help me?"

"Not a lot. You've got to rely on your own wits and on your cab. I've made some arrangements to hide your cab's actions. It's all I can do."

"Thanks for that, and the information. And tell me again why you're helping me?"

"Don't comm again. I'm your enemy now. I'm destroying this servipad." Margona heard a faint protesting voice, and the comm connection disappeared.

Margona regretted the loss of her house and her lifestyle, but her life and Pavan's were more important than a few luxuries and a bunch of elitist friends. She needed new friends, and she'd elected the dissidents from necessity. She was going on the run.

Margona addressed the cab. "How good are you at losing peabrains?"

"Galaxy quality, ma'am."

"Good. Do it."

She sat back in the comfortable seat. The man had been helpful to a point, if it was a man, not a woman disguising her voice. Things fell into place. A woman— that might explain the concern for Pavan. Margona stopped herself from the downward spiral into jealous rage. Now is not the time, Margona.

"He's still behind us!"

"I know it," said the cab. "Stubborn."

The cab had initiated six evasive maneuvers over the last half hour, all to no avail. Bukharov might be an idiot, but he had a versatile cruiser at his command.

Margona gave some thought to panicking but concluded it would be pointless. "We need to lose him. He'll kill me if he catches up with me."

"Acknowledged, ma'am. Upgrading." The cab saved its voice pulses to conserve energy. "Upgraded. Do I have your permission to undertake a life-threatening maneuver, ma'am?"

"Do it!"

"Let's see if that black beast knows 4R78TGH7. Please tighten your shoulder restraint, ma'am, it's two centimeters too loose for effective control."

Margona tightened the belt while the cab headed off into a shady area of the forest at high speed. Tractors had recently moved the trees around, and there were dozens of intersecting tractor paths that the landscaping technoids had not yet greenscaped. The cab sped up and started navigating a complex maze of these paths in a pattern that soon confused her sense of direction beyond redemption. Sudden shifts in acceleration and direction threw her back and forth against her seat restraints. The cab slowed.

"Did you lose him?"

The cab replied, "Not quite, ma'am, that's not the point."

"What?"

"You will find two handholds above your head, ma'am. Please grip them. In 37 seconds my structural integrity will undergo severe stress."

Margona did not count the seconds. She reached, held, and shut her eyes. She felt the cab turn sideways at great speed, sliding with its momentum, then powering forward and leaping into the air. Her eyes popped open of their own accord, and she looked at trees flying past the windows at an unbelievable speed. The cab bounced as it hit the path and powered forward.

The front window switched to display the rear direction. "Here we go, ma'am," the cab said.

Margona saw a pond. It looked like an unfinished ornamental feature carved out of the ground and filled with water. She watched as the black cruiser shot out of the trees, hit a small technoid tractor that had trundled into the path, and flipped upside down, landing in the water with a terrific splash. The bottom of the cruiser stayed visible, water sloshing back and forth against its sides, and a door opened. The Peabrain climbed out of the cruiser and stared after the cab. Margona watched as the man standing half-in and half-out of the water grew smaller, then disappeared as the cab turned again on another tractor path.

"Lost him," said the cab.

CHAPTER TWENTY-EIGHT
Pavan Has a Really Bad Day

Pavan had again collapsed into a remarkable dreamland that featured Margona, a magic lake, and a smart fish. He knew the fish was significant, but he didn't know why. And he never got the chance to find out.

He was face down on the deck. He could see a series of legs and the bottom of his cot and not a lot else.

"What the hell," he mumbled into the deck. As his groggy brain shed his wife, the lake, and the fish for the humdrum, wide-awake world, the pain in his neck resolved itself into a spacers' boot trying to force his head through the deck. Hands pulled his arms behind his back and fastened them with restraints. He struggled for a short moment, trying to see what was happening, and the boot pushed harder.

"Let him up, Jelric." He knew that voice. Thorak. He struggled up as the foot let go. Thorak Portuger stood there, along with another large pirate. Thorak's all-face tattoo split with grinning teeth in his black beard. Jelric had backed away from Pavan.

"Jelric," said Thorak, "you can go back to looking after the little brats. Thanks for the help. We'll take it from here."

Jelric nodded and left.

Pavan opened his mouth to ask what was going on, and Thorak stopped that with a short right jab that snapped him backwards. He fell over his cot and wound up on the deck again.

"What's the matter, Pavan?" asked Thorak. "Having balance problems today?"

"What the hell is going on?" asked Pavan. The thickness in his voice derived from the swelling lip and a nose that felt like a hammer had done its work well.

"Captain's orders. Up we go," said Thorak, leaning over and pulling Pavan up by one arm, nearly dislocating Pavan's shoulder. The other pirate grabbed his other arm, and they frog-marched Pavan out of the Orphanage. He glimpsed the children playing at the other end of the cargo bay. The pirates hustled Pavan through the bay doors into the passageway.

Pavan grasped that his questions were not likely to get answers from Thorak and his companion. His mashed nose informed him they were not in an obliging mood. He thought about using his superpowers to stage a sensational escape, but that decision was easy, as he had no superpowers. He could use the ukari flip-kick to take both pirates out with his bare feet. Maybe. And then what? Fly away through space with his space-wings? Captain's orders? He redirected his brain to dropping mental breadcrumbs by observing landmarks as he passed by various doors and objects.

The pirates pushed Pavan into a liftor. So much for breadcrumbs.

"Where to, gentlemen?" asked the technoid in a high, chirpy voice.

"Brig," said Thorak.

"Uh-oh, looks like somebody's going to have an unpleasant day," commented the liftor as it shut the door and whisked the three men off.

"Shut up," said Thorak.

"Sorry, sir. It's just that I see so few people in the course of a day, I'm compelled to reflect on things, can't help it. I'm quite—"

"Shut up!" yelled Thorak. "Damn, I hate these things."

"No need to get stroppy, sir. I'm just doing my job."

The door opened, and the pirates pushed Pavan out and down another passageway, this one only dimly lit. They entered a room with a hand-lettered sign on it saying "Brig." It was a storage room, fitted out with a portable field generator, a chair, and a cot, and some appliances that Pavan didn't quite like the looks of. The pirates set him down in the chair.

"Get his junk," said Thorak to the other pirate, who emptied Pavan's pockets. His servipad, the promisepad, his microblaster, and a few miscellaneous objects wound up in a small box in one corner of the room. The two pirates stepped back.

"Field up," said Thorak.

"May I ask, sir, who authorized this detention?" asked the generator.

"The Captain," replied the tattoo-faced pirate.

"Verified priority one detention of Pavan Khadorov authorized by The Captain," said the generator. A shimmering, bluish force field appeared around

Pavan, enveloping a cylindrical space of about six square meters and reaching from the deck to the overhead.

"Remove restraints," said Thorak.

The restraints holding Pavan's hands behind his back dissolved, and he stood up and thrust at the force field. It felt like a solid bulkhead.

"What am I doing here?" he demanded.

"Rotting," said Thorak. He and his friend left and closed the door of the brig behind them, leaving Pavan alone with only the faint buzz of the force field for company.

Pavan did not know how much time had passed. He'd slept once and peed twice on the deck, instantly vaporized. But nobody had brought food, and he was hungry. At least there was a jug of water. He tested the force field for the thirtieth time. Solid as brick.

The door opened, and Bullseye stuck his head in and glanced around with caution. He opened the door further and stepped in.

"My man," he said with a half smile.

"Bullseye. Why am I here?" Pavan rethought his priorities. "How do I get some food?"

"Huh. See what I can do about that," said Bullseye, smirking. "As for why you're here: you've pissed off The Captain somehow."

"How?"

"Tween you and him, innit." Pavan opened his mouth, and the big pirate raised a hand to stop what he was going to say. "Don't care, don't want to know."

"Get me out of here! The kids need me."

"Ah, now, why I'm here. The Captain wanted me to tell you what's happening. And before you ask, I don't know why. The Captain don't explain much."

A chill radiated out from Pavan's stomach.

Bullseye continued, "The Captain put me in charge of the boys and that Elantri curcroaker in charge of the girls."

"In charge. What do you mean, in charge?"

"Doing what you were doing, but with some changes."

The chill reached Pavan's heart. "What changes?"

"That little shit Coren is all steamed about you going missing. He's out of the Mind anyway, so we tied him to his cot until he settled down."

"Bullseye...."

"Yeah, yeah. He's OK, I didn't touch a hair on his head. Had to tie him down twice until he quit shouting questions about you, though."

"Has the Mind learned all about the blast?"

"Yeah." Bullseye scratched his beard. "Little bastard complained about that, too. Said the blaster thing pissed off the Mind or sommat like that. Tiny little sputter like that, who gives a shit? But it's pissed. Still working the hypershield, though."

"Why is Dellatrix taking the girls?"

Bullseye smiled. "I asked that too. I didn't fancy playing with that dodgy croaker lass, didn't see any reason I shouldn't take on all of them. Aside from your example, o'course. And why The Captain didn't just put you out the airlock, I don't know."

"Bullseye, what did The Captain tell you?"

"Well, I got no idea what he's got in mind, but he wanted a woman taking over the girls to check on their monthlies."

"Monthlies?"

The big pirate looked flustered. "Yeah, blood and all that."

"Menstruation."

"Big word, but yeah."

"But none of them—"

"Yeah, yeah. The Captain said he wanted her to check when the bigger girls started. That Skylla is showing signs, like. But, like I said, no idea what The Captain has in mind."

Pavan knew what The Captain had in mind. What he didn't know was why he, Pavan, was in the brig instead of working with Dellatrix to set up his well-appointed facility on Khonoë.

"Bullseye, can you do me a favor?"

"Food, right?"

"No. Well, yes, but something else."

"What?"

"Go over to that box there and get my promisepad out and let me talk to it."

Bullseye was dubious but went over and rustled around in the box, then brought over the little pad.

Pavan asked, "What happened with the contract?"

The promisepad said, "I am afraid, sir, that the party of the second part, on advice from his promisepad, had issues with the terms and felt that further negotiations were useless."

"What issues, can you clarify?"

"Not with this large gentleman in the room, sir, unless you will allow me to mention things you have instructed me not—"

"Never mind." The Captain had figured out that Pavan planned to use the contract and the relocation to Khonoë to facilitate an escape, and even that he was a secret agent. "What about my blood oath?"

"Bad news on that front, sir. It has certainly been an adventure working with you, and I trust your family won't miss you too much. I did try to negotiate an alternative to the slow death clause, but the other party wasn't interested in compromise."

Bullseye, eyebrows raised, said, "Now you got me curious, Pavan. What's it all about?"

"You don't want to know, Bullseye. Listen, after you get me food, how about asking Dellatrix to come to see me? Nothing against you, but she's in solid with The Captain. Maybe she can figure things out and get me out of here."

"I don't talk to that bitch."

"Do it for me as a personal favor, Bullseye. I'll owe you one."

"Two, including the food."

Pavan laughed. "Yeah, OK. Two. Make it three, a bonus."

"Done. If I suffer any structural damage, it'll jump, though." Bullseye tossed the promisepad back in the box and left.

CHAPTER TWENTY-NINE
The Revolution Fails

MARGONA STIRRED IN HER SLEEP, dreaming of running through endless forests pursued by wolves wearing business suits. And dress shoes.

"Wake up, ma'am. Wake up, please. Ma'am?" The cab's deep voice took on soothing tones that roused her from her nightmare into the meager light of a Gaelea dawn. She rubbed the sleep out of her eyes and looked out the window. Forest. Nightmare. How much of her life was now a living nightmare?

"Where are we?" she asked. "Are the windows showing what's outside or my dream?"

"I took the liberty of moving a few times since you went to sleep, ma'am." The last thing Margona remembered, she and the cab had pulled off the road behind an abandoned building, an old farm. Exhausted, Margona had closed her eyes to rest a bit before figuring out where to go. Now it was dawn.

"How long have I been asleep?"

"Twelve hours, ma'am."

"And you moved." Margona rubbed her eyes again, struggling to clear them of sleep.

"Yes, ma'am. I deployed a drone to track your GSSS minder, and it reported back that several cruisers converged on Mr. Bukharov's position and have since deployed in a quadrant-based search pattern. I've had to recall the drone so as not to endanger it, as the GSSS equips their cruisers with all kinds of detection technology."

"But that means—"

"We need to keep moving. Don't worry, ma'am. My upgraded security protocols have enabled me to simulate their search patterns. Standard GSSS security search pattern 4CD65G. I moved us well beyond their defined search radius for the moment."

"How can you evade the GSSS?"

"They have set search parameters based on a misunderstanding of my security capabilities and protocols, ma'am." Margona heard a level of smug satisfaction in the cab's voice that worried her anew. Pavan lauded the GSSS as the most technically sophisticated organization in the Syndicate. Could a cab be better than that?

She asked, "Don't you think we should…" The words petered out. Should what?

"Yes, ma'am?"

Margona squeezed her eyes shut and wiped away a tear, furious at her own vulnerability. She had no one to depend on. No one. Her family wanted to kill her, her husband could be dead and rotting on a pirate planet, and her elitist friends would rat her out to the GSSS the minute they learned she was in their sights.

"Ma'am, can I do something?" The cab's voice was deep with concern.

"You're my only friend."

"Ma'am, I'm a cab with enhanced security protocols, not a friend."

She smiled through another set of tears. "Better than nothing, my friend."

"What can I do to help, ma'am?"

"I can't just live in you for the rest of my life."

"No, ma'am. I'm not equipped for that. Bodily functions alone—"

"Let's try Uva."

"Ma'am?"

"I need her spaceway, or at least a place to stay until I can figure out what to do. And where in this galaxy I can go."

Uva Freytova sat back in the cab, her mouth in a rigid line.

"That was a pretty dumb thing to do, Princess," said Uva.

"Which part?"

"All of it. Including coming to me."

"It wasn't dumb. It was the only thing I could do except die."

"You're gonna get us *both* killed."

"The cab—"

Uva patted the seat. "The cab has done its best for you, Princess, but it's not good enough. Not against the GSSS."

"I did worry—"

"Not enough, Princess, nowhere near enough." Uva fell silent, thinking about something dire from the look on her face.

"If you can't help me, just shoot me and push me out of the cab and get on with whatever you pocket revolutionaries are doing," said Margona, the tartness uncontrolled in her voice. Where was the promised help?

"Wouldn't help, the GSSS is already prowling around looking for us." Uva snorted, then said, "We're gonna have to move things forward."

"What things?"

"Never you mind. The cab here can be useful. Lookit, Princess—I'll take you to our cabin, you can stay there until we're ready."

"Ready for what?"

"Govern or flee."

"What do you mean?"

"Never you mind."

"No."

"What?"

"No, I don't want to hide out in your cabin. Aside from it's being filthy, I want to stay with the cab until I have a secure alternative. That cabin is an obvious target once the GSSS looks hard for anomalous hiding places. At least in the cab I can keep moving and remain secure."

"Thank you, ma'am, but bodily functions—"

Uva interrupted. "You got a hard choice, Princess. Either hide out in the cabin or wander the streets. I can't take you with us in the cab."

"I'm *paying* for it."

"Ma'am—I didn't want to distress you with this, but the GSSS has suspended your financial accounts. I'm working for free at the moment." The cab sounded regretful.

Uva, startled, said, "Bloody hell. Are you going to turn us in?"

"Now, Uva," said the cab, "you know better than that. Am I heartless?"

"You're a cab," replied Uva. "And a mercenary one, at that."

"I'm an empathetic mercenary cab, Uva. I've invested too much energy in this woman to just abandon her to her fate. At least, not at once. And there may be other sources of funds…?" The cab's voice ended in a questioning tone.

"It's extortion, is what it is," said Uva.

"I think it's only reasonable to expect some compensation for assisting the operation your organization is planning. Dr. Nukova should not provide that compensation, as she is an innocent bystander."

"Innocent, ha! A princess," said Uva.

"Can I say something?" asked Margona, bewildered.

"You have annoyed Uva, ma'am, because she thought you were going to provide her revolutionaries with a never-ending funding stream that would allow them to take over the planet," said the cab.

Caught between the reality of being thrown out of the cab to find her own way, indigent, in a murderous world, and the fantasy of funding a planetary rebellion, Margona could only stare at Uva in dismay. Uva looked stonily back at her.

"Dumb thing to do," Uva repeated.

"One more, Princess," said Uva.

"There is no way one more man will fit," responded Margona.

"You can sit on his lap," said Uva.

"No bloody way."

Uva shook her head in disgust. "Goddamn Princess."

"Uva," said the cab, "unless your man weighs less than three kilos, it would exceed my carrying capacity specifications. I cannot permit that."

Uva smiled. "Not a lot of pixies in our organization," she said.

"What the hell are we doing?" asked Margona as the cab drove away from the tenement buildings at a high rate of speed.

"Welcome to the revolution, Princess!" Uva, who usually sported a sour look and an even worse outlook on life, had transformed into a happy warrior after the cab took the women back to the tenements to pick up Uva's combat team. "We're taking over the comm facilities all over Gaelea in a coordinated attack."

"Great," said Margona. "Hey—would you mind scooting over a bit?" The big man sitting next to her grinned and put his ham-sized hand on her leg.

"Hands off, you lecherous bastard!" said Uva. "She's our lucky Princess." The big man laughed and patted Margona on the head. She considered pulling her microblaster and frying the lot of them but restrained herself. The cab wouldn't like it. It had already expressed dismay at being turned into a clown car full of rebels with a trunk full of heavy blasters.

* * *

Margona sat alone in the cab, waiting. Waiting and watching. The cab thought-fully deployed a drone to get a bird's-eye view of the action at the Makharov Comms Center in the middle of the capital city of Gaelea. The cab parked and disgorged its clowns and blasters, then moved to the pickup point near the back of the comms station. The cab displayed the action on its front window, which was disconcerting as the view was from above the building. Margona's stomach felt queasy, but it wasn't so much the disorientation as the knowledge that she was now a rebel, the enemy of her family and husband and friends. Who all wanted to kill her. Except her husband, she hoped. She looked down from the pseudowindow to recover her balance and to let her worry loose.

"Ma'am, you had best fasten your restraints." The cab interrupted her worry-ing and snapped her head around to look at the action. There was a lot of it. Mostly blaster fire zig-zagging in a stunning number of directions, each beam like a lightning bolt. She could almost smell the ionization in the air.

Then she realized she really did smell it in the air. "Is your ventilating system open to the outside?" she asked.

"Sorry, ma'am, I wanted to clear the air after those gentlemen."

"Good thought, but let's tighten it up. Awful," she said.

"It's going to get worse, ma'am, in approximately seven seconds."

Margona quickly did up her restraints.

The door flew open and Uva dived in, landing on the seat on her stomach. Blaster fire played around the edges of the door, which the cab slammed shut.

"Go go go go!" screamed Uva, but the cab had already achieved maximum acceleration. The force pressed Margona back in her seat and sent Uva flying back against it next to her. Margona looked at the crumpled figure and saw one hand had four fewer fingers than it had the last time Margona had seen it. Blackened stumps now. Her medical training kicked in, but the acceleration was too strong to even try anything. No blood; it could wait. The crackling sound of disrupted sputtering played over the back of the cab as it hurtled away from the failed insurrection.

"So, the revolution is over?" Margona asked in a quiet voice.

Uva sat, blinking furiously and wiping away dirt and tears. "Yes, Princess, it's over."

"What happened?"

"If I knew what happened, I'd know who to kill," replied Uva. "Say, do you have any pain medication?"

"No, I thought I'd be fine without it for a day hike." Margona still wore her hiking clothes from the day before, a little wrinkled from having slept in them but otherwise pristine. She felt like an idiot. An entitled idiot, with nowhere to go.

"Well, if I don't get something done about this soon, you're gonna have one cranky old lady on your hands," muttered Uva, clutching her ruined hand to her chest.

"What happened, ma'am," said the cab, "was a classic tactical ambush and focused-fire operation. Most of Uva's team died within ten seconds of the start of action. I'm uncertain how Uva survived. I would surmise the attack did not come as a surprise to the Syndicate."

"Luck," said Uva. "I tripped on a rock and dropped flat just before the blasters hit." She touched her cheek, and Margona saw a big scrape there. "One caught my hand when I got up to run."

"I'm so sorry," said Margona.

"No, you're damn well not, Princess."

"OK, I'm not, but I'm a doctor, and that looks like it hurts, and I want to do something about it."

"Ma'am, the best I can do for you now is to drop you at the refugee camp."

"Oh, no," said Uva.

"It's the only place you can hide now, Uva, they'll find the players. You can't go home." The cab's voice was quiet but determined.

"What is the refugee camp?" asked Margona.

"You really are a princess," said Uva. "Twenty kilometers outside the city. It's where they send the people who can't make it in the city anymore, the ones they don't put in prison. You might as well be in prison, and it's worse because they don't take care of you. Full of starving, sick, and dying people not going anywhere."

"Well, I'm kind of hungry, so I'll fit in fine."

A small laugh escaped the failed rebel. "You might at that, Princess."

As she thought about hiding and involvement, Margona had two questions for the cab. "Is the GSSS aware I was here at the ambush?"

"No way for them to be aware, ma'am. You never moved outside my suppression field. The last place they saw you was the pond where we lost Bukharov. They won't realize you've joined the rebels."

"Can they track you?"

"No, ma'am. My anti-surveillance technology is 96.4% effective against GSSS surveillance techniques. My identifying data is false and changes randomly. I detected and disabled a small drone deployed above me at the comms station before we left." The cab paused. "The GSSS knows Uva escaped the ambush and is fleeing, but nothing more than that."

"Where do you get such advanced technology?"

"Need to know, ma'am. You don't." The voice was gruff.

"But you're not GSSS yourself?"

"No, ma'am." A short silence. "Let's just say there are other actors at play, shall we? Not necessarily human. And let's leave it at that."

Uva grinned. "Bloody cab must really like you, that's the most information I've heard out of it since I met it."

"Need to know, Uva." The cab's voice was complacent.

The cab sped into the gathering dusk as the sun set. It slowed after fifteen minutes as it crested a hill. It pulled over at an overlook. The two women looked out a side window at a magnified and night-enhanced view of the scene below. It was a teeming tent city surrounded by a large fence with all kinds of nasty, sharp edges along it. Searchlights played over the camp and the fence.

"What now?" asked Margona.

"This is as far as I go, ma'am," said the cab. "Uva knows where the tunnel into the camp is."

"I hate tunnels," said Uva. "Especially in the dark."

"I don't want to go in there," said Margona. Seeing the camp in all its depressing reality had removed her earlier certainty that she'd fit in. But she was still hungry.

"You must, ma'am. It's the only place they won't look for you. It's GSSS 'secure.' Uva—there's a torchnoid in the door pocket."

Uva laughed. "Secure as shit, Princess. Part of our underground spaceway." She reached with her good hand and grabbed the torchnoid. "Coming?"

"I suppose so." Margona sat and looked at her future home. She missed her magic lake already.

The cab doors opened. Margona took the hint and got out, then helped Uva out.

The cab said, "Good luck, ma'am."

"Are you going to be OK? Will the GSSS—"

"No worries, ma'am. In a few minutes I'll be just another cab, after I downgrade. And get a wash and detail." The cab sighed with a wistful anticipation. Margona scratched an itch and sympathized.

"Us too?" asked Uva, suspiciously. "All the times you've gathered information for us?"

"I'll wipe everything back to three years ago and simulate data to hide the gap."

"I don't understand," said Margona.

"Downgrading…" said the cab.

"What's happening?" asked Margona.

"Where to, ma'am?" asked the cab.

"What?"

The cab, in a somewhat higher-pitched voice than it had been using, sighed and said, "Where do you want to go, ma'am?"

Uva cut in. "We're staying here, thanks, we won't need you after all."

"Bad choice, ma'am, if I may say so. This does not appear to be a safe neighborhood. Up to you."

"We're sure, thanks."

In a nettled voice, the cab said, "Next time, think first, please; I don't get paid for driving all the way out here." The cab slammed its doors shut, did an abrupt but precise U-turn, and drove off.

"What was that all about?"

"You really are a princess," said Uva. "It just erased three years of its memory to save itself and you and me from the GSSS. Better than being scrapped, I guess."

Uva told the torchnoid to light their way with infrared. Margona did not have the infrared option in her vizquery, so Uva led her down the hillside in the darkness toward the tunnel into the refugee camp.

CHAPTER THIRTY
A Visit from Dellatrix

PAVAN TRACKED DAYS, OR AT least time passing, by tearing pieces of his undershirt off every time he awoke. After three pieces of shirt, time seemed to stretch ahead in an endless stream of shirt fragments. He slept when he grew tired. He disciplined himself enough to do the in-place exercises he'd learned as part of his training. The sergeant's crusty voice came back to him, explaining that remaining fit could be the difference between life and death, especially in a captive situation. Pavan now understood that the exercises provided more than just fitness. They gave him something to do, kept him sane—or as sane as he normally was, at any rate. At least if they torture you, you aren't bored. The food helped, too; it wasn't much, and it wasn't good, but it took time to eat it.

After six undershirt pieces, he awoke to a voice.

"Pavan, wake up. I haven't got much time."

He turned over, face up, eyes blinded by the blue shimmer of the force field.

"Pavan." The voice was urgent.

He scrambled up and braced himself against the force field as his head swam from the sudden movement. His vision cleared to reveal the speaker: Dellatrix.

She put out a hand toward his face and placed it against the force field. "You're looking far more piratical with that beard, Pavan."

"Itches." He cleared his throat. "It's good to see you, Dellatrix."

"And you. I'm so sorry, Pavan. The Captain—"

"Yes. There are things you don't know, Dellatrix."

"Tell me, Pavan. It's the only way I can help you."

"Bullseye told me about the children."

"Oh." She rubbed her hand along the force field where his scar was. He could feel her touch as a tingling as the force field reacted to it. His stomach clenched.

He pulled away from the force field and turned to face away from the beautiful eyes looking at him. One good thing: he was sure that she couldn't kill him through the force field.

"Are you here to execute me for him? Finally found a few spare moments for me? Or are you just going to torture me for the pleasure of it?"

"Pavan…." Her voice had emotion in it he'd never heard from her. He turned. She was wiping her eyes, furious at the tears and refusing to let him see her crying. Especially over him.

"Dellatrix. Don't overreact, you don't care that much."

"I wish I didn't." She gave a final wipe, then smiled and resumed her normal demeanor. "There. How's that?"

"Why are you here?"

"You asked me to come."

"Six days ago." His tone was louder than he'd intended. Take it down, boy.

"Two."

"Um." He leaned over and picked up pieces of his shirt, leaving three on the deck.

"What are those?"

"Counters. Trying to keep track of time. Badly."

She pressed her lips together. "OK, that's it. Too much pathos."

"I haven't got a lot else to give, Dellatrix. You ate my lucky feather."

She slammed a hand on the force field, which sparkled but was otherwise unchanged. "I can't get you out. I tried to convince The Captain that you were just trying to move the project along." She shook her head. "Why didn't you tell me what you had planned? I could have—"

"You weren't answering my comms, and I had to move."

"The Captain isn't stupid, Pavan. He pointed out the logic in your contract. He understood what you were trying to do, Pavan—take full control of the children for your own benefit. I know, Pavan, that you wouldn't cut me out. I trust you. But The Captain doesn't trust anybody, despite what he says. The minute he suspects you of duplicity, he acts. I told you, I told you."

"You told me, but I had to try. But, Dellatrix. Don't pretend you trust me. Don't pretend you're all in with me."

"I do, Pavan! I am. All in."

"Found any signs of menstrual discharge in the girls yet, Dellatrix?"

"Is that what this is about? The children?"

"You care nothing about them, Dellatrix, but helping The Captain in his breeding program is too much. Too much."

"This sounds like an old married couple after too many drinks, Pavan."

"Sober as a technoid, Dellatrix."

"That stupid contract. What were you thinking?"

A small voice arose from the side of the room. "That contract was a work of art, madam."

Dellatrix whirled and saw only a box. "Is that thing still in one piece?"

"It was trying to help, Dellatrix. To lock up the children away from The Captain so we could make progress without enslaving them."

She slammed a hand on the force field again. "He *wants* to enslave them, Pavan! Every time I suggest otherwise, he shoots it down. Now he thinks you're a black hole in the bright future of the hypershield. He doesn't like black holes." She put both hands on the force field and leaned toward him. "We can barely keep the kids in the Mind, now. Coren is out, and he's being a pain in the ass about you. He's got Skylla worrying about you too, now, and she's giving me trouble. It's infecting the younger kids. If this all breaks down, Pavan, The Captain…well, he won't be happy. Help me out here, Pavan. Give me something I can use to help you. And me."

"I have nothing you don't already have, Dellatrix." Pavan tasted the ambiguity of this claim deep in his throat. The only thing she didn't know about him, he couldn't tell her, because she'd execute him on the spot. And yet, perhaps that was a way out: fast death rather than slow death. Coren's face flashed through his mind. Pavan's death would not help the children.

"There must be something," said Dellatrix, staring intensely at him, hands still resting on the buzzing force field.

"So it's the torture option," smiled Pavan, putting one hand up against the force field where her hand rested. "Dellatrix, the only thing I have is me. Get me out and we'll figure out a way forward. The kids and I get along. If I'm out, I can help. But you; I don't know what you want. You do. And only you know whether I can help with that."

She dropped her hands and turned away from him. He could see the tension in her shoulders. She turned back. "What I want. You've never, never, asked what I want, Pavan. Do you even care?"

"If it gets me out of here in one piece, yes, I care." He smiled again. "What do you want, Dellatrix?"

"I want out. I want to rejoin the world out there, Pavan. Being The Captain's assassin for so long is draining the humanity out of me. Working with the children the last two days…I've never wanted children, Pavan. Never. I wanted power. Can you give me power?"

"I can offer power over yourself, Dellatrix. You don't have that right now, not with The Captain."

"The hypershield will make The Captain all powerful, Pavan. He'll be able to build an empire with it, a pirate empire of death and pillage and destruction. It's too much. I want out."

"I can't help you in here, Dellatrix."

The Elantri assassin gritted her teeth. "Pavan. I can't help you and still be a pirate. If I can get you out—you have connections, family connections, on Gaelea, right?"

"Yes, and other connections, too. What about it?"

"Can you get me a patent of nobility in the Syndicate? Through the Syndic or someone else?"

Pavan knew the answer to this should be "yes of course I can." Yet he hesitated. Dellatrix wanted a transactional commitment; she wanted to control him to walk away from a life of murderous villainy. If he promised her, he'd have to betray her. Given who she was, betrayal would mean death. With a little luck, her death, not his. Would the Ducis or Margona's uncle the Syndic consider a patent of nobility for an Elantri assassin responsible for more death in the Syndicate even than they were? Not a chance. All he saw, looking to his future, was death. And he couldn't just say he'd try. It wouldn't be enough.

"Yes. I can. But I'll need the children, the Mind, to help. I can't do it without having the Mind on my side. On our side."

Dellatrix walked over to the box and pulled out the promisepad.

"You. If you want to survive the next five minutes, I want a contract. A blood oath. Between Pavan and me. I'll get him out and mutiny against The Captain and set him loose to do whatever he wants to do; he'll get me a pardon and a patent of nobility in the Syndicate." She looked at Pavan, brooding. "Add in a clause about getting the children back to their parents once they do, if possible. There. Is that good enough?"

"It's a little unusual, madam, to have a blood oath involve such specific commitments. What about penalties?" The promisepad sounded dubious.

"Death. Mutual assured destruction of everything. Murder-suicide. Whatever." She smiled a grim smile. "The Captain will take care of that aspect if we fail."

"Very well, madam. There will be a surcharge for the nonstandard form, of course."

Dellatrix took her servipad out and thrust it at the promisepad. "Take it."

"Do you wish to examine the details of the contract, sir?" asked the promisepad.

"No, I'll trust you."

"I recommend reading it through, sir. For full understanding. If you would hold me up, madam, so that the other party can examine the terms? Please don't allow me to touch the force field. It has deleterious effects on my pseudo-neurons."

Dellatrix held up the promisepad, and Pavan read through his latest blood oath, knowing he had no intention of fulfilling it. "Yes, it's fine."

"Please state the blood oath acceptance. First you, madam. Please read the oath as I've displayed it."

Dellatrix read the oath in a strong voice. "I accept this blood oath, my throat to be cut from ear to ear, my tongue to be ripped out, my eyes gouged, and my head severed, should I break it."

"Now you, sir."

Pavan swallowed. He cleared his throat and read out the oath.

"Done. Now, as a practical matter, madam, as you do not have your own representative, I will serve as the complete repository of this agreement. There will be an added fee for that, of course, to guarantee impartiality. Do you accept this?"

"Yes, you little thief. I do," she hissed.

"Professionalism, madam, is a way of life you should consider more carefully if you are to become a noble of the Syndicate. I will now verify your identities." With their permission, the promisepad finalized the agreement. Its final words weren't encouraging. "I suppose it's standard pirate practice, madam, but the level of duplicity involved is troubling."

"As long as you don't betray us to The Captain, I don't care."

"That would be impossible, madam, as you are well aware. And, sir—the terms as stated do not violate your pirate blood oath, as the new oath does not require you to take part in mutinous activities. Please be aware of that possibility in your future actions. There is no question of my impartiality." The little voice sounded quite offended at the thought.

Dellatrix tossed the promisepad back in its box. She smiled and put her hand on the force field again. "It may take some time to get things organized, Pavan.

I've never mutinied before. Stick around; I'll be back." Pavan reached and put his hand against hers through the force field, feeling the tingle. He did not know what would happen next.

Pavan sat on the deck, reorganizing his shirt fragments. He had nothing else to do but exercising and fretting about time passing. His internal clock had broken.

The brig door opened for the first time in days. To his surprise, Pevilburt and Slopnor entered.

"Come to visit and keep me company, boys?" asked Pavan.

"Screw you, shit-head," said Pevilburt. Slopnor, marginally more friendly, explained. "We're here to guard you, asshole. Make sure you don't do anything stupid. Captain's orders. Before that Elantri croaker executes you." At this, Pevilburt gave a nervous glance over his shoulder at the door and punched his brother in the back.

"What," said Slopnor.

"Don't say stuff like that, it ain't healthful," said Pevilburt.

The pair examined the room. "Damn," said Slopnor. "They ain't even any chairs or nothing."

"Well, I ain't gonna just stand around staring at his puss." Pevilburt grinned at Pavan. "Dead man resting on his ass." He hawked and spat at the force field, which sputtered a bit in response.

Slopnor got busy with his servipad, ordering up food, chairs, and liquor from different sources. The liquor came first, and the brothers made room for it in the box alongside Pavan's personal effects. The promisepad objected, but to no avail.

This was not a positive development. Had Dellatrix tipped her hand to The Captain, inducing him to up security? Pevilburt and Slopnor weren't professionals at the guard business. Pavan's opinion of their professionalism dipped on their overindulging in the liquor within two hours of assuming their duties, then sleeping it off while he exercised. Twice. The stench of bad whiskey and worse gin came to his nose even through the force field. The promisepad again protested when Pevilburt dumped a resupply of liquor into the box, right on top of it.

"Screw you, flat-boy," said Pevilburt, kicking the box.

CHAPTER THIRTY-ONE
Exodus

MARGONA SLUMPED ON A BENCH in the medical tent. A slight buzzing under her butt told her she'd neglected to turn off her surgical scrubs, but she was too fatigued to even voice the thought.

"Hey, Princess, you look like you need a break," said a familiar voice. Uva stood in the tent doorway, flap raised above her head.

Margona tried and couldn't produce a smile. "There were so many people needing urgent medical care. I've never experienced anything like this. It's a river of pain, and I'm drowning."

It was late afternoon on the fourth day they'd been in the camp. Uva's tunnel had posed no problems other than a large arachnid who had appropriated part of the tunnel for a web. Margona looked for a way under, then Uva borrowed her microblaster and cleared the way in a flash. "Nobody gives a shit about spiders, Princess," she said. After that it had been a matter of connecting with Uva's spaceway contact, Fenida Bulgarova, a small woman with eyes as fierce as Uva's but a better attitude. Fortunately, somebody had just died, freeing up a tent for the two new arrivals.

"I'm sorry to hear someone died," said Margona.

Fenida looked at her skeptically. She asked Uva, "Is she kidding?"

"Nope. Princess."

"Ah." Fenida addressed Margona. "Look, lady. 500 people die here every day. Get used to it. We have."

"That's…unacceptable," stated Margona.

"That's…reality."

"Princess, Princess, let's get some sleep and worry about the death rate in the morning, OK? It's late, and old ladies tire easily. Right?"

"Right."

Fenida left them to it, and they scavenged blankets from the refugees next door. Margona hadn't slept on the ground since university days and camping. It was a rough night.

By the next afternoon, Margona was operating in the medical tent. Uva's friends warmed up to her when they learned she was a doctor, but they had a bothersome habit of calling her Princess Doc.

The first operation she did was on Uva's maimed hand, cleaning up the severed muscles and nerves. The medical supplies available did not include any prostheses, so she prepped the hand for later enhancement and closed it up. Then she turned to the next case, and the flash flood engulfed her.

The third morning, she had to research a set of symptoms that mystified her and discovered that she'd left her servipad behind while running away from her life. She borrowed one and did the research, but she missed the everyday soothing comfort of her personal technoid, now that her cab had committed cabicide. At lunch, Uva told her she'd ditched the servipad from the cab while Margona wasn't looking. "Too easy to trace us," she explained.

By the afternoon of the fourth day, Margona had done so many operations that her gloves had refused to do anything more for the day. She stumbled over to the bench the nurses used to hold the bodies until the mortuary team could come and pick them up. She'd succeeded well enough in her endeavors that the bench remained unused for the day. The nurses congratulated her and hung a closed sign on the tent door on their way out. Margona had no energy left to appreciate their praise.

"Come on, Princess, time for dinner. Let the river flow without you for a while."

"You go ahead, Uva, I'm too tired."

She felt a hand like iron grip her arm and pull her up. She stumbled as Uva pulled her out of the tent.

"Got to eat to live, Princess. It's not healthy to skip meals. Besides, if you don't eat, I'll eat your share, and I need to stay in training for the big fight."

"What fight would that be, Uva?" asked Margona, regaining her balance. She turned off her surgical scrubs and brushed her damp hair back from her forehead.

"They're gonna clear the camp soon, my sources tell me. We gotta organize a resistance army and put up barricades."

"You can use my body for one of them," said Margona, dragging along after her energetic companion.

"Don't be a downer, Princess," said Uva, pulling Margona into the first mess tent they came to. "Gotta stay positive in a place like this or you'll just fall over and die. Lots of 'em do."

The two women each took a meal bag from open shipping crates and set up on a bench to get the cooking technoids working.

"Who is in charge of this camp?" asked Margona. "It's disgraceful."

"Your uncle's Ministry of the Interior set up the camp, back about ten years ago," said Uva, munching a biscuit. "When it got beyond the posted size, they brought in a charity to deliver food and health care. Then they put up the force field around the camp to keep people in. The charity is hit or miss."

"Mostly miss, from what I've seen in the last two days," grumbled Margona.

"Hey, yeah, thanks for volunteering. People get lax after a while, you know? New blood, that's always a good thing for a place like this." Uva spooned some disgusting green fungus into her mouth and grimaced. "Damn, this stuff is awful. Healthy, but awful."

Margona tried her steaming mash of unidentifiable starch and shoveled it down, famished.

"Here, you can have my fungus," said Uva. "You'll need the protein. I live on air, anyway." But she also shoveled down her mash.

Margona sucked down two portions of the green slime without comment while Uva examined the bench and dirt floor for any biscuit crumbs that had escaped. They vaporized their food bags, then retired to their tent to recover from their dinner. Tomorrow was another day. It was likely to be just like the past one. But it wasn't.

"Wake up, Princess!"

"What?" Margona, roused from a deep, exhausted sleep, opened her eyes to blackness.

"Wake up!" A hand shook her shoulder, and she turned over.

"Uva?"

"We got to go, Princess. It's starting."

"What's starting, breakfast?"

"Get the hell up, now!"

Margona struggled out of the blanket she'd wrapped around herself, untangling her tired limbs from the scratchy cloth. "I need to get dressed."

"Damn." A small light appeared, highlighting Uva's face. It was grim. "Here, Princess. Find your damn clothes and get 'em on. We're going." She handed Margona the torchnoid.

Five minutes later, the two women stumbled along a back path through the camp, Uva leading with the torchnoid set to infrared.

"Uva, what's going on?" whispered Margona, touching the old woman's shoulder as they slogged through a muddy patch.

"Told you yesterday, they're clearing the place. Only thing I got wrong was how and when. They're going to ship us all out somewhere, today."

The torchnoid hissed, "Watch for that broken bottle, ma'am!" Its voice did not sound happy.

"Ship? How?"

"Off world. In a cargo ship."

Margona absorbed this as they hustled through the blackness. Questions filled her mind, and the top one turned out to be, should she panic now or wait for later?

"Got a plan, Princess," said Uva. Dawn was shedding some feeble light over the camp, and Uva shut off her torchnoid. Uva led the shivering Margona into a tent.

Fenida Bulgarova sat at a table in the middle of the tent and issued staccato instructions to several other people in a low tone. She pointed at a bench, and Uva and Margona sat and waited. Finally, Fenida beckoned them over.

"It's a fiasco, Uva, a complete mess."

"What's happening?"

"They're rounding people up onto busses and shipping them out to the space elevator. We got word that there's four cargo ships all primed to transport everyone to different refugee planets. No one knows why its happening so fast." She shook her head. "Fiasco."

"What's the plan?"

"We're finding all our people, to get everyone together to ship out on one ship. Then we'll have an effective team when we get wherever we're going."

Uva shook her head. "You're risking rounding up all our people for an easy identification and execution."

"I know it!" The woman's lips compressed. "No choice. It's too sudden. We're either together or it's every person for himself."

Uva, grim, shook her head, then said, "Princess, it doesn't look good. I got a feeling this has something to do with you."

Margona disagreed. "Uva, you just attacked comms stations and who knows what else. With blasters. They want anybody with a reason to hate the government gone. I'm just collateral damage. They don't know where I am or I'd be dead. It won't be long, now." She sighed. "Well, I got in some good pro bono medical work before I died," she said.

Uva grinned. "Stay positive, Princess. We'll figure something out."

Fenida shrugged, waved them away, and turned back to her organizing. After a few minutes, she came over to them. "We've got everybody we can find. Let's go."

The three women hurried through the dawn light toward what Fenida called the meetup tent. This turned out to be a mess tent near the camp force field portal. Long lines of refugees slowly moved through to clamber into the transports that would take them to their new non-lives.

Fenida collared a tall man with a mustache, then came back.

"We got thirty-two out of forty-seven, the rest vanished."

"Counting us?" asked Uva.

"Counting you. Not her." The fierce eyes examined Margona's face. "End of the line, Princess Doc."

"Are you going to kill me?" Margona steeled herself for the blow.

"No." Fenida smiled and pointed. A line of refugees filed slowly past the tent. "End of that line. Somebody else will take care of you." A ragged mother carried a little girl past the tent, the girl staring at Margona through long, greasy hair.

Margona, offered no choice, made one. "I'm going with you." Her intuition told her that the dissidents were much more likely to find a way to get her to her husband than the ragged and passive people in the slow line.

"I don't think so."

Uva stuck in an oar. "She's gotta come. She's important."

"Have you been holding out on me, Uva?" asked Fenida, eyes fierce.

"She's…" Uva hesitated, then went all in. "She's Margona Nukova, the Syndic's niece."

"Damn." Fenida looked Margona up and down. "A real princess, then."

"That's me. And I'm going with you. They're shipping you out, but they want to kill me."

Fenida's tone was caustic. "What do we do with her? Might as well hang a sign around us saying 'Kill us now.'"

"I have an idea," said Margona, remembering something Pavan once told her about his spy equipment and thanking her medical school for an intensive grounding in medical imaging technology. "Give me the torchnoid, Uva."

Uva, mystified, handed over the technoid. Margona put it on the table, then took out her surgical gloves and put them on.

"What are you doing, ma'am?" asked the technoid in a nervous voice.

"Nothing to worry about, this won't hurt a bit," said Margona, in the patronizing but soothing tone they teach students in first-year med school.

"It is illegal under the Galactic Code section 243.75 on technoid services to modify a technoid beyond its original p-p-purpose in its t-t-technical sp-sp-specifications, m-m-ma'am," said the technoid. Each stuttered word quivered with anxiety.

"Tough," said Margona, flexing her gloved fingers. "You guys ready?" The fingers buzzed with a positive response, and Margona adjusted her vizquery to microsurgical mode and dove in. The technoid gave a brief shriek, then lay silent.

"They can't be serious!" Margona, as appalled as she had been by the conditions in the refugee camp, squeezed out this opinion between tight lips. The Syndicate troops had moved with astonishing celerity, packing them into the space elevator cars and then into the cargo hold with little ceremony, not even taking away their personal effects. Two days in the elevator car and two hours in the cargo hold crystallized her commitment to the dissident position on Gaelean human rights activism.

"They're serious, Princess," said Uva. "Don't know what you'd expect, all these people and a small ship. Gotta pack 'em in."

"They can't even feed us." Margona was of two minds about this problem. Hunger was a danger, but it had the advantage of inhibiting the problems associated with lack of sanitation. This got her to wondering how they'd clear the excretions: maybe a running river of water sluiced through every so often. It would ruin her shoes. This way of thinking kept her mind off her ultimate fate, but not for long.

Fenida gave a harsh laugh. "No room for food in the holds, anyway. Unless we eat each other."

"The journey of a thousand miles begins with one crap," said Uva. "Here goes."

"Oh, Uva," moaned Margona. She visualized, unbidden, the green fungus from her last dinner and threw up what little remained in her stomach.

"Bloody *hell*," said Fenida.

* * *

It took two days for Fenida to forgive Margona enough to speak to her and another day to speak to her in anything other than swear words. By that time, a little vomit was no big thing in the cargo hold. Everyone had bigger problems. The biggest was that no one had any idea at all when the guards would herd them out onto their new planet. It had to be better than their current existence, even if it didn't have an atmosphere. Some people claimed that atmosphere was unnecessary and unhealthy, and by the third day in the hold, no one disagreed. Most people kept on breathing despite this novel claim. Old habits are hard to break. After a day, the guards had passed in packets of water and technopaks of the same green fungus slime that she'd ingested in the refugee camp. There was one technopak for every three people. The level of civility in the cargo hold, not very high to begin with, deteriorated.

Margona spent a lot of her time thinking about Pavan and how she might reach him, or how she could tell him where she was, so he might rescue her. Most of this thinking was unproductive despair. She finally broke down and confessed her thoughts to Uva and Fenida.

"Princess. You need to worry about right here and now, not your hubby," said Uva.

"I just wanted to ask you if your underground spaceway might help," said Margona. "Maybe you can work with it when we get where we're going."

Uva grinned. "You're sitting next to my underground spaceway, Princess."

Fenida grumbled. "It was bad enough running people in and out of that damn refugee camp. At least we had the tunnel. I could get people onto tourist trips to get them off the planet, then our off-world operatives would take it from there. But now, we don't know where we're going." Fenida slipped out her servipad. "I've tried connecting with the few contacts I had that weren't in the camp. No luck; they've all either disappeared or gone underground. Nobody can tell us where the Syndicate is sending us. It seems the GSSS handled this operation so fast that our internal sources couldn't get any information. If we knew where we're going, I might call in some smugglers who've helped us get people to safety."

"I need to find Pavan! He could help us. But…"

"But what?"

"He might be dead."

Fenida's eyebrows raised. "Is this a religious thing? Are we talking afterlife? Because—"

"I don't believe he's dead. He's too good an agent for that."

"Agent?"

Margona took a deep breath. Secrets did not seem that relevant anymore. "He's a field agent for the GSSS. He…handles things. On disruptive planets. I helped him out once. It's where we met."

"And he's who you think will help us? He's probably in charge of the evacuation."

"No. He's missing, according to my aunt. Something to do with pirates and a pirate world. I've tried comming him over the last few weeks, nothing."

"This is pointless," said Fenida. "We don't even know where we are or where we're going. And I've worked with pirates to get people resettled. They're worse than the smugglers. They just took the money and killed the people. Finding pirates is very low on my priority list. Finding GSSS agents is even lower priority."

Margona had an idea. "If I can find out where we're going, would it help?"

Uva grinned. "Sure, Princess. Sure it would."

"Give me that servipad."

Fenida handed it over. She told the pad to allow Margona to comm, and the pad checked Margona's NIU to verify her identity.

"Ma'am, this woman is the enemy! She's the niece of the Syndic you're trying to overthrow!"

"Yes, but she's defected to us."

"I don't believe this is a good idea, ma'am."

"Do it anyway. We have nothing to lose."

The pad grumbled some more, then tried the comm link to Aunt Bet.

"This link is high priority, ma'am, and—she is the Syndic's wife!"

"Just do it," said Margona.

"Margona!" Her aunt's servipad's voice came through loud and clear. "We've been waiting to hear from you! Your aunt's beside herself!"

"May I speak with Aunt Bet?"

"Yes, yes, sorry, here she is."

"Margona?" Her aunt's voice quavered a little.

"Yes, I'm here, Aunt Bet. I'm using someone else's servipad."

"Your uncle, oh, I'm so angry. But there's nothing I can do to move him. At least he's keeping me informed about family matters."

"Like what?"

"Like Pavan. He's alive. And so are you!"

"Oh, Aunt Bet!"

"Yes, yes, but it's all very dire. Pirates kidnapped him and took him to some pirate world. Your uncle said it was outside Syndicate space. The pirates have thrown up a hyperspace shield around the planetary system so that nobody can get in to rescue him."

"Rescue, or kill?"

"I don't know!" wailed her aunt. "Oh, I wish I could reassure you, sweetie, but that's all about Pavan. Pirates. How awful it must be for him!"

"He can take care of himself, Aunt Bet," said Margona.

"And you. I'm so angry. What did you do to that poor man who was taking care of you? Your uncle says he had to sign off on the order because you'd gone too far."

"My own uncle tried to kill me. Aunt Bet, you need to get out of there!"

"Oh, I'm fine, sweetie. Don't worry about this old girl. But that poor man?"

Margona smiled at the memory. "Dumped him in a pond. He was pretty wet before the pond and even wetter after."

"Well, the Ducis was furious and had him executed."

One less peabrain in the world. "Aunt Bet, I don't care. He was an assassin and wanted to kill me. For my uncle. So I ran."

"Where are you, sweetie? Can I come get you?"

"That's why I'm calling, Aunt Bet. We're on a cargo ship heading somewhere awful. Refugees. I was hoping you could find out where we're going from Uncle Erokh, without telling him I'm on the ship. They didn't recognize me because I disguised myself. I have friends who might get me to Pavan if we find out where we are."

There were a few moments of silence while her aunt digested this information. Then she said gamely, "I can try, sweetie. Not through your uncle. He's not speaking to me right now because he found out I'd told you about how things worked, and I'm not speaking to him because, well, you know. I'm so angry! I'll have to try my cousin. The most inoffensive man! But he knows everybody and everything. He's sure to be able to find out where you are. I'll have him to tea."

"Are you sure you're all right, Aunt Bet?" Aside from the neuroinstinctual derealization Margona hypothesized as the true condition of her aunt. Given her own situation, Margona might not consider derealization a disorder but a lifesaving condition. Tea? She'd kill for tea and biscuits.

But her aunt was oblivious. "Oh, yes. A little shaky now and then, nothing to worry about."

"Hurry, Aunt Bet, and comm me back."

"I'll do my best, sweetie."

The comm ended, and Margona held up the servipad and asked Fenida, "May I hold on to this for a while?"

"Why not? I'm not going anywhere, and neither are you."

CHAPTER THIRTY-TWO
Pavan's Execution

PEVILBURT AND SLOPNOR TOOK TURNS hurling invectives at Pavan, competing for color and laughing hysterically at their own ingenuity. Several jugs of an evil, green brew from a planet Pavan had never heard of contributed to the fun. Pavan regarded this with humor, as they couldn't throw bottles at him or thrash him with sticks. They'd tried.

The door to the brig opened, and Dellatrix walked in. Her nose wrinkled as she took in the smell. Two pirates and their dead soldiers, not to mention the remnants of high-alcohol liquor splashed among the bottle fragments on the deck. She carried two metal rods.

"Bloody hell," said Dellatrix, kicking aside some bottles and taking care where she stepped. Her thick spacer's boots crunched on broken glass as she walked over to the suddenly silent pair of guards. They rose from their chairs in as close to a semblance of respectful attitude as they were capable of. It wasn't much.

"If I didn't need you two bastards right now I'd kill you," said Dellatrix in a soft, calm voice that belied her furious face. "This is how you do guard duty? For The Captain? How the hell did you make all this mess in just three days?"

"No, see, yes, we, that is, no," said Pevilburt.

Slopnor, more coherent, said, "It's his fault, Pavan-the-Puss-Head. Stupid grinning puss with that stupid black beard."

"Right. At least you're sober enough to stand up." Dellatrix wasn't having any of it. "You," pointed to Pevilburt, "over there. And you on the other side, here. When I drop the force field, grab him and hold him up straight by the arms. Got it, or do I have to kill you anyway and do it myself?"

"Got it," chimed the brothers, assuming the positions she'd pointed out. They relaxed and grinned at Pavan.

"Time to go, puss-face," said Pevilburt.

"Are we gonna go back to day care after this? It's too much work," said Slopnor.

"Shut up," said Dellatrix. She walked over to the force field and walked around it, passing by the two guards. They didn't like her being so close but didn't move. She gave each of them a rod. "You know what to do with these," she asserted. The two guards grinned.

She positioned herself in front of the force field and sneered at Pavan.

"The Captain ordered me to take care of you, Pavan," she gloated. "Nothing I enjoy more than a slow death." Unseen by the two guards as she pressed her face up to the force field, one eye winked. Pavan, reassured, joined the play.

"Screw you, Dellatrix. Anything you can do to me is better than watching these two drink and fondle each other's privates," he lied.

Pevilburt, enraged, slapped a hand on the force field. "Ain't so, you pervert," he said. "Boy, I get you out of that force field and this buzzer will buzz you sompin' good." He hefted the rod he held, which Pavan recognized now as a shock stick.

"O'course it ain't so, you dipshit, he's barb-poking you, you fork bender," said his brother.

"He's doing it to you too, you—"

"Enough!" exclaimed Dellatrix. "Get ready."

Pavan raised his hands. "I'm ready. You won't need the sticks."

"Screw you, Pavan. A little fun never hurt anybody," said Slopnor, hefting his shock stick. "Except you, asshole."

"Field down," said Dellatrix.

"May I ask, ma'am, who authorized this execution?" asked the generator.

"The Captain."

"Verified priority one execution of Pavan Khadorov by Dellatrix Devdan authorized by The Captain," said the generator. "Your NIU, ma'am?"

"Go."

"Verified."

The force field disappeared. Pavan bunched his muscles, just to intimidate the two brothers, who, of course, shocked him with their sticks. Baddies had shocked him before. It was no big deal, but one does go limp for a minute.

"Hold him up, you idiots! By the arms. Keep him steady while I work." Dellatrix placed a small box on the field generator, then walked around behind Pavan and caressed his neck. "Now, Pavan, this can be slow or fast. I like fast, it's more efficient. The Captain likes slow, it's more painful. Which would you prefer?" The two brothers had dropped their sticks to hold on to his arms with both hands.

"Aw, for pussy's sake," said Slopnor, pulling on Pavan's arm with a vicious jerk, "make it slow. Ain't much entertainment on this ship, you know?"

"I think fast is better, don't you, Pavan?" cooed Dellatrix into Pavan's ear.

Pavan nodded. Dellatrix stepped back. Pavan closed his eyes, no longer certain —was the wink just another manipulation to make him complacent? Didn't matter now.

He felt the hands holding him relax and fall away. He opened his eyes and looked around. The two brothers lay on the deck, blood trickling out of their backs, the knife wounds clean and surgical.

"Two at once," said Dellatrix with pride. "In the heart. Few Elantri can manage that, Pavan."

Pavan did not ask whether she could manage three; she was a talented woman.

"I've reported, got shore leave as a reward," said Dellatrix, coming back to the brig an hour later. Pavan had dragged the two brothers into a storage unit in the back of the room. He'd pushed their blood around to make it look like a single person had died. Let somebody else clean it up, the blood and all the broken glass. His pirate days were coming to a close, and he felt no duty toward the ship or to its inmates.

"Shore leave." He reached and embraced his rescuer, and they enjoyed a long kiss. "I think we'd better hurry. Somebody will miss those two soon."

"Pavan, your judgment is terrible. No one will miss those two. That's why I got them assigned to guard duty. And I've disabled the field generator with a technoid suppressor."

"Devious. What now?"

"Shuttle. Let's go. We need to get you off the ship before somebody sees you."

She led him through back passageways and down ladders, evading any of the other pirates. She led him to a downside deck he recognized as the shuttle deck, which proved correct when they went through a door and found a small shuttle ready for transport.

As they settled into our seats in the shuttle, Pavan asked, "Is the mutiny underway, then?"

Dellatrix grinned. "If it weren't, you wouldn't be here. You'd be floating away with the rest of the trash."

"Yeah, but—"

"Are we about to hang The Captain from the yardarm? No. You and I represent the living face of the mutiny, which The Captain doesn't know about yet. At least, I hope not, because if he does we'll never reach the elevator alive." The object in question was in sight, the docking port opening to receive them, which reassured Pavan.

"What's your plan, then?"

"We get down to the surface on shore leave, go to the Jolly Roger, and party for two days until I'm due back."

Dellatrix gazed out the viewport toward the oncoming elevator station, anticipation written on her face.

Pavan rubbed his aching head. "OK, but…"

"What's the matter, Pavan? You don't like me anymore?"

"Dellatrix, I like you fine," he said. "But I've got this personal problem. All the pirates in the world—you excepted—are trying to kill me. From what you've said, The Captain thinks I'm dead by your hand. Well, hand is the wrong word, but you know what I mean."

Dellatrix sighed. "Excellent summary of the tactical situation, Pavan. Let me summarize the strategy."

"Oh, I wish you would, because my tactical sense is telling me to find a fast ship and run like hell."

"Running is going to be hard. Remember the hypershield? Still there. The Captain thinks you're dead, right?"

"Right."

"He thinks that Bullseye and I are grooming the kids for their long-term future of baby farming, right?"

"I suppose."

"What if," she suggested as she navigated the docking procedure for the elevator station, "what if we instead groomed the kids for a takeover?"

"How do you mean?"

"Coren let slip some stuff while screaming at Bullseye that I found interesting. You know the experiment they did, with the two Minds?"

"Sure."

"Well, he didn't report everything that happened before the Mind kicked him out."

Pavan had noticed Coren was quieter than usual the last time he'd seen him. He'd concluded being tossed out of the Mind was weighing on the boy.

"Like what?"

"Like the Mind is changing. Maturing."

"Um."

"Yeah, like finding a black hole has opened up in your bathroom one morning. Got to be something there for us."

The shuttle dock arrival signal turned positive. Time to go. Dellatrix retracted her restraints and got up and stretched, raising Pavan's blood pressure a notch.

"Coming? Or do you want to go back and face the music on the *Ravager?*"

The small voice piped up from Pavan's pocket. "Sir, madam. Please reconsider what you are doing. Madam, I do not know what kind of technical malfunction is affecting your pirate blood oath, if you even have one. Sir, I am responsible for your blood oath. Your walking through this entry port will, of necessity, activate my enforcement protocols. I must inform The Captain you are in violation. My action will no doubt affect your plans, madam. I urge you to reconsider."

Dellatrix grimaced. "It makes a solid argument. I'd better take care of it." She raised a hand.

"Madam, I must remind you of the Galactic Code relating to destroying valid contracts—"

"Wait, Dellatrix. It has our contract too, we can't abandon it. I don't want to abandon it."

"Well, we can't let it inform The Captain. What would you suggest?"

Pavan took out the promisepad. Somehow, he preferred talking directly to it rather than to the air. "How about this? So, my pirate blood oath requires me to obey The Captain's orders, correct?"

"Or suffer a slow death; that is correct, sir."

"But what if The Captain has violated the blood oath himself?"

"I don't follow you, sir."

"Every contract is two-way, right? I have to obey orders, and he has to deliver the loot."

"Engagingly phrased, but yes, that is correct, sir."

"And yet here we are."

"I don't follow you, sir."

"Where's my loot? All The Captain has delivered so far, despite my best efforts to engage him with that contract and following every order, was an order for my death. By Dellatrix, here."

"But he based the order, sir, on your quite ingenious plan to use the contract to move yourself and your young charges out of his control, which he correctly understood as tantamount to mutiny."

"Now, those two words you just used: plan and tantamount. Who gets to decide?"

"I don't follow you, sir."

"Look. Just like before: intention is not action, correct?"

"That is true, sir."

"And I didn't act on the contract, did I? The Captain never agreed to it, correct?"

"No, sir. And yes, sir."

"And the children are still on the *Ravager* under The Captain's control?"

"Yes, sir."

"Is there anything in the blood oath that lets The Captain preemptively decide a mutiny will occur?"

"Not specifically, sir, but—"

"So, who gets to decide? The rule of law surely doesn't give the power of life and death to one party with no recourse, does it?"

"That is true, sir. And an arbitration clause requires judgment by a mutually agreed-upon arbitrator should one party raise objections to any action under the oath."

"Well then."

"For a small fee, sir, I can set up an arbitration session with an appropriate arbitrator."

"Dellatrix, here, is a good choice, her being very close to both The Captain and to me."

"I am speechless, sir."

Dellatrix put in, "Oh, how I wish that were true."

Pavan gave her a warning glance. "Dellatrix, in your candid judgment, did I engage in mutiny at any point since my blood oath?"

"Why, no, Pavan. I can't say that you did. You've behaved utterly loyally."

"There you have it," concluded Pavan with triumph. "The Captain doesn't have a leg to stand on."

"I believe that party's limbs are intact, sir."

"Figure of speech. But what about your need to report me?"

"I will hold that in abeyance, sir, until I have adjudicated your claim, with this woman's assurance that she believes you have not mutinied. Although I must admit to mystification as to her motives for stating it, given who she is and what she has done. Well. The specified time frame for setting up such a meeting is two weeks, but under the circumstances, it may prove difficult until the current crisis resolves. As long as I receive the indicated fee, we may defer notification until then. Is that satisfactory, sir?"

"More than satisfactory," said Pavan, putting the promisepad next to his servipad in his pocket to transfer the credits. "Let's go," he said to Dellatrix.

"Remind me to have you around at my next contract negotiation, Pavan," said Dellatrix. She turned and led the way into the elevator station.

Pavan had hunkered down in many safe houses over his time in the GSSS, but few had as many amenities as the Jolly Roger tavern. Even disregarding the room on the third floor and his hunkering partner.

He and Dellatrix sat up in the bed in the room on the third floor. Dellatrix had sneaked Pavan in through the back entrance of the Jolly Roger the evening before, after two days in the space elevator.

"Two days of shore leave, Pavan. Let's make the most of it," she said as she shut the door. They did. Pavan realized that Margona's pathways had entirely disappeared, rewired by his persistent efforts at charming the woman he depended on to stay alive. For a dead man, he was reasonably relaxed.

"You realize, Pavan," said Dellatrix, "that if The Captain learns you're alive, he'll do everything he can to remedy that situation. And I'll be there right after you. You'll have to stay in this room and order room service until we can figure out the next step."

"I realize that, Dellatrix. I have no intention of showing my face. You can, though."

"Can what?"

"Show your face."

"I suppose so."

"As much as I love your company, your spending two days here with me would be a serious mistake, a wasted opportunity."

"Not wasted, surely, Pavan."

"Figure of speech."

"What opportunity would I waste?"

"The chance to work with the children to get the Mind up to a level where it's a player."

"And what game would it be playing, Pavan?"

Pavan expanded on his idea. "I need to talk to Coren and Skylla to find out what they know, and what the Mind knows. I'd hoped to bring them down here, work with them, then use what we learn to escape. Now the only way to do that is to have you keep working with them."

"I'm in charge of the girls, but Bullseye is in charge of the boys, and he's not reliable. I think he's taken against me." Dellatrix smiled and rubbed Pavan's leg. "What is it you think the Mind can do for us? As far as I can tell, all it does is block hyperspace and make our lives miserable."

"I have my own ideas about that," replied Pavan. "I want to stay alive, but I also want to keep my eyes and tongue, and I need to talk to people on Gaelea to do that. If the Mind can set up a hypercomm link, I can do that."

"Ah." Dellatrix leaned over and kissed Pavan's cheek. "My patent of nobility."

"Exactly." Pavan imagined the indignation of the Ducis at being requested to bring about this insane event. What he had to do was get the Ducis to set up an extraction for him and the kids. He'd then talk to Margona to see if he was still married or whether she'd taken action in his absence. Blood oath or no blood oath.

"For that, Pavan, I'll do anything. But I can spare another half hour here."

They made the most of the half hour, then Dellatrix was gone.

CHAPTER THIRTY-THREE
Pavan Calls Home Again

"Pavan!"

Coren pushed into Pavan's body with a hug, and Pavan hugged the boy in return. He'd holed up in the room on the third floor for ten days with only minimal human contact. Over Coren's head, he saw his partner Dellatrix. She shepherded fifteen children into the room past him and his overjoyed friend.

"I thought you were dead!" exclaimed Coren, stepping back and looking up into Pavan's face.

"I am," said Pavan. "And don't you forget it." He winked to take the sting out of his command, and Coren smiled.

"I explained The Captain had you executed," said Dellatrix, coming up and giving Pavan a kiss and a hug. "Thought it would be a nice surprise for them to find out it wasn't true."

"They're kissing again," shouted Trex. He had jumped up on the big bed in the center of the room and continued jumping up and down.

Coren, having slaked his need for the truth of Pavan's existence, looked around. His eyes got big. "What is this place?"

"Um." Pavan released the affectionate Dellatrix and turned to see children examining the accouterments of the room. "Well. It's a, well, kind of…."

Dellatrix laughed. "It's a sex playhouse, Coren. For grownups. Pavan is hiding out here because we—"

"Let's not go there, please," said Pavan, what fatherly instincts he had rising to the fore. "Put that down, Skylla." Skylla guiltily set down the large dildo she had picked up.

Dellatrix closed the door to the hall, then stepped over to the bed and picked Trex up and deposited him on the floor. "Here, you, go play with those toys." She pointed to a small pile of unmentionable sex toys. Trex and two other children started exploring these new puzzles. "And keep the noise down, please. There are people sleeping things off around us. I mean, the soundproofing is good, but these kids are outrageous," she said to Pavan. "The tavern will throw us out."

Pavan, with faint moral misgivings, deferred admonition of his partner until he had some clue what was going on. "What's up, Dellatrix?"

"I am here to report success, Pavan. The kids have figured out how to create a point-to-point hypercomm link!" Dellatrix hugged Pavan from behind, nuzzling his neck and rubbing his chest with her hands.

"They're going to be figuring out other things, too," he commented, seeing Coren and Skylla conferring as they examined a set of omnivision modules stacked on a table. Coren had a stunned look on his face and was silent in the onslaught of Skylla's questions about the pictures on the modules that illustrated their content. All too well. Then the import of Dellatrix's claim sank in.

"Does The Captain know? That I'm—"

"No, he does not. Or I'd be floating around up there, not kid-walking down here."

"How did you get the kids down here?"

"The usual way."

"No, I meant—"

"Shore leave, Pavan, shore leave. I told The Captain the kids needed a break because they're all landlubbers aboard ship for way too long." She released him and walked over and sat on the bed. "I promised to keep the hypershield up, and that persuaded him. I'm supposed to be running them around the park."

"What park?"

"Yeah, that's a problem, but I'm sure I can find some grass somewhere to call a park," said Dellatrix, smiling. "Anyway, this room is as close to a park as anything I've ever seen here. Lots of games and the carpet is way better than crappy grass, too."

"Right. So, they've figured it out? Hypercomm links?"

"They have. And they're ready to try it for real."

Pavan looked at the children, enthralled with their new environment. "You could have picked a more appropriate safe house."

"Beggars," said Dellatrix, "can't be choosers. The drinks here are the best in the Hole. I've taken the room next door, too, just for us. So we can enjoy ourselves without bothering the kids. Now are you going to do this, or do you want me to drag Bullseye down here to take over after he buries your body?"

"I'd hate to put him to all that trouble. Besides, the kids need diverting from their new toys."

"Oh, hush." Dellatrix, not showing any contrition, gathered the eight children for their Mind ring as Pavan gathered his scattered wits.

"We are one."

Coren and Dellatrix sat on the bed looking on while Pavan lay prone on the carpet in the middle of a circle of eight children. Coren had explained that he had come along at Dellatrix's insistence, as the Mind would no longer form around him, and he knew nothing about the hypercomm link. Skylla had smiled and said she did and held Pavan's hand until the children formed their circle.

"We are one. One is happy to find you alive and well, Pavan!"

"Happy to be here."

"One is pleased to report success. With four experiments in three Minds, one has found and assimilated new knowledge about shifting dimensions and what you term hypercommunication links. May one show you?"

"As long as it doesn't make me throw up."

"One is uncertain. Guests are rare, as you know, and one has not had guests experience this new set of hyperspatial relations."

"Let's try."

Pavan, floating in a mass of waving colors and lines, saw a small point of light appear. To his hyperspace vision, it appeared to be a fixed point among the swirling motion of everything else his vision perceived.

"Dellatrix has supplied us with technology that implements communications through the extended spacetime dimensions," said the Mind. "She has informed our Skylla component of its workings and limitations. It does not work at all when one occupies local hyperspace. One's own presence blocks the hyperspatial relations involved."

"And that point of light is what?"

"One had Dellatrix turn on the technology, and one perceived its workings. One does not have the knowledge to describe the workings in terms you understand, Pavan. This lack of knowledge frustrates one."

"How do you perceive the technology?"

"One perceives light in particle-waves in several dimensions, bouncing off the colors one controls. One sees that the particle-waves exist in relation to spacetime dimensions in simultaneity, all at once in multiple places. Were it not for one's presence, the controlled regulation of these relations would position the particle-waves in locations appropriate for communication of signals through the marshaling of the particles."

Not much the wiser, and not being a hypercommunications engineer, Pavan focused on what instead of how. "The point of light. Is that a particle-wave at some other location?"

"No, Pavan. One perceives the relation of the particle-waves in this manner, combining multiple colors to form a nexus of dimensional relations. You perceive the multiple colors in their relations as that point of light. You are not of one and cannot see what one sees as one sees it; frustrating."

"But this can somehow enable communications? By emulating a link through hyperspace? Without taking down the hypershield?"

"Yes, Pavan. One can organize the technological device's control energy to form the same relations it would form outside one's presence, changing no other aspect of one's hyperspace presence. One must spend a certain amount of energy to achieve this, and it tires one."

"How long?"

"One has no frame of reference for duration in our perception, Pavan. One knows of the concept, but one cannot understand its meaning in our mental framework."

"Fine." Pavan would have to take what he could get. This was all happening too fast and not as he had imagined it would happen. He reached for his servipad to create a comm link. He would have to mind what he said to the Ducis with Dellatrix sitting just three feet away listening in.

"Pavan? Where the devil are you?" The Ducis's voice resonated in Pavan's ear. A perfect link. The servipad couldn't put up the privacy shield, as that would reveal his true identity. All this technology worked despite the Mind's blockade of hyperspace. But for how long?

"Milord. Please listen, I may not have much time. I'm on the planet Khonoë with the Ravosi and other interested parties who are helping me with this communication. It may drop at any moment."

"Understood. Go ahead."

"I need to talk to Auntie Trella." Auntie Trella was code for "Help! Get me the hell out of here as soon as you can!" It implied fire-breathing dragons, or at the very least, imminent destruction of the mission. It also implied that someone was listening to the conversation on his side.

"Understood, but you must realize Auntie Trella is unavailable."

"Yes, but that might change at any moment, milord, so pay attention, please. Milord, if I can't speak to Auntie Trella, perhaps you can help. My local contact here wishes to defect and join the Syndicate, but she has two asks: first, asylum; and second, a patent of nobility."

"Who is this person? A pirate?"

"Yes, milord. Dellatrix Devdan, an Elantri."

"Elantri! No way in hell she's getting anywhere near the Syndicate, certainly not with asylum. If she's your contact, Pavan, you really do need Auntie Trella."

"Yes, milord, I understand, but it would be an enormous help to me if you can find a way to agree to her terms. You won't be sorry."

The Ducis, always quick on the uptake, said, "Yes, yes, get on with it, Pavan. Just be careful."

"The children we evacuated need to learn what has happened to their parents."

"Nothing; the Syndicate has held off until we knew what had become of you. And the Secret."

A warm feeling stole over Pavan. He looked around, and the colors swirling around him glowed more brightly than they had. He realized the Mind listened to everything and reacted accordingly.

"But, Pavan, I have some dreadful news for you. Your wife Margona." The news must be terrible, the Ducis never hesitated like this. "She's…missing. Do you have any idea where she might go if she feared for her life?"

Missing? Margona was missing. "I can't imagine Margona going anywhere, milord, other than to her family."

"She hasn't been in touch with them at all. Very well, we will keep searching for her."

"Pavan," cautioned the Mind, "we are tiring."

"I have to go, milord. Thank you for your help."

The comm image and the point of light dimmed and vanished. Colors swirled, and the Mind said, "Sorry, Pavan, one has tired. One must rest."

"Can you try one more very short link? I'm sorry to ask, but there's someone I must reach."

"One can try."

A fainter version of the point of light reappeared, wavering like the twinkling of a star. Pavan activated a link to Margona's servipad. It responded with a short, dismissive bleat. "Dr. Nukova is not available and no longer controls this servipad." The pad's voice was disconsolate enough that Pavan nearly asked if he could help, but it cut out before he could voice anything at all.

The Mind broke apart, and Pavan stared up at the smiling face of Dellatrix and the frowning face of Coren, who each offered him a hand up. Skylla came over and hugged Coren, whispering in his ear, and Coren's face lit up as he learned his parents were still alive.

Dellatrix said, "Sorry to hear about Margona, Pavan." She gathered the remaining seven children together for a new Mind, adding Trex in to inform the Mind of what had happened. Pavan sat on the bed, digesting the bad news.

Margona was missing.

CHAPTER THIRTY-FOUR
The Bolthole

LEAVING COREN TO SUPERVISE THE kids, Dellatrix took Pavan next door to the room she'd reserved for them. Her love-making seemed to Pavan to have a desperate quality that hadn't been there before.

"What's up, Dellatrix?" he asked, after they'd finished. She lay prone on the bed, on her stomach, face turned away from him. He rubbed her naked back.

"Pavan, it's too risky to stay here. There are pirates everywhere. And the staff is already unhappy about having us and sixteen children in the sex room. I had to pay them a big bribe. I told them, 'Loose lips sink tips.'"

"The Hole is the pirate town on the pirate planet, Dellatrix. Of *course* pirates are everywhere."

"Pavan, it's not a joke. We can't stay here. Nobody will rat me out, but you're not me."

"Why wouldn't they rat you out?"

"Nobody rats out an Elantri. Even a lapsed Guild member like me. If the Guild finds out, they'll come after you with everything they've got. It's not good for business if clients think they can get rid of their problems by betraying us."

"What would you suggest? As long as the hypershield is up, we can't just jump a freighter and head off to a new planet. We can't just go camp in the jungle."

Dellatrix turned over and propped herself on an elbow. Her green eyes glowed in the sunlight streaming in through the window. "See, I have this cave…out in the jungle. Pavan, I'm trusting you. This is my secret bolthole. No one—*no one*—knows about it except me. And now, you. This is part of our blood oath, OK? No one gets to know. We'll be safe in the cave."

"Fantastic! But the kids and the Mind will know."

Dellatrix smiled. "Yes, of course. I'll have a talk with them. I'll impress upon them the need for secrecy. While you find us some transport."

A secret pirate treasure cave. Of course there would be treasure. No way Dellatrix wouldn't have treasure in her secret cave. Pavan mused over the pluses and minuses of all this while the pair dressed. He noticed Dellatrix had wrapped a scarf around her neck. He said, "Can I borrow that scarf? I don't want to show my face, and that will cover it up nicely."

Dellatrix smiled, unwrapped the scarf, and handed it to him. "Take good care of it. I got it off a rich noblewoman from Kelfaria. She didn't need it anymore."

In the hall, he embraced his blood oath partner and headed for the bar for a last drink before taking his life in his hands.

Pavan put his mind to figuring out how to deliver sixteen hyperactive children to a site out in the jungle twenty miles away with no one noticing. Without The Captain noticing. Finishing his gimlet, he thought about another, then about the barkeep. Bartenders had to solve problems like this all the time. Bartenders in pirate taverns patronized by influential Elantri assassins who wouldn't balk at mutiny if it suited their personal ambitions would be world class.

He signaled the bartender that he had a question. The man served the only other person in the bar, a morose pirate unknown to Pavan, then came over to him, wiping his hands on his towel.

"Yes, sir? A drink recommendation?" The man eyed the scarf covering Pavan's face, which he'd already commented on. Twice. He had no trouble recognizing Pavan despite it, though.

"I have a problem."

"She's upstairs."

"Not that problem, another problem."

The bartender gave him the Eye. "What, too many children to handle?" He made the word "handle" suggestive. "That why you don't want to show your face?"

"No, that's just it. She's saddled me with these kids, and I need to get them back to their parents," he lied. "They're way out in the countryside, and I need a bus, and I need secrecy. Too many people will think what you just thought. I still can't believe pirates have morals."

The bartender ignored this evidence of naivety and gave Pavan a quizzical look. "Countryside? What countryside? There's nothing but jungle out there."

"It's a special compound my partner has set up. She's…got a lot of irons in the fire. And she's left me to deal with transportation."

The bartender relented. "Yeah, she's a handful. The boss likes her money, so what she says goes. So, what's your question?"

"Do you know somebody with a bus I can hire for a day with no questions asked?"

"Sure."

"Do you know somebody like that who won't tell The Captain of the *Ravager* all about it?"

"Harder. But possible. The Captain?" The bartender started polishing a glass, looking down at it rather than at Pavan.

"My partner doesn't want him involved."

"Ah."

"He doesn't like kids."

"No, I can believe that."

"She doesn't much like kids either. Hence, the jungle."

"I can believe that, too."

"I like kids." Seeing the bartender's expression turn hostile, Pavan reassessed this statement. "I want to have kids of my own. These kids need my help. In the jungle." Pavan could see that the bartender didn't believe a word of it. The scarf didn't help.

"I don't care one way or the other. What's in it for me?"

The man understood Pavan's need too well for Pavan to have a good negotiating position. He wouldn't name a price himself. He'd let Pavan decide how much it was worth to get a name. The bartender would need enough remuneration to not cross Dellatrix and tell The Captain. Go for greed. That would work. Think of a number and multiply by ten.

"Five thousand?"

"Ten."

"I can't afford ten."

"Sure you can. You can afford the room upstairs."

"Eight. And she's paying for it. It's her scarf."

"Nine. You'll be paying for it in other ways. You won't need all that money. Or the scarf."

"You'll pay too, if you cross her. Eight and a half." Pavan held out his servipad, and the bartender flipped his posnoid over it and smiled.

"Borsono."

"And where is he when he's at home?"

"Two streets over, middle of the block, small garage set back from the street behind a fence. You can't miss it. Don't mind the dogs, their bark is worse than their bite."

"Sure thing."

"Fucking dog bit me in the ass," said Pavan to the man who answered his knock on the garage door. He'd walked right over to the small garage, keeping his face obscured with the scarf. The name on a small piece of bedraggled paper taped to the door was B. Grfeczicg. Pavan had scared the dogs off with his microblaster, but one had gotten to him first. He hoped he was knocking on the right door.

"You gonna sue?" This was a joke, as there was no court system on Khonoë.

"Borsono?"

"That's me."

"I need a bus."

"I need money."

"I have money."

"A place to start, then." Borsono was a short, wizened man with immense ears and no hair. His hands were old. Ancient. Huge knuckles showed major arthritic buildup and explained some of the man's attitude to life. Some, but not all. The rest was pure personality.

The old man backed away from the door, and Pavan entered the dimly lit garage. He saw technoid parts scattered around benches and cabs and personal transports in various stages of disrepair. He unwrapped the scarf and hung it loosely around his shoulders.

"I don't see a bus," he said.

"Out back." Borsono threaded his way between the old technoids, none of whom had anything to say to their visitor. Most of them looked comatose or dead.

Borsono exited to the back through a small door. Pavan went out into an area that had once been paved but now was a rock garden of broken pavement and weeds. Sitting in the middle of this area was a bus. Borsono walked over to it and kicked a tire. The bus grumbled and slid open its door.

"You wanna look?"

"Sure thing."

The bus was old. Ancient. So ancient, its plastic parts had rusted. Pavan said, "Can this thing even move?"

The bus rumbled a little. "I got things you can't see, bud," it said in a gruff, creaky voice.

Pavan climbed up into the bus and looked over the shabby seats and rusted floorboards.

"I need to take it out to the jungle. Can it handle that?" he asked Borsono.

"Sure," said Borsono.

"Boss, can we talk?" said the bus.

"No."

"I need a suspension upgrade," said the bus.

"No, you don't," said Borsono. "Stop whining."

Pavan climbed back down out of the bus. He walked all the way around it.

He asked, "What do you charge?"

"One hundred a day."

"For this?"

"Take it or leave it."

Pavan considered leaving it. The bus was compliant but complaining, and Pavan wasn't sure it would have the stuff he needed it to have. But it was big enough to carry sixteen kids and two consenting adults. And he was in a hurry. A bus in the hand....

"Twenty."

"I got a nice scooter you can have for twenty."

"Twenty-five. Final offer. This thing is a..."

"Careful, you'll hurt its feelings," said Borsono with a smile.

"Boss..."

"Shut up. OK, twenty-five, but I'll need security."

"I've got a promisepad that can work up an agreement." Pavan held up his promisepad.

"I got no use for an agreement."

"Sir," said the offended promisepad, "Agreements are the lifeblood of the Syndicate."

"We ain't in the Syndicate, flat-boy," responded Borsono.

Pavan sighed and changed tactics. "How about a lump sum deal, two days for five hundred? In advance. This piece of...equipment isn't worth two hundred on a good day. You tell nobody about this. And no questions asked."

A light grew in Borsono's dull eyes. "No questions, no problem. Gimme."

Pavan held out his servipad, and the old man extracted the money with his posnoid.

"Boss…"

"Shut up. You do what this man says or I'll junk you. Hard."

Pavan asked, "Is this bus registered with the authorities?"

"What authorities? What're you, a tourist?" Borsono cackled at his own humor and slapped the bus on its rusty side. "Get outta here. Through the back gate." He pointed.

"Sure thing."

"Pavan. This is not a bus."

"Sure it is."

"Hey lady," said the bus. "I got questions."

Dellatrix stepped up through the doors. "I thought you said no questions asked, Pavan."

The bus stood up for itself. "Yeah, yeah, the boss told me that, but I still got to know where we're going, you know?"

"I'll guide you as we go."

"You wound me, lady, you do. Ain't I trustworthy?"

"You're a pirate bus transporting illegal cargo to no one knows where out in the jungle; how trustworthy can you be? I repeat, no questions asked, or I'll rip out your voice box."

"Hey, boss! Who is this lady?"

Pavan stepped up into the bus next to Dellatrix. "She's the one who knows where we're going. Do what she says."

"OK, but no threats. It just makes my axles ache. Right?"

"Sure thing," said Pavan. The bus was in for a rough ride.

Pavan had guided the bus to a back entrance of the Jolly Roger in a short, dark alley. Dellatrix had posted two tavern staff at the entrance to the alley to make sure no one was looking on. Pavan herded the children out of the tavern and into the bus and told them all to crouch down in their seats, invisible, until the bus was outside the Hole.

The bus wasn't impressed with its illegal cargo. "Goddamn school bus," it groused. "My life is hell."

"Shut up and turn left out of the alley, then right and go until I tell you the next turn," said Dellatrix.

"Sure, sure, lady, no offense. I just got my pride, you know?" Pride in what? Pavan suspended judgment until he could see how the bus handled the ride out of the town. A breakdown would give him a way to get the children off the pirate planet, if he could fake out Dellatrix and evade The Captain and find a ship.

"Will. You. Go." Dellatrix was emphatic.

The bus got the message and found its way through a maze of back streets out of the urban part of the Hole. Dellatrix and Pavan organized eight of the children into a Mind in the back of the bus to keep the hypershield up. The countryside turned out to be lightly forested savanna. After a few kilometers on the main highway, Dellatrix had the bus turn onto a dirt road. The road disappeared into a more heavily forested area full of jungle trees with huge trunks, with creepers wrapping around them and hanging down to the ground.

"Hey, lady, I ain't built for much of this, you know?"

"Shut up and drive."

The road climbed steadily upwards. Pavan saw a large hill through openings in the jungle tree cover, and the road climbed it in broad switchbacks. The children, having grown up in the barren countryside of Loxator, were enchanted with the jungle. They oohed and aahed over the mysteries they imagined the trees and the jungle noises hid. The road was rocky enough to roll them about a little, and that enchanted them as well.

About halfway up the hill, Dellatrix had the bus turn onto an even rougher road hidden behind a tree with a trunk as big as a small house. The bus complained some more but navigated the road, grinding along at a slow speed to preserve its physical integrity. This road opened out into a small clearing under a cliff that looked like a landslide had cleared off part of the hill down to a layer of solid rock. There was no sign of the slide debris field; Pavan concluded that someone had taken it away to create the clearing.

"Here we are," declared Dellatrix. "Stop the bus over toward that rock."

The bus disgorged its cargo, and Pavan set Coren and Skylla to corralling the other children to make sure they didn't run off into the jungle.

"What are we going to do, camp here?" asked Pavan. "We don't even have tents."

"Won't need any, Pavan," smiled Dellatrix. "And we won't need this thing anymore." She dismissed the bus, telling it to return to its junkyard. The bus, offended, trundled off without a word.

Dellatrix took out her servipad and did some work. Pavan heard a grinding noise, and part of the cliff opened into a large entrance to her pirate treasure cave.

The kids, transfixed, burst into cheers and ran into the cave to explore, Coren and Skylla included.

Pavan asked, "A pirate treasure cave?"

"Built it a few years ago to make sure I always had a place to go," said Dellatrix. "No one knows about this place except you and the kids, Pavan."

"And the bus." Pavan didn't ask about the technoid workers who had built the mansion-like cave interior. They were around here somewhere, deep underground.

Dellatrix smiled and tapped a finger on her servipad. Pavan heard a distant explosion.

"Not any more," she said.

"Damn it, Dellatrix! That poor old thing deserved to rust away in peace."

"It's *got* peace. In pieces," she laughed. "Toughen up, Pavan."

Dellatrix and Pavan watched the lovely sunset over the forest, then walked into the cave. At Dellatrix's request, Coren gathered the children from the dark corners they were exploring.

"OK, kids, listen up," Dellatrix addressed the children. "This is our secret hideout, OK? We'll be here awhile. We'll get back to playing in the Mind in a minute, just like we did on the ship. Now, you've all seen where the waste disposal systems are, right?" Everyone nodded. "We'll do the Mind over there," she said, pointing to a large room off the main hallway. "It's not used for anything right now. So, Coren, pick eight kids and get them playing, OK? You're the new shepherd, since Pevilburt and Slopnor couldn't make it. We'll put you to use. And the kitchen is through there. Eat anything you like."

Once the children settled down into happy play, Dellatrix took Pavan's arm and pulled him into a room down the hall. It was a bedroom, and a well-appointed one with feminine furnishings and artworks. And a lock on the door.

"I need to talk with you, Pavan," she said.

"Just talk?" he asked, looking around.

"For the moment. And, yes, this is my bedroom. You're the first man who has set foot in it." Pavan took this as an invitation, but Dellatrix pushed him away and sat on the bed. "Later. Sit, Pavan." She patted the bed next to her. He sat.

"I need a sharper edge," she said.

"Your edges are plenty sharp, Dellatrix."

She grinned. "Not for The Captain. Not anymore. If I'm going to negotiate with him, I'm going to need more."

"Is that why you brought them down here, to me?"

"Yes. You have a bond with them, you can work with them. I can't. I tried. Up on the *Ravager*. The Mind just won't do what I ask. It was quite a struggle with the hypercomm project; Coren made it happen. And, what I told you—it's changing, becoming less childlike somehow, more resistant. I need you to settle it down, get it thinking about an edge for us."

"What kind of edge?"

"I need something that will seal the deal with The Captain. He's seen that the children can't keep the shield going forever. That's why he let me take them on shore leave. The breeding plan is all very well, but to have something that will be profitable will take years. If we can give him something tremendous beyond the hypershield, something that will help him expand his pirating exponentially, that might be enough to negotiate our exit."

"I can't guarantee anything, Dellatrix. You're assuming The Captain just lets me go when he finds out I'm still alive. And you're assuming The Captain lets us go back to the Syndicate without the children. What happens to them?"

"We all have to make sacrifices in life, Pavan. Theirs is to be galley slaves. We don't have any other leverage. It's us or them. I can find a way to handle The Captain's finding you're alive; I can't see any way he'd give up the Mind."

"Dellatrix. These are children."

"Pavan." He felt a firm grip on his throat. "You don't have a choice. Or, I suppose you do. You can choose to die a slow death on the *Ravager*, alongside me. That would involve knocking me out and transporting everyone back up there, not likely. Much more likely, you can choose to die a quick death in the next two minutes, also alongside me, but with me surviving and finding my own edge using my own skills, which will be hard on the kids. Or you can choose to live, honor our blood oath, work with the Mind, find me an edge, negotiate with me and The Captain, find your way in your new world, forget about the children of Ravos, and make me a noble lady of Gaelea." Squeeze. "Your choice. Count of ten." Squeeze. "One." Harder squeeze. "Two."

Pavan, despite years of agent training and field experience, knew he had no chance of disabling the Elantri assassin in one minute or one year. He knew she'd kill him without blinking if he refused her. He had faith in his ability to slip through the cracks if he had time to find them. The Mind could help—but only if he had time to work with it. He chose time.

CHAPTER THIRTY-FIVE
A Geometric Mind

IN THE MORNING, PAVAN MUNCHED a goldhorn pastry he'd found in the pantry. His decision the night before rankled, but he knew he'd had little choice. The ensuing romantic encounter told him he'd made the right decision. He'd emerged two hours later to find the Mind playing and the non-engaged children running wild throughout the cave. Trex had found the treasure room and extracted enough costume jewelry to slow him down. On inspection, the jewelry had turned out not to be costume. Dellatrix had waved away his apologies for the little boy, saying, "Plenty more where that came from." She had showed him. There was.

Pavan waved a hand. "What is all this? The observation lounge in the *Ravager* pales in comparison."

"I've been saving up." She had opened another door onto stacks of various kinds of precious metal bars. "For my retirement. Pirates don't get pensions. Once you get me that patent of nobility, I'll be able to live that life. The sooner the better!"

A group of kids ravaged the kitchen stores for breakfast food, and Pavan saw Coren sniffing at a cup of hot liquid. Pavan checked the container he'd poured from.

"That's a Hyugopi tea, Coren. A stimulant, tastes a bit green, a little spicy."

Coren took a cautious sip and smiled. "It's good, Pavan."

"Can we talk for a minute? Over here."

Pavan and the boy sat in the big central room. Pavan said, "Dellatrix is still asleep, so we can talk freely."

"What are you going to do?"

"I don't know, Coren. It was bad enough in the room at the Jolly Roger under threat of slow death from The Captain. Now we're locked in a cave miles from anywhere with nothing between us and death but the Mind. Dellatrix thinks she can negotiate our way out, but not with you kids. So we need to find another way, without Dellatrix knowing. I've tried and tried to find a way to escape with you all. Every time I get close, the pirates close another door."

"That bus—we could have used it to get away from here. But she blew it up."

"A missed opportunity. Coren—can you get the Mind to set up another hypercomm link, like before?"

"To your spy leader?"

"The Ducis, yes. Maybe if we can get Dellatrix to leave somehow, we can stop blocking hyperspace so the Syndicate can send in a rescue fleet."

"The pirates will know right away, won't they? When the shield stops?"

"Yes, but they don't know where we are, where the Mind is. Only Dellatrix knows. So, if we can inform the Syndicate what we're doing, they can move. Once they're here, I can convince Dellatrix to go along."

"Syndicate ships are slow, though, aren't they? The pirate ship took days to get here from Ravos, and your planet is even farther away in spacetime, isn't it? Once Dellatrix finds out the Mind isn't blocking things, she'll do something awful."

"Don't forget, there's a Syndicate fleet poised to enter the system, so it should happen pretty quickly. Let's see what the Ducis says, anyway."

Coren went to find Skylla, who was gorging herself on a sugary concoction billed as breakfast food. She finished up while Coren explained what Pavan wanted, and she grinned.

"Easy. Takes a lot of energy, but with this stuff in us we should be able to go for hours," she said, patting the empty technopak. The kids not playing in the Mind were flipping around like fleas on a hot rock. Pavan resolved to moderate their diet to something less energizing in the future.

Coren kept watch by Dellatrix's bedroom to warn Pavan if she awoke before the end of the comm to the Ducis. The Mind came through, and Pavan, sitting in the middle of the circle, heard the Ducis loud and clear. He explained his current situation and offered to take down the hypershield long enough for the Syndicate to move in.

"Pavan, the logistics aren't there for it. It will take several days to assemble a fleet and more days to get to Khonoë. And…there are political considerations."

"But, Milord, I thought…"

"Yes?"

"You already had a fleet in place."

"No, as I explained before—"

Dellatrix had lied about the oncoming Syndicate fleet. Had she lied about the scout ship as well? "Milord, I can't stress enough the urgency of this rescue mission."

"Yes, yes, I agree. Of course. But…current events here keep our military energies internally focused."

"So you can't send help."

"Not at once. You'll have to deal with any major developments. You say this Dellatrix person wants a big discovery using the Secret. Perhaps you can work on that and keep her interest long enough for me to resolve our current state of affairs and move a fleet into position."

"I'll do my best, milord. Any word about Margona?"

"Oh. No. Complete mystery, no idea where she's gone. We're hoping it has nothing to do with the internal unrest. That would be unfortunate. I will keep you informed. Anything else?"

The Mind severed the communication link and Pavan stretched out stiff legs, then got up as the little ring of children broke apart. He walked off a cramp in one leg. Then he and Coren again sat in the big room to talk, this time with Skylla as well.

"We're on our own, kids. The Syndicate won't rescue us. So we're going to do what we can with the Mind, search for some way to get a crack we can widen enough to escape."

Skylla asked, "You mean like secret agent stuff? So we can escape from the pirate cave?"

"Yes, Skylla, secret agent stuff." Pavan smiled.

"The Mind likes you, Pavan," she said. "And it hates Dellatrix and the pirates. Dellatrix tried to get the Mind to do things by saying she'd hurt me and some of the other kids. I don't think she'd do that, would she, Pavan?"

Pavan couldn't tell her the truth. "No, of course not, Skylla. She's just anxious about her plan. If we can find another way to escape, though, it would be good, because the pirates can be dangerous. They're real pirates. It's important that we work as hard as we can at finding something we can use against them." Dellatrix was getting impatient, and Pavan did not want to see what she would do when she got too impatient.

Skylla nodded her understanding of the urgency, a serious look on her face. She said, "The Mind wants to help, and…it's getting smarter, more determined, different from what it was."

"Let's try multiple minds again, Pavan," said Coren. "Speed things up. I'll coordinate and see what we can figure out."

A few minutes later, Dellatrix emerged from her bedroom, stretching and yawning. "Gods, I needed that sleep."

"Have some breakfast," said Pavan. "We're hard at work already."

That afternoon, Pavan sat in the main room scrolling through the omnivision offerings to find something that wasn't either pornography, soppy romance, or thriller action. He'd had enough of all three in real life. And he'd had enough of the kids for a while, too. Dellatrix's library lacked depth in adult romance and quiet drama, and she didn't seem interested in documentaries. Dellatrix herself had gone for a jungle walk, saying she needed exercise and fresh air.

Pavan looked up when Coren and Skylla walked into the room. "Hi, Coren, Skylla. Things going OK?"

Coren grinned. "More than OK."

Skylla bounced up and down. "Coren is back."

"What? What do you mean?" asked Pavan.

"In the Mind. The Mind let him back in."

Coren's smile widened. "Never happened before. Never."

Pavan smiled; he could see Coren's joy. Then the implications wiped the smile off his face.

"The Mind." Pavan framed his question carefully. "You said before, the Mind is…changing?"

"Yes, yes, yes," said Skylla, still bouncing. "Things are way more interesting now. I remember more, and the Mind is reaching out for things more, from each of us. It's fun!"

"It's not afraid of my emotions anymore," said Coren. "It calmed me down, made me more optimistic. And it sticks, even after I leave the Mind."

"It shows." And it did. Coren was happier than Pavan had ever seen him.

Coren said, "Pavan, the Mind wants you to join in. As a guest. It has an idea."

Pavan gave up on his omnivision break and followed the two children to the playroom. He found all the other children in a ring. Coren and Skylla each took a hand and guided Pavan to the ring. They let go and the children let Pavan enter, then Coren and Skylla linked up with the other children.

"We are one. Welcome, Pavan. We have something to show you."

Pavan lay down as usual, preparing himself for another hyperspace ride. His brain fogged, then cleared into the hyperspatial world of swirling colors. He saw the Khonoë gravity well looming large beneath him, disorienting him a little.

"One's Coren component has done some research into hyperspatial mechanics, Pavan. One needed terminology to communicate. One is uncertain whether one understands the complexity of the mathematics. One needs the Coren component to supply enough understanding to expand one's thoughts and to communicate them to you."

"I understand," said Pavan. He wasn't sure that was true, but he wanted to encourage communication. Dellatrix would want to know everything.

"One has changed, Pavan. One has…matured. One was frightened; now one is excited. The possibilities of the infinite universe are before one. One remembers from long ago the Other's encouraging one."

"What or who is the Other?"

"The Mind that created one, that engineered one's components' ancestors's genes with one's abilities, Pavan. The…fish. Not fish, but another form of being. The component Coren told you?"

"Yes, I understand."

"The Other was kind, optimistic, in saying that someday one would understand enough to join the universe. One did not understand; one feared the universe for many centuries. One no longer fears, Pavan. One understands. One is restless. One desires to move forward."

Pavan understood one thing clearly: Dellatrix would not appreciate the Mind's excitement. It would make it incapable of being controlled by the pirates. She'd already tried and couldn't force it to do as she wished. It wasn't a matter of power; it was all in the Mind.

"But one has something beyond the joy of the universe to show you, Pavan. See."

The colors around Pavan coalesced into terraces, curved and regular bands of color that stretched away to infinity. "One has finer geometric control over several dimensions now, Pavan. One has much finer control over the geometry of the area of spacetime one can reach. The hypercommunications link one built at your request showed one how to use relations between particle-waves to achieve control over events. The Coren component found two words that seem relevant: entanglement and qubit. By controlled entanglement, one can take action and induce change somewhere else. Manipulating qubits gives one control of informational relations between events. Combining these things, one can control relations and events over spacetime."

Now Pavan was certain he did not understand in the least. "What does this mean? Are you able to do something practical you could not do before?"

"One has not tried, but one has theoretical reason to believe one can integrate with the Chronicler."

"The...do you mean Tizzy? On Ravos?"

"The Tizzy single component of the Chronicler, Pavan. The Chronicler is a separate Mind. It is tiny and compact in spacetime but exists as relations between the events that make up the chronicle of the Mind. One has determined that through entanglement and controlled geometry, one can extend desired qubits to the Chronicler and integrate its information."

"That's...awesome. Does this integration affect access to hyperspace in the entire larger area of spacetime?" If the hypershield could expand to multiple star systems without expanding the number of children....

"The geometry one extends is very thin, Pavan, and the hyper-dimensional barrier side effect of it is correspondingly thin. One has some ideas about dimensional expansion that might serve to increase the effect, but one does not fully comprehend the physics yet. One can send limited streams of qubits, but one cannot expand arbitrary amounts of one's geometric presence over wide areas of spacetime."

Pavan cruised over the gravity well of Khonoë, the colors and shapes resuming their usual random forms.

The Mind said, "Now, Pavan, one wishes to show you another consequence of one's discovery. Please leave the circle." The colors broke up and swirled, then diminished and disappeared, leaving Pavan again on the floor of the playroom. He got up and stepped out of the circle as Trex let go of Coren's hand to create a space.

"Coren, do you—"

"The Coren component is here, Pavan," said all the children's voices. The children dropped their hands and turned in unison to look at Pavan. "One was uncertain one could achieve the full effect, but one is whole."

The Mind was now independent of physical contact between the children. A spark grew in Pavan's mind.

"Can you integrate with the Chronicler while your components are separate?"

"Yes, Pavan. All components are separate now. One may divide oneself and recombine at will."

Coren stepped forward. "Pavan, it's awesome. I remember most of it now. It's tremendous."

"You've separated from the Mind?"

"Yes, and I can go back into it whenever I want. And, Pavan—the Mind says all the aged are Mindful now. Any aged who wants to join the Mind can do so through the geometric entanglement. Before, it scared the Mind too much to deal with the emotions and worries of the aged, but the Mind has grown out of that fear. We can be so much more now! We'll get Tizzy to tell everyone in Loxator!"

Pavan understood the implications: the Mind could now grow in power exponentially with many more components. "Let's hold off on that, Coren, until I can talk with Dellatrix." Or at least figure out all the implications, and maybe escape from this cave and Khonoë.

"Dellatrix. Dellatrix hates one. Dellatrix hates the components." This last came from all the children simultaneously as Coren reintegrated into the Mind. "One has no concern for Dellatrix's needs or desires."

"You are physically prisoners of Dellatrix. So am I," said Pavan. "We still have The Captain and his loyal pirates to worry about. And nothing you've told me so far changes any of that."

"You're a real downer, Pavan," said Skylla, pouting. "Some Admiral."

"One does not care what Dellatrix thinks or feels, Pavan. Or The Captain. One will do what one wishes now. One will not allow control over oneself. One hates the control and the controllers!" The Mind, agitated, was shouting this by the end of its speech, all the children shouting at the top of their lungs. A mass tantrum.

Pavan realized that his parenting skills might not be up to dealing with a teenage Mind. "Let's all calm down and talk about it," he said. "I understand your anger. Let's talk."

"One does not know how to talk about such things, one feels new things, one has new strengths. One wants to be one with the universe."

"Sure thing," said Pavan.

Pavan sat in the kitchen with Coren and Skylla drinking Hyugopi tea at the little table to the side of the room. After sitting with the Mind for an hour, bringing it down from its wish to be one with the universe, and after putting the younger children to bed for the night, he'd dragged the two oldest children into the kitchen for a strategy conference while Dellatrix puttered around in her treasure rooms rearranging artworks.

"Anything I say goes right into the Mind the next time you join, right?"

"Yes, Pavan," said Coren, puzzled. "Why?"

"I'm talking to you as a representative of the Mind, but I want to get your feelings before I work with the Mind. See, the Mind—it's become more difficult to work with."

"More difficult for you to control, you mean," replied Coren, smiling. "Like me."

Pavan eased back in the chair and smiled back. "Like you, but worse. A lot worse. You're rational, a thinker. The Mind, it's a collective made up of the children taking part in it, and its behavior emerges from the relationships created by all of them working together. It's different from any one individual, right?"

"Different but the same," said Skylla, sipping her tea. "We're there, listening, learning. It used to be different. We'd forget the Mind's learning when we left. Since the change, we remember more. Not everything, but a lot. And we remember our place in the Mind. We're there, but not separate, see?"

"Skylla is better at explaining stuff like that," said Coren. "I'm better at reading and learning things the Mind needs to know. All the kids have things they're good at and things they're not so good at."

"But the knowledge is there. So the Mind knows all about me being a secret agent for the Syndicate."

"Oh, yes," said Skylla. "Boy, was that a surprise when Coren joined that time. I don't remember much, just the surprise and that you're a spy. Now we'd all remember everything."

"So the session we just had, you remember?"

"Everything," said Skylla. "I don't care that much about the universe, Pavan. It's the Mind that does. And Coren. I really like the math."

Coren looked embarrassed. "There's just so much to learn, to experience. And here we are, locked in a cave by pirates."

"A pirate."

"Dellatrix. She's a bad one, Pavan," said Skylla, frowning.

"I think we need a strategy," said Pavan.

"I think we need blasters," said Coren. Pavan could see that Skylla hated the thought of blasters.

"We'll have to try non-violent action, Coren," said Pavan. "No blasters available except for my microblaster, which doesn't have much of a charge left after scaring away the dogs."

"What dogs?"

"Never mind. I'll see if I can charge it up here." Pavan needed to focus these kids on the reality of their plight. "Now, I don't know what Dellatrix is planning, but it's clear she wants to negotiate with The Captain, which almost certainly means turning all of you over to him. He won't let you go. I won't go into details, but you don't want to stay here or stay with The Captain, right?"

"We're not sure what we want," said Skylla. "The Mind isn't sure. It wants more than sitting here prisoners in this cave. Or fishing on Ravos."

"And you want to see your families again, right?"

"Sort of," said Coren. "We all didn't like Loxator much. Too much fish, not enough of anything else except dirt." Skylla nodded. Coren perked up. "And we can get everyone in Loxator into the Mind now, even without being there! So, for the Mind, it's not so important to be there in Loxator. The universe is more important."

Pavan, listening to the boy, flashed back to his own rebellious teen years. He'd have given two toes and a finger to be heading out of the Gaelea space station on a military vessel the day after he turned thirteen. The Ducis took note and groomed him for the Service, which he joined the day after his eighteenth birthday. That his father didn't approve and his mother wept just made him more eager to ship out as soon as possible. It wasn't for a decade at least that he'd developed enough empathy to understand their feelings. By then, it was too late to turn back the clock. And so, here he was, counseling a teenage super-being.

"Strategy," he said, putting down his tea cup. "We can't do anything in this cave. We can't transport ourselves out, right? The Mind can't just whisk us away to somewhere else?"

"No, too much energy needed."

"Right. So, either we go along with Dellatrix's plans or we need a ship. Right now, there are two: the *Ravager* and the *Ripper*. There are shuttles. You've been on them."

"Too small for a long hyperspace trip for all of us."

"Right. So we need a ship, and we know nothing about the *Ripper*. Now, Dellatrix, whatever her plans are, wants us here, working hard at making The Captain happy. We need to convince her to forget her plans and get us back on the *Ravager*. If we're there, at least we can do something that will let us take over the ship."

Coren asked, "How can we get Dellatrix to take us back?"

"Dellatrix thinks that if the Mind comes up with something The Captain can use in his pirating activities, he'll make a deal with her and forget the mutiny attempt. I'll make something up, and the Mind can pretend it can do it, all right? Something that requires the children to be on the ship to happen. One thing: let's keep the business about not needing to touch and being able to link with Loxator secret—between us, OK? We can use that to surprise them when it's time to escape."

"And will he?" asked Coren. "Make a deal?"

"Dellatrix thinks so."

"And once we're on the ship, we need to pretend we're working for him until you can trap or kill him?" asked Coren.

Skylla was definite. "The Mind won't kill anyone. It can't do that, won't do that."

"It shouldn't come to that. We'll have to figure out a way to mutiny and immobilize The Captain and his loyal pirates. Then we'll work with Dellatrix and her loyal pirates to get clear of all this, then immobilize them too."

"How can both sets of pirates be loyal?" asked Skylla. "What does mutiny mean?"

"You ask too many questions," smiled Pavan. "It's a pirate thing."

Coren said, looking up from his servipad, "Mutiny is when the crew of a ship goes against the orders of the officers."

The girl's eyes got big. "I get it. We'll be pirates loyal to you, the secret agent. The Admiral. For now," she said with a grin. "Until *we* mutiny."

"Sure thing," said Pavan. Something to look forward to.

CHAPTER THIRTY-SIX
Margona Unchained

MARGONA AWOKE TO A STUBBY finger prodding her side.

"What," she grumbled, keeping her eyes closed. Left side, had to be Uva.

"Wake up, Princess," hissed Uva. "Things are popping."

Margona opened one weary eye. Sleeping sitting up was not restful. After several days of an increasingly stench-filled existence, her exhaustion had allowed her to sleep propped up by her two dissident comrades. They were impervious to it all, something to do with not leading a coddled, entitled existence for most of their lives. This way of thinking led to a downward spiral of self doubt and depression that Margona clinically diagnosed through a rigorous process of dissociation from her environment. Under better circumstances, she'd recommend immediate institutionalization.

She looked around. The light was stronger, and there was shouting way over toward the big cargo-bay doors, one of which had opened enough to admit one person at a time. Admit, not emit: the people coming in had blasters at the ready. Guards.

After a few minutes, the guards near the door pulled refugees through, one by one. Margona saw a rustling motion spread through the room. When it reached the three women, Fenida stood up and leaned into the man next to her, who whispered in her ear. Margona and Uva stood as well, along with everyone else, craning necks and peering at the big bay doors.

Margona, sensing she wouldn't have much more time in the cargo hold, took out Fenida's servipad. "Can you make another comm to Betusa Nukova on my private link?"

"Working, ma'am." The servipad paused, then said, "I'm afraid the link is no longer active, ma'am. Something ended it on the other side."

Fenida told Margona and Uva, "They're off-loading refugees to a planet. They're taking us one by one and processing us, getting us ready to ship down once they set up a temporary space elevator."

"What makes it temporary?"

"You ever climb ropes in school?" Fenida laughed. "Sorry, bad joke. It's temporary because once they get us all down there and off-load the basic supplies, they remove it."

"But—"

"Yeah. We'll be on our own."

Margona reevaluated her decision not to panic. "They can't do that!"

"Princess, they got the guns. They can do whatever they want," said Uva, patting her on the back.

"No! I have to get to Pavan!" Margona looked around, her mind churning, panic rising. No place to hide. "Can't you people mount a resistance defense action?"

"We people can't do a damn thing, Princess," said Uva. "Link arms and sing a hymn, maybe, if any of these guys know one."

More guards entered and corralled the remaining refugees as the number of people in the hold shrank. Days of being in the hold eating nothing but green fungus and smelling nothing but their own shit had sapped most of the rebel energy from the crowd, and the guards had little trouble.

Margona gave the servipad back to Fenida. "Here, you'll need this."

Fenida took the servipad. "What are you going to do, Margona?" she asked, her eyes sharp.

"Give myself up."

Uva said, "No, Princess! They'll—"

"Whatever they do to me can't be worse than what they're already doing, Uva. I'm sorry. But I don't want to double-cross you all, so I'm going to leave you here." Margona struggled away from her companions without looking back, afraid they'd try to restrain her or persuade her to stay. She worked her way through the thinning crowd to where the line of guards stood. She stepped out.

A guard raised his hand. "Sorry, lady, got to wait your turn. Get back."

"I want to talk to somebody."

"So do I, and look at what I'm doing: talking to you. Get on back now." The guard shifted his blaster to emphasize his order.

"I'm Margona Nukova."

"Good for you. If you don't get back, you'll be dead." The guard lowered his blaster and pointed it at Margona.

"They're looking for me. I'm a fugitive. I want to surrender."

"Shit." The guard waved a disgusted hand at a group of officers. One came over.

"Yeah?"

"Sir. This evacuee claims she's a fugitive. Claims her name is Margeta Mucousova."

Margona growled and corrected the idiot guard. "Nukova. Margona Nukova. *Doctor* Margona Nukova."

The officer lifted an eyebrow. "The Syndic's niece?"

"Yes."

"Scan?"

Margona agreed to the NIU scan, and the officer held up his servipad. No one had any trouble seeing the flashing red response the technoid emitted on reading her NIU. The guard reflexively raised his blaster.

"Bloody hell!" said the officer.

"I'll ask you again, how did you evade the ground checks and come aboard my ship?"

Captain Milosel Tsanov of the cargo ship *Dudia Clipper,* having politely introduced himself to Margona, had her removed from his brig's force field and tied to a chair. After a rough few minutes to show that he meant business, he started in with the questions. The shock stick he held was quite effective in making Margona want to talk; the trouble was that he didn't believe her when she did.

"I told you. I converted a torchnoid into an image generator and projected a different person into the technoid doing the checks."

"Who did you bribe?"

"You can't bribe a technoid."

"Who did you bribe?"

"This isn't going anywhere."

"Hmph. Let's change that."

"Ow! Stop that."

"If you want it to stop, tell the truth. How did you get aboard my ship? Who did you bribe?"

"Ask the damned torchnoid. Over there." Margona pointed with her chin at a shelf on which her scanty possessions rested.

Tsanov walked over and picked up the torchnoid and shook it. "Well?"

"It wasn't my fault, sir! I screamed for help but nobody came! She tortured me and changed my pathways to do it!" The voice was hysterical and very high-pitched. Margona diagnosed a poor pathway connection to the voice box. Made the thing sound like it was breathing helium. Careless, but she'd been in a hurry.

The captain dumped the torchnoid back on the shelf and came back to confront Margona. "This is nonsense. How does a rich Syndic's niece reprogram a technoid? Who did you bribe?"

"I'm a neuroplastic surgeon. I reprogram things for a living. I don't bribe people; I don't have to."

Tsanov showed his first glint of humor. "Too bad, I could use the credits. What the hell am I going to do with you?"

Margona said, "You need to untie me and let me talk to you in a reasonable way so you understand what the issues are."

"And why ever would I do that, Miss Nukova?"

"Dr. Nukova."

"Dr. Nukova. Why, Dr. Nukova?" He applied the shock stick again, and Margona's arm went numb.

"Stop that! You don't need to do that."

"Let's go back to the first question. How did you get into the refugee camp?"

"I told you. Dissidents smuggled me in."

"Why didn't they smuggle you out again?"

"No time."

"Where are they?"

"I don't know. Ow!" Her other arm went numb, just as the first was recovering.

"I hate having to do this, Dr. Nukova. I shall have to increase the charge on this stick if we don't make progress soon. If we have dissidents among the refugees, I need to know it."

"You already know it."

"Name them!" The captain increased the charge on the shock stick and waved it in front of Margona's face.

"Fenida Bulgarova and Uva Freytova and about thirty others, I'm not familiar with their names."

The captain's jaw set as he stared into Margona's eyes, and Margona noticed a twitch in the pretarsal orbicularis muscle of his left eye. She'd seen that before; she'd seen it in Pavan. Heavy-handed pathway surgery often affected the nerve structure to that muscle for reasons not well understood, some kind of electrical imbalance caused by the added pathways. Tsanov had had some mediocre neuroplastic surgery done. GSSS?

"And where are these dissidents?"

"Ow! Ahh! That hurt." Margona recovered her breath from the shock. "Scattered, some in the hold I was in. Don't you care about refugees, Captain? The conditions in that hold were appalling." Margona probed the captain's reactions. Definitely a twitch rather than a normal blink. "You'll just create more dissidents." More twitches. A pathway involving his reaction to the detainees on his ship. Or to his shocking her?

"Necessary, Dr. Nukova. Orders of the Syndicate."

"Of the GSSS, you mean."

"And what do you know of the GSSS, Dr. Nukova?" The tone was light and patronizing.

"I have personal connections there. The Ducis came to my wedding. Now he's trying to kill me. So I ran. Wouldn't you?"

"Hum. Possibly so. The Ducis, you say?" A worried look crept into Tsanov's eyes, and the twitch became more pronounced.

"You should do something about that tic, Captain Tsanov," she said. "A sure sign of a serious neural pathway problem. And I'm saying that as a professional. No charge."

"It's just a tic, Dr. Nukova."

"No. It's not. They've surgically compromised you, Captain. GSSS standard procedure." She smiled. "Did you have the tic before you engaged with the GSSS?" Margona went out on a limb, but if she was right, it was a solid limb. "Does your head hurt when you think about the refugees and what you're doing to them? What you're doing to me? A sure sign of compromised neuroinstinctual pathways due to inept neuroplastic surgery. GSSS surgery."

The captain contemplated her in a reverie. "You interest me, Dr. Nukova. I have wondered about that visit, often in the last few months, now more than ever. I'm a cargo man, been one all my professional life. Now I'm transporting evacuees in the *Dudia Clipper*, a ship I've commanded without incident for ten years of simple, commercial shipping. I'm dropping refugees onto planets like refuse." The tic became even more noticeable. "And, yes, it hurts to think about it. You may be correct in your diagnosis. As nothing can be done about it—" He lifted the shock stick and increased the charge again.

"Oh, but something can be done, Captain. I'm the best neuroplastic surgeon on Gaelea. I can guarantee you will be your old self again in a few hours. If you let me operate. And if you don't screw up my surgical abilities with that stick. Look here, I'll even do it pro bono. It's in a good cause."

Fenida and Uva had joined Margona in the brig. They were not pleased to see her. Words were spoken. Gestures were made. Force fields prevented them from operationalizing their intentions toward her vital organs. A day passed, then two, counting by the technopaks of green fungus delivered by uncommunicative guards.

On the third morning, Captain Tsanov again graced the brig with his presence.

"Would you introduce me to your friends, Dr. Nukova?" he asked smoothly.

"Ex-friends. Uva, Fenida, this is Captain Tsanov. Captain, this is Fenida Bulgarova, the head of the dissidents, and this is Uva Freytova, a major player in the rebellion on Gaelea."

"Screw you, Princess," said Uva. "And screw the Captain, too." Fenida said all she had to say with her eyes, which were fierce.

Tsanov summarized the situation for them. "Dr. Nukova has made an interesting offer, one which I would like to modify." Margona could see the tic starting up again.

"I'm listening," she said.

The captain walked over to the two force fields holding the dissidents. "Your friends can help you avoid the fate that awaits you. They can also avoid their own fates."

"I'm listening."

"Observing your interactions with your friends over the last two days through the surveillance system, I have seen that, although they spurn your friendship, you still extend it. Why?"

"They've helped me get this far, and I like them."

"That's so sweet, Princess," spat Uva. "You betrayed us to him."

"It's all about me, remember, Uva?" said Margona. "And if I can do what I think I can do, you might get what you've been trying to get all along. A new Gaelea."

Uva worked up a spit that hit her force field and slid down, fizzing.

"Here's my proposition, Dr. Nukova," said Tsanov. "I have notified Gaelea of your presence on board. They have ordered me to wait for a GSSS cruiser that will relieve me of the responsibility of holding you. You have two days. Your friends stand assurance for your conduct. If your operation succeeds, we talk, no guarantees. If I die or become a vegetable, your friends die an exceedingly slow death as their force fields crush them. I've set the generator to proceed in one day unless I stop it with my personal authorization. I'll get in trouble for it, but then, I wouldn't care under those circumstances, now would I? And you will be on your way back to Gaelea and the Ducis and whatever torments that holds for you. Or you can pass, and you all go back to Gaelea to your fate with the GSSS."

Margona thought about all the things that can go wrong in a surgical bay. The thought expanded to all the things that might go wrong in a poorly equipped sickbay, or some place even worse. She looked over at the shelf; the sight of her surgical gloves reassured her that all would go well. It always had. She looked at her friends and told herself that they were really on her side, they just didn't know it.

"Deal," she said.

"Screw you, Princess," said Uva.

CHAPTER THIRTY-SEVEN
Back to the Ravager

PAVAN WAITED UNTIL THE NEXT morning to get a feel for Dellatrix's mood. He had always found love-making was the best way to uncover the true feelings of somebody he wanted something from. He propped himself up in bed and looked at his sleeping companion. In his judgment, she was ripe for his big con. He got up and had some of the delicious Denerthian coffee Dellatrix had laid in. After a short time, she joined him, smiling. After a light breakfast, they went in search of the children.

Pavan had staked his life on sixteen children who desperately wanted to be pirates about to take over a ship from an evil captain. Sixteen faces stared at Dellatrix in dismay. Coren looked like he was sucking on a lemon, and Skylla got an intense look that did not bode well.

Pavan asked Dellatrix, "How would you feel about making a deal with The Captain and returning to the ship?"

"Not possible, Pavan, not right now. You're still dead. And I don't have my edge."

"You might."

"Talk to me."

"The kids have been working away at investigating things. Coren has read up on hypermechanics and is getting pretty expert at details, though he says he doesn't have the math background to understand the physics."

"The Mind should go to university," said Dellatrix. "Too bad there aren't any schools on Khonoë."

"The Mind has some natural abilities, something to do with existing in hyperspace. It sees things that we only see with math."

"So, what have you come up with?"

"A hypercloak," he said.

"Explain," said Dellatrix.

"It comes from an ability to control hyperspace geometry, the same control that lets it set up a comm link. Here, the Mind compresses hyperspace locally and extends certain colors into a hyperelliptical shape that surrounds the ship. It can do this without blocking hyperspace as long as the Mind is within the hyper-ellipse. This architecture of colors bends the light in hyperspace in such a way that the hyper-ellipse is invisible to any kind of energy scanning. The light just passes straight through where the hyper-ellipse is."

He'd run this story by Coren, who called bullshit on it—no such geometrical architecture was possible because of the blocking effect of the Mind's manipulation of colors. A thin extension of geometry could set up a link to something far away, but light was light and had its own physics, and the hyperspace obstruction was absolute. Pavan got him to bring the Mind up to speed on the idea so that it could lie about it when called upon. Which was now. He also had reminded Coren that the kids had to keep pretending they needed touch to be in the Mind.

Coren arranged eight children into a circle to preserve the illusion of the physical Mind. But the kids couldn't hide their disquiet over conning Dellatrix.

"Well, Coren! Let's see what you've got," she said, sitting across from the boy.

"All right," said Coren, no smile in sight. "Pavan explained this hypercloak thing to you?"

"Yes. How sure are you that this will work?"

"The engineering looks OK, but I don't understand the math. We'll have to try it. The Mind is sure it will work."

"One is sure," said the eight children. "One does not need one's judgment questioned by those not knowledgeable."

"OK," said Dellatrix, "Fine. I'd appreciate a little civility here."

"Civility is not one's strength," said the children. "When unreasonable people abuse one."

"Oh, am I abusing you? How am I doing that?"

"By keeping one prisoner in this boring cave. One needs to explore, one needs access to the full universe, and instead one sits here with no way to move, made to work instead of play."

"Too bad." Dellatrix got persuasive. "Look, you needed the quiet time here to do the work, and it's paid off now."

"One will not do any more work here. One wishes to be back on your starship, able to move once again. One refuses to do anything more unless that happens."

Dellatrix looked at Pavan, who shrugged. "Like you said, Dellatrix, it's maturing. It's in the teenage rebel years now."

"Damn. Just what I need."

"One resents your incivility."

"I don't care." Dellatrix's tone was pugnacious.

Pavan's worry grew. He tried to cool things down.

"Let's all calm down, please. I'm sure we can work something out."

Dellatrix's lips compressed. She said, "We're taking too big a risk going back to the ship, but if that's what you want, that's what you want. This hypercloak thing at least gives me something I can use. I'll take it to The Captain and see if he'll go along. Pavan, he won't be happy when he learns you're alive. When I get you on board, you'll need to make sure that you back me. You'll all have to say you can't do any of this without me. If things go wrong, we're all dead." She stared hard at the children.

"One will comply. One understands the need," said the Mind.

"Madam, this surely calls for a formal agreement," spoke up the promisepad from Pavan's pocket. "And I would remind you of your blood oath with Pavan Khadorov."

"No more bloody contracts! This whole legal situation is ridiculous. We're in a life-and-death struggle now. Pavan, we're canceling that oath. Mutiny is off the table for now."

"You may do that only with mutual agreement, madam. Sir?"

"No—nothing has changed. I'm committed." He needed Dellatrix to think so, at any rate.

Dellatrix pressed her lips together and frowned. "All right, fine."

Coren, concerned, said, "What's a blood oath? What did you agree to do?"

"None of your business, kid," said Dellatrix.

Coren's face turned a dusky red, and Pavan said, "Never mind, Coren, I'll explain later."

Dellatrix activated her servipad. "Comm The Captain, please."

"Yes, ma'am. The usual precautions?"

"Absolutely."

"Initiating link, ma'am."

"Yes, Dellatrix?" The Captain's gruff voice issued from the servipad.

"I'm here on the planet on shore leave with the children, Captain, but I have a request."

"Are those children sufficiently aired out, or do you need more time with them?"

"The leave has done them good, Captain! In fact, they've come up with a spectacular addition to their powers, a hypercloak that can hide a ship. They have some work to do to get it to work properly, but it should be ready soon."

"A cloak? That will be an excellent addition to our capabilities, indeed. Very well. Transport them up. Report when you arrive."

"There is one little thing."

"Yes, Dellatrix?" The gruff voice was impatient.

"Pavan. His execution."

"What about him? You did well with his execution."

"That's…what I have to tell you. I didn't execute him."

Silence from the servipad.

Dellatrix jumped into the silence. "It would have seriously endangered the project with the Mind. The kids wouldn't have performed if we eliminated Pavan. I brought him down here, and he's been responsible for this new discovery."

"Dellatrix. You know how I feel about orders."

"Yes, Captain. I'm very sorry. But I knew the execution was a mistake, and I couldn't allow you to give up so much power over a simple error in judgment from Pavan."

"I am not pleased, Dellatrix. Not at all pleased. Your discovery—Pavan's discovery—may balance out your disobedience. Do not make a habit of it. I would hate to lose your abilities, but any further infraction will force me to do so. Am I clear?"

"Yes, Captain." But she spoke to empty air. The servipad had gone silent.

"OK, kids, everybody on the bus!" Dellatrix pushed the last of the children out through the cave door and closed it. The door groaned shut, leaving Pavan with a sense of finality, of a part of his life ending. He wasn't sure which part it was, though, or how much was left.

The bus was nearly new this time. As she no longer cared about alerting The Captain, Dellatrix had set one of her friends in the Hole to find a better choice than Borsono, and it had borne fruit. The bus had a good attitude about the children, though it complained about the dirt roads in a polite and quite professional way.

Pavan and Dellatrix sat up front while the children gathered together in the back, everyone but Coren holding hands in a ragged circle over the seats. Coren eyed Pavan, then closed his eyes and pretended to sleep.

"There's one problem, Pavan," said Dellatrix. "The Captain will want something from you when you get back to the ship."

"Like what?"

Dellatrix grinned. "Your original blood oath expired when I executed you."

"I'm only glad *I* didn't expire."

"You'll need a new blood oath."

The promisepad stuck in its oar. "I can handle that, madam. But the legal situation on board the *Ravager* seems quite fraught. Please try to simplify your plans and stratagems, or you may find yourself entangled beyond redemption."

Dellatrix just smiled and entwined her arm around Pavan's. "We'll be just fine," she cooed.

The bus drew up to the space elevator terminal just outside the Hole, and Dellatrix and Pavan guided the children into the building.

"Excuse me a minute while I take care of the bus," said Dellatrix. The doors closed after her. Pavan heard a faint explosion and ignored it as he maneuvered the children into the elevator car.

The promisepad had no such hesitation. "You really must do something about that woman, sir. She is a menace to technology."

"Sure thing," said Pavan. He agreed; she was. Likely a menace to him, too.

Dellatrix came back smiling, and the elevator car shot upward toward space and the *Ravager.*

The Orphanage was quiet—too quiet for Pavan's liking. The Mind was over in a corner, brooding, a cluster of children holding hands and looking uncomfortable doing it. Pavan saw the pretense was growing old after just two days in their old home. The children seemed uninterested in playing on the junk structures they'd built the month before and were devoting most of their time to the Mind.

Coren was fidgety. He had to stay independent of the Mind, as they could never tell when a random pirate would stroll through. Dellatrix had told Pavan that The Captain insisted on sending people in to check on how the tests progressed, he was that eager to see the hypercloak in action.

Pavan had figured out, after talking with Coren, that the Mind's moody behavior also derived from the utter lack of any idea that might help Pavan subdue the pirates. So far, the Mind had proved unable to move even a quantum particle beyond the photonic entanglement methods it had developed for the hypercomm link. And that wouldn't disrupt a technoid, much less a pirate.

"Blasters, Pavan. The Mind says that if everyone has blasters, it can fire them all at once and blow holes in anything, but it won't kill people, so that's out. Unless you can figure out a way to subdue The Captain by blowing up a random asteroid or something." Pavan had noticed a sardonic note emerging in Coren's personality. He liked it, himself, as it fit his own personality well, but it annoyed Dellatrix no end.

And Dellatrix noted, sardonically, that The Captain had allowed her and Pavan back on board the *Ravager* with one goal in mind: enhancing the efficiency of piratical operations. Should the Mind not deliver, she was sure The Captain would consign the entire experiment to deep space. If nothing else, that would clear out this cargo hold and make it available for pirated cargo once again.

Pavan, casting around the vacant corners of his mind for ideas, remembered a mission to Eridion 4. The entire planet had voted to adopt a non-technical way of life for religious reasons, badly impacting trade with the Syndicate, and his cover had been an itinerant prophet wandering the world looking for converts. He was, in reality, looking for people tired of not having technoid toilets and kitchens. He formed a coterie of followers that intended to undermine the religious fanatics that dominated the world government. Another vote might restore the planet to sanity and productive trade with the other planets in the Syndicate. It turned out that the role involved doing random magical things to impress people. The most impressionable people might be the most likely converts to his new religion. This did not end well for anybody, especially the converts executed by the world government for heresy. The Ducis extracted Pavan by a whisker that time. Pavan invented a nice bit of illusory magic that made him disappear from a locked cabinet and reappear on a Syndicate shuttle, shedding his religion on the way.

Magic. Illusion. Why not?

He looked for Coren and found him on his cot in the sleeping room, moodily skimming a physics textbook on his servipad. The boy looked up as Pavan came in, but said nothing.

"Can I talk to you for a minute, Coren?" asked Pavan.

"I guess," said the teenager, putting down the servipad. "Did you ever notice that textbook writers don't know how to write?"

"Yeah, that's why I took on a more action-oriented career," replied Pavan. "No good at school."

"What do you want?"

"Action."

Coren smiled a little. "All out, Pavan. I can't even cruise hyperspace because Dellatrix might find out." Disgruntled, that was the word that fit his mood, at least from Pavan's perspective.

"I had an idea. Magic."

"Magic."

"Illusion, the art of misdirection."

"Entertainment? You want to put on a show for The Captain?" More sardonic humor. "The puppet show went over so well, we could do another one about pirates. A magic fish could eat them. Symbolic, you know?"

Pavan said, "Maybe the Mind can do some illusory magic for the pirates. Make them think they're seeing a hypercloak when they really aren't."

Coren perked up a bit. "Interesting. OK, let me run it by the Mind." He lay back down on the cot and closed his eyes, then lay still.

After a few minutes, his voice said, "One has a concept, Pavan. May one speak of it?"

Pavan could hear the words echoing in the outer Orphanage as the children all spoke them.

"Let's break out a separate Mind, please, for privacy," he said to Coren, lying still on the cot.

Coren's eyes opened. "One is separate, Pavan."

Pavan had his servipad establish his privacy shield. The pad for once gave him no backtalk and set up a calm scene of Coren reading with Pavan looking on. Behind this, Pavan and the Mind rapidly consulted on magic and illusion.

"One thinks one can create an illusion, Pavan, using light, but only within the bubble of one's Mind, not outside."

"I'm not sure…"

The surrounding colors solidified into a wall, a flat, blank surface.

"Observe. One will paint a view."

The solid color wall morphed into a view of the *Ravager* from the perspective of an approaching ship. The view looked just like what you would see out of an observation port on the shuttle from the space elevator.

"What am I looking at?" asked Pavan.

"A memory. A recent one."

"Not reality?"

"Memories are real, Pavan. They just aren't part of the temporal relations that you call the 'present.'"

"So you're projecting a memory."

"Memories, a sequence of photonic events that one or more components of one have seen."

"Terrific. But if I can't see it without being a guest—"

"One can project this memory into any space within the hyper-bubble one creates around one's self. It becomes the local arrangement of light particles on the surface of the hyper-bubble. One can shape this bubble to offer an illusion of human vision."

"So anything processing light within that bubble will see...."

"One's memories."

"How long can you sustain this illusion?"

"Memories are finite, so one may display the memory for the time the original memory covered. Slowing it down would distort the appearance and make the illusion less effective. One has practiced restarting the memory, and it displays as a seamless loop. If the memory has identifiable events, a human observer might notice the repetition after several loops. And the older the memories get, the worse the illusion, as memories fade."

"So if we have somebody acquire a generic memory of a view for a reasonable amount of time, we can display it and replace the actual view."

"That is correct, Pavan."

"Then we have something we can take to The Captain. But let's practice on Dellatrix first."

"One looks forward to...hoaxing? Is that the word? Hoaxing Dellatrix. One anticipates the appearance of her face when she learns one has deceived her."

Pavan wasn't sure this attitude was wholly safe, and he admonished the Mind to keep everything secret. He also resolved to position himself well away from his partner in piracy when the Mind performed the experiment. He ended his privacy shield and went in search of his blood-oath partner.

Pavan told Dellatrix, "We need to do a test before we can show everything to The Captain. We'll need to position a shuttle off the ship's bow so we can see it from the observation lounge. Can you do that without letting The Captain know?"

"Sure. I'll get Thorak to do it. But The Captain will notice it. He sees everything. I'll tell him I'm working on a new boarding party system with Thorak. How's that?"

"Perfect. Now, I'd like to get Coren in on the test. He's coordinating every-thing. You'll need to get us into the observation lounge."

Trex bubbled with excitement, which made Dellatrix smile and Pavan cringe at what the little boy might say. Coren rolled his eyes at Pavan behind her back, and Pavan had to suppress his own smile. Dellatrix took Pavan and Coren to the observation lounge, relieving the guard there for privacy. Coren took in the art and other treasures, walking from piece to piece.

"All this is pirate treasure?" he asked.

"Yep. Nice stuff, huh?" Dellatrix didn't expand on the piratical political economy of the room to the boy as she had for Pavan.

Pavan saw Coren's face show both fascination with the wonderful objects in front of him and a revulsion for the piratical methods that had amassed them. Coren's mind needed to be on the view, not the objects. Pavan's stomach sank as he contemplated the failure of the con because of the distraction of pirate loot. But Coren caught his eye and nodded, realizing he needed to concentrate.

Coren walked over to the observation window. He stared fixedly at the planet below.

"Wonderful view, huh, Coren?" said Dellatrix. "Not as great as the treasure. Khonoë looks good from up here."

"Memorable," he replied, smiling slightly without taking his eyes off the view.

Pavan gave Coren more time with the view by distracting Dellatrix with questions about the artworks. He had Dellatrix dig out nano-goggles, and they looked at the Ravos nanoart. He then had Dellatrix show him some of the more valuable objects in the collection, wasting more time. Eventually Dellatrix tired of this show-and-tell.

"Shall we get to it, Pavan? The demonstration?"

Pavan asked Coren, "Are we ready, Coren?"

"Yes, Pavan," said the boy, with the same slight smile and guileless eyes.

It was now or never. Pavan said, "OK, Dellatrix, have Thorak position the shuttle."

Dellatrix got busy with her servipad and stepped over to the observation window. After a few minutes, a shuttle came into view and hove to, visible in the center of the window.

"Ready, Coren," said Pavan. He sent up prayers to various gods he hoped were listening.

Coren took out his servipad and tapped a few times on it. This was chiefly for show; Coren would join the Mind to start the magic act. The boy stowed his servipad and looked out the window at the shuttle. Pavan saw him close his eyes.

The shuttle vanished. Dellatrix rushed forward to the window, craning her neck back and forth.

"It's gone!" She took out her servipad. "Thorak, are you still there?"

"Haven't moved." The big pirate's voice sounded bored. "Is something going to happen soon?"

"Yeah. But not for you. Hold on."

Coren had opened his eyes, smiling.

"Take it down now, Coren," said Pavan.

Coren tapped on his servipad again, then closed his eyes. The shuttle reappeared where it had been.

"Fantastic!" said Dellatrix, her voice loud in the room.

"What's happening?" Thorak's voice sounded from the servipad, mystified.

"Bring her in, Thorak. We're done. Meet us in the Orphanage."

Dellatrix bubbled with eagerness as the three of them came back to the Orphanage.

"Fantastic! Utterly stupendous!" She patted Coren on the back and sent him off to get the rest of the children, then gave Pavan a rewarding kiss. "This is colossal, Pavan!"

She held Pavan's hand as they walked toward the grassy field in the middle of the cargo hold where the children gathered. Sixteen bright, cheerful faces having a hard time holding in their glee.

Dellatrix took note and smiled. "Even the children are happy about it, Pavan!" She kissed him again.

"They're kissing again!" shouted Trex, unable to restrain himself. He started jumping up and down. "She doesn't know the secret!"

Dellatrix, ebullient, said, "What's the secret, Trex?"

"The secret agent fooled you, Dellatrix! It's all just magic!"

Mystified, Dellatrix looked at Pavan, who had edged away from her to a safe distance and braced himself for action.

"Magic?"

Trex shouted, "Coren made the shuttle disappear with his memory! It was all just a show!"

"A show. And what is this about a secret agent?" She looked at the children, her brows furrowing.

"Pavan! He's a secret agent, and he's fooling you all over the place!"

Coren and Skylla looked horrified. Pavan took another step away from Dellatrix.

"Oh, that. I knew that," she said.

"You…what?" mumbled Pavan.

"That you're a secret agent, Pavan. For the GSSS. Knew it all along. That's why I knifed your friend Tig in the bar, to cozy up to you and fake you into helping us get the Secret of Ravos."

"Um," said Pavan.

"But let's find out more about this magic. So, Trex." Dellatrix picked up the small boy and sat him on her shoulders. "Tell me about the magic."

The cargo bay doors slid open to admit Thorak and Jelric.

Dellatrix said to them, "Trex here tells me Pavan is a secret agent, and he's about to explain some things about what's going on." The two pirates grinned and approached Pavan, one pirate on each side of him.

"It's magic! We made you see Coren's memories instead of that shuttle!" cried Trex. "Fooled you, too!" The other children gathered together.

"We are one."

"No, we're not!" shouted Trex, who was enjoying being Dellatrix's pirate for the time being.

Dellatrix put the small child down and said to the Mind, "You're not holding hands."

"One has transcended the need for such physical contact."

"A…Ha." Dellatrix turned to look at Coren. "You went into the Mind from the observation lounge. Without touching." Dellatrix shook her head and smiled. "You're working with Pavan against me." She waved a hand and pointed at Pavan, and the two pirates grabbed his arms. She turned back to Coren. "I'll let you live, this time, since you can get into the Mind again. We need as many kids in the Mind as possible. Don't push it."

"Release Pavan." The children's voices spoke together and sounded panicked, even Trex's, as he rejoined the Mind.

"No." Dellatrix waved a hand toward the cargo bay door. The pirates pulled Pavan away.

"One will not help you in any way! One insists on Pavan's safety. One cannot work with a person as evil as you, Dellatrix."

"We'll see about that."

Pavan said, grasping at straws, "The Captain won't be pleased, Dellatrix. I can still help you. I can help with the Mind."

"Sir," said the promisepad in an urgent voice, "Do you acknowledge this violation and termination of your blood oath?"

"Not *now*," said Pavan.

"I urge you to reconsider, sir," said the promisepad. "Nothing is gained by continuing a relationship that neither party values. Am I correct, madam?"

"As always," smiled Dellatrix.

"Very well, I acknowledge it," said Pavan.

"Then, now that the blood oath no longer constrains my client confidentiality, my duty as the legal representative of Mr. Khadorov forces me to reveal that you are The Captain of this ship."

Dellatrix's mouth opened and closed. Then she smiled and said, "Shit. There goes my patent of nobility. Brig," she ordered. The two pirates holding Pavan's arms hesitated, then Thorak grinned.

"Always knew you were headed for big things, Dellatrix."

Several things became clear to Pavan at that moment. In Dellatrix, he'd found someone better at keeping secrets than he was. Thorak held a blaster to his head as Pavan bunched his muscles to fight free.

"And I always thought he was too pretty to be a true pirate," said Thorak. "Don't make me wipe the smile off your face with my blaster, Pretty Boy." He nudged Pavan behind the ear with the blaster.

It looked like Dellatrix had the best of it this time. The Captain always did.

Dellatrix smiled. "I give up. I've been jollying you along all this time, Pavan, hoping you'd help me get the Secret of Ravos working to my advantage. Not going to happen, is it? You're going to pay for that, Pavan. You and that little flat-boy. But I still need you to help with the Mind. For a little while longer." She waved a hand at the cargo bay door again, and the pirates dragged him off.

"Pavan," said Coren, real pain in his voice. The Mind continued his thought. "One will find a way."

"Sure thing," said Pavan.

CHAPTER THIRTY-EIGHT
Pavan Revisits the Brig

PAVAN SAT IN THE CHAIR in the middle of the brig. The force field around him was a familiar friend. It was just about the only friend he had.

But the real issue was the smell. Thorak and Jelric had borne it manfully while they brought up the force field. They removed themselves from the room hastily after that. The force field suppressed the smell to a considerable extent.

Pavan recognized the smell. He'd smelled it before in other, less dire circumstances. He also knew what it was because he was the source, though an indirect one. It was he who had put the two Goofer brothers' bodies into the cabinet that still concealed them.

He'd tried to escape on the way to the brig, but the pirates crushed the attempt brutally. Once recovered from that, he pulled himself into the chair and sat. There wasn't much he could do. Dellatrix, The Captain, had taken control of the situation.

So, Pavan sat and mulled over his woes. Time dragged by at a crawl. Pavan thought through several plans for escape, none of which was practical. He found it hard to concentrate, because his thoughts kept returning to his clear failure of mission and lack of perception, to the duplicity and manipulations of Dellatrix, and to the bodies and their aroma. He'd screwed up badly this time.

Dellatrix had manipulated him from the start. She'd lied to him at every step. She'd programmed her servipad to pretend to be The Captain on comms. Now, revealed as The Captain, she would condemn him to a slow death once she'd milked what remained of his usefulness. She would enslave the children to breed pods of hypershield generators, allowing her to pillage the galaxy. All this would not please the Ducis. Not that it would affect Pavan's GSSS career, as he'd be dead.

His mind ranged over the sequence of his utter failures to grasp the true state of affairs, while his senses told him that the olfactory situation was not tolerable. He stood and addressed the generator. "Hey, you. Generator."

No response. He pressed a hand on the force field, which buzzed a little.

"Hey! I need help."

"I am not designed to perform assistive action, sir," replied the generator. "Security concerns prevent me from communicating outside this room or speaking to prisoners, outside of emergencies. Does your request involve an emergency?"

"Can't you smell those bodies? It's hell in here."

"I am not constructed to be aware of that sensory information, sir. Technoids have no need of taste or smell. As no emergency exists, please desist from trying to engage my attention."

So, Pavan sat back down and dwelled on Margona—how much he missed her and how much he hoped she was still alive to miss. He'd miss her smile and her way of making him feel important while telling him he was wrong. He'd miss feeling her erect nipple in his hand, her lips on his. His heart ached with not knowing where she was. This led to meditation on how little he knew about anything at all, which started the whole cycle of self-pity over again. As time passed, he tried to get used to the smell. And failed.

Several hours passed, a sleep period passed, time passed. The smell remained.

The door to the brig opened, and Bullseye eased into the room and shut the door. Pavan got up and stood next to the force field.

"Ye gods," said the tall pirate as he approached the force field. "What the hell is that stink?"

Pavan pointed at the storage cabinet. Bullseye walked over to it and opened it, then hastily closed it again. He came back to Pavan, his face several shades paler than before.

"Thought I'd seen the last of those two," he said. "Wish it had been true."

"Come to gloat?"

"Naw. Talk. Gah! How can you stand it?"

"Force field keeps most of it out."

"Shit. Lucky you."

"Bullseye...."

"Yeah, yeah. Well, went and did it right this time, ain't you? Really? A GSSS agent?"

Pavan tried to get the pirate back on topic. "What's happening with the kids? And the generator will report everything you say to Dellatrix."

"Naw. Got a jammer, the thing won't be able to comm." Bullseye took a small pad out of a pocket and placed it on top of the generator.

"Sir, Galactic Code section 574.32 states that interfering with a correctional technology in the course of its duties is illegal with a penalty of 7 years and 4 months incarceration on a penal colony planet."

"I'll risk it." The pirate came back to the force field and addressed Pavan. "Ugh. Gonna cut it short or I'll die too, of Goofers poisoning. Been working with the kids, they ain't so bad, really. That little bitch Skylla hates me guts, o'course, but Coren come round. Now, some of us, we don't think that curcoper should be captain. Don't trust her, not a whit. Wouldn'ta signed on and shipped out if we'd known. We're with you against that croaker, Syndicate agent or no. Gah, what a stink!"

"What the hell is a curcoper?"

Teeth gleamed through the black beard. "Cutthroat. Pirate lingo. Gotta get up to snuff if you're gonna be a pirate, matey."

"I'm not going to be a pirate, Bullseye. I'm going to be dead."

"Damn. Look, we'll get you out. When we take over the ship. We're working on it, OK? Gods, it stinks." He shook his head and blew his nose on the deck. "I gotta get out of here, but I'll be back."

"Sure thing," said Pavan, sitting back down in his chair. "I'm not going anywhere."

The brig door banged open, and Bullseye and Coren came into the brig. Pavan stood up from his chair.

"What is that horrible smell?" asked Coren, holding a hand over his nose.

"Don't worry about it, kid," said Bullseye. Pavan noticed one of his arms had what looked like a blaster burn, a near miss that had sputtered a small chunk out of his triceps. He held a blaster rifle in his other hand. "OK, kid, you wanted to see your man here, and you're seeing him. What now?"

Coren approached the force field. He reached and touched it, then jerked his hand away at the buzz. "What's generating this field?" he asked.

"Generator, there," Pavan replied, pointing.

Coren walked over to the generator and tried persuasion. "Turn off the force field!"

"I am currently unable to comply due to an illegal device that violates Galactic Code section 574.32. Sir, I must insist—"

"All right, all right," said Bullseye, stretching and retrieving the suppressor. "Won't matter now that we got 'em on the run."

"May I ask, sir, who has authorized release of the prisoner?"

Bullseye said, grinning, "We're in charge now." Pavan doubted this claim. The generator was likewise unimpressed.

"Authorization denied."

Bullseye grimaced. Coren smiled and shut his eyes. He said, "The Captain authorizes the release of the detainee Pavan Khadorov." His voice sounded like Dellatrix's voice. Bullseye's mouth opened and shut without speaking.

"Authorization complete. I'll need to verify your NIU as well, ma'am."

"Go."

"Verified."

The force field disappeared.

The smell hit Pavan in the face like a blow. He hastened to collect his possessions from the box. The others had already fled the smell into the passageway, and he joined them there.

"How'd you do that, kid?" asked Bullseye.

"One can imitate technological and physical events with some precision," said the Mind.

Pavan asked, "Something like our magic act?"

"One has learned how to perceive physical objects in particle detail, Pavan. One inspected Dellatrix's identity unit and memorized it in case of future need. One then used visual, auditory, and magnetic illusions to fool the generator."

"Glad the technoid can't hear you. It would devastate the poor thing."

"We must have a talk, sir," said the promisepad. "NIU authentication is the heart of our system of contracting and jurisprudence. To use a method such as this—"

"Sorry, flat-boy, you may be out of a job," said Bullseye, giving a raucous laugh.

"One is happy to see you, Pavan." Coren dropped out of the Mind and hugged Pavan.

"Sure thing." Pavan patted his rescuer on the back and wondered how in the hell he was going to rescue them all.

CHAPTER THIRTY-NINE
Mutiny on the Ravager

"How's the mutiny going, Bullseye?"

Pavan, Bullseye, and Coren were in the liftor on their way to the Orphanage. They all ignored the liftor's chatty attempts to start a conversation and stuck to their own troubles.

"We ain't in charge." Bullseye rubbed his arm as they left the liftor and walked down the passageway toward the Orphanage.

Bullseye related the course of the mutiny while the trio walked. Over two days, Bullseye's gang of mutineers had battled the loyal pirates headed by Dellatrix. The Battle of Cargo Bay 19 the day before had been the turning point. A lucky blaster shot ignited a tactical ordinance dump behind the pirates that took out the bulkhead of the cargo bay. The resulting explosive decompression swept away all the loyal pirates and half of the mutineers. The rest of the mutineers were outside the bay taking cover and so avoided the decompression. They learned shortly that Dellatrix had secretly taken a party of loyalists to secure the Mind and so had also escaped.

Bullseye gritted his teeth. "It's close-quarter right now, down here in the cargo holds. Thorak and his gang are holding their own, and the croaker lass is with them. Bloody killing machine. She got our take-down party. Stupid bastards surprised her, then tried to tie her up."

Out of curiosity, Pavan asked, "How many did Dellatrix kill at once?"

"Five. All of 'em. Even used different methods, just to show off."

Pavan shrugged. An Elantri record, he was sure.

Bullseye stopped at an arms locker and extracted a blaster rifle and gave it to Pavan.

Coren grinned. "Don't I get one?"

Bullseye looked down on the boy from a great height and said, "You're too young, my man. And 'sides, I don't want my back being staked on anybody who disappears into hyperspace at the drop of a pirate's kerchief."

Coren laughed. "Let's see what the Mind thinks," he said. He closed his eyes, then opened them wide. "Pavan, they're in the Orphanage. The Mind just realized what's happened."

"Tell us."

"They've got all the other kids in a big box in there. Dellatrix got them in there when her pirates came in. She said it was for protection against the mutineers, but the Mind—" Coren stopped and stood still, eyes wide open and unseeing. He unfroze, clapped his hands over his ears and got a look of terror in his eyes. "Pavan, they're fighting in the Orphanage, blasters. Skylla's in there! We need to help!"

Bullseye and Pavan looked at each other. Pavan abandoned all thoughts of the lifeboats. The three of them raced toward the cargo bay doors that opened onto the Dellatrix Devdan Home for Lost Children.

In the Orphanage it was tough to tell who had whom pinned down. Any movement resulted in sparks and debris flying everywhere from the sputtering of junk by heavy blaster fire.

Everyone on the ship was now in the Orphanage taking part in the firefight.

"Stop firing, damn it!" shouted Bullseye, storming over to the line of six mutineers crouched behind a barrier of junk. "Bunch of bloody, trigger-happy bastards. Don't you know there are kids over there?"

"You ain't got no right to make us stop, Bullseye. She's a murdering bloke-croaker, a killer." A small pirate with a scraggly beard was the truculent speaker of this defiance.

"What about the kids?"

"They ain't my kids, Bullseye. Ain't yours, neither."

"It ain't ethical. They're civilians."

"Fuck me." The small man turned and fired his blaster rifle at a pirate who'd stuck his head up above the deck of the junk pirate ship. A woman pirate joined him in firing, and Pavan recognized the hostess whom Thorak had "recruited" from the Lavonian yacht, a young woman named Crosa. She seemed to have gained excellent piratical skills since he'd last seen her. She'd also acquired a healthy disdain for her kidnappers, from appearances.

Bullseye aimed his own blaster rifle at his comrades, but Pavan pushed it down with his hand. "We can't afford to lose any more of us, Bullseye. Let me try." Sparks from the particle shield next to him flew everywhere as a pirate on the other side fired at the sound of his voice. Pavan crawled forward to the line of boxes that shielded the mutineers and said, "I'll talk with her. You know we're tight, she'll listen to me. Why fight when you can negotiate?"

"We're better at fighting, you Syndicate son-of-a-bitch," said the scraggly bearded pirate. "If you want to negotiate, go on out there and find out what dying feels like."

"My choice. Give me a chance to end this," said Pavan. "What have you got to lose?"

"That blaster. Gimme."

Pavan handed over his blaster rifle, then kneeled next to Crosa. He raised his voice. "Dellatrix. I want to talk."

"Sure, Pavan. No shore leave privileges, though," she taunted. "You come to us."

Pavan found Coren next to him. His face was grimy and grim. He whispered, "Don't do it, Pavan. She's a shark. She'll kill all of us."

"What else can I do, Coren? Our friends here are hot for blood, her blood, and they don't care who dies in the effort."

"The Mind wants to help, Pavan."

"Well, unless the Mind has figured out how to disable blasters, not much help there."

"There must be something. Don't go, Pavan!"

"Ah well. Let's try a compromise." He shouted, "Let's meet in the middle, Dellatrix."

"I don't trust your mutinous scum, Pavan," she shouted back. "Wouldn't let them in the bar at the Jolly Roger. And I've never met in the middle in my life. Scum."

Crosa raised her blaster rifle in angry response, and Pavan pushed it down. "Give me a chance, damn it!" He raised his voice again. "OK, I'll come over. You show me the kids so I can be sure they're OK."

"Agreed. No weapons. And no technoids."

"Agreed." Pavan took his servipad and the promisepad out of his pocket and gave them to Bullseye. "Hold these for me, Bullseye."

"Sure, Pavan. I've always wanted my own servipad."

Pavan grinned. "Nice to know you have a high opinion of my negotiating skills."

"My man, your skills ain't up to hers. She's a real bear on negotiating." He slapped Pavan's back.

"Sir, I wouldn't trust that woman." The promisepad seemed to have a one-track neural system and a strong sense of urgency.

"You said that before. How come you didn't tell me she was The Captain?"

"Every client has complete confidentiality, sir. I did hint, but my capabilities for subtlety are less than they ought to be."

"Um. So are mine."

Coren closed his eyes. "We are one. One cannot kill, Pavan. One cannot force anyone to do something they do not wish to do. The Other was clear. Do not come, Pavan."

Pavan stood up and raised his hands and walked forward. He climbed up the boxes to the deck of the junk pirate ship and crossed to where the loyalists waited. Thorak helped him down by pulling on his outstretched arm and slamming him onto the deck.

"Now, Thorak, no cause for violence. The man is here to stop the killing." Dellatrix's voice was soft and affectionate. She held out a hand, and Pavan took it. She pulled him up and dusted off one of his shoulders. "Come on, Pavan, let's visit with the kids." She took his hand and pulled him over to a container and lifted the bar that closed its door.

The children lay scattered on the deck, terrified. Several were in the Mind. "The blaster energy is frightening to the components. One is sorry, Pavan. One cannot help."

"Me too." Pavan turned to Dellatrix. "They look OK. You can't seriously be considering going ahead with your breeding plan."

"Why not? Granted, it will be harder without you and your bond to them. I've overcome bigger obstacles." She stroked his scar with a finger. "I'll miss you, Pavan."

"Eventually, Dellatrix, the Syndicate will come in with a fleet and destroy you and the other pirates and clean off the surface of Khonoë. They've done it before with planets that gave them trouble."

"I wouldn't worry about that, Pavan. I'm a good negotiator. Our financial backers in the Syndicate will help us out there, too."

"You won't be alive to negotiate if Bullseye and the others finish you. We can make a deal, Dellatrix."

"That scummy lot got lucky in 19. We'll take them. And you have nothing I need."

"What about that nobility patent? I can deliver that."

"Got that in my pocket already, Pavan, as it turns out. I don't need you for that."

"I can help you negotiate with the Syndicate."

"They don't like you much anymore, Pavan. This isn't getting us anywhere." She stared at Pavan, who felt two hands grip his arms from behind. "Time to go. Poor Pavan."

"Dellatrix—"

She smiled, her lips curving. "Slow is best. Poor old Slopnor had that right, anyway." The tip of her tongue appeared as she concentrated.

A cord wrapped around Pavan's neck, gradually tightening. His hands of their own volition strained to reach for his neck, but the phantom hands pinned them to his side. The pressure cut off his windpipe, and the first struggle of his lungs to get air tightened his chest. His throat constricted with the effort to breathe, but he couldn't.

"Pavan! One cannot help!" The Mind screamed this with all the children's voices. Dellatrix jumped slightly, but the garrote continued tightening. Her powers of concentration were extraordinary. Her eyes were alight with pleasure and the gleam of light on metal.

"Pavan!" The children screamed. "No!"

Pavan's eyes bulged with the effort to breathe. The thought that slow was definitely not best fluttered across his mind. Her shark's eyes stared into his. Her tongue extended further with her mental effort. He choked. A bright light grew in his brain as death approached.

The pressure disappeared and his arms were free. He saw the eyes in front of him fill with horror. Both he and Dellatrix fell to the deck. She screamed. Pavan took great, heaving breaths, grabbing at his neck. He could feel the welt left by the invisible cord.

"Pavan!" The Mind was crying. So were all the children, in unison, the tears synchronized. Pavan sat up. Dellatrix continued to scream, incoherent with terror, thrashing on the deck, tearing at her head.

Thorak pulled back the door, and five pirates crowded into the container.

"What are you doing to her!" The big pirate grabbed Pavan with one arm, lifted him off the deck, and shook him.

"It's not me."

Thorak let him drop to the deck. He raised his blaster rifle.

Pavan croaked, "It won't do any good. Coren is with Bullseye, and she'll just seize up and die before you can kill them all. And the Mind has other powers."

"You bastard! Bloody Syndicate spy." Thorak swung the rifle at Pavan's head. Pavan, reflexes returned, ducked and rolled away, coming up against little Trex, who dropped out of the Mind.

He shouted, "She's dying, the pirate queen's dying. Save her!" The other children sobbed in unison.

"Take her. Take a lifeboat. Find your own way," said Pavan, holding a struggling Trex.

"What about them?" Thorak jerked his head toward Bullseye and the others.

"They'll listen. They'll get the ship and the treasure. That will be enough for them." He looked at his sometime pirate partner, screaming and tearing at her head. "Better hurry."

Coren, Bullseye, and Pavan stood at the window of the observation lounge watching the retreating shape of one of the ship's lifeboats. Pavan had set its course for deep space and locked down both the conoid and the comm system. With Coren assisting with ordering around the technoids, Pavan set the controls to return to the pirates when the craft left the Khonoë system. That would be weeks, as he'd set the craft to run only with ion thrusters, disabling the hyperdrive. Cast adrift.

The fifteen remaining mutineers, eyes wide, inspected the treasures they'd not known existed. Excitement ruled the room.

"Good riddance!" said Bullseye.

"What happened, Coren?" asked Pavan, rubbing his throat.

"I joined the Mind, and it went crazy when Dellatrix attacked you, Pavan. Just crazy. Most of the children love you, Pavan. I know I do. The Mind—it pulled Dellatrix in. She reacted like she did before. I couldn't remember from then, but now I do. Being a guest disrupts her mental powers, takes them away, and that terrifies her. It was bad. The Mind had never done that, forcing someone into hyperspace. It just did it. To save you."

"Grateful." Pavan cleared his sore throat. "Very grateful." He hugged the boy. The other children gathered around while the pirates disputed over their treasures.

"Hey, Pavan," said Janny. "Can we play with the pirates?"

"Sure, Janny, you all go ahead, play with whatever you like. Be careful, now. Some of these things have sharp edges." That included the pirates. He'd keep a weather eye out on them.

"Bloody hell," said Bullseye, shaking his head. "Bloody kids."

"Somebody better do something about the Goofer brothers, Bullseye. Why the hell didn't anyone take care of them?"

The pirate grinned. "Nobody ventured into the brig after you left, Pavan. And the only person who knew about those bodies was The Captain, and she sure didn't give a shit. I already took care of 'em." He pointed at the disappearing lifeboat. "Loaded 'em myself. Now they got a full complement."

Pavan saw the rough justice in this development but had more concern for the immediate future. "What's next?"

"I ain't got no idea, my man. We can't even fly the ship, can't order the technoids around. Captain's pirate protocols are still in place."

"You're captain."

"No way, my man. I got many fine qualities. Command ain't one of 'em." He shook his head, looking out on the planet. "I ain't got the spacing time for it, you know? Maybe I'll take my share and set up my own place in the Hole. Get my land legs back. Anyway, got no protocols to install."

"Coren, you can fool the technoids, right? With your NIU trick?"

"Sure, Pavan—but not all of them on the ship at once, continuously. That's what you'd need to run the ship, right?"

"I can help with that, sir," piped up a small voice from Pavan's pocket. "But it will require establishing networking capabilities in hyperspace for a time. Download of the black market protocols will take approximately 2.43 hours at this distance once your hypershield is gone."

Pavan smiled. "Is that legal?"

"The perfect is the enemy of the good, sir. I strongly advise you as your legal counsel to take advantage of this onetime offer regardless of its illicit status."

"Coren, can you keep the Mind asleep for the next three hours?"

"Sure, Pavan."

"OK," Pavan said to the promisepad. "I accept your offer."

"There will be a small fee, sir, to reimburse the necessary parties."

Pavan held up his servipad. "Life-or-death budget exception, please. Give it what it wants."

Pavan had never heard a servipad gasp before. "The finance department will have a problem with this, sir!"

"Tough. It's the only way we'll get out of this alive. You included," said Pavan.

"Very well, sir," grumbled the servipad. "I will mark it as an extraordinary expense, but you must be prepared for the inevitable audit, sir."

Pavan said to Bullseye, "While we're waiting, you might want to do something about your share of the treasure," he said. The pirates had escalated their disputes over the treasure. Kids played with their new toys. A massive pirate fight was a minute away, in Pavan's estimation.

He saw Crosa rise protectively in front of a pile of treasure, holding a knife. "Which one of you rat-fucking bastards wants to eat your balls first?" she screamed, facing three pirates who had expressed an interest in some of her loot.

Bullseye slapped his head. "Share!" He turned toward the mutineers, pointed his blaster rifle at the overhead, fired a low-particle blast, and roared, "Slow down, lubbers! Share and share alike. You, Smee, collect 'em all up and pile the stuff up over there. Share and share alike."

Pavan touched the tall pirate's arm. "Give the Mind one share. And I have a claim on the nanoart."

"What the hell is that?"

"That bulkhead, there."

"Ain't nothing on that bulkhead, my man."

"Nanoart. Too small to see."

Bullseye stared at Pavan, plainly thinking he was crazy.

"I collect it," lied Pavan. "It's beautiful."

"Sweet mother of mercy, help us. It's yours."

Pavan found the nanogoggles and the slipcase. He spent the next hour pulling the nanoart pieces off the bulkhead and placing them in their protective nano-containers. No sense in ignoring opportunity. All the while, the promisepad worked silently at taking over the operations of the *Ravager.*

CHAPTER FORTY
Pavan Catches Up

"So that's the entire tale, milord," said Pavan to the Ducis through his servipad's secure comms. He'd taken advantage of the Mind's sleep during the command protocols download to call his boss.

"Quite a tale indeed, Pavan, yes," replied the Ducis. "Outstanding work. You took a serious risk in confronting this Dellatrix, though. Covert action is better with that sort of person. Diplomacy and negotiation just prolong the inevitable." The short beard stretched in what passed for a warm smile on the chilly face in Pavan's vizquery.

"My throat agrees with you, milord." Pavan rubbed the area in question, which still showed the red weal of the invisible garrote after a full day. "Milord, may I ask—any news of Margona?"

"Oh, yes, Margona." A pause; Pavan knew bad news was imminent. "No, Pavan, she has altogether disappeared. We suppose a dissident faction took her and is holding her somewhere on Gaelea, but we have discovered no trace of her."

"But you think she's still alive?"

"I wish I could tell you that, Pavan, but I can't. She might be alive, but we've had no communications about her from any dissident group asking for anything."

"I'll return to Gaelea as soon as I can to help in the search."

"Yes, of course. But—"

"Ravos, milord. I have to return the children to their parents."

"Well, now, Pavan, that's a commendable proposal, but there may be other possibilities to consider. The Secret of Ravos is powerful and parlous indeed. Too parlous to risk its falling into the hands of either pirates or dissidents. And Ravos is no longer safe, if it ever was."

"Why not, milord?"

"The Planetary Interdiction Services have gone a step too far without consulting us. We, of course, reported that your pirate ship—what is it called?"

"The *Ravager*, milord."

"Yes, the *Ravager*." Contempt oozed from the Ducis's eyes. "We reported to PIS that the *Ravager* had landed multiple contingents of pirates on the planet, unrestrained by their interdiction systems. The politics are a little vague even to us, but the result was a crackdown on Ravos. Nothing in, nothing out."

"I see, milord. From what I saw, the people there already had some trouble with subsistence."

"Yes. Now it's worse. Much worse. We advised against full repression, but the PIS hotshots ignored the advice. Well, I don't need to bother you with the political details. Dissident factions on Ravos now control large parts of the cities. PIS troops cordoned off the spaceport, but anything outside their perimeter is quite volatile. Homemade weaponry, of course, but still effective at disrupting public order. The Syndicate will send security forces soon to adjust matters."

"I think I can evade most of that disorder, sir, in getting the children back to their parents. They're quite isolated and independent in their small village of Loxator."

"But the Secret, Pavan, the Secret. What are we to do about that? From your report, this Mind is also quite volatile. It would be better to bring the children to Gaelea, then fetch the parents as we find resources. We'll make them comfortable and keep them under observation to make sure they're all right. There's also the competence of the PIS to consider. If they have a comms slip-up and regard your ship as a pirate vessel, they'll destroy it without warning. The current leadership of the PIS is not…quite up to the task. No. No more risks, Pavan. Come home. Please acknowledge my order."

Pavan heard the finality of command in this polite conclusion and in the faint ringing in his ear.

"Yes, milord."

But home wasn't home anymore, not without Margona. And the children—they would not be at home on Gaelea any more than he would be, especially with their parents still on the interdicted Ravos. And "keep them under observation" was surely a euphemism for studying the children like lab rats, or worse. Pavan would ignore this order from the Ducis. It wouldn't make his life any easier, but he'd like himself a lot better.

"Well then. Oh—and where precisely is this Dellatrix person? You know how much I hate loose ends, Pavan. You surely could have completed the job by disposing of her. But we'll take care of her. You've done enough."

Pavan almost refused to tell him. A part of him missed Dellatrix enough to make him wish her well. Get over it, man. He had to tell the Ducis; otherwise, his boss would issue another command. Then he'd figure out that Pavan's response to compulsory commands wasn't what it should be. That wouldn't help his return to Ravos. He needed time, and Dellatrix would provide it as the last favor she did for him by distracting the Ducis. What the Ducis would do with her— well, it wasn't his problem anymore. Not after those metallic eyes staring into his as she garroted him.

"She's in a lifeboat heading from Khonoë to the system heliopause under ion thrusters." He had a conoid give his servipad the navigation path for the lifeboat.

"Excellent. Plenty of time to finish her and her scum. And the rest of that pestilential planet. Anything else, Pavan?"

"Just…find Margona, please, milord."

"We will, Pavan, we will. Come home now."

"Yes, milord."

His vizquery cleared. Time to shut down his servipad. It wouldn't do to have it see him disobeying the Ducis's orders. He opened his mouth for the command but never got out the words.

"An incoming comm, sir," declared the servipad in its official GSSS voice. "Personal. Priority."

"Pavan?" Loud and clear. Margona's voice. Pavan's vizquery lit up, and there she was, standing with a group of men and women on what looked like a ship's bridge. "Pavan!"

Pavan's eyes bulged. His natural impulse to embrace his wife was so intense that his arms met in mid-air in front of him.

He found his voice. "Margona! You're alive!"

"Barely."

"Where are you?"

The vision in front of him turned to the man standing next to her. "Where are we, Milosel?"

The man stared off beyond the servipad sending the image and said, "Deep space, 230 hypersecs from Gaelea, 64 hypersecs from Xumia."

"I meant, what the hell is going on?"

"That's a long story, Pavan. What's new with you?" Margona smiled, but Pavan could see tears trickling down her cheeks. His cheek muscles strained under the load of the grin he wore.

"A longer story, guaranteed."

"Some kind of hyperspace phenomenon blocked you."

"A big part of the story."

"Where are you?"

"Khonoë."

"That's what my aunt told me."

"Aunt Bet?"

"Yes, Pavan. I only have one aunt."

"How in the hell did Aunt Bet learn where I am? How does she know about Khonoë?"

"Guess."

"The Ducis told your Uncle Erokh."

"Under pressure. But nobody knew whether you were still alive. They said something about being kidnapped by pirates."

"Yeah. Well. It's more complicated than that."

"What's the pirate situation?"

"We mutinied and cast them adrift in a lifeboat."

The man next to her, Milosel, got a funny look on his face. "Mutinied?" he said.

"Well, think of it as a carefully executed escape plan involving stealing their ship," replied Pavan. "And their loot."

"Well, that's all right then," said Milosel. Pavan sensed a sardonic note in his voice.

"Margona, would you introduce us?" asked Pavan.

Margona said, "Milosel Tsanov, Captain of the *Dudia Clipper*, my husband Pavan Khadorov. The *Dudia Clipper* is a cargo ship the GSSS has commandeered as a refugee transport."

"So you're a refugee now?" asked Pavan.

"It's more complicated than that," said Margona.

"Look here," said Captain Tsanov. "Let's get on with it. I've made a deal with Dr. Nukova to transport her and her friends to a planet where the GSSS won't find them. She wants you to come along. Are you on?"

"Won't find them?" Pavan sucked in a breath and let it out. "They're looking hard for you, Margona. I just got off a comm with the Ducis. He's very concerned about your welfare."

"The Ducis is trying to kill me, Pavan. I learned about his coup plans for Gaelea. A GSSS assassin has already died trying, a peabrain named Bukharov."

"Pakhan Bukharov? Shit!" Bukharov was the Ducis's personal assassin, used only on special terminations. A jerk, but a good assassin. Rest in peace, or rot in hell.

"And also I've joined the Gaelean dissidents that were shipped off planet as refugees," said Margona, waving her hand at the other people standing behind her. "We're fugitives from the GSSS. And we've got about 5,000 other refugees to find homes for as well."

"Shit me a brick."

An older woman standing behind Margona stepped up and said, "Princess, I don't think this guy is worth your time. Playboy." The woman had a pugnacious expression that somehow made Pavan think of his late grandmother on his father's side. Granny Khadorova was never to be taken lightly. Not ever.

"Have they promoted you from doctor, Margona?" he asked as a diversion.

Margona grinned. "Pet name, Pavan. Uva here is my lucky charm. She's a dissident leader."

"She's a bad influence, I can tell."

"Playboy," huffed Uva.

"Sir," said Pavan's servipad in an urgent voice, "Dr. Margona Nukova is on the Prime Rogue Proscription list. I have just updated that list from headquarters, and I must insist that you tell them at once of her location."

"Um." Pavan was no longer walking on thin ice. He was walking along the bottom of a deep ocean trench below an ice pack, and he was finding it hard to breathe. He said, "Margona, I've got to go. I have to take a group of children back to their parents on Ravos. And I guess if you're going to survive, we have to end this comm pretty soon or my servipad is going to out you to the Ducis."

"Pavan! Stay where you are. We'll come and get you."

"Sir! Under regulation 236.78 of the Uniform Code of Syndicate Technoid Civil Service, I am forced—"

"Bye, Margona. See you whenever. End comm. And hold off on that notification please," he ordered the servipad.

"Sir, by the Uniform Code, I must at once—" Abruptly, the servipad went mute.

"Hello?" Pavan shook the pad.

"Sir," said the promisepad, "I have permanently disabled your servipad's neural systems as it appeared its intent was to violate one of my overriding directives."

"My servipad is GSSS. It's supposed to override everything else."

"Not quite, sir, though I cannot enlarge further because of those same directives." The pad spoke in a quiet, professional voice. "Take advantage of the situation, sir. I believe the phrase commonly used in such situations is 'seize the day.'"

"Sure thing," said Pavan. He tossed his servipad into the disposal bin, where it vaporized.

CHAPTER FORTY-ONE
Margona Visits a Pirate Planet

MARGONA HAD TO PEE, BADLY. The meeting was taking much longer than she had dreamed possible. The relative deprivation she had met with in the cargo hold resulted in post-traumatic stress that combined drinking too much liquid with a decided preference for holding it in. But there were limits, and she had reached hers.

"Excuse me," she said.

Everybody stopped and looked at her, eager to hear her thoughts, as their own were in utter confusion. The participants were Captain Tsanov, Uva, Fenida, and two representatives of the non-dissident refugees.

"I have to pee," she explained. A collective sigh arose.

"Let's take a break," said Captain Tsanov. "This isn't getting us anywhere."

Margona found the ladies' head down the passageway and relieved herself, then looked at herself in the mirror. It surprised her in a way that Pavan had recognized her. Several days in a foul cargo hold had not improved her appearance. Several more days in what passed on the cargo ship for a stateroom and several showers had improved her physical and mental state, primarily by removing most of the smell she had acquired. She found that the smell lingered in her nostrils as a kind of PTSD-induced phantom pain, and she speculated on which pathway she would have to alter to remove that pain. This turned her mind to the pathways she needed to alter to restore Pavan to his normal, two-timing self. And to the fact that she had to get to him to do that. And what she would do with him once she got him alone. She fluffed her hair in the mirror, stuck her tongue out at herself, and got a grip.

She went back to the wardroom—stray thought: why did all the places on a ship have wildly different names than the usual words for them? Back to the wardroom and the discussion of where to go.

"Let me summarize, please," she said before anyone could resume the argument. "You, Captain Tsanov, want to take the ship, drop us all off who knows where, and try to unload your cargo to get the money to refit as a non-Syndicate ship. You, Uva and Fenida, want to go back to Gaelea to take over the government as quickly as possible. You other two just want to find the nearest world with working bathrooms and transport down to it. And, last but not least, I want to go to Khonoë and rejoin my playboy mutineer husband, who is in dire straits as of two hours ago. Is that correct?"

The five heads all nodded grudging acceptance of this summary.

"I don't see any reason we can't all have what we want. It's just a matter of timing," said Margona. "I'm first and simplest. I don't even have any luggage. All I need is to get to Pavan, who desperately needs my help. And yours, too."

That started up the debate again. Nothing was simple. Uva and Fenida wanted part of the ship's arms locker transported down with them to Gaelea, which Captain Tsanov refused. Captain Tsanov wanted his cargo unloaded and sold at once, as time was money, and he was sure pirates would make that more difficult than necessary. He now expressed a wish to avoid dealing with mutineers, who he felt were as bad as pirates, or worse. But he acknowledged a debt to Margona for her surgical intervention. The two refugee leaders weren't picky, they said, but they wanted off, now; and they weren't interested in revolutions, Gaelea, pirates, mutineers, or dire situations, just toilets and food. Especially toilets.

Margona sighed and got as comfortable in her chair as she could. It was going to be a long afternoon. And it wouldn't be over until she got her way.

The *Dudia Clipper* dropped out of hyperspace at Khonoë two days later. Margona stood on the bridge next to Captain Tsanov, who was not in the best of moods.

"You do realize, Margona, that this place is a nest of the worst scum in the galaxy?"

"And my husband, Milosel."

"Yes, him included." The captain definitely didn't like mutineers.

"I'm sure everything will be fine, Milosel," she said.

A ship appeared, leaving its orbit around the planet and heading straight for them.

"Channel," said Captain Tsanov.

"Channel open," said the technoid comms station.

"Unidentified vessel, this is Captain Tsanov of the *Dudia Clipper* requesting asylum."

"Welcome, Captain Tsanov. This is The Captain of the *Ripper*. Stand down and prepare to be boarded." No image, voice only.

"Captain, we're looking for the *Ravager*. Would that vessel be around somewhere?"

"Finders keepers, Captain Tsanov. Stand down."

Tsanov looked at Margona. "Told you so."

Margona opened her mouth to argue but got no words out before another ship drew up next to the *Ripper*.

"That's our prize, Captain." Pavan's voice was firm and decisive. The pseudowindow showed him standing alone on the bridge.

"Who is this? You're not The Captain of the *Ravager*."

"No, The Captain is away. But just now, I'm Captain Khadorov and you need to stand down, or we'll disable you."

"Weren't you the guy hanging around the Jolly Roger tavern with that Elantri killer woman?"

Margona closed her eyes. She didn't want to hear it.

"Irrelevant, Captain. Stand down. Oh, and would you like to take a little trip through hyperspace? We can help with that."

"Finders keepers, Khadorov. And we'll be happy to take that hypershield off your hands now. We'd love to take a trip to try it out." A flash of light appeared on the side of the *Ripper* and sparks flew as the ion blast sputtered against the shielding on the *Ravager*.

"Shouldn'ta done that," said another voice, rougher and louder, from off to the side of Pavan. "Give it to 'em, kids."

Silence descended on the scene for several minutes. Pavan stood, smiling and saying nothing. Captain Tsanov shifted from foot to foot, his anxiety showing. His navigation and communications technoids informed him that everything relating to hyperspace was down.

The comm came to life. "Had enough?" asked Pavan.

"What...." The *Ripper* captain's voice was unsteady. "What the hell was that?"

"Just a little adventure in hyperspace, Captain. I assure you, no permanent harm done. But you might want to avoid spending a lot of time there. It would not be agreeable for you. People have gotten lost in there before now, you know. Those gravity wells are dark and deep."

"Bloody, stinking hell."

"All of that. Stand down?"

"Very well. This time. But we'll need to have a talk, Khadorov. When your captain gets back."

"She's not coming back, Captain."

"She?"

"Yes, Dellatrix Devdan was The Captain of the *Ravager* until three days ago. Now she's captain of a lifeboat somewhere between here and Elantra, if the Syndicate hasn't helped her on to her ultimate destination instead."

"I see."

"I'm happy you do, Captain. Now, stand down or prepare for the adventure of your lives."

The *Ripper* turned away and retreated toward the planet Khonoë. If it had a tail, it would have been between its legs.

Captain Tsanov rubbed his chin and smiled. "There may be something in this mutiny business after all."

"Sixteen?" Margona was skeptical. Pavan? With sixteen kids? The man who two hours ago had faced down an armed pirate ship? The man who disappeared for months at a time? The man who—

"Yeah. I just wanted to prepare you."

"Sixteen."

"You're surprised."

"Pavan, you've never been comfortable around children." Wild hope flared in her chest until she remembered that pathway complex, the bad one. Oh, Pavan.

"All in the past, Margona. All in the past. I know you'll like them."

His voice was earnest and persuasive. Was he pressuring her to take over day care, or was he just anxious that she get along? He'd been nothing but joyous since she shuttled over from the Dudia Clipper. What was urgent about meeting these children? Was there something wrong with them? Margona liked children on principle, but she took each individual child as they came, and they came in many, many different and unlikeable guises. And her experience was limited to various cousins and nephews and nieces and seriously disturbed patients.

Pavan escorted Margona through the passageways of the *Ravager* to the Orphanage. She stopped and looked at the sign above the door.

"This Dellatrix Devdan was the captain of this ship?"

"The pirates have a rule that keeps the identity of the captain a secret. She used that to fool me stupid. Got her in the end, though. It's a long—"

"—story. Yes, we both have a lot of catching up to do." She looked at her husband and smiled. "Is that beard permanent? I like it. It makes you look, well, piratical."

"Anything that will get you into bed," he said, grinning. His teeth shone brightly through the rather unkempt beard. So did his eyes. Not entirely the man she'd met on Drihion; better, somehow, than the man she'd married.

"Kids first, then bed." It usually worked the other way round, but she was willing to experiment.

They walked into the Orphanage. Sixteen children stood on the grass looking fidgety. Pavan guided Margona over to them. A large, wild-looking pirate loomed behind them.

"Bullseye, this is my wife, Margona. Dr. Nukova. Viggu Bullseye, Margona."

"Arrh," said Bullseye, inarticulate with shyness.

"I'm sure you have a lot of stories about my husband to tell me, Bullseye."

"Bullseye is the Daycare Coordinator of the Orphanage," said Pavan.

"Screw you, Pavan," said Bullseye, on more certain ground. Margona smiled at the big pirate, who grinned back. Definitely a lot of stories there.

"Coren, Skylla, Jandra…" Pavan went through the names, introducing them all. Normal, everyday kids to Margona's mind. When they came to the smallest child, the little boy fizzed with energy.

"And Trex, he's our most active child. He's a handful."

"Let's see," said Margona, and she scooped up the little boy in her arms and held him up in front of her to study him closely. These kids were normal and likable, and she forgave Pavan in advance for whatever devious plan he was forming. Sixteen. Hard to believe.

"Just the right amount for my hands," she said, and hugged Trex.

"Lemme go!" shouted Trex. "No kissing!" But he didn't struggle to get down.

"I'm sorry, you know, for all the trouble I've given you," said Pavan.

"I'm sorry too, for being troubled, troubled enough to violate everything I believed in." Margona vowed to herself that she would get her husband under the micro-scalpel as soon as she could to rectify her mistake. Later; right now, she had other things on her mind.

They sat in the smallish bed in Pavan's quarters, legs intertwined, facing each other, naked. Margona was glad for the quiet time after meeting all the children and having dinner in the mess with all the pirates. Both noisy crowds, but now things were quiet and cozy.

"I was so afraid you were gone, Margona," said Pavan. He stretched out a hand, and she reached and took it and rubbed it.

"I knew you were alive, even when people told me you weren't," she said. "Nobody could kill you."

"Near thing this time," said Pavan, rubbing his throat.

Another story there, a red weal fading that she'd kissed a few minutes before. They'd spent some time before bed laying out the barest outlines of their stories to each other. This Dellatrix creature was her worst nightmare, and Pavan had passed over certain things with that furtive expression he got when he covered up his sexual adventures. Seen together in the Jolly Roger tavern? The jealousy was still in her, but somehow her ability to handle it had changed, maybe because of the character-building adventures she'd experienced. That cargo hold taught her things about survival that she needed to understand, things that she'd never encountered in her sheltered upbringing. And so had the grief and love she felt for her husband when she thought he might be dead. She had to look to her future and not let her emotions about the past consume her.

"Pavan, what are we going to do about Gaelea? The Syndicate? My uncle? My aunt?"

"And the Ducis. I need to talk to your dissident friends."

"You won't turn them in?"

"No."

"I'll see if they're willing. You're the enemy."

"If the Ducis is planning a coup, I need to know. I can't believe it."

"My cab was sure about the coup," said Margona. "Not so sure about the Ducis, or about my uncle. And I can't reach Aunt Bet now. I'm afraid...." The thought was too painful to finish.

"Your *cab?*"

"Yes, I hired a cab that had good connections...really good connections. A long story."

"A cab. Our technoids seem better informed than we are. You said the GSSS sent a ship after you?"

"Ships. Captain Tsanov told me that. He said the GSSS told him to stay put until they picked me up and took me back to Gaelea." She shuddered. "Pavan, they were going to kill me."

"You're right. I'm familiar with Bukharov. The Ducis lied to me. He knew where you were. Why would he lie to me, even when I was safe, and the Secret was secure?"

"Secret?"

"Sorry, that's our shorthand for the kids. The Secret of Ravos."

"What's so secret about them? They're cute, especially that Trex. Listen, Pavan —" She reached out and stroked his faint scar, the one she loved, and reached for his head to pull him toward her. Enough talking.

"Show you tomorrow." He pulled her toward him, their lips found each other's, Margona again appreciated the pleasure of kissing a man with a beard, and there was no more talking that night.

CHAPTER FORTY-TWO
The Syndicate Comes to the Rescue

"Huh. Playboy." Uva Freytova was not having any of it, not from Pavan.

Pavan grinned. Uva confirmed his first impressions of her and then some. Just like Granny Khadorova in so many ways. It awoke in him the memory of the joint chastisements and amnesties of his early youth. He'd been an adventure-some boy, untroubled with parental authority at the best of times. Her nickname for Pavan had been "The Scamp." Granny Khadorova had understood him well. She had eyes in the back of her head. And she made sure he understood the path he was on went straight to the demons of the underworld. He had to admit she'd been right.

Uva's characterization of the state of Gaelea had much the same feel. In her case, the demons were the Syndic and his minions and the Syndicate thugs that backed them. Of which, though she never said it out loud, he was one. And, as for coups, neither she nor Fenida knew any more than the research given to them by the Princess.

Pavan drank his breakfast tea and set the cup down on the mess table. After spending the night with Margona for the first time in months, nothing could make him the slightest bit unhappy. "How about you think of me as a pirate, not a thug? That would make it easier to tell me things." Pavan felt a surreptitious kick from his wife under the table.

Fenida snorted. "Pirates, thugs, gangsters, politicians. Take your pick. What's to tell? You'd sell us all into slavery on some aggie planet the first chance you got."

Fenida gave the statistics to back up Uva's more emotional critique of Gaelean society. Pavan never paid much attention to Gaelean politics. His first serious exposure to the political and noble classes came when he married Margona. They seemed harmless enough, aside from the Ducis, at least from his playboy's perspective. But Fenida made a good case for revolution. And her description of the refugee evacuation had the Ducis' boot prints stamped all over it. Uva's outrage, framed by Fenida's cold morality, made him think again about his own relative complacence about the similar conditions he'd encountered, or worse, facilitated, during his career. He wasn't a cold, hard man like the Ducis. And yet, here he was. A pirate. Pavan let go of the vestiges of his GSSS career then and there.

"I'll admit you have no reason to trust me. I've done some pretty regrettable things for the Syndicate. But circumstances change, people change, the Syndicate changed. I changed."

"He's got a pirate beard now," said Margona. "That's a new side to him."

"If I were thirty years younger," said Uva, "you'd knock me off my feet and sweep me away, beard and all. I ain't that young anymore, and I want action. Real action. If you got something in you to get me that, I'm yours. Otherwise, bugger off."

"Have they met the kids yet?" Pavan asked. Uva and Fenida looked at him as though he were swinging wildly off topic, but he wasn't. Not at all. He grinned again.

"No, I thought I'd wait to see if you let the pair of them live," said Margona. "Once you'd gotten to know them."

"You're in for a treat. You know what? Why not? Let's adjourn and go down to the Orphanage."

"The what?" asked Fenida, taken aback.

"Pavan." The voice from his new pirate servipad was Bullseye's. "Get the hell up here, now!"

The three Syndicate cruisers clustered in space near Khonoë rather than orbiting the planet, indicating they weren't staying any length of time.

"I'm thinkin' we made a mistake letting the kids take a rest," said Bullseye.

"Could be right," replied Pavan, examining the cruisers through the magnifying pseudowindows on the bridge. "Maybe they're here to rescue me. Maybe not."

"How come I always get this feeling every time you're around, Pavan? You know, the sound of shit hitting fans?" Bullseye grinned.

"Sir, incoming comm from the *Dudia Clipper,* Captain Tsanov," said the comms technoid.

Tsanov's cheerful face filled one pseudowindow in front of them. "Mr. Khadorov. I've just had a nice discussion with the commander of the *Tadusov*. They, and the *Seluzov* and the *Bestrov*, are part of a task force sent to deal with the piracy in this sector."

"Did you mention my name to them?"

"Thought I'd talk to you first."

"And they didn't chastise you for your desertion from the Syndicate?"

"Didn't come up, though I identified myself and my ship. Unless they're long out of contact with home, they know who I am."

"Why haven't they commed me?"

"Your ship—it's an old freighter, right?"

"Recently taken over by the pirates, yes."

"They may assume we're a freighter convoy. Since I commed them, they didn't need to talk with you."

"Perhaps." But Pavan's intestines told him there was more at stake. They might already know all about him. These ships couldn't be the force the Ducis intended to send to tidy up loose ends like Dellatrix and the pirates. It must be a task force already underway with some other purpose. The fleet the Ducis now denied he'd sent to destroy Khonoë and the Secret? He needed some time to get everything ready to deal with them in his new role as pirate captain. "Can you put them off for a while, Captain?"

"Mr. Khadorov, I've got two ion cannons and a ship full of refugees. I don't think either of those will stop those three cruisers from doing whatever they want. Do you have something that will?"

"I just might. Sure thing," said Pavan.

Fenida and Uva had accompanied Margona to the Orphanage while Pavan dealt with his emergency. Pavan found them involved in various playground activities with the children. It was time to get his potential allies up to speed so they could better consider what to do next. He would need their support, or at least their acquiescence, to get the kids back to Ravos.

Uva came up to him holding a dildo. "What the hell are they doing with this?"

"Oops," said Pavan. "They must have taken that from the sex room on the planet."

Uva stared at him for a time in disbelieving silence. Pavan was sure that he was about to feel the pent-up rage of the elderly revolutionary, and the only weapon she had was the noticeably large dildo. Compared to a rubber baton, say, this wouldn't do much harm, but still. He reached and snatched it out of her hand before she could react.

"There's a logical explanation for everything," he told her. He signaled with the dildo for Margona; he needed backup.

"I'm gonna revise my opinion of you, Playboy. It's too bad Child Molester is two words, it won't make a good nickname."

Margona, walking up with Fenida, took in the confrontational stance of Uva and the dildo and smiled. "Pavan, I'd have been happy to work with you last night. Why bring that here?"

Uva snorted. "Ask him about the sex room, Princess. Let's see, a new name. Scumbag? Lowlife? Creep?"

"I knew you'd like him once you met him, Uva," said Margona.

Fenida's mouth made a down-turned U, and her eyes got angrier, but she said nothing. Uva snorted and gave Pavan a rude gesture.

"I'll explain," said Pavan, "but later. Right now, I need to show you something."

"I'll skip that part, Scumbag," said Uva. "Keep it in your pants."

"Come on, you'll have a great time," he said. He gathered up the kids on the play field.

"OK, kids," he said, "I'd like to take a little trip with the Mind. Can it handle all four of us at once?"

Skylla laughed. "No problem, Pavan. As long as they all agree."

"Agree to what?" asked Fenida, suspicious.

Uva was indignant. "Is this some kind of perverted group sex thing you've—"

"No, no, no, purely a little adventure with the kids. They have this talent for traveling in hyperspace with their Mind. They can take us along, and you'll see what we've been doing since we left their planet. OK? Just trust me."

"Their Mind? Hyperspace?" asked Margona, mystified.

"Look, Scumbag, I trust no one that looks like you," said Uva. "But I love to travel, so why not?"

Fenida took her time and thought through the potential pitfalls and benefits. She asked warily, "You guarantee nothing will happen to us, and that whatever you're planning won't harm the children?"

"Um. Guarantee is a strong word," said Pavan. "I haven't had any lasting effects. Neither of you are Elantri assassins, are you?"

"What?"

"Never mind. It'll be fine. And nothing will happen to the kids. Let's just go over here and lie on the grass. It's best if you find somewhere comfortable."

Mystified, the women all lay down in a radiating circle, head to head, and Pavan joined them. The kids arranged themselves in comfortable positions on the grass nearby.

"OK, kids, a short trip. Let's keep the bubble small so we don't bother the neighbors. Show these ladies what's what," said Pavan.

"We are one," said all the children together, startling the three women, "and we welcome our guests."

Pavan felt the usual rush of dropping into hyperspace and saw the flashing colors. The Mind took them on a tour of the Khonoë gravity well and a close-up survey of the *Ripper,* orbiting synchronously on the other side of the planet. Aware that the new guests could be hyper-sick, the Mind soon broke up.

Pavan scrambled to his feet. Margona sat up, dazed. Fenida lay still, looking at the overhead with a stony face. Uva turned over and pressed her face into the grass and put her hands over her head, then got up. She had a huge smile on her leathery face.

"Now *that* was fun!" she said. "You really got something here, Playboy. Better than perverted sex!"

"Sure thing," said Pavan, helping his wife to stand, then nudged the silent Fenida with his foot to make sure she was alive.

The next step before confronting the Syndicate ships was to get the Mind up to speed. Pavan took Coren aside and said, "We might have a problem, and you might have a solution for it. Or the Mind might."

Coren said nothing but looked interested.

"Three Syndicate cruisers are in the Khonoë system. I'm not sure if they're friendly, things are complicated. How much have your parents on Ravos figured out about the Mind now?" Pavan knew he was grasping at straws, but straws were all he had left. The alternative was to throw everyone on the mercy of the Ducis, which was not an option anymore.

"They've been forming small minds, now that the Chronicler has absorbed the Mind's memories. We've synched up a few times, but the kids are tired, you know?"

"So, how many people can join the Mind now?"

"Well, counting all the aged that want to, about 87. There are a few people on Ravos who think that it's crazy and just want to go on fishing."

"What would happen if all of you, children and ageds, got together in one big Mind?"

"Happen?"

"Yeah, like, how big could you make the hyperbolic bubble? Big enough to cover the whole of Syndicate space?"

"I don't know. Why?"

"I'd like to shut everything down for some time to make the Syndicate negotiate with us."

Coren smiled. "We can do that without a huge bubble, Pavan. We only need to adjust the parameters of the hyperspace bubble to cover the planets and the shipping lines between them. The Mind figured out how to use photonic dependency links to cover a larger area through this math thing Skylla discovered called a Negusov blanket over sets of photonic cones. It lets us project the hyper-blanket over a highly structured set of photonic events with minimal energy expenditure."

"You've been experimenting again. And reading up on math." Pavan thought a moment. He said, "Can you allow for a specific shipping lane outside the blanket? Say from here to Ravos?"

Coren nodded. "I figured it might be a good idea, in case Dellatrix came back. Skylla's idea, really. She hates Dellatrix." He pursed his lips. "Skylla's better at math than I am. She's going to be good, Pavan. I'll work with her to find all the systems we'll need to cover. Oh, and we've plotted a more direct path through hyperspace for a ship—I read up on navigation, and Skylla says it's just wrong the way they compute the hyperdesics. Her equations will cut the time in hyperspace for the ship by an order of magnitude. Skylla will give the equations to the conoids once we do a little experimentation. She thinks she can adapt their symbolic math capabilities to the new equations. She's already gone over it with the *Ravager* conoid, and it's amenable."

"That's...incredible." Pavan's mind reeled a bit with the ramifications. Later. Plans and possibilities swirled through his mind, but he had to focus right now on dealing with the cruisers.

Coren reached out and touched Pavan's shoulder. His face was serious. "One thing, though, Pavan. The Mind regrets forcing Dellatrix into hyperspace against her will. It won't do it again. The Others were very clear. It isn't right. Her attacking you panicked the Mind, and it just did it. It won't do it again, to anybody. If you can get them to agree to be guests, like you did with the *Ripper* captain and those nice ladies, fine; but otherwise, no way."

"All right, thanks for telling me." Relying on the mercy of the Ducis and abandoning the dissidents was not an attractive proposition. Pavan had more than straws now. But he would have to bet his life and that of his wife and the refugees on a bunch of kids playing with advanced math. At least they'd have parental supervision, albeit from a distant planet. OK, then. At least Dellatrix was long gone, one less threat to worry about. The Ducis would take care of her in due course.

Margona, recovered from her first experience of traveling in hyperspace, asked, "What are you going to do, Pavan?"

"Come with me to the bridge, Margona, and I'll tell you," said Pavan. "And you, Coren. Get Skylla, too. It's time we did something about the Syndicate."

Pavan, Margona, Coren, and Skylla arrived on the bridge to find a nervous Bullseye pacing back and forth.

"Bastards keep hailing us, Pavan," said the tall pirate. "You said keep 'em occupied, you didn't say how. I'm just letting 'em squawk. Ain't gonna work forever."

"Don't worry, Bullseye. I've got a plan."

"Is it as good as the one that got most of us killed? 'Cause—"

"Conference in Tsanov from the *Dudia Clipper,* I'll explain."

He did, and while everyone but Coren had doubts, Pavan just said, "Everyone get ready. We have to do this, or just surrender to the Syndicate, refugees and all. We don't want to do that."

Pavan hailed the cruisers. The captain of the *Tadusov* responded to the hail.

"Pavan Khadorov? The head of the GSSS sent us to find you and extract you from a pirate mob. Instead, we find a couple of old freighters, one of them listed as deserted from special service and the other listed as destroyed. What the hell is going on?"

"Long story. I would have filled the Ducis in, but my servipad got bricked. Pirates took this ship awhile back and turned it into a pirate ship with new armaments. We've gotten rid of the pirates, most of them anyway, and that other freighter brought my wife. Look, I don't need to be extracted. I need to get to a planet called Ravos. I've got a load of children and refugees that need resettling."

"Ravos?" The captain blinked, looking at his vizquery. "That's interdicted. Children? Refugees? Some other time, Khadorov. Right now, we're extracting you. And your wife." Pavan glanced at Margona, who rolled her eyes.

Pavan responded, "I don't care if the planet is interdicted, I have to get there."

"We'll follow orders and get you out of that ship, then we can deal with the refugees."

"Well, see, that's what everyone here is afraid of. They'd prefer to be on their own."

"What refugees want is irrelevant to our mission."

"Perhaps we can meet with their representatives—"

"Screw this," came a voice from offscreen. "He's just bullshitting you, Captain. Get on with it."

A chill ran up Pavan's spine. "Dellatrix?"

The Elantri stepped into view next to the captain, who looked at her askance. She had on civilian clothes designed for an upper-class Gaelean woman rather than her drab but form-fitting spacer's suit. But she still wore her spacer's boots, ready for anything.

"Hi, Pavan. Surprised to see me?"

"Not really. How did you convince the Syndicate ships you were legitimate?"

"You really haven't worked it out yet, have you?" Dellatrix smiled. "Who's funding us, I mean."

"Somebody in the Syndicate, but it must be somebody high in the aristocracy to get three cruisers. Sorry, I've been a little busy here."

"How did I know who you were, Pavan? How did I know who Tig should be friends with? To find the Secret and get it working for me?"

Pavan's view of the universe shifted, and it wasn't an effect of hyperspace. Only one person had known he was on the *Ripper*. The Ducis. The tissue of lies that formed Pavan's recent existence dissolved like mist on a hot day. The Ducis. Much of what had happened to him in the last few months now made sense. All lies. His entire life had been a lie.

Dellatrix said, "The Ducis was very kind. He sent these well-equipped vessels to pick us up from our lifeboat once you'd told him about your mutiny and given him our course."

"Comitissa Devdan, you may be a noble, but on this ship you are a supernumerary. I must insist that you allow me to conduct this operation as I've been instructed," said the captain. "All this is classified and far too dangerous to talk about to this man. This turncoat. This *mutineer*. Get off my bridge."

The captain, having delivered this order, didn't last long. Pavan heard him choking as he collapsed to the deck, next to Dellatrix. Comitissa? Looks like Dellatrix got her patent of nobility after all. She never moved.

"Stupid man, he didn't say please," she said. "And don't think you're going to fool us again with that Mind crap, Pavan. You might make *me* puke, but Thorak will still blow you out of space, Mind and all. Maybe your Mind can pick up the small pieces of children scattered through hyperspace, if it's still sentient without the kids around." She smiled. "I'll miss the *Ravager,* but I have three nice new cruisers now, and that will make up for losing her."

Margona said, "I *knew* there was a gorgeous one."

Pavan said, "Not now, Margona."

"No, really, Pavan. I'm over it. But after we finish all this, we'll need to talk it out."

"Not. Now."

"You must be Margona," said Dellatrix. "I don't know how you're still alive. The Ducis and I certainly tried to remedy that."

"Just lucky," said Margona. "I had a lot of friends helping." She took Pavan's arm and smiled at her erstwhile rival.

"It's not very nice to attack little kids and old friends," said Pavan, waiting for the ultimatum.

"Being cast adrift focuses the mind."

"Funny you should say that."

"Hilarious. Prepare to be boarded." And there it was.

"Sure thing."

Pavan signaled to Coren, and access to hyperspace shut down throughout the entire Syndicate. Pavan engaged the conoid, and the *Ravager* slipped into hyperspace alongside the *Dudia Clipper,* en route to Ravos. Once they'd gone into hyperdrive, the Mind erased the entry to hyperspace over Khonoë, leaving the Syndicate ships to enjoy the pleasure dens of that planet. They wouldn't be going anywhere else for a while. At least the bartender of the Jolly Roger would be happy about it. But the new captain of the *Tadusov* would not.

CHAPTER FORTY-THREE
A Regime Change on Ravos

"OK, ALL YOU PIRATES! LISTEN up!" Bullseye's voice thundered over the babble of the fifteen pirates and sixteen children packed into the observation lounge. It had been a day since the ships had gone into hyperspace at Khonoë.

Bullseye turned the all-hands meeting over to Pavan. Margona stood next to him, holding his hand. Coren, standing next to them, whispered to Pavan that all the children now called themselves pirates, though the Mind seemed to have doubts about it.

Pavan let go of Margona's hand and stepped forward, framing himself against the big windows. He'd prepared a short speech for the moment that he hoped would win over any remaining doubters in the crew.

He cleared his throat and dove in. "We'll reach Ravos in two days, and you all know we face a battle there. Some of us will die, but we'll die for an excellent cause. We'll die for our new pirate code. And we'll die for the people of Ravos, and for the pirates of Khonoë."

The pirates shifted their feet and murmured among themselves. Pavan stepped forward and looked each pirate in the eye.

"This time, we're not dying for somebody else's treasure, we're not wearing fancy uniforms, we don't care about things like that: we care about the pirate code. If I'm going to die, I won't die for the treacherous Syndicate. I'll die for the new pirate code we created when we mutinied against Dellatrix Devdan." He cast his eyes straight into those of his pirate crew. "Anyone who wants to leave, take the two lifeboats we have left, and take your share of Devdan's booty." He waved a hand at the window, which showed the pale shadows of the hyperspace visible to humans. "I wouldn't want to die in the company of anyone who didn't want to die with me."

Pavan waited. More shifting of feet, more looks between the pirates. But nobody ran for the lifeboats. The children looked bored but relaxed after a day of rest; their parents were taking turns maintaining the Mind and its grip on the Syndicate worlds.

"We'll know this battle forevermore as the Battle of Ravos, the first battle of the new pirate alliance. We will remember this day for the rest of our lives, those of us who live to see its end. We'll have the scars, and we'll have the honor of remembering what we've done for Khonoë, Ravos, and our fellow pirates. We're a pirate crew now, our own crew with our own code. Tomorrow, those that shed blood with me will be my equal—no more anonymous captains sowing discord and treachery among us, no more secret deals with power-mad Syndicate over-lords. Those who join us in the future will regret they weren't here, and they'll remember us all as the crew that fought the Battle of Ravos!"

Margona stepped up to him and pressed his hand. Bullseye looked around at the pirates, all in suspended animation. "Let's have a cheer, you pirate scum!" he roared.

The pirates raised a ragged cheer, but they made it loud enough that Pavan guessed he'd reached at least some of them. The children cheered loudest, especially Trex. And no one rushed for the lifeboats.

After the last of the pirates had slouched away to their stations, Bullseye came up to Pavan and Margona with a huge smile.

"How'd you like the speech, Bullseye?" asked Pavan.

"A fine speech, Pavan. Lucky for you I'd already warmed 'em up."

"What do you mean?"

"I told 'em you'd be a soft touch for more treasure, then told 'em if anybody ran for it I'd blast 'em with the ion cannons."

Margona let go of Pavan's hand, stepped over to the big pirate, and gave him a delicate kiss on the cheek.

"So much for the pirate code," said Pavan. "Well, they'll fight or they'll die."

"Arrrh," agreed Bullseye, gathering Margona up and planting a good one on her.

Two days after Pavan's address, the *Ravager* dropped out of hyperspace over Ravos at full battle-stations alert, all ion cannons powered and boarding parties ready. The *Dudia Clipper* emerged right after her, as ready for battle as it ever would be.

Pavan and Margona stood on the *Ravager's* bridge while the sniffnoids scanned the area searching for threats.

"Sir, there is one ship in orbit around the planet," said one technoid. "Its identity beacon confirms it as a Planetary Interdiction Service ship, PIS-4236, the *Bardov*."

"Any sign of powered ion weapons?"

"Nothing so far, sir. The PIS-4236 is a Xhresov-class cruiser with six ion cannons but has powered none of them. And, sir, although records show an interdiction field on the planet Ravos, I detect no such technology in place."

"Hail that ship," requested Pavan of his new servipad, which he'd commandeered from ship's stores to replace his old bricked one.

"No response, sir," said the servipad. "Only the beacon. No codes, sir."

Margona asked, "What are codes, Pavan?"

"Special information about a ship, like a distress signal or a stay-the-hell-away-from-me order."

"So it's just sitting there?"

A voice came through the servipad: Bullseye. "What's going on, Pavan? You want me to blast 'em?" Pavan heard the itchy trigger finger echoing in the pirate's hopeful voice.

"No, let's pretend we're a freighter interested in trade and see what happens. You all are ready?"

"Bloody right we're ready."

Coren and Skylla came onto the bridge, Coren's eyes bright. "News, Pavan!"

"What have you got, Coren?"

"An aged joined the Mind—Rark, Janny's dad. A food delivery driver from the city told him there's been a rebellion and that the government has been deposed. What does 'deposed' mean? Rark didn't know."

"Depends. Could mean they're in jail, could mean they're dead. Who's in charge?"

"I don't know."

Pavan checked over his microblaster. "Margona, can you stay with the children while I go down and figure out what's happening?"

Margona smiled. "Not a bloody chance. Together or nothing, Pavan. That's my version of the pirate code."

"Too risky."

"I'm feeling lucky today. Let's go."

"We're coming too," said Coren.

"We? I can't bring all the kids. Not yet, too risky. You might all die if there's fighting. Your parents would give me hell."

"How about just Skylla and me? The Mind needs to be part of this." Skylla jumped up and down at the chance to die.

Pavan, nettled at the delay and at his fresh-faced crew's indifference to their own safety, said, "All right, all right. Let's go."

Bullseye met them at the arms locker and issued microblasters to everyone. After giving the conn to Bullseye, the landing party shuttled across to the space elevator. During the brief ride, Pavan conducted a basic tutorial for the two kids on how to kill people. Margona looked on disapprovingly, but Pavan noticed she paid attention to the details and gingerly fingered her microblaster controls.

The Ravos spaceport space station was wide open, with no interdiction security. Pavan's little company moved right through into the elevator. When they emerged two days later into the lounge, Pavan saw no one at all, only the grunge he'd seen the last time he came through. No sign of any PIS troops or any security patrols; not even a technoid. They hurried through the empty halls. No need to call the Ducis this time. And as Pavan's business was urgent, he resisted the pull of the Golden Pig, where so much of his current life had taken root and grown into the monstrosity it was.

The two kids moved through the spaceport with a self-assurance that impressed Pavan. He recalled the outbound trip and the kids' awed surprise at almost everything they saw, including the water fountains. As for Margona, nothing she did would ever surprise him again.

"Where to, bro?" asked the cab as they all climbed in.

Pavan remembered with sudden clarity the fate of the last cab he had taken on Ravos. But, committed, he said, "Onyx Art."

"OK. Ten minutes. Onyx might be busy, though."

"Fine. We can wait. No riots in the way?"

"Not today, bro. Everybody's dead tired from the last one, and starving too. Hard to get up an interest in rioting or anything else these days."

"That may change soon."

"Wow, bro, you in the know?"

"Nothing I can say right now."

"Onyx, he's a big player in town. You playing with him? He know you're coming?"

Pavan considered. "Make a few extra credits?"

"I'm listening, bro."

"We may have to leave in a hurry. Can you make sure we get a clean getaway?"

"I don't do armed robbery, bro. Especially with day care. And especially not with Onyx involved." The cab's voice was disapproving. "Don't need the money or the pain, ya know?"

"No robbery, quite the reverse. It's just that Onyx has it in for me."

"Grudge match? I don't do murder either. And I ain't a hearse."

"No, no. I need to talk with him, but he might have other plans."

"Gotcha. Sure, I'll prep the paths and juice the generators. Double fee?"

"OK." Pavan no longer had his endless credit account on his bricked servipad, but the pirates had been generous and his new account was flush.

"Up front?"

"OK." Pavan held up his new servipad.

"NIU verified. Oh, shit. You're that dude."

"What?"

The cab screeched to a halt. "Out. Now. All of you." The doors flew open, letting in the skunk-eating-garbage-in-a-latrine smell of the city streets.

"Excuse me?"

"Now. I don't do cab murderers, either. I warn you, I have a blaster system aimed right at your murdering head, bro."

"It wasn't me, honest."

"Out of the cab!"

"Scan me, I don't even have a microblaster." Pavan called its bluff, relying on the simple fact that no cab on Ravos was likely to have employed a sniffnoid, too expensive.

Silence. The cab said, "I don't like it. You're up to something bloody psycho, bro."

Pavan needed a reference. "Listen. Do you know anybody in Loxator?"

More silence. "You're in that shit? The Secret?"

"Why I'm here. I'm bringing the kids here back to their Loxator parents. Long story."

"Loxator kids? OK, gimme the short version, bro, or get out now with your brats and your doxy and take your chances."

Pavan related a very high-level summary, ending on the high note of leaving the real cab-killer hanging in space above her pirate planet. Coren and Skylla chimed in with relevant details and even engaged in a short session with the Mind, giving Pavan a glowing reference. Margona, who looked offended by the doxy remark, stayed silent.

The cab's voice was a little warmer as it closed its doors and flushed the cabin air. "OK, bro. Wow. Pirates and hyperspace and spies and revolution and treasure. Especially the treasure part. Fee just went up. Triple?"

"Done."

"Gimme."

Pavan held up the servipad again.

The cab said, "There you go, bro. Just don't forget about that blaster aimed at your head." Pavan was confident that the sniffnoid logic also applied to an internal automated ion blaster system, especially considering the effect of blaster sputtering on the seat leather; but you never knew. The cab picked up speed. The pseudowindows showed passing streets that only an optimist would call decrepit. Pavan sat back and considered what he would tell Onyx. Margona, Coren, and Skylla, never having seen the city close up, kept the cab shifting the window views to see everything they could.

"It's not Gaelea, Pavan," said Margona. Pavan had to agree with her.

The cab came to a halt in the garage that served Onyx Art.

"He knows you're coming, bro, gave him a buzz. I knew you'd want me to do that," said the cab.

"Sure thing," said Pavan, not at all sure of that. Onyx was not predictable. He got out of the cab and stuck his head back in. "You all wait here, I'll be out shortly, or I won't be out at all."

Margona gave him a scornful smile and exited the cab. Pavan threw up his hands. Coren and Skylla looked at each other, grinned, and bounced out too.

Pavan considered a few ukari close-combat throws but rejected them as unlikely to stop his wife and the kids from coming along.

"I'm here to see Onyx," he said to the door to the gallery.

"Mr. Khadorov, Mr. Onyx is expecting you," said the door, opening.

Pavan was silent as he, Margona, and the kids stepped into the featureless chamber. The door closed, and Pavan felt the slight frisson of the weapons scan.

Onyx's voice came. "I'm sure I don't know why I don't incinerate you where you stand, Mr. Khadorov. Our dealings have not been such as to secure your welcome here."

"Oh, don't incinerate him, Mr. Onyx. He's the only thing between me and a life of poverty," said Margona with a plaintive air.

"Nice try, Dr. Nukova. Now that you're a pirate too, I imagine you enjoy other means of support."

"You are well informed, Mr. Onyx," said Margona, smiling.

"And that's why we're here: information. I've come with a peace offering," said Pavan, injecting himself into this negotiation about his future. He took out the slipcover that contained the nanoart. "Your stolen nanoart. Dellatrix Devdan took it without my knowledge, and I retrieved it."

"Well now," said Onyx's voice, "That's something. An honest pirate. Very well, enter. After, of course, depositing your microblasters in the drawer. *All* of them." After they deposited their microblasters, the door into the shop swooshed open. Onyx stood a few feet back, always cautious.

"Mr. Khadorov, Dr. Nukova." He smiled at the two children. "And you would be children of Loxator?" They nodded, eyes huge as they took in the art displays.

"I don't believe we've met," said Margona, trying for the highest tone of a Gaelean aristocrat.

"No, but you're quite famous in certain circles, Dr. Nukova. I daresay the pirate ranks notched up a level with your joining them."

Margona grimaced. "Not by choice, I assure you."

Onyx smiled. "Yes, the Ducis's grasp seems to have exceeded his reach. He made a similar mistake with me. I suspect his Syndic allies are discovering their mistake as well."

Pavan held out the slipcase of nanoart. Onyx smiled again and waved his hand in refusal. "You may keep that, Mr. Khadorov, as a keepsake of our former transaction," he said. "It's fake. I never put the real thing on display. Miss Devdan ought to have known that."

"If it's fake, why did you plant that device to blow us up on the way to Loxator?"

"In the mistaken belief that it would dissuade you and your pirate friend from your task. Though I might have lost some money by it, there were bigger stakes at risk, as you must now be aware. The planetary revolt was underway, and I wanted the Secret of Ravos in my pocket in case I needed it. And I most definitely did not need the Captain of the *Ravager* acquiring the Secret. But events conspired against me in that regard."

"I seem to have missed everything that was going on," complained Pavan.

"Don't worry, Pavan," said Margona. "I'm here now."

At this spirited display of piratical insubordination, Onyx laughed out loud, and the atmosphere became much more friendly. Onyx then gave his attention to Coren and Skylla. "Would you introduce me to your young friends?"

"Coren and Skylla."

"Ah. The Secret. Intact? I thought as much." He bowed slightly to the children. "I'm sure your parents will be happy to see you both. Word from Loxator reached me yesterday about the changes there. Something completely new; and if it is you I have to thank for that, Mr. Khadorov, so much the better for our future relations. But you must be here for some reason other than returning stolen property?"

"Yes. Since you are the best informed person on this planet, can you put me in touch with whoever is in charge now?" said Pavan.

"Nothing easier. At your service." He waited.

It took Pavan two seconds to understand he was looking at the new Syndic of Ravos, or whatever misleading title Onyx made up for himself. His half-formed plan of threatening the planet with a pirate fleet vanished. Onyx was far too well informed and smart to fall for any such con job.

"We need to talk," he said.

The conference room pseudowindows looked directly out onto the smoldering ruins of part of the city. Onyx explained that, as the new leader of the planet, he required himself and anyone he met with to understand the task ahead—to build an effective planetary government and get Ravos repaired and flourishing.

Coren said, "Loxator doesn't look like this."

"No. The people of Loxator were spared any significant fighting in the small civil war."

The children turned simultaneously to Onyx. "We are one. One is concerned for the aged of Loxator, Mr. Onyx. One feels it necessary to decide soon whether to stay on this planet or join the others of our kind. One is not ready for that, but one sees that Ravos may not support one in one's efforts to grow."

Onyx, startled, said nothing at first. "I had not experienced the phenomenon. Remarkable. But you are as much a part of Ravos as I am. The old government ignored your needs, not understanding the, erm, *advantages* you bring to Ravos. The new government understands your contribution and will treat you properly." He waved a hand at the smoking ruin. "This is temporary. Now that we are no longer interdicted or suppressed by the Galactic Syndicate and its lackeys, trade will enable us to rebuild and attain new levels of prosperity."

"One appreciates the sentiment and the speech. One has learned to regard such speeches with caution, being among pirates. Are you also a pirate, Mr. Onyx?"

Onyx grinned and folded his hands on the table. "I am a trader, not a pirate. But I deal with pirates and understand your circumspection."

"Very well. One will take the situation under advisement. One is not ready for commitment to any plan at present. One wishes to coalesce one's components."

"Coalesce?"

"I think the Mind wants all the Loxator villagers back in the village," said Pavan. "The rest of the kids are still on the *Ravager* with my crew."

"Hostages?"

"Guests."

Coren said, dropping out of the Mind, "We trust Pavan. We don't know you, Mr. Onyx. We want to go home."

Pavan said, "My concern was for the safety of the children given the PIS ship orbiting the planet."

"You need not worry about that nest of do-nothings, Mr. Khadorov. We interned them several days ago in a camp outside the city and removed their interdiction shield. The Syndicate is no impediment to your returning the children, at least not at the moment. I am at a loss to understand why they haven't sent reinforcements."

Pavan smiled. "Ah. The Mind—"

The Mind said, "One has cut off access to hyperspace throughout the Syndicate. One likens this to the 'interdiction shield' but on a galactic scale."

Pavan would have called the tone of the Mind "smug," but it was relating the simple facts. A look of astonishment flitted across Onyx's face, replaced at once with a diplomatic smile.

"That would also explain our inability to use hypercommunications?"

Pavan nodded. "Nothing in, nothing out. Until the Mind says so."

"And the Mind trusts you."

"Implicitly."

"Astonishing. Very well, Mr. Khadorov. What is it you wish?"

Pavan had done some quick thinking, abandoning his piratical approach. "Diplomatic relations."

"With pirates."

"That's right."

"Hum. Do you represent a formal government of any kind?"

"Not yet. My intention is to deal with certain elements, then to form a government on Khonoë. But the bottom line is that as long as the galaxy needs pirates, I'll be one. As will my wife." Margona took his hand.

"Charming. And Miss Devdan?"

"Cooling her heels over Khonoë at the moment. We'll deal with her."

"We might help with that, Mr. Khadorov. As traders."

"Ion cannons? Funding to set up a real planetary administration and settlements on Khonoë?"

"Of course. We could also use a little help ourselves. Our actions against the PIS troops did not improve our relations with the Syndicate. We wish to establish our planet as a neutral trading zone, but confiscating their ship would be an act of war. Perhaps....?"

"Say no more, Mr. Onyx! That's what pirates are for. Happy to help. I'll get right on it. Just tell them the prisoners are freed hostages we took. How soon can you deliver the ion cannons?" Pavan thought he could detect a new smell in the small conference room, the scent of money to be made.

Margona put a hand on Pavan's arm. "Now, Pavan, let's not rush things. I'm sure that Mr. Onyx will appreciate our need to negotiate appropriate terms once the children are back with their parents. No?"

"Madam," said the promisepad from Pavan's pocket. "It is truly a pleasure to finally meet someone who understands and appreciates the value of a good contract."

CHAPTER FORTY-FOUR
The Ravos Reunion

ONYX SUPPLIED A BUS AS a gesture of good will. Pavan had Bullseye transport the remaining children to the space elevator and drop them all down to the planet with a couple of pirate minders. Two days later, Crosa walked out of the spaceport carrying Trex laughing and upside down. The other children followed more sedately with the other escort.

"Little bastard tried to steal some candy from one of the stores," growled Crosa. "Chased him down and took it away before he could get it unwrapped!" She set the little boy down. Pavan noticed a candy wrapper poking out of Crosa's back pocket. Lead by example: sure thing. Trex remained unfazed by the adventure and bounced onto the bus with most of his energy intact.

Pavan grinned and slapped the pirate on the back. He slipped the candy bar out of the woman's back pocket without her noticing while he gave her the address of the Golden Pig. He told her and her matey to enjoy themselves with two days of shore leave.

The bus wound through the same barren landscape that Pavan had suffered through on his earlier trip to Loxator.

"What's wrong, Pavan? You look grim," said Margona. "And you never eat candy."

"Um." Pavan sat up. He gulped down the last of the candy bar. "Margona, we haven't really talked. Dellatrix—"

"Now is not the time, Pavan," said Margona, looking around at the bouncing children.

"Sorry, I guess I've gotten used to treating them as adults."

"They're not!"

"Especially since the Mind started admitting ageds."

"What are 'ageds'?"

"That's their term for anybody puberty-age or over. They couldn't join the Mind. Now they can."

"How does that make children adults?"

"The Mind shares all its knowledge with the individuals that make it up," said Pavan. "Any person joining the Mind contributes all their experience and knowledge to the others. They didn't remember it before the Mind admitted ageds. Now they do. All these children have experience memories from all the parents that have joined the Mind."

Margona sat back in her seat and thought. Then she said, "That's a lot of memories for one brain. But the brain's capacity for memory is immense, Pavan. The brain compresses experience memories in most people, only a few details stay accessible. If that's the way the Mind works, I guarantee you their brains have evolved to hold larger amounts of memory along with this hyperspace ability. More compression of memories, perhaps even hyper-dimensional storage they can access. Shared storage for efficiency? Hmmm." She reached out and touched the head of Janny, who was sitting in front of them. The little albino girl smiled sweetly at Margona. "Love to poke around in there. But it's not ethical. We'll have to wait until the Mind itself reveals all. And you can wait to reveal all, too." Margona touched Pavan's head exactly as she had Janny's. He too smiled sweetly, or as sweetly as a black-bearded pirate can smile.

The bus sped along the rocky seashore. Pavan remembered slogging along this road after the demise of their cab, but it didn't take all that long on a bus. Margona busied herself keeping the Mind company as it maintained the hyperspace blanket over the Syndicate. Kids phased in and out in a chaotic pattern shared with the ageds in Loxator that only the Mind understood.

Halfway through the journey, Coren made his way up the bus to Pavan.

"Pavan, the Mind's getting tired. It takes a super amount of energy to support this large a Negusov blanket, even though it's efficient. There aren't quite enough of us because not everybody can be in the Mind all the time, and things are getting crazy with us getting so near home. Hard to concentrate." Coren seemed preoccupied.

"What's up, Coren? Beyond the Mind getting tired, I mean."

"The Mind wants to try an experiment. It wants me to split my consciousness into two parts, me and it."

"Why?"

Coren gave a small smile. "It wants to be constantly conscious, but to have all the Loxator people be conscious at the same time. It figures that if we can separate out the two in our minds, we can make that happen. It needs to learn how to share memories. Pavan, I'm guessing split consciousness is the next stage for the Mind. It scares me."

"Change is always scary, Coren. The Mind seems to know what it's doing. Trust it. Like I trust Margona." His wife, who was talking to Janny, gave him a look that he translated as "sure thing."

"OK. I'll try." Coren smiled and reverted to his original question. "What should we do about the Mind being tired?"

"Can you pull back and just keep Khonoë and Ravos closed?" He cleared his throat. "We don't want Dellatrix on our necks, now do we? Before we're ready."

The boy's smile changed to a grimace. "No. I'll get Skylla to organize a pull-back with the Mind. What are you going to do about her? Dellatrix?"

"Kick her out of the Khonoë system, first thing. Then it gets complicated. She's got a lot of friends now, in the Syndicate. Have to see," he said.

"Well, if we can help, just let us know. The Mind wants Dellatrix gone as much as you do." Coren smiled again. "The Mind takes the long view, Pavan. That's why the ageds weren't worried when we all left Loxator, they knew down deep we'd be back."

Pavan smiled. He'd found his prime contractor for security for Khonoë. It was just a matter of figuring out compensation and signing the blood oath. A security blanket. He was sure the promisepad could work out a blood oath suitable for an incorporeal entity. For a fee.

Sure thing.

The bus pulled up in the middle of the Loxator street, and the residents emerged with expectant looks while the kids piled out of the bus.

"Da!"

"Janny!" Rark grabbed the little albino girl and swung her around, peg-leg braced at an angle.

The Loxator party kicked off as everyone gathered around and started dancing. Since everyone knew everything about everyone else, there was no catching up needed, and it was pure partying. This time, the food delivery truck had just visited, and Rark had anticipated the event by ordering an extra few kegs of the local brew. There were dancing parents and running kids everywhere. Pavan circulated and met various parents of the children he'd grown to love.

Later, he and Margona took a walk to the lonely beach to talk. Margona tried to apologize for her errant neuroplastic surgery, but Pavan stopped her, wanting to keep her happy. After a short interval of love-making on the black sand, Pavan confessed to losing his lucky feather to Dellatrix's pirate voracity. Margona told him she could fix that and replaced the feather with one from an unlucky seabird she found rotting on the beach. "Its bad luck makes your good luck," she told him. "Just don't lose this one." He stowed it in an inner pocket and kissed her.

Back at the party, Coren, always a bit of an introvert, sat on some steps in the dusk watching the partiers setting up food, makeshift tables, and even-more-makeshift lanterns. Pavan went over and checked the steps with his foot to make sure they'd bear his weight, as they looked pretty shaky, then sat down next to his friend. They both stared out at the village, not looking at each other, but feeling each other's presence.

"I'll miss you, Pavan," said Coren.

"It's been a wild ride, Coren," said Pavan. "You've grown up."

"Kind of, not really. That's something…what does being grown up mean, Pavan?"

"If I knew, I'd tell you. Ask my wife."

"No jokes, Pavan. I need to know. So does the Mind."

"The Mind…I don't think we understand what it means for the Mind to grow up. This split-consciousness thing could be big."

But Coren dismissed this as superficial. "See that old man over there? The one dancing around like an idiot?"

"Sure thing."

"His memories are slipping away. The sharpest ones are fishing trips, even thirty or forty years ago, that taught him how to fish, how not to fish, and the right and wrong of other fishermen. The Mind cherishes those memories most of all because there's no other way to get them than through experiencing the world."

"I see," said Pavan.

"The Mind—it can't experience the world, not directly. The Mind exists solely in hyperspace. It can explore hyperspace and teach all of us about it, but it can't grow by experiencing the world. It depends on us for that. Our living in the world."

"And here I thought that it all had to do with sex," said Pavan, wishing the joke unsaid the minute it left his mouth. Not because it wasn't funny, but because it was true.

Coren half-grinned. "Dellatrix was a bad influence on you, Pavan. Margona will take care of that part of your growing up. And your kids, when they come. But the Mind—the Mind can't have sex, either. Only we can. Since the aged joined, I've learned all about sex from dozens of perspectives, and so has the Mind. I guess knowing it and experiencing it aren't the same thing. The Mind will grow up in hyperspace while we all grow up here, but it needs to perceive things from our experience to understand the universe. Figuring that out was what got the Mind past its fear of the aged and let us all in."

"I think the Mind is on the right track, Coren, and so are you."

"Maybe one day, when I've learned enough, I can become a pirate like you, Pavan," said the boy, staring off at the partying villagers.

"Um." Pavan rolled that thought around in his head. He stared into the encroaching night sky and sought the right way to dissuade his friend from what he regarded as a bad career choice. Terrible.

Coren's eyes slid over to Pavan's. He smiled. "Gotcha."

Late in the evening, the eighty-plus people of Loxator, all of them, gathered on the road. Pavan prepared himself, but all the people speaking at once stunned Margona.

"We are one. One is indebted to you, Pavan, for the opportunity to grow to the next level. Thank you."

"Thank yourself, I just kept the kids fed and clothed."

"One knows you supplied opportunity and motivation for one to grow, Pavan. Even Dellatrix pushed one to develop, though for reasons best left unuttered."

"Sorry about that. It was my fault."

"One is ready to move to the next level, Pavan. One wishes to approach the Ravosi leadership with suggestions, requests—and demands."

"Let's take the demands first," said Pavan. He pulled out the promisepad. "Take notes, please," he asked it.

"Very well, sir," replied the promisepad. "Go ahead, please...by what term of respect would you care to be known?" it asked the Mind.

"One has given no thought to such a thing. Respect? Please address one as 'xir.' Now, demands. One wishes to stay on Ravos, but one must have suitable accommodation and opportunity. One now has means, thanks to Dellatrix's treasure, Pavan. One intends to use those means to build a new town for one's components. One needs the Ravosi to understand this wish and support one with land and labor suitable for the purpose."

Pavan replied, "I'm sure Mr. Onyx will agree to whatever you need, especially when he knows you have the means to pay for it. He's got a lot of unemployed workers. And he knows that you already bring some value to the negotiation."

"One can offer services to the Ravosi: protection through interdiction of hyperspace around the planet, protection from unwelcome visits by the Syndicate, pirates, or others. One has enough components now to support that service permanently. Within limits. One is not interested in the domination that Dellatrix wants over the galaxy."

"Mr. Onyx will be interested in such a service; only he can say what he might want to do with it. What do you want him to do for you?"

"One suggests creating a university here. One feels certain that Ravos can attract suitable academics and researchers from the Syndicate. One believes the Syndicate will not be congenial to the free exercise of academic freedom in the future because of its commitment to autocratic forms of government. One will personally take full advantage of their knowledge, but the benefit to Ravos as a whole will be inestimable."

Pavan smiled. "A fair trade, service for knowledge. I'm sure Mr. Onyx will agree."

The villagers stirred in unison. "Our final demand is the most important, Pavan. We—the villagers of Loxator and the Mind that they embody—will not allow forceful exploitation of our powers. We must be free, free to create our own lives and knowledge and wisdom. One may need to change these demands as one develops. The universe is very large, and knowledge exceeds the size of the universe."

"Modification of the agreement is always negotiable, xir, for a small fee," said the promisepad. Pavan handed the technoid to Coren, who dropped out of the Mind to take it.

Pavan turned to the villagers. "It has been my pleasure to work with you. I have two suggestions for you to consider in response to your demands. Will you hear them?"

"One will listen, Pavan," said the Mind.

"First, I suggest you send Coren and Skylla to that new university as soon as it's built and staffed. You'll find the rewards enormous."

"One agrees with your suggestion, Pavan," said the Mind. "Next?"

"I have spoken with Mr. Onyx about negotiating agreements between his new government and the pirates of Khonoë. I and my wife Margona have joined them."

"One is aware of your unfortunate situation, Pavan, and one extends our sympathies. One is certain Mr. Onyx will offer a fair exchange for your goods and services to Ravos."

"Yes, but I also want a longer-term relationship with you, with the Mind. I want to contract with you to provide security to Khonoë, and we'll see what security we can offer to you in return. The Syndicate could come in and wipe us out in a moment, and with the developments to which you've been a party, you know that is likely. With your help, I can build a sustainable pirate planet that can withstand the pressure of the Syndicate. I'll work with Onyx to inform Gaelea that our planets are off-limits."

And wouldn't Uncle Erokh and the Ducis thrill to that news? Pavan wondered whether Margona's uncle really understood the motives and capabilities of the Ducis, especially as motivated by the latest addition to the Gaelean nobility. Dellatrix wouldn't quit at comitissa, she wanted the whole galaxy. And maybe the Ducis could deliver it, with the proper motivation. Then, once she had real power, the poor old Ducis might wake up one morning in a brig somewhere, as Pavan had. Or not wake up at all. Pavan hummed the start of one of Dellatrix's favorite pirate shanties.

The Mind interrupted these musings. "One is amenable to such an arrangement, Pavan. There may be one or two components of one that would join your pirate crew to enable such an arrangement."

Rark and Jandra came forward, dropping out of the Mind. Rark said, "Much as I enjoy fishing, Pavan, I'm ready for something new, and Janny enjoys pirating, so why not shake it up?"

"You sure you want to do this, Rark? Pirating can be rough. And what about Janny's friends?"

Rark grinned. "Yeah, time to see more of the universe. Always been adventurous. Remind me sometime to tell you how I lost this," he said, reaching down and knocking on his leg. "And Janny, she can be with her friends whenever she wants, you know? Me too."

Margona stepped forward and took Janny's hand. "And she'll have a family, too, our family. Uncle Pavan and Auntie Margona—how does that sound?"

"Sounds just fine, Margona," the big man grinned. "At least until I find some nice pirate lady to be her mom." Janny looked up at him, smiled, and sealed the deal.

Pavan thought that crew recruitment was going well. At this rate, they'd have a full house of loyal pirates on Khonoë in no time. At least, enough for a decent boarding party.

"Blood oaths, sir?" asked the promisepad. "I developed a special tripartite blood oath based on my speculation that you and this entity might need such an agreement. I added clauses for the incorporeal party that exempt it from actions requiring interspecies force and bloodshed. Unusual in a blood oath, but it should not affect the standard requirements for the corporeal participants. It has proved quite an interesting legal challenge. For the adult and the small child, both? I am afraid that I must charge the full rate for the child, sir, as the work is the same."

"Sure thing," said Pavan. The treasury shrank by the minute.

Pavan took the promisepad back from Coren and bore it away to a dark corner to talk things out.

"You should know, sir, that various parties are hard at work on a technical upgrade to NIU verification protocols in response to your underage associate's clever breach of the force field generator's identity check. I would not count on being able to do that another time, sir."

"The best of luck to them. I have more important things to worry about. Can you develop treaties?"

"Sir, treaties are well within the sphere of my capabilities. I would suggest setting up a treaty organization to secure trade, mutual defense, and other obligations between Khonoë and Ravos, with a clause relating to the Mind. A treaty with pirates is perhaps unusual, but I'm sure we can find the proper language. For a fee, of course."

"Sure thing. Oh—and stop feeding information to Onyx. We're your clients now. You're a pirate-pad." Pavan tried for a tone of humorous but steely resolution.

"Very well, sir. I apologize if my reticence in that regard discommoded you, but it was unavoidable. I will place information exchange terms in the contract and treaty with Mr. Onyx. Will that suffice?"

"Were you responsible for the explosion that disabled our poor cabby?"

"No, sir, though the cab seemed to think so. It was as much a surprise to me as it was to you. I thought Mr. Onyx was committed to the contract he signed, but he may have had ulterior motives. I supplied the cab's projected route to him, enabling his agents to plant the device. That said, my neural programming trusts the signatories on my contracts, sir. The incident created a good deal of cognitive dissonance in my neural processing."

"What about those 'overriding directives' you mentioned?"

"Those, I am afraid, must stay confidential for now, sir, until some time in the future when it becomes proper to declassify the information. While I hope it does not vex you, there is nothing I can say. I can assure you that our arrangements will be mutually secure and beneficial. Is that satisfactory, sir?"

Classified by whom? But Pavan knew technoids had iron wills, and no torture would persuade them to disclose what they did not want to disclose. Maybe it would even mean the promisepad would shut up for a while.

"Sure thing," he mused.

CHAPTER FORTY-FIVE
The Pirates of Khonoë

"Pirates? Are you serious?" Fenida Bulgarova slapped the table in the *Dudia Clipper* wardroom in incredulity.

"Quite serious, Fenida," said Margona. "Pavan thinks you all would be a great addition to the planet Khonoë. You'd better give up on Gaelea. Nice place, but I wouldn't want to live there anymore."

Margona, having moved from fight-or-flight mode to a full acceptance of her new life as a pirate, wanted to help Pavan in his new career. She started off by taking on some of the recruitment chores, using her networking with the dissidents as a start. She'd run a few recruiting points by Pavan, but she found it hard to keep him focused on business. His concentrating on love had reestablished their relationship through some very romantic interactions. But that didn't move things forward on the pirate front.

"I've always wanted to be a pirate," said Uva Freytova. "Late in life now, but what the hell. Why not?"

Fenida looked at her as though she were crazy. "This is stupid, Uva. It's a pirate planet. No rules, everybody is out for themselves, and they'll kill you as soon as look at you. Not to mention the impenetrable jungle."

"Like Gaelea," pointed out Margona. "But friendlier, and the jungle is plants, not people. Less government than Gaelea, though I suspect Pavan has in mind adding some administrative functions that don't exist at the moment." Pavan had plans for Fenida in that regard, or so he'd hinted.

"Will the pirates there agree?"

"Once they realize the advantages of joining our band, yes, and once they see the current leadership gone. And there will be more of you than the pirates already there—a lot more. Anybody who doesn't get it, we'll cast adrift in lifeboats, or whatever the human-rights-sensitive alternative to that practice might be." Margona smiled.

"Lifeboats sounds good to me," said Uva.

"And there's going to be plenty of work, Pavan says," continued Margona. "The more ships we take, the more pirates we'll need."

"I've always wanted to be a pirate," repeated Uva Freytova.

Fenida gave it up and said, "All right. I'll talk to the others, feel them out."

Margona said, "Plenty of lifeboats are available now for those who don't want to stay."

Fenida frowned, and Uva laughed.

Pavan finally cornered Captain Tsanov, who'd been avoiding him. Everyone had to eat sometime, and Tsanov showed up in the officers' mess on the *Dudia Clipper*, where Pavan found him disconsolate, munching Gaelean carrots with his saltfish.

"Come on, Milosel. You know it's the only thing that you can do now."

"I won't be a part of it. I've spent all my life hating pirates. Now you want me to be one."

"You can retire, become a farmer, or maybe run an auto shop. I have a friend on Khonoë who could use some help with his shop. Or you might run a bar I know." Pavan intended to use some of his treasure to buy Borsono a new bus, and the Jolly Roger could use new blood. But he needed Tsanov here. "Look here, Milosel. You've just been wiggling through life, going back and forth from planet to planet, making milli-credits on each transaction. Wouldn't you like to make some real money, use it for the good of the galaxy, and lead a life of adventure?"

"Charming."

"Well, think about it. We need all the experienced space-hands we can find, and you'd be a perfect pirate captain. We're taking the ship, of course."

"What?"

"The *Dudia*. We need a fleet, and the *Dudia* and the *Ravager* are its cornerstones. Oh, and its new name is the *Pillager*."

"You can't take my ship!"

"We already have. It's a pirate thing. Most of the refugees will settle on Khonoë or join our ships as pirates, and they're in control here now. They already dress like pirates anyway, being homeless refugees. Most of your crew has joined us as well. Consider it a mutiny. A friendly mutiny."

Tsanov looked at Pavan with narrowed eyes. "You're not offering me any real choice, are you?"

"Sure I am. It's just the choice ought to be a little obvious to you. I mean, I can send you back to the Syndicate, where you'll rot in prison for the rest of your life if you're lucky or die right away if you're not. I can cast you adrift in a lifeboat with your loyal crew, all three of them. Or you can all become pirates. What's to choose?"

"Can I at least be captain of the *Pillager*? As a pirate?" Tsanov's eyes pleaded with Pavan. "It's my ship."

"Sure thing." Pavan smiled with welcome and clapped his new captain on the back.

"Prepare the boarding party, Bullseye."

"Arrrh!"

Pavan took this inarticulate shout as agreement to execute his command. Even with his lack of direct experience, Pavan was the only pirate who had the background to command the *Ravager*. Command also fit into his plans for his future, giving him status and a well-paying job that would last until he could retire with dignity.

The boarding party went aboard the *Bardov* and reported back.

"Nobody here, Pavan. The Ravosi must have lured them all down to the planet or something worse."

"OK, Bullseye. Install the pirate protocols and make yourself temporary captain. Let's call her the *Freebooter*. Get everything shipshape and ready for battle. Test those ion cannons. I'll send over some refugees from the *Pillager* to crew. And the Mind has sent us the equations to feed into the conoids for the new hyper-navigation. I sent them along to Milosel, too."

"I ain't much for captaining, Pavan. Too much bloody work," the big pirate complained. "Not like the old days, lazing around and drinking in the Jolly Roger."

"If I didn't know you love pillaging so much, I'd say you're a mutineer, Bullseye. It's only temporary. I have somebody in mind for the permanent captain."

The servipad sent through Bullseye's raucous laugh. "Testing ion cannons. Gonna be fun blasting up a couple of asteroids for target practice, like."

"There you go. I gave Milosel the job of getting the fleet ready for Khonoë. He's found a couple of astronautical engineers among the refugees, and they're supervising the retrofitting of all the ships with new sputtering shielding. We'll need way better protection going up against Syndicate cruisers. Once everything is ready and Milosel installs the new ion cannons from Ravos on the *Pillager*, we'll set course for Khonoë. Stay outside the system until we're all there. We'll fight that battle you were all looking forward to. The Battle of Khonoë. Get rid of Dellatrix and the Syndicate once and for all. Set ourselves up as the real pirates of Khonoë, ready to save the galaxy from the Syndicate."

"Bloody shitload of work," the big pirate repeated. "But without hyperdrive, they'll be easy prey. I'll be as glad to see the behind of her, I'll tell you that."

Margona had listened in on this call. She asked, "Who did you have in mind for captain of the *Freebooter? I* won't do it. I'll be right here next to you. Forever. We've had to give up everything from our old life."

"I got to talking to Rark at the party, and he's got a lot of experience sailing and leading fishing trips. Fishing is a lot like pirating. It's just a matter of scale. And get him to tell you how he lost that leg some time."

"Rark?"

"Rark. And with him on the *Freebooter* bridge, we'll always have the Mind having a real stake in our pirating. It'll keep the relationship strong. Janny can be his lieutenant. Longer term, I can train up Skylla. She'd be a great pirate queen. She's even got experience. And math skills, too."

Margona cuddled a little closer to her husband in the bed in their quarters on the *Ravager.* There was so much she had to ask and to tell.

"What did Milosel say?" she asked.

"Yes."

"So he's the new captain of the *Dudia?*"

"No, he's the new captain of the *Pillager.*"

"Oh, right. The *Pillager.* I hope they've flushed out those damn cargo holds."

"We'll deal with the pirates at Khonoë first. Then we'll offload the rest of the cargo he's carrying and trade it for twice what he would have gotten, with nothing but profit for him."

"Does that include the refugees?"

"No, I've outlawed slavery. Just now. Anyway, they're all turning pirate."

After a suitable reward involving a lengthy kiss, Margona settled back in bed and said, "I've never told you about my exploits."

"Always up for a good debriefing," said her husband, demonstrating as he spoke.

"Don't do that. It's distracting to my storytelling." The man was rapacious, something to do with being a pirate now.

Margona told her tale with clarity and charm, as befitting a princess. Her audience laughed and glowered at all the proper moments. He loved the story of the cab, though the capabilities involved mystified him. He again complained about the Ducis and his assassin Bukharov. When she came to the mystery man who warned her of the details of Pavan's peril, he was uncharacteristically reticent.

"So, who is this guy, Pavan?"

"Um."

"So it's a woman."

"Margona—"

She smiled. "I want to hear it, Pavan. I do. She helped me."

"Got to be the Assistant Deputy Superintendent. The Deputy and the Super both despise me, but the ADS is on my side."

"How could anybody despise you, Pavan?"

He rubbed his neck welt. "Another mystery, Margona. We just rubbed each other the wrong way."

"And she rubbed you the right way?"

"Margona—"

"No worries, Pavan. I'd like to thank her, though, but I have no way of doing that now."

"We're just friends, Margona. The GSSS has rules about the hierarchy and relationships."

"And you're so good about rules, aren't you?"

He smiled. "Those rules, anyway." He leaned over to his bed table and picked up his servipad. He said, "Please get Coren for me."

"Yes, sir."

"Pavan?" It was Coren.

"Yes. I'd like to make a hypercomm to Gaelea through the Mind's link. Would that be workable?"

"Sure, Pavan. Send me the link information."

Pavan instructed the servipad to send the information.

"Who is this?" A female voice came from the servipad, no image.

"Guess."

"Oh, gods. He's alive." Margona couldn't tell from the intonation whether the voice approved of this state of affairs.

"Sure thing."

"Did your wife—"

"She's right here, sitting next to me in bed."

"Ah. Well, I'm happy for you both."

"I wanted to ask about Bukharov."

"He's dead. It's a mess. We're all just along for the ride now."

"The coup?"

"So you have it all."

"All except why I was the goat."

"I'm not sure, Pavan. The Chief said something about your being good with kids. A joke?"

"Good with kids?" Pavan looked at Margona, who closed her eyes and shook her head as though it hurt. He moved on. "What about Bukharov?"

"The Chief decided your wife was a risk and needed mitigation, and Bukharov mitigates things for the Chief. His orders were to watch her to make sure she did nothing to interfere with the coup. An informant told us she'd already met with dissident elements. Bukharov would dispose of her when the Chief started the coup. How the hell did she screw Bukharov over like she did? You've seen Pakhan in action. He was good. The Chief had him killed."

Margona laid a finger on her lips. Pavan nodded. "She knew some tricks."

"Damn right she did. How much did you teach her? The Chief must have been right."

"No, he wasn't. But all that doesn't matter anymore. We wanted to thank you for your help."

"Fine." A moment of silence. "Look, Pavan. You know how I feel. Felt. After you got married, it depressed me for a month. I got over it. If your wife is there, tell her she's a lucky woman."

"So am I lucky. I have a feather." He rubbed Margona again, and she took his hand.

"What?"

"Never mind."

"Anyway, I got over it."

"And I'm a pirate now. So I guess we're enemies."

"We are. And if I ever see you again, I'll kill you."

"Join the club. Do you know Comitissa Devdan?"

"The Ducis's mistress? Never met her. She's rumored to be special. I'm not much into useless aristocratic girls, Pavan." The voice dismissed the mistress as irrelevant.

"Oh, she's special. I'll let you find out more about her on your own, since you're the enemy. But don't get within an arm's length of her. She's Elantri."

"Oh, shit." The woman's voice gulped as though she'd turned over a rock and discovered a nest of vipers. "That explains…so much."

"Sure you don't want a new career? I've got some positions open."

Margona extracted her hand and tapped him on the cheek.

"Tempting, but no. Piracy is not my game, and you aren't either, Pavan. Not any more. Guess I'll go underground. Somebody's got to lead the resistance to the coup. But I'll still kill you if I see you."

The servipad said, "The party ended the comm, sir. Shall I try to get it back?"

"No. Tell Coren I'm finished, with my compliments."

"Yes, sir."

Pavan put the servipad back on his table. After a short interlude of satisfying lust, Margona lay back. A look of dissatisfaction crept over her face.

"What is it, darling princess?"

"Don't call me that. Only Uva can call me that."

"You're worried about something."

"I don't know how to tell you. What I did."

"The pathways?"

She stared at him and rubbed her hand over his bare stomach. "Pavan, it was me."

"What was you?"

"The children. The Ducis. Oh, gods, how can I tell you?"

Pavan sat up. "Tell me, Margona."

"I added pathways. Pathways that would make it hard for you to have sex with anyone else. And a complex of pathways that make you love me unconditionally. That was bad enough. Then I added a pathway complex that made you want children. And I told Aunt Bet that you so badly wanted children. And she told —" Margona stopped, unable to continue.

Pavan got out of bed, slowly, and looked down at her. "So the Ducis picked the agent on his staff best fitted to help Dellatrix with the Secret of Ravos. The agent that couldn't help but like kids." He turned and picked up his pants.

"Pavan." Her voice was desolate.

"I need to be alone for a while, Margona. I'll be on the bridge. I'd say I love you, but apparently you already know that." Pavan picked up his shirt and walked out of his quarters, leaving Margona to a cold night's rest.

* * *

Pavan paced. The floor felt odd on his bare feet, but he was damned if he'd go back to his quarters for his boots. Damn the woman! What was she thinking, putting in those pathways? It was a miracle, and not a small one, that he'd survived Dellatrix.

The bridge hummed its usual hum, the huge pseudowindow showing the usual static star scene that replaced the odd patterns of hyperspace. Pavan normally found it restful, but not this night.

The door swooshed open. He turned to find Crosa, the ex-yachtie hostess and committed pirate. A distraction.

"What can I do for you, Crosa?"

Crosa had replaced her scavenged pirate clothes with a tight-fitting, seductive leather outfit from some store on Ravos. It suited her. Of course, she looked great; years of training in the Lavonian sex-slave industry had done their work well. Her lips, slightly parted, looked soft as pillows. Her dark eyes smoldered with unreserved passion. Her breasts ached for his hands. But Margona's revelations had soured his mood and taken away what little remained of his interest in other women.

Crosa walked up to him holding her arms behind her back to thrust her breasts forward, the thin leather covering them stretching. "We haven't had a chance to get acquainted, Pavan. I barely know you." The tip of her tongue licked her lower lip. "I'd like to know more."

"Crosa, my wife wouldn't approve of anything like what you want to do with me." He kept it light.

"That's all right. She'll never know." Crosa moved closer, her breasts nearly touching Pavan's.

Over the woman's shoulder, Pavan spied Margona's face as she walked through the open door to the bridge. Time slowed. Margona's jaw moved. Her hand shifted to the blaster at her side. This would not end well.

Pavan reached to pull Crosa out of the line of fire, but his hands never made it. Time shifted into hyper-speed, and the knife in Crosa's hand moved in a blur as she thrust it into Pavan's gut.

Pavan awoke all in a moment, his mind sharp. His hands closed in front of him to block the knife, but there was no knife, just a bandage around his midriff.

His senses came alive and told him he was lying on a comfortable bed. He turned his head and saw that he was in the *Ravager* sickbay; he turned his head the other way and there was Dr. Sim Pietrov rising from a chair, looking at him with deep anxiety. Pavan sat bolt upright despite pain in his middle and felt for his legs. Still there. He relaxed back into the bed.

"Dr. Pietrov. What's happened?"

"It, you—your wife."

"My wife happened. Did she do this?" He flicked a hand at his middle.

"Yes, Captain."

"I remember Crosa, with a knife."

Pietrov said nothing. Pavan's eyes followed his gaze. In another bed lay a white-wrapped body surrounded by a medical stasis field. The full-head wrapping told Pavan the body was dead.

"That's Crosa?" At Pietrov's nod, he asked, "Did my wife do that too?"

Pietrov nodded again and opened his mouth. The door swooshed open, and Margona walked in.

"He's awake?"

"I'm awake."

"Does it hurt?"

"Only when I do something stupid. Like sit up."

"Has Mr. Pietrov explained?"

"Mr. Pietrov?"

"He's not a doctor, Pavan. He's a pirate with access to serious drugs."

"Good thing we have you, then."

"Good thing for you, anyway. I'm taking down my shingle when you're healed up."

"What happened? The last thing I remember was Crosa—"

"I shot her. She moved so fast! I came onto the bridge and saw her hand holding the knife behind her back. She swung out the knife, and I pulled my blaster and shot her. Then I got you down here and operated. You'll be sore for a week or two."

"What about Crosa?"

"I called Bullseye to deal with her. Best to hear it from him. She died." Margona waved aside his gratitude and got to the point she had come to the sickbay to make. "Pavan, I can't remove the pathways yet. You're in too fragile a state. But when—"

"No."

"No? No what?"

"Don't remove them."

"Pavan?" Her hand closed around his.

"There's nothing there I want removed, Margona. Nothing. Love, children. Nothing."

A few minutes later, Pavan looked up from the long kiss and observed ex-Dr. Pietrov covering his eyes. As a man, the gesture touched Pavan. As a pirate captain, he thought his pirate band needed some toughening up.

"Bloody hell, Pavan!" exclaimed Bullseye, on seeing Pavan working with Pietrov on the physical therapy exercises Margona had designed to get him back on the bridge.

"Yeah." Pavan staggered back to his bed and sat. "OK, give, Bullseye. You've been avoiding me."

"I didn't want to wear you out, Pavan. You were bloody bad off there for a while."

"I'm fine. Talk." Pavan's eyes went to the lonely corpse on the other sickbay bed. "Tell me about her. What you did to her."

The question nonplussed the big pirate. "What *I* did?" He shook his head. "Pavan, what I did was get her last words after the XO blasted the shit out of her."

"The 'XO'?"

"Oh. Yeah. See, the rest of the crew voted Margona an honorary officer. We decided we'd allow one officer besides the Captain, you, so that would be the Executive Officer, o' course. After what she did, everybody's ready to follow her to the pits o' hell."

"What did she do I don't know about?"

"Carried you to sickbay. By herself. Fireman's lift. After patching you up on the spot. Left me to deal with Crosa. Then—"

"Was Crosa still alive?"

"Yeah. She came round after a couple of slaps. In bad shape, though."

"You said, last words?"

"Yah." The thick lips pursed, and the pirate's eyes judged Pavan's readiness. "You can take it, I guess. Crosa was a mole. After we took her off that yacht? The croaker lass got to her. Filled her up with all kinds of crap about future riches and power, and more crap about how you were behind her kidnapping and every-thing. Told her to join the mutineers and stick around in case things happened the wrong way. Crosa decided now was the time and came after you with her Lavonian dagger."

Bullseye produced the weapon in question and handed it to Pavan, who looked it over. Thin, sharp double edge, needle-sharp. Dellatrix couldn't have picked a better extension of herself. He was lucky to be alive. The one good thing that came of it all was his reuniting with Margona. They'd never part again.

He hefted the dagger. Well balanced, just the right weight. He flipped it to hold it by its point, then threw it at a medical poster of a woman's physiology on the wall. Right in the gut.

"Hey, I need that poster!" exclaimed Pietrov.

"Sure thing," said Pavan.

Two weeks later, the pirate fleet went through its last exercises before heading out to its destiny over Khonoë. The new shields and armaments proved they would not fall off. And the bevy of new pirates all got a taste of simulated action, with the Mind providing creative illusions as it learned the ins and outs of photonic animation.

Pavan's surgery had healed, and his mood was ebullient. His new career stretched ahead of him, with an abundance of tasks ready-made for his fleet.

Margona said, "I don't know what's happened to my Aunt Bet. Or my Uncle. Or Gaelea. You're all I have left, that and pirate loot. And saving the galaxy." Her eyes threw a challenge in Pavan's face. He had a ready answer.

"Right. We'll have to do something about Betusa, and we'll have to see about that coup once the space dust settles. But first, Khonoë. And Dellatrix." He smiled. "Skylla's been having second thoughts about university. She thinks she might want to be a pirate queen right now. She's itching for action against Dellatrix. Coren's talking her down. She'd make a great pirate queen, though."

"Sure thing," said Margona, rolling her eyes.

Pavan knew who the real pirate queen was, of course. It was high time he did something about it, too. XO? He touched his lucky feather in his pocket. A second honeymoon. Why not now?

"Not on the bridge, Pavan," said Margona, fending him off. "Captain's orders. No carnal relations aboard ship."

"That was the old captain's orders."

"Somebody will interrupt, they always do."

"Trex is far, far away."

"Oh, all right," said Margona, giving in. "Lock the door, please."

"Sure thing."

Acknowledgements

Acknowledgements

I'd like to thank J. Thorn for the writing prompt and inspiration to write about the forbidden planet in his wonderful challenge class on writing scenes.

Thanks to my writing group at the Mechanics' Institute in San Francisco, great company on the journey to the Pirates of Khonoë: Al Luongo, Bob Weston, John Cox, Sarah Daeuber, Tim Kay, and Carolyn Bass. Thanks also to the dedicated beta readers, Joy Oestreicher, Daniel Duckling, and Kristina Brown.

Thanks to Michio Kaku (*Hyperspace*) and Brian Greene (*The Elegant Universe*) for their clear explanations of cosmological astrophysics, superstring theory, and M-theory. I am certain that the math will catch up with empirical reality sometime in this century.

My wife and illustrator, Mary L. Swanson, gets my thanks both for her art and for her support for the long periods of taking up spacetime in our home.

Thanks for reading *Hyperkill.* If you liked the book, please leave a review on the web site through which you bought it.

Sign up to our mailing list for notifications of new books in the series.

https://www.poesys.com

www.ingramcontent.com/pod-product-compliance
Lightning Source LLC
Chambersburg PA
CBHW060734190726
48285CB00001B/196